T0302918

BANNED & CENSORED

OTHER LOTUS TITLES

Aitzaz Ahsan	*The Indus Saga: From Pataliputra to*
Ajit Bhattacharjea	*Sheikh Mohammad Abdullah: Tragic Hero of Kashmir*
Amarinder Singh	*Honour and Fidelity: India's Military Contribution to the Great War 1914–1918*
Amarinder Singh	*The Last Sunset: The Rise and Fall of the Lahore Durbar*
Anil Dharker	*The Romance of Salt*
Ashis Ray	*Laid to Rest: The Controversy over Subhas Chandra Bose's Death*
Bidyut Chakrabarty	*Mahatma Gandhi: A Historical Biography*
B.M. Bhalla	*Kasturba Gandhi: A Biography*
E Jaiwant Paul	*Baji Rao: The Warrior Peshwa*
E Jaiwant Paul	*Annals and Antiquities of Rajasthan*
H.L.O. Garrett	*The Trail of Bahadur Shah Zafar*
Kuldip Nayar	*Beyond the Lines: An Autobiography*
Khushwant Singh with photographs by Margaret Bourke-White	*Train to Pakistan*
Lakshmi Subramanian	Singing Gandhi's India
Manohar Malgonkar	*The Men Who Killed Gandhi*
Mohammed Hyder	*October Coup: A Memoir of the Struggle for Hyderabad*
Moin Mir	*Surat: Fall of a Port, Rise of a Prince*
M.J. Akbar	*India: The Siege Within*
Pramod Kapoor	*1946 Royal Indian Navy Mutiny: Last War of Independence*
Pramod Kapoor	*Gandhi: An Illustrated Biography*
Shashi Joshi	*The Last Durbar*
Shrabani Basu	*Spy Princess: The Life of Noor Inayat Khan*
Thomas Weber	*Going Native: Gandhi's Relationship with Western Women*
Thomas Weber	*Gandhi at First Sight*
Tr Imtiaz Ahmad Sahibzada	*The Frontier Gandhi: My Life and Struggle/ The Autobiography of Abdul Ghaffar Khan*

FORTHCOMING TITLE

Vandana Shiva and Shreya Jani	*Slow Living: What You Can Do About Climate Change*

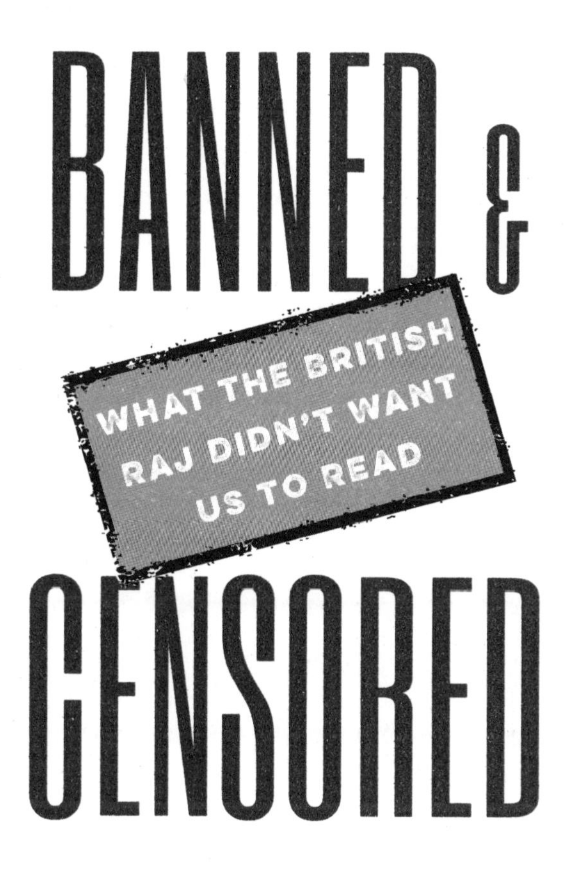

Selected and Introduced by

DEVIKA SETHI

Lotus Collection

ISBN: 9789392130649

First published in 2023

The Lotus Collection
An imprint of
Roli Books Pvt. Ltd
M-75, Greater Kailash II Market
New Delhi-110 048
Phone: ++91 (011) 40682000
E-mail: info@rolibooks.com
Website: www.rolibooks.com
Also at Bengaluru, Chennai, & Mumbai

Editors: Neelam Narula & Ushnav Shroff
Design: Sneha Pamneja
Pre-press: Jyoti Dey
Production: Lavinia Rao

Typeset in Minion Pro and Archer by Roli Books Pvt Ltd
Printed and bound at Nutech Print Services, India

CONTENTS

PART II: 1911–1920 132

PART III: 1921–1930 170

INTRODUCTION

Censorship – by the state, market, mob or even self – seeks to destroy ideas after they are uttered, and sometimes even before they are articulated. How does one resist or defeat censorship? Texts (defined here as books, pamphlets, posters, newspapers, journals or printed matter in any medium) that are banned often continue to circulate in a clandestine manner, at times at great personal costs to their authors, editors and publishers. In the long run, however, such texts are often consigned to the dustbin of history. The fact of censorship may be remembered but the words of authors, both famous and anonymous, fade away with time. Even as scholars of censorship focus on its tools (legal, administrative) and even resistance to it, the material itself gets obscured.

This anthology will take you on a journey of words and ideas that were deemed dangerous and seditious by the British colonial state in the eventful first half of the twentieth century in India. It includes non-fiction writings by figures famous, obscure and anonymous of events immortalized and forgotten, by Indians and non-Indians by people jailed and free by politicians and intellectuals, revolutionaries and students. The well-known figures included in this selection include S.C. Bose, Bhikaiji Cama, Hay Dayal, M.L. Dhingra, M.K. Gandhi, Aurobindo Ghose, H.M. Hyndman, Shyamji Krishnavarma, M.M. Malaviya, S.P. Mookerjee, Jayaprakash Narayan, J. Nehru, M. Nehru, Lajpat Rai, C. Rajagopalachari, Sampurnanand, V.D. Savarkar and B.G. Tilak. Each excerpt illuminates not just its author's thought processes, but the times in which the text was composed and circulated. Some of these banned ideas are provocative even today while others seem tame; certain arguments have stood the test of time while others have lost currency. If censorship gives us an insight into the weaknesses of a state – its many Achilles' heels, as it were – these texts collectively map the anxieties of the colonial state. They also reveal to us individuals, events and ideas that have shaped India's present. Changes in the tone and tenor of these banned texts reveal the limits of tolerance as the century progressed.

Colonial censorship laws are still in place in India, supplemented but not replaced by post-colonial legislation. Given their long afterlife, it is only fair that once-banned texts too are retrieved and remembered. When we read the words of banned writers, we access – as best as possible, after the intervention of time – their worlds, their world-views and their aims and rationale for action.

* * *

In 1907, the anti-colonial public intellectual Bipin Chandra Pal (1858–1932) denounced British rule as 'maya', illusion or hypnotism. He could not find any other explanation for the hold that the British had over India, given that most districts had Englishmen who could be counted on the fingers of one hand: two, or three, or four, 'but never more than half-a-dozen.'[1] Twentieth-century Indian anti-colonial publicists succeeded because they destroyed the illusion. By recognizing that colonialism in India rested on the twin pillars of coercion and patronage, and by drilling away at the latter through their persuasive speeches and writings, they weakened the fundamental base of colonial power. Over the course of five decades, they convinced millions of Indians that colonialism's visible benefits only served to disguise ugly structural exploitation. Colonial officials soon recognized that the printed and spoken word could influence Indian students and also silence moderate or pro-British Indian opinion by giving vent to extremist and anti-British ideas, which they thought to be held by a minority. Many officials believed that display of weakness in dealing with provocations in print would make it difficult to hold India; undecided or neutral Indians could yet abandon their loyalty to the Raj.[2] To the colonial state, certain kinds of publications were simultaneously 'a symptom and cause of unrest.'[3]

Control of public opinion via control of the written or spoken word was therefore high priority, even as anti-colonial nationalists vied to control and direct public opinion into channels of their making. The audience for Indian publicists comprised not just Indian masses or specific constituencies (students, women, caste or class groups, and so on) but also international observers, most importantly in Britain and the United States. The battle for the hearts and minds of these constituencies was fought not only in the well-known mass movements of the twentieth century but also on the terrain of print.

Print technology, which had arrived in India in the 1550s, had colonized the Indian public sphere by the twentieth century.[4] It is estimated that by 1905, there were two million subscribers in India of over 1,300 newspapers and journals, of which 200 commented on political issues.[5] Despite low literacy levels (just about ten out of every hundred Indians were literate in 1931, for instance), the printed word had magnetic appeal in India, as it jumped out from the page to be read-aloud, acted or sung. Circulation figures of publications disguised the fact that the number of readers was far more than the number of subscribers, and that print could reach the unlettered through other means. In his study of propaganda in colonial India, Milton Israel gives print the role of an opposition party in a colonial context and analogizes the press to a weapon of war deployed by the state and Indian nationalists of various hues against each other.[6] The texts assembled in this anthology are united by their patriotic sentiments, their sense of mission and by the fact of their all being banned. However, they also reveal to us the differences among patriots in terms of their objectives, and certainly in their methods, despite the considerable exchange of ideas and ideologies among them.

ASSEMBLING THIS ANTHOLOGY

For the historian of censorship in colonial India, the problem (in terms of locating primary source material) is not of paucity but of plenty. Many censored texts were preserved, often both in India and in Britain, with a view to providing administrators with precedents and resources for taking decisions about subsequent cases. The large volume of material censored is such that there exists no comprehensive catalogue of all material that was banned, only of material that has been preserved in official collections.[7] The number of proscribed items is staggering; the only scholar to have attempted a calculation estimates that between 8,000–10,000 individual titles were banned in the last forty years of colonial rule in India, and about 2,000 newspapers were subject to some kind of legal restraint.[8] Over 1,000 individual items were banned by name during the First World War (1914–1918) alone, for instance.[9] In one year (1930), as many as 150 collections of nationalist poetry were banned[10] and over 1,000 items were banned in the four years between 1931 and 1935.[11] The Customs department prevented (multiple copies of) 450 individual titles from entering India between 1935 and 1938.[12] If getting banned was a badge of honour in the context of an anti-colonial struggle, then there were many wearers of the badge in India as well as abroad.

The texts in this book have been collected from a variety of sources. Some are available in their original form as individual items in the proscribed-material collections of the National Archives of India (New Delhi) and at the British Library (London). Some pamphlets' translations (and, more rarely, the original as well) are to be found in the files of the Home & Political departments of the Government of India. Publications by prominent authors or those deemed especially dangerous are easier to locate as the file name bears their name. Yet others are buried more obscurely in various kinds of communication between the Government of India (the central government) and provincial or local governments. For instance, when the Government of India sought the opinion of local governments before passing or amending a law relating to publications, the latter would occasionally include samples of publications that they had prosecuted. Prosecutions under section 124A (sedition provision) and 153A (inciting class hatred provision) of the Indian Penal Code were regularly reported to the Government of India, and such files too yield a mass of material. Some excerpts deemed particularly inflammatory are quoted in government reports and confidential handbooks produced for use by officials.[13] Fortnightly reports of the Central Intelligence Department,[14] lists compiled by or sent to Customs officials and reports on the 'tone' of vernacular publications prepared by various provinces are additional sources for such information. In addition to the publications themselves, the history of why they were banned – the dissenting views among officials at times, the rationale, the hand-wringing about the desirable and undesirable effect of a ban – are also recorded in various files and need to be retrieved. Concerns about certain bans can be gauged from questions asked in the Indian Legislative Assembly and the British Parliament. Files prepared by the government to answer such questions also contain information about publications deemed offensive. It is not always the case that the banned publication and its curriculum vitae, as it were, are both found in the same file.

The collection assembled here has relied mainly on translations by state officials, except for some documents in Hindi (Devanagari script) which I have translated myself. Translators, usually native speakers of Indian vernaculars, were employed by various levels and branches of the government in India in order to translate and render intelligible documents in language other than English. Apart from the utility of such translations as evidence in court proceedings, these translations were required because each local government was required to send weekly newspaper reports and abstracts to the Government of India after translating and abstracting from articles that showed the trend of public opinion. Translation arrangements could vary quite a bit. In Madras presidency, civilian officials translated newspaper articles themselves, in addition to their regular duties, while military officials translated Persian and Hindustani articles. On the other hand, the Government of the United Provinces (hereafter UP) employed two full-time translators, one Hindu and one Muslim, and the Police and the Criminal Investigation Department (CID) worked closely together. Bombay

Pandit Jawahar Lal Nehru's Speech.

Pages 106-107.

Transliteration.

"....Panditji ne bataya ki kis prakar wah larka itna vikhyat tatha logon ka path-pradarshak ho gaya. Kiya karan hai ki hinsa ke virodhi ahinsavadi bhi uske liye samman prakat karne ko ichchhuk ho rahe hain. Yeh Sardar Bhagat Singh ke uchch tyag aur virta hi hai jiske karan aj use itna uncha asan mil raha hai. Lekin is uttejna aur josh ke same hamen yeh na bhul jana chahiye ki hamne ahinsa ke siddhant se swaraj prapati ka nishcheya kiya hai. Mujhe hinsa ke siddhant se koi lajja nahin parantu vartman saman men hinsa ka siddhant desh ke labh men hanikarak hai aur bhaye hai ki yadi talwar myan se nikal pari to kahin sampradayak yudh na chhir jaye.

Dil men kuchh rakhna aur uske virudh prakat karna kamjori ki nishani hai. Is liye prastav men spasht kar diya hai ki ham hinsa marg ka samarthan nahin karte........

...Bhagat Singh ke balidan se hamen yeh shiksha leni chahiya ki manushya ki bhanti bahaduri se ham desh ki liye maren aur hamara desh jivit rahe".

Translation.

"...Panditji showed how the boy had become so famous and a leader of people. What is the reason why to-day even the followers of non-violence or the opponents of violence are desirous of showing their respect for him. It is Sardar Bhagat Singh's great sacrifice and bravery that has today secured him such a high position. But during this time of excitement we should not forget that we have decided to obtain Swaraj through non-violence. I am not ashamed of the principle of violence but during the present time the cult of violence is harmful to the interests of the country and there is danger of civil war if the sword is unsheathed.

To believe in one thing and to appear to believe in something else is a sign of weakness. Therefore it has been made clear in the resolution that we do not support the cult of violence.....The lesson we should take from the sacrifice of Bhagat Singh is that we should die brave like men for the sake of our country and our country may live".

An unusual sample of side-by-side transliteration and translation by official translators. Source: Home Political File 208, 1932. National Archives of India, New Delhi. (Digitized collection).

presidency, on the other hand, employed one Oriental translator at a handsome salary of Rs. 800 per month (in 1907).[15]

The exactitude of translations commissioned by the state, especially when used for legal purposes, can be questioned, and was indeed questioned by Indians accused of sedition. To take one example: during his second sedition trial in 1908, fiery nationalist (and lawyer) Bal Gangadhar Tilak (1856–1920) himself cross-examined the official translator (an Indian) at length about several terms that he thought had been mistranslated.[16] The issue of translation could, however, also be to the advantage of writers in language other than English. James Campbell Ker – who had worked closely with the Director of Criminal Intelligence and authored the influential confidential handbook for officials titled *Political Trouble in India, 1907-1917*[17] – was of the view that the *Kesari* (Tilak's Marathi language newspaper) was more outspoken that its English counterpart, the *Mahratta*. This, in Ker's view, was because the *Kesari* could base its defence in court on allegations of mis-translation whereas the *Mahratta* could not do so. Contemporary scholars too have been sensitive to the centrality and problems of translation of vernacular texts in a variety of colonial contexts, specially the court room. In fact, the scholar of comparative censorship, Robert Darnton, has argued that 'literature under the raj was political in itself, down to its very syntax.'[18] Having noted this, if we want to understand what colonial officials including judges *thought* they were reading, and which so inflamed their censorial urge, then reading the texts in officially commissioned translations serves our purpose. At the same time, given the geographical and linguistic spread of the texts in question, this officially collected data allows us to include texts in ten languages in this anthology.

Texts are often produced in one context and read in others. In order to make sense of them, one therefore needs an insight into the times and circumstances in which they were produced. The five sections of this book cover one decade each. These sections are prefaced with context notes that flag important milestones in the political sphere that provoked the circulation of specific critiques of colonialism. The first decade of the twentieth century in India witnessed very significant changes in Indian politics. The landmark event of the decade was the partition of Bengal by Viceroy Curzon in 1905, an event which can be said to have changed the style of political activity in the country. The rise of the 'Extremists' – who no longer wanted to discuss constitutional arrangements politely, but wanted to mobilize the public via secret societies and dramatic acts of violence – and the increase in the number of 'political crimes' such as assassination and robberies meant that the government not only had to deal with them, but had to rally moderate opinion on its side too. Public opinion, whether that of 'moderate' leaders or the undecided Indian 'masses' became more important than ever before. Although prosecutions for the offence of sedition commenced in the closing years of the nineteenth century (the first sedition trial dating to 1891), it was only in the first decade of the twentieth when various strategies of censorship were applied in tandem. How was this done?

THE NUTS AND BOLTS OF CENSORSHIP

Objectives, policies and plans framed in London (at the India Office) or at the highest levels of the British government in India (the Government of India, centred in Calcutta till 1911, then in Delhi) had to be implemented by district officials, including ICS (Indian Civil Service) officers (both English and Indian). We would do well to remember that by the 1930s, Indianization of the ICS was well under way. By 1937, the service had 1,893 British and 1,319 Indian officials. Proscription notifications in the provinces were therefore increasingly signed by Indian officials, and at the level of the Government of India, Indian officials' opinions were often sought before instituting prosecutions. Officials of the Central Intelligence Department (headed by the Director of Criminal Intelligence) as well as provincial Criminal Investigation Departments (hereafter CID) had to coordinate with officials from other branches of government in matters pertaining to the circulation of unwanted texts, including postal communication. We often assume that state censorship is an unthinking application of a homogenously repressive opinion held by state personnel. A careful analysis of state censorship in colonial India, however, reveals it to be more akin to a well-thought out, discussed and debated policy, with divergent opinions and consensus-building. Not only did provincial governments have different priorities, but there could also be difference of opinion among administrators, which is amply on display in the official files of the colonial period. Conciliation or persuasion of political opponents, issue of warnings to them and finally frontal attacks (via legal proceedings, arrests, imposition of terms of imprisonment and fines): all these strategies had their votaries and were deployed depending on the assessment of the gravity of the threat.

The terms 'censorship' and 'banning' are used in this book to cover several methods by which the printed word was removed – or more accurately, sought to be removed – from the public eye. These included prosecution under the relevant sections of the Indian Penal Code (more about which later), demand for security from printing presses (a bond for good behaviour, which could be forfeited), and proscription by notification (forbidding the entry of a publication into India, or its transmission by post, or its forfeiture). In addition to provisions of the Penal Code and the Code of Criminal Procedure, a variety of press acts, postal and Customs acts and emergency provisions (war-time acts and ordinances) were marshalled to wield control over print.

The colonial state exercised both preventive and punitive censorship. The former, in the form of pre-censorship, was exercised mainly during the two World Wars (1914–18, and 1939–45). Two provisions of the Indian Penal Code were employed to punish transgressive publications. One was section 124A, the provision that defined the offence of sedition as:

> ...words, either spoken or written, or by signs, or by visible representation, or otherwise, (which) brings or attempts to bring into hatred or contempt, or excites or attempts to excite disaffection towards Her (His) Majesty, or the Government established by law in British India...

The law of sedition was formulated in 1870 and amended in 1898. The 1870 section only mentioned 'disaffection' and not the terms 'hatred' and 'contempt'. As amended in 1898, it covered words (spoken and written), signs and visible representation, though the addition of the term 'or otherwise' after this listing made its application much broader. The punishment prescribed for exciting 'hatred', 'contempt', or 'disaffection' against the government ranged from transportation for life, imprisonment for three years or the payment of a fine. The original section 124A of 1870 as well as its amended version in 1898 made it clear that comments on or criticism ('disapprobation') of any action of the government, or the attempt to get the government to change its policy ('with a view to obtain their alteration by lawful means') was *not in itself* an offence.[19] Although this clause was used in their defence by many publicists, it did not prevent the state from achieving its ends of punishing outspoken critics. The other important provision that was used to ban or otherwise push undesirable publications out of circulation was section 153A, which made incitement of 'class hatred' (broadly interpreted to cover race, economic class and caste, more often the first two) a punishable offence.

Some years stand out in the history of free (and un-free) expression in India. In 1835, unlicensed printing was allowed, with only registration of the printer and publisher, and the name of the publication, required to comment publication. The same was reiterated in 1867, as registration of publications was made mandatory. Licensed printing – which may be considered pre-censorship – was resurrected for a year after the revolt of 1857. Two years, 1878 and 1882, are important for the institution and then repeal of the Vernacular Press Act, resented by Indians as it targeted only non-English publications. In June 1908, the Newspapers (Incitement to Violence) Act was passed following a spate of political assassinations. This act empowered the government to forfeit presses used to print newspapers inciting certain offences, including murder, violence, and those offences listed under the Explosives Act of 1908. Since this act did not cover the offence of sedition, the Indian Press Act was passed in 1910. New newspapers and presses had to, as a preventive measure, submit a security by default (unless exempted by a magistrate) which could be forfeited in certain circumstances. This security deposit could range between Rs. 500 and 1,000, and could be asked of a newspaper or press at the discretion of a magistrate. At a time when the per capita income of an Indian was just under Rs. 200 annually, this amount had a deterrence value since it could then be forfeited in the event of a transgression; it was only forfeiture alone and not the demand itself that was subject to appeal. Old printing presses and newspapers did not have to deposit the same, unless they offended against the act and were called upon to do so. In the event of a violation of the act, the security as well as all copies of the newspaper or book would be forfeited, or removed from circulation. However, such a stringent demand did have an unintentional result. After several years of its implementation, the government appointed committee to study sedition noted, 'This act drove much of the seditious literature to secret presses.'[20] Although the 1910 Press Act was repealed in 1922, the state continued to wish to exert control over print. Between April and July 1930, the Government of India promulgated as many as seven special ordinances to deal with the Civil Disobedience movement; some imposed restrictions on the press, while others dealt with intimidation and 'unlawful instigation'. Less than a decade after the repeal of the 1910 Press Act, the Government of India made a case for greater control of the press by stressing that the tone of the press had 'deteriorated' since 1922. This led to the passage of the Indian Press Act of 1931, which was to provide the central framework for action against the press until the end of colonial rule in 1947.

Despite these attempts to tackle both 'indigenous' and 'imported' sedition (the former through press acts and the latter through the Sea Customs Act), determined publicists were able to exploit several loopholes in order to subvert official censors. Strategies included the registration of dummy editors, the issue of 'unauthorized news sheets' and posters, publications by anonymous authors, clandestine circulation, using court room trials as avenues for gaining notoriety and publicity, and of course innovative strategies to smuggle or transmit banned texts.[21] The colonial state's concern with preserving its *izzat* (honour) meant that prosecutions were undertaken after seeking legal opinion and only after preparing a water-tight case.

* * *

Colonial officials tasked with monitoring seditious activities had no doubt at all that there was a direct connection between the act of reading and acts of violence against the state. As Ker put it in his handbook:

> It is easy to see how the course of reading contained in the books described in this chapter [titled 'The Literature of Revolution'] would lead a young man by easy and direct stages from the study of religion and philosophy to the use of the revolver and the bomb.[22]

This necessitated (at times, absurd) surveillance on reading material. To cite but one example, Ker went to the extent of remarking on how many times a book was issued from the library of the Anusilan Samiti (a revolutionary organization in Dacca [Dhaka], then in India): *Jaliyat Clive* (Clive the Forger) was issued thirteen times, and biographies of Rana Pratap (a sixteenth-century ruler from Western India) and Nand Kumar (an eighteenth-century Bengali official who was executed after coming into conflict with Warren Hastings), the *Bhagawad Gita* (part of the Hindu epic poem, the Mahabharat) and *Anand Math* (a historical novel authored by Bankim Chandra Chattopadhyay in 1882) were popular in terms of issues to patrons.

The Sedition Committee report of 1918 expressed certainty that:

> The connection between this leaflet literature and the outrages has over and over again been accepted and dwelt upon by the courts. These leaflets embody a propaganda of bloodthirsty fanaticism directed against the Europeans and all who assist them.[23]

The report cited a letter written by a schoolboy from Sylhet (then in Bengal and now in Bangladesh) to the *Jugantar* (see chapter 4 in this anthology) where he credited the newspaper with making him 'alive to wrongs'. The committee believed that newspapers and pamphlets thus incited 'racial hatred of the most virulent form conceivable' among Indian youth. Words were monitored because they mattered.

The question of how far ideas shape material reality, and therefore the course of history, is far from being a settled one. In the context of North India between the eventful decades of the 1920s and 1930s, the historian Gyanendra Pandey has argued that a large-scale political movement is caused neither by poverty nor by political naiveté; as he puts it, 'It has taken stirring ideas and persistent propaganda to draw discontented men into open and extended political action.'[24] This anthology represents an attempt to showcase the powerful appeal of these arguments, ideas and ideals that shattered the myth of colonial invincibility.

Finally, the texts included here have not always been chosen for their literary merit, but for their rhetorical value, and also for their value as historical artefacts that reflect individual authorial views at times, and at other times a wider zeitgeist. Various streams of thought, often antithetical to – or in uneasy alliance with – each other, fed into the river of anti-colonialism in the twentieth century. For every banned text expressing sympathy with the Congress or with Gandhian methods, there were texts criticizing the methods of moderate nationalism and advocating violence. Schisms within the national movement which colonial authorities noted with relish in confidential file notings were nevertheless hidden from public view when the texts in which they appeared were banned for other reasons. Anti-colonial voices appear more like a jazz ensemble, with improvisation and spontaneity, than an orchestra with one conductor and a set repertoire.

No anthology can ever please every reader, especially when the terrain is as packed as that of late colonial India with exceptionally exciting events and scores of inspirational personalities. Neither does all proscribed material deserve our admiration. Material inciting conflict among religious communities, what we would recognize as 'hate speech' today, was also proscribed as it was understood to provoke violence, and caused law and order problems. In material produced by Indian anti-colonial nationalists of various hues, we encounter aggressive calls for violence, reverse racism (labelling the British as monkeys, dogs and snakes for instance) and – to our minds – problematic notions of gender roles (asking men to participate in movements by taunting them for being 'unmanly', or by citing the example of 'even women' having done their part).

Censorship can both succeed and fail, depending on the timeframe we assess. In the context of late colonial India, Gerald Barrier notes (what we would call today) the short-term 'chilling effect' of censorship measures on Indian publicists, even as he argues that in the long run censorship could not 'stem the tide of nationalism'.[25] Seventy-five years after the termination of colonial rule in India, the seventy-five chapters that follow reveal, represent and revel in the eventual triumph of free speech over repression.

NOTES

1 *Speeches of Sri B.C. Pal Delivered at Madras* (Madras: Ganesh & Co., 1907), 22.

2 Literally, the term 'Raj' refers to realm or kingdom. It is used to refer to the colonial state and British rule in India.

3 N.G. Barrier, *Banned: Controversial Literature and Political Control in British India 1907-1947* (Columbia: University of Missouri Press, 1974).

4 For perspectives on book history in India, see Abhijit Gupta and Swapan Chakravorty (eds), *Moveable Type: Book History in India* (Delhi: Permanent Black, 2008). A.R. Venkatachalapathy, *The Province of The Book: Scholars, Scribes and Scribblers in Colonial Tamilnadu* (New Delhi: Orient Blackswan, 2015) and Francesca Orsini, *Print and Pleasure: Popular Literature and Entertaining Fictions in Colonial North India* (New Delhi: Orient

Blackswan, 2017) are wonderful accounts of the production, circulation and consumption of print in different parts of India.

5 Barrier, *Banned*, 9.

6 Milton Israel, *Communications and Power: Propaganda and the Press in the Indian Nationalist Struggle, 1920-1947* (Cambridge: Cambridge University Press, 1994).

7 Two such catalogues are listed in the Further Reading section at the end of this book under the heading 'Catalogues of Proscribed Publications'.

8 Barrier, *Banned*, 160.

9 Ibid., 70.

10 Ibid., 116.

11 Ibid., 124.

12 Ibid., 137.

13 Three such reports/handbooks are listed in the Further Reading section at the end of this book under the heading 'Government Reports and Handbooks on Sedition and Revolutionaries'.

14 Not to be confused with the provincial level Criminal Investigation Department. Both are discussed in the next section and find mention in the rest of the book.

15 Home Political A (Proceedings), 64–74, January 1909. National Archives of India, New Delhi. Dadabhai Naoroji, famed nationalist and Britain's first Indian Member of Parliament, had estimated India's per capita income to be Rs. 30 (annually) in around 1870. At the beginning of the twentieth century it has been estimated to be at just under Rs. 200 (annually).

16 Translation Studies scholar Padma Rangarajan has focused on Tilak's second trial for sedition, in 1908, when he quizzed the official translator at length about the validity of translating terms, challenging him to explain why 'vaddh' should be translated as 'assassination' and not 'killing', for instance. Padma Rangarajan, 'Translation, Discursive Violence, and Aryanism in Early Indian Nationalism' in Christopher Rundle (ed.) *The Routledge Handbook of Translation History* (Routledge: London and New York, 2021), 289–92. For a complete account of the trial, see *Trial of Tilak* (New Delhi: Publications Division, Ministry of Information & Broadcasting, Government of India, 1986).

17 James Campbell Ker, *Political Trouble in India, 1907-1917* (Calcutta: Editions Indian, 1960; originally published 1917).

18 Robert Darnton, 'Literary Surveillance in the British Raj: The Contradictions of Liberal Imperialism', *Book History* 4, 2001, 143. See also Sukeshi Kamra, 'The Vox Populi, or the Internal Propaganda Machine, and Juridical Force in British India', *Cultural Critique* 72, 2009.

19 For more discussion on this, see Devika Sethi, *War over Words: Censorship in India, 1930-60* (New Delhi: Cambridge University Press, 2019). For a wide-ranging history of the evolution of sedition law in India right till the present day, see Chitranshul Sinha, *The Great Repression: The Story of Sedition in India* (New Delhi: Penguin Random House India, 2019).

20 *Sedition Committee, 1918: Report* (Calcutta: Bengal Secretariat Press, 1918), 34.

21 These strategies are discussed at length in Robert Darnton, *Censors at Work: How States Shaped Literature* (New York: W.W. Norton and Company, 2014); in Sethi, *War over Words*; and in Gerald Barrier, *Banned*.

22 Ker, *Political Trouble*, 28.

23 *Sedition Committee, 1918: Report*, 73.

24 According to Pandey, Congress propaganda played an important role in turning grievances into agitation, Gyanendra Pandey, *The Ascendancy of the Congress in Uttar Pradesh: Class, Community and Nation in Northern India, 1920–40* (London: Anthem, 2002), 61–64.

25 Barrier, *Banned*, 160.

NOTE ON EDITORIAL INTERVENTIONS

The original formatting of each text has been preserved as far as possible. Italics and bold type as they appeared in the original have been retained in the excerpts. None have been added. Unless indicated otherwise, translations are officially commissioned translations that were used in court or administrative proceedings, or accompanied ban notifications. Wherever I have translated the original (from Hindi to English), I have indicated that in the introduction to the respective chapter.

When there are spelling or other typographical or grammatical mistakes in the original, [sic] has been used to indicate these. Unusual usage has been retained as in the original text.

Round brackets ( ) where they appear in the excerpts are in the original text as well. Translations of texts by official translators often included brief explanations in such brackets. These have been retained.

Square brackets [ ] have been added by me for editorial comments, definitions, translation to English terms, new names of places and so on.

Ellipsis … indicate omission of sentences or paragraphs in the process of choosing the most important and revealing excerpts. Three periods (…) have been used when word(s) in the middle of a sentence have been omitted. Four periods (….) have been used to indicate the omission of entire sentence(s) prior to or after the sentence reprinted. Urdu script refers to the Perso-Arabic script.

There are three sets of Context Notes. The first one is for the first two sections, covering the period 1900–1920. The second one is for the third section, covering the period 1921–1930. The third one again covers two sections, covering the period 1931–1947. These notes highlight major trends and events in anti-colonial activities that served as the backdrop for the production and persecution of these texts. A brief biography of each text precedes the excerpt itself.

The Further Reading section contains seminal books and articles on the major themes and personalities that feature in the text. These books mentioned are easily available in bookshops and libraries, and the journal articles are available on the journals' web-sites and/or on databases such as JSTOR and Project Muse.

PART I: 1900-1910

&

PART II: 1911-1920

CONTEXT NOTE

In 1905, the province of Bengal was partitioned into a Hindu-majority Western Bengal, and a Muslim-majority Eastern Bengal. Though the official reason was stated to be administrative convenience, Indians were convinced that the intention of the colonial state was to drive a wedge between Hindus and Muslims in what was then the heartland of British India. Thereafter Bengal became a centre of radical anti-colonial activities and witnessed the articulation of new aims and the deployment of novel techniques in opposition to the colonial state. This partition provoked the Swadeshi (self-reliance) movement, and tactics such as Boycotting (of British good, educational institutions and employment avenues with the state). In the Western part of India, Bombay [Mumbai], Poona [Pune] and Nasik had already emerged as centres of a new radical politics.

From December 1907 began a coordinated campaign of political assassinations (employing bombs and guns), train derailments targeting officials, and assaults on symbols of government power (such as treasuries). One such event referenced in many of the banned publications in this section occurred on 30 April 1908, when Mrs and Miss Kennedy, two Englishwomen, were mistakenly assassinated in place of the intended target, a judge called Douglas Kingsford (who features in chapter 4). This case came to be known as the Alipore or Muzafferpore Conspiracy bomb case. The teenage assassins, member of the secret revolutionary society known as the Anusilan Samiti, were to become legends. Khudiram Bose (1889–1908) was executed in August 1908, while Prafulla Chaki (1888–1908) committed suicide. This event, and the praise of the heroes in the case, finds repeated mention in banned publications (see chapters 5, 8, 10 and 17).

In addition to Bengal, the Bombay presidency (primarily Poona [Pune], Nasik and Bombay city itself) emerged as a centre of both revolutionary ideas and their implementation. The official response to political assassinations was the passage of the Newspapers (Incitement to Offences) Act, 1908, which authorized the forfeiture of printing presses.

In the meantime, Indian revolutionaries abroad were activating transnational networks, exchanging ideas, and ensuring that anti-colonial ideas were made accessible to the Indian public as well as to well-wishers in other countries. Japan's victory over Russia in 1905 was an inspirational moment for many Indians (see chapter 9 for Tilak's reference to it) as it challenged European claims to inherent superiority. The establishment of India House (a hostel for Indian students) in London in 1905, thanks to the efforts of Sanskrit scholar and philanthropist Shyamji Krishnavarma (1857–1930), was a significant development as Indian students in Britain made it a hub of both the production and dissemination of nationalist views of revolutionary hues. Several of the chapters in this section highlight some of the most famous and widely circulated periodical publications that entered India from abroad.

In Europe, Indian expatriate Madame Bhikaiji Cama (1861–1936) served as the central conduit for the creation of anti-colonial content in Europe, as well as for the transmission of publications from the United States (specifically from the Yugantar Ashram at San Francisco) to Indian recipients. The Hindustan Ghadr (also spelt Ghadar, Gadar or Gadr) party, founded in 1913 in the United States with Har Dayal (1884–1939) at its helm, was active in dispatching material to India, often via Indians in far-flung corners of the globe from this decade till the Second World War. In 1909, an Indian student called Madan Lal Dhingra assassinated Sir Curzon Wyllie in a public meeting in London. A statement found in his pocket was later circulated – and banned – in India. Many of the chapters in these first two sections draw upon this rich vein of material; see chapters 9-12, 15, 19, 20-27.

Although more than a million Indians participated voluntarily as soldiers and camp followers in the First World War and witnessed action in Europe, Africa and the Middle East, yet other Indians continued to criticize the very basis of colonial rule and challenged its claims to benevolence. The Jallianwala Bagh massacre, which occurred on 13 April 1919 in Amritsar in Punjab, radicalized an entire generation of Indians, and served as a rallying cry for anti-colonial agitation in the decades that followed. The firing by (Indian troops under British command) on an unarmed crowd of political agitators led to over 400 deaths (Indian estimates put it at upwards of 1,000). This traumatic event, and the two men held responsible for it (Col. Reginald Dyer, who ordered the firing, and Sir Michael O'Dwyer, the Lieutenant Governor of Punjab) are referenced in many of the excerpts in this anthology; see chapters 30, 32, 35, 36, 41, 52, 66 and 67. The name of the park itself was enough – then, as now – to summon up an entire assemblage of images and sentiments associated with the humiliation of being subjects of a foreign king.

Indian anti-colonial nationalists were by no means united in their approach to the colonial state; passion for the cause of greater role for Indians in managing India's affairs was the one unifying thread. Proscribed publications in these as well as subsequent decades contained criticism – often vitriolic – of rival approaches. When such publications were banned, schisms among nationalists were therefore also hidden from public view.

PART I: 1900-1910

1

1905 ›› BHALA [THE SPEAR]

Original: Marathi | Article: 'A Durbar in Hell', 11 October 1905

THE *BHALA* WAS A MARATHI POLITICAL NEWSPAPER STARTED BY the Bhopatkar brothers in Pune on 5 April 1905. For an article titled 'A Durbar in Hell', the editor, Bhaskar Balwant Bhopatkar, was sentenced to six months' simple imprisonment and a fine of Rs. 1,000. During the trial, Justice Batty of the Bombay High Court accepted the defendant's contention that he had not written the piece but had only published it, thinking it was 'some thing like the allegories of old English Literature'. Nevertheless, the judge held him responsible for publishing something which led the public to regard government authorities with 'suspicion and distrust', which was 'far from being a patriotic action'. The judge also took into account the fact that *Bhala* enjoyed a wide circulation since it was priced low – its readers bought it for half an anna. One hundred and twenty copies were sold in Bombay, 205 in Poona and the vast majority (1,322) in the mofussil or rural areas. Could the latter category of readers be guaranteed to be, asked the judge, 'persons of reasoning power and sufficient calmness of judgment and understanding' to take a mature view of the article? In other words, the judge acknowledged that the identity, location and status of the reader also determined the power of the words they read. The defence lawyer in this case was Dinshaw Davar (who was later to serve as the defence lawyer for Bal Gangadhar Tilak's sedition trial in 1897, and as Judge during Tilak's prosecution for sedition in 1908). He rested his defence on two aspects – showcasing other articles where the editor had professed loyalty to the British, and arguing that there was no evidence that it was the British government and not any other that was being referred to in the article. Even as the jury pronounced a verdict of guilty, Justice Batty elaborated on the meaning and application of section 124A of the Indian Penal Code. While Bhaskar Balwant Bhopatkar was serving his sentence, his brother, Laxman Balwant Bhopatkar edited the paper. The paper suspended publication in 1910. It resumed as a weekly paper from 1925 till 1935.

The offending article, excerpts from which are reproduced in the following pages, merged fact with fiction in an imaginative rendering of a gathering in hell.

It described a meeting organized by the 'Emperor of Hell' to choose a worthy successor. Claimant after claimant described his brutal deeds but the winner – a thinly veiled allegorical portrayal of an Englishman in India – won the contest hands down.

* * *

11 OCTOBER 1905

'A DURBAR IN HELL'

Once upon a time a great Durbar was to be held in the Empire of Hell. A grand and extensive Mandap [hall] was erected there for that purpose.... At last only one member was left (to speak). But none imagined from his attire that he would prove to be pre-eminent in deeds of cruelty. For, his complexion was most attractive, that is, reddish white. His attire too, was very simple. He wore trousers, boots (and) a coat; and he had, as his head-dress, a turban shaped like a mason's hod. He carried in his hand a cane carved at one end, and he had in (his) mouth a wooden pipe from which smoke was issuing. The member (attired) as above got up and began to harangue as follows:— "Your Majesty, many persons have till now sung the praises of their own accomplishments; but all these must pale before a narration of my qualifications. Your Majesty, a short while ago, a member gave you some idea of civilized oppression, and you also nodded your head (in approval) at the time. From that I am perfectly convinced that I alone am (destined) to obtain your kingdom. For, I have practised oppression fully in conformity with that very mode. Your Majesty, therefore, may be pleased to hear (an account of) my cruelties. In the first place, I entered, under the pretext of trade, a country in which I possessed no rights and with which I had no connection; and, by gradually fomenting dissensions among the people there, commenced to deprive them of their kingdom. Then I began to assume the authority of a King (by acting) on the principle of might is right. I made many forged documents, 1 plucked out the teeth of the queens there and robbed them of their wealth by starving them. I ruined the money-lenders of that country by confusing documents and sent them to Hell. Then I became a king and usurped the kingdoms of many (persons). I robbed all of their independence. I removed their wealth from there to my distant country so that there could be no fear of its coming back. I then saddled them with different taxes. I taxed (their) incomes and (also) levied an impost upon (a commodity) which

ORIGINAL CRIMINAL.

Before Mr. Justice Batty.

EMPEROR

v.

BHASKAR BALVANT BHOPATKAR.

1906

February 14.

Criminal Procedure Code (Act V of 1898) Sec. 292—Right of reply by prosecution—Tendering of evidence by the defence—Indian Penal Code (Act XLV of 1860), Sec. 124A—Sedition—Ingredients of the offence.

Where the defence puts in documents while the case for the prosecution is going on, the prosecution is entitled to reply.

Changes is policy and changes in measures are liable to criticism, and to criticise and urge objections to them is a special right of a free press in a free country. But any effort which aims at impairing the confidence with which the public is entitled to look to Government, and at producing an unwillingness to accept the intervention and protection of the Government, for the purposes for which Governments exist, is within the mischief contemplated by s. 124 A of the Indian Penal Code, even though there be no intention to excite a rising or actual violence of any kind.

The provisions of s. 124A of the Indian Penal Code explained.

THE accused Bhaskar Balvant Bhopatkar was the editor and publisher of a Marathi newspaper called the "Bhala" (a) printed in Poona. The charge against him was that he published an article under the heading of "A Durbar in Hell' in the issue of "Bhala" dated the 11th October 1905, and thereby attempted to bring the Government into hatred or contempt and to excite feelings of disaffection against the Government established by law in British India, an offence punishable under s. 124A of the Indian Penal Code, 1860.

Report of the Bhala *case. Source: The Bombay Law Reporter, Vol. 8, 1906.*

is vital to their existence, that is, salt. I gave them bribes of money and made them hate their own country. Then I deprived them of their arms and thus arranged that they should not be able to defend themselves even if torn and devoured by wild beasts. I hanged many of them and ill-treated their women and children. I consumed kine which are held sacred by them. I held many Durbars like this without any reason and made a parade of my own greatness thereat, and mixed earth with their food. I changed the direction of the education (al) system, and banished the qualities (i.e. sentiments) of patriotism etc. from their minds and turned them into donkeys for bearing loads. By telling them that we (I) would come to their assistance, I gave the beggar's bowl and wallet into their hands. I incessantly trod them under (my) boots (heels) and made their hunger vanish by systematically pinching their bellies. I made a bon-fire of their lives, their wealth, their homes, their religion, their reputation, their honour, their independence and everything (else) belonging to them. Can there be any more civilized mode of oppression than this? I alone, therefore, deserve the throne." The Emperor of Hell was highly gratified to hear this (speech), (and), getting up, he cordially embraced that member. He gave three cheers in his name (honour) and said:— "You alone are fit to conduct this Government after me. You have perpetrated many acts of cruelty up to this time and it is only in consequence of this that you have obtained this kingdom by right; we will, therefore, very shortly crown you." The Ruler of Hell having spoken thus, the Durbar was dissolved as it was rather late.

* * *

2
1906 ›› INDIA AND HER PEOPLE

Original: English | Author: Swami Abhedanand
Book Excerpt: Chapter III - 'Political Institutions of India'

SWAMI ABHEDANAND (1866–1939) CARRIED FORWARD FAMED spiritual leader Swami Vivekanand's (1863–1902) legacy in the United States, following the latter's successful visit there in 1893. *India and Her People* was published in 1906 by the Vedanta Society New York, and proscribed by the Government of Bombay. It contained six lectures delivered at the Brooklyn Institute of Arts and Sciences, plus an additional chapter on 'Woman's Place in Hindu Religion'. The first two chapters of the book summarized ancient Indian philosophical systems and Hindu beliefs and practices. It was the third chapter that led to the ban. It drew upon arguments of Indian nationalists about the drain of wealth from India and blamed British rule for famine and misery. Excerpts from this chapter are reprinted in the following pages. The author thanked the economic historian Romesh Chunder Dutt (1848–1909; who had been both a member of the Indian Civil Service, as well as President of the Indian National Congress) whose books had, he stated, provided him 'numerous valuable facts and statistics'. Swami Abhedanand also cited many British authorities in the chapter, including British government records and committee reports, in addition to House of Commons reports. These gave this book more credibility but also made it more dangerous as a well-researched critique. Furthermore, the circulation of such a book, in English, among the American public, was considered to be undesirable as it would prejudice the claims of the British empire to benevolent governance in India.

* * *

Cover of India and Her People.

CHAPTER III

POLITICAL INSTITUTIONS OF INDIA

To-day in British India this self-government of the Hindus has been destroyed by the short-sighted policy of the British autocrats, and its place has been given to a most costly system of judicial administration, unparalleled in the history of the world. They talk about English justice. Of course there is justice in English government, but it is very expensive and one-sided. Indians have justice among Indians, but if an Indian's rights are outraged by a European he cannot hope for similar justice. The poorer classes, furthermore, cannot pay for justice under any conditions; it is too expensive. The present oppression of the police and the cruelty of revenue

INDIA

AND

HER PEOPLE

BY

SWAMI ABHEDANANDA

Author of "Self-Knowledge," "How to be a Yogi," "Spiritual Unfoldment," "Divine Heritage of Man," "Philosophy of Work" etc.

PUBLISHED BY

THE VEDANTA SOCIETY

NEW YORK

Title page of India and Her People.

collectors under British management have already driven the masses to the verge of absolute despair and rebellion....

The government of India is as despotic as it is in Russia, because three hundred millions of people who are governed have neither voice nor vote in the government. The interest of the British nation is the first aim of the present system of government. People pay heavy taxes of all kinds, and that is all. The government sends out expeditions to Soudan [sic], Egypt, China, Tibet, and other places outside of India, and then the poor people of India are forced to pay the enormous cost of these expeditions, amounting to millions of dollars....

To-day the masses of people in India live on from two to five cents a day and support their families with these earnings. Expecting to have their grievances removed by the government, they have been agitating for the last

Portrait of Swami Abhedanand printed in the book.

Below: Dedication, India and Her People.

TO THE

PEOPLE OF INDIA

WITH DEEP FELLOW-FEELING

AND

EARNEST PRAYERS FOR THE RESTORATION

OF THEIR ANCIENT GLORY

AND

NATIONAL FREEDOM

twenty years by calling annual public meetings and special public meetings, where the best classes of educated people have been represented. Although the Indian Government has spared no pains to stop all such agitations, still the people have been passing resolutions and sending them to the Viceroy and to the Secretary of State. Not one single word of encouragement has ever come from the despotic rulers, who are determined to follow the steps of the Russians in their methods of administration....

Ambitious, unsympathetic young civilians go out to India for a few years to exploit the country, satisfy their greed and self-interest, and return come to live like lords, drawing upon the taxes of the impoverished millions. I will give you an illustration of Lord Curzon's administration. Lord Curzon [1859-1925; in office 1899-1905] was the most unpopular Viceroy ever in India. His policy was one of interference and distrust. He is no believer in free institutions or in national aspirations. He took away the freedom of the press, which was steadily gaining in weight and importance, by passing the Official Secrets Act. The policy of his administration was to keep all civil as well as all military movements of the government secret. He sent the expedition to Tibet. He wasted the resources of the country on the vain show and pomposity of the Durbar [Delhi Durbar of 1903] while millions were dying of famine and plague. He condemned the patriotic and national spirit of the Indians, and lastly he carried out the Roman policy of divide and rule by partitioning the Province of Bengal, simply to cripple the unity of the educated natives, as also of seventy millions of inhabitants. All these and many acts he carried out with such despotism and highhandedness, against the unanimous opinion of seventy million people, that they were driven to boycott all English goods and manufactures....

The natives of India are now determined to stand on their own feet, but it is a hard problem for an enslaved nation to raise their heads while the dominant sword of a powerful alien government is held close to their necks. If the people of America wish to know what would have been the condition of the United States under British rule, let them look at the political and economic condition of the people of India to-day.

* * *

3

H.M. HYNDMAN (1842–1921)

Original: English | Pamphlet
3.1: Pamphlet: The Ruin of India by British Rule, 1907
3.2: Pamphlet: The Emancipation of India, 1911

HENRY MAYERS HYNDMAN WAS BORN IN A WEALTHY FAMILY, WHO began life as an ardent supporter of British imperialism, and then turned into a socialist and equally ardent anti-imperialist. Till the 1860s he was an ardent supporter of the British empire in India; reading a pamphlet on the Orissa famine converted him into a strident critic. He was an associate of Shyamji Krishnavarma's Indian Home Rule Society and was present at the inauguration of India House in London, which was to become the centre of revolutionary activity in the West. Having established contact with famed Indian nationalists in London – including with Dadabhai Naoroji (1825–1917) who articulated the Drain of Wealth theory to challenge British claims of benevolence – he began speaking and writing passionately about issues connected to India. The excerpt reprinted in the following pages is taken from a sixteen-page report written by Hyndman in 1907 on behalf of the British political party, the Social Democratic Federation, and presented at the International Socialist Congress at Stuttgart, better known as the venue where Madame Bhikaiji Cama unfurled the first nationalist flag of India. The many-pronged critique of the British Raj, made by an elite English public intellectual, was considered to be very damaging by the colonial state, as Hyndman also linked colonialism to capitalism.

* * *

3.1

1907

THE RUIN OF INDIA BY BRITISH RULE

IN THIS PAMPHLET, HYNDMAN DREW ATTENTION TO THE PERKS enjoyed by colonial officials in India, presenting them as opportunists and not as self-sacrificing men on a civilizing mission. He spoke not only of the economic but also of the cultural costs of colonialism. This pamphlet was banned entry into India under the Sea Customs Act, as was *Justice*, a journal edited by him.

* * *

The British Empire in India is the most striking example in the history of the world of the domination of a vast territory and population by a small minority of an alien race. Both the conquest and the administration of the country have been exceptional, and although the work has been carried on, save in a few directions, wholly in the interest of the conquerors, we English have persistently contended that we have been acting really in the interest of the subdued peoples. As a matter of fact, India is, and will probably remain, the classic instance of the ruinous effect of unrestrained capitalism in Colonial affairs. It is very important, therefore, that the International Social-Democratic Party should thoroughly understand what has been done, and how baneful the temporary success of a foreign despotism enforced by a set of islanders, whose little starting-point and headquarters lay thousands of miles from their conquered possessions, has been to a population of at least 300,000,000 human beings....

According to an official return to the House of Commons, obtained many years ago, with great difficulty, by the late Mr. John Bright, the conditions not having materially changed in the meantime, out of 39,000 officials who drew a salary of more than 1,000 rupees a year, 28,000 were Englishmen and only 11,000 natives, or in the ratio of more than five to two. The Englishmen, however, received on the average in salaries more than five to one what the natives are paid. Of 960 civil offices which really control the civil administration of India, 900 are occupied by Englishmen and only 60 by natives. The Indians have no control whatsoever over their own taxation, nor any voice at all in the expenditure of their own revenues. The entire civil government is now carried on by men who live lives quite remote from the people they govern, who have no permanent interest in their well-being, and who return home (which they have visited frequently in the meantime) at forty five or fifty-five years of age with large pensions. India is, in fact, now administered by successive relays of English carpet baggers, men who go out with carpet-bags and return with chests having ordinarily as little real sympathy with the natives as the have any deep knowledge of their habits and customs....

In the last resort we English hold India by the sword. A well-known Anglo-Indian official of high rank, walking with a great Afghan chieftain, many years ago, on the ramparts of Peshawar, held forth to him on the importance of the British power in India and the overwhelming forces it could bring to bear. "Your power in India," replied the Khan coolly, "is 70,000 men. Well armed." The European forces in India are now somewhat in excess of this, and the native army, officered in all the higher grades by Europeans, amounts, including reserves, to 180,000 men, without artillery since the mutiny. The cost of this army is entirely thrown upon the revenues of India, and amounts to upwards of £19,000,000 a year—a terribly heavy tax in itself on a very poor population, and the heavier that so large a proportion is paid away in salaries to foreigners.

It is claimed by the supporters of European domination that this army, though admittedly entailing heavy charges, is cheaply purchased; seeing that by its presence peace is ensured from one end of Hindustan to the other. But the horrors of peace, even in the Western World, are often worse than the horrors of war, and in India this is unfortunately still more apparent. The vigour and intelligence of one-fifth of the human race is being destroyed by this despotic peace. Beautiful arts are falling into decay; native culture is being crushed out; agriculture is steadily deteriorating. Anything in the shape of patriotism or national feeling is discouraged, and its advocates are persecuted and imprisoned. Denunciation of the wrongs of British rule is treason, and legitimate combination to resist tyranny is a pernicious plot. Peace is not worth having at such a price, even if accompanied by increasing wealth. But when such peace goes hand in hand with growing impoverishment for the mass of the people, then clearly we are face to face with an utterly ruinous and hateful system....

The total gross value of all the produce of British India for 225,000,000 of human beings cannot be put, at the outside, at more than £1 per head. The late Mr. William Digby put it at not more than 12s. 6d. per head. No such dire poverty over so large an area was ever before known on the planet. And the impoverishment is increasing. Mr. Digby, himself an official of one of the great Famine Agencies, and with special opportunities for obtaining information, calculated that the ryots [peasant] in the districts outside the permanent settlement get only one-half as much to eat in the year as their grandfathers did, and only one-third as much as their great-grandfathers did. Yet, in spite of such facts, the land tax is exacted with the greatest stringency, and must be paid to the Government in coin before the crops are garnered! Thus, apart from other drawbacks, our system forces almost the entire agricultural population into the hands of the native money lenders, from whom alone money to meet the tax can be obtained; and then we hypocritically lament the usurious disposition of the men who lend on the crops! When it is remembered that every improvement which a ryot makes in his holding he is taxed for; that fallow land in British territory is taxed as high as cultivated land; and that little allowance is made for famine periods, it is easy to comprehend the crushing effect of our ruinous system upon the miserable agriculturists, who constitute four-fifths of the Indian population. But for the money-lenders—if, that is to say, the native usurers refused to lend on growing crops—the Government of India would at once be bankrupt....

This drain, or economic tribute, from which most conquered dependencies suffer, is specially severe in the case of India. Making every possible allowance, it is clearly established that, comparing the Indian exports and the Indian imports, the overplus of exports for which there is no commercial return now amounts to more than £35,000,000 a year, or considerably in excess of 50 per cent more than the total land revenue obtained from all British India. This drain has been going on in an increasing ratio, and necessarily with deepening effect, ever since the British occupation. It means that India, naturally a country with the greatest possibilities for wealth-production in every department, is being steadily bled to death, in order to pay pensions, interest, home charges, dividends and remittances in Great Britain to the capitalist and landlord classes with their hangers-on. Wherever it is possible to throw a charge upon the Indian revenues this is at once done, and, as the Indians are wholly unrepresented either in India or in Great Britain, they are unable to complain effectively in any way whatever. It is very doubtful whether the Spaniards ever exacted anything approaching to this tremendous tribute from their American possessions, even in the hey-day of their ruthless extortions. When to this drain of £35,000,000 annually is added the amount paid for the services of Europeans in India, including the 75,000 white soldiers, which runs up to many millions sterling, it is clear we need look no farther for the real cause of India's frightful impoverishment and the continuous famine and plague which now steadily prevail in some part or other of our territory....

* * *

3.2

1911

THE EMANCIPATION OF INDIA

PUBLISHED IN LONDON AND PRICED AT ONE PENNY, THIS PAMPHLET advertised itself as a reply to the Secretary of State for India, Viscount Morley, on his article on 'British Democracy and Indian Government'. Hyndman mentioned in the preface that he had 'done my utmost for five-and-thirty years to warn my countrymen how impossible it is that our hold in India should be permanent.' Eighteen years before the Indian National Congress declared, at its annual session at Lahore in 1929, its goal to be Purna Swaraj [complete independence], Hyndman had argued for the 'complete emancipation' of India. He had been writing against British rule in India since the 1880s, comparing it to ancient Roman tyranny and as something much worse than the Spanish conquest of South America and Mexico. After detailing the financial burdens imposed by Britain on India by way of taxation and home charges, that is, by summarizing the 'drain' theory, Hyndman moved on to address his compatriots. He also explained the reasons for the rise of patriotic sentiments among Indians of all creeds. Indian translators of Hyndman's pamphlets were prosecuted as well.

* * *

....Most of our recent dealings with other nations have been guided by Asiatic rather than by European considerations, and the possibilities of disturbance in India affect prejudicially our influence in Western affairs. Nearly all those, likewise, who return from holding office in India join the ranks of the reactionary party; while the few who take a wider view of the prospects of humanity are of opinion that British rule in India is a necessity, and are thus drawn more or less themselves into the vortex of Imperialism. Nor is it far from the exercise of despotism abroad to an attempt to stifle public opinion and exalt the power of bureaucracy at home. This in itself may be a serious danger. For the British Democracy, about which Lord Morley writes, is in fact non-existent. We have all the drawbacks of a plutocracy and none of the advantages of a popular Government at the present time. A Referendum to the whole of the people would, however, I am convinced, decide even

THE EMANCIPATION OF INDIA.

A Reply to the Article by the Right Hon. Viscount MORLEY, O.M., on "British Democracy and Indian Government" in the "Nineteenth Century and After" for February, 1911.

By H. M. HYNDMAN.

ONE PENNY.

THE TWENTIETH CENTURY PRESS, LIMITED (Trade Union and 48 Hours), 37, 37A & 38, CLERKENWELL GREEN, LONDON, E.C.

Hyndman, Cover page of The Emancipation of India *(1911).*

now in favour of giving self-government to India. English workers are not Imperialists in the bureaucratic sense at all....

A population of 44,000,000 of people exercising practically despotic rule over 300,000,000 of civilised Asiatics several thousand miles away from these islands. Is it not enough to state that one fact to show plainly that sooner or later this connection must come to an end? Is it not also reasonable, when that truth is admitted, to consider seriously how soon the change is likely take place, and to prepare for bringing it about in a satisfactory manner with the consent of both parties? At the present moment there seems little probability of this being done, and it is the loss of all confidence in the intention of Great Britain to act reasonably in this direction that more than anything else has led to the growing unrest and dissatisfaction throughout Hindustan.

But we have it now on the highest official authority that this unrest exists, and that quite probably it will continue and will spread. Lord Morley may be right when he says that disaffection prevailed in Bengal long before partition. Nevertheless, it is also true that this cutting in two of a great historical province, in order to give the Mohammedans, who are supposed to be favourable to British rule or at any rate hostile to Hindu dominance, a majority in the severed portion brought the disaffection to a head. It did more. This was no economic oppression; it was an outrage on local sentiment and the general feeling of Indian patriotism. What was the result? This purely sentimental grievance aroused a spirit among the Bengalis which Anglo officials still seem unable to understand. This "cowardly" race as our people were never tired of calling them -- though the history of the Bengal Sepoys and of the Bengal Moslem Wahabi Crescentaders passed up by the secret committees from Benares to Agra, and thence on to the frontier to fight on the Black Mountain in 1868, might have taught them better -- this pusillanimous set, I say, suddenly developed a succession of cool, desperate, self-sacrificing young assassins who reckoned their own lives at nothing, and who, when they gloried in their condemnation and went triumphantly to their deaths, were regarded as martyrs by their countrymen.

No such imposing religious demonstration has been seen in India in our day as that secretly-summoned crowd which attended the cremation of the body of one of these popular heroes after his execution in Calcutta itself, the presence of many well-to-do women lending special significance to the ceremony. Much as we all detest assassinations, it is madness to shut our eyes to the importance of such a public outburst of religious feeling in favour of an assassin, because steps have been taken to prevent renewal of the display.

Nor is this exhibition of sympathy with opponents of the Government confined to actual criminals or manifested only in the towns. When Mr. Bipan Chandra Pal, a convinced pacifist, was released from the imprisonment to which he was condemned, for refusing to give evidence in a political case, his portrait was carried crowned with flowers through most the villages of the partitioned province, and it is said that Mohammedans joined with Hindus in their appreciation of the service he had rendered to the common cause by his action. Why should they not? They are of the same race after all, and are placed under similar disabilities. Certain it is at least that, so far as Bengal is concerned, the suppression of newspapers, the putting-down of public meetings, the deportation without accusation or trial of political suspects, and the flogging of young political offenders, have not checked the development of and discontent among the 80,000,000 Indians, Hindu and Mohammedan, who constitute the population of them undivided province. These measures have only, as might have been expected, driven the propaganda underground. The demand for Swaraj is more persistent than before, and the cry of "Bande Mataram" arouses more enthusiasm than ever.

But it is just same in the Mahratta country. There, though serious economic and social causes are at work to account for permanent unrest, it was the arrest and condemnation of Bal Gungunder Tilak, for an article dealing with the history of the Mahratta race and drawing encouragement for the future from the records of their past, which stirred agitation throughout the province of Bombay, and led to the extraordinary action of the Bombay Municipality in actually closing the markets of that great city for eight days in order to show disapproval on the part of the commercial classes – the chief supporters of our rule -- with the policy of Government. Here, again, not only in Bombay and in Poona, but throughout the whole of the villages, the same view was taken of the trial and judgment. Tilak to-day in his prison is still leader, not only of the Mahrattas, but of the whole of Western India. The agricultural population may be poor and ignorant and superstitious; but if we have failed, after 150 years of victory in the field and "successful" administration in the bureau, to convince them that our presence and leadership are preferable to the counsels of men of their own race and faith, then what probability is there that we shall be able to deal any better with this growing dissatisfaction the future?....

I do not pretend to speak with any knowledge on military affairs, but the famous march of Sir Hugh Rose's column through Central India during the Mutiny could never have succeeded if the agricultural population had not been friendly to the English troops. I do not myself believe that our removal from India will be brought about by an armed rising; but with only 70,000 European troops in Hindustan, and a large part of them unavailable at a given moment, it is well to bear in mind that we cannot hope to hold our own by military force against an unfriendly, to say nothing of a hostile, India. Nor is it well to overlook such a statement as that made by Mr. Donald Smeaton at Glasgow, immediately on his return to England, to the effect that what is going on in India would lead to a revolt "besides which the Mutiny would be child's play." In fact, I do not suppose the most bigoted Imperialist would seriously argue that we can keep down India with European troops alone. We conquered India and we reconquered India with the help of native armies and with, in the main, the good will of the native population. If the conditions have completely changed within the past fifty years we are bound in common prudence to take account of this....

Lord Morley, giving in his article a summary of what Indians urge against us, voices a portion of their complaints thus: "You have shown yourselves less generous than the Moguls and Pathans, though you are a more civilised dominant race than they were. Hindus were willing to embrace Islam and to fall in with the Moslem regime because the equals of the dominant race. With you there has been no assimilation." That is true, and assimilation is not now possible. But surely the duty which we owe to India is not fulfilled by mere refusal to understand her demands or to give an outlet to the higher conceptions of her people. To continue to repeat the hypocritical statement that we remain in India for the good of India deceives no one - not even ourselves. To say that we will never be driven out of India is to predict a permanence for our rule which does not depend upon us. To enlarge upon Indian shortcomings in the past and in the present is little more than a pharisaic belauding of our own virtues, which men of other races do not regard as transcendent. Yet, if we would but see, there is a glorious task lying immediately to our hand. We have done mischief enough. Here is a magnificent Empire, with a splendid record behind it in every branch of human achievement, slowly stirring with a new life which will be a glorified and ennobled resuscitation of the old. Great art, great architecture, great public works, great industries, great agriculture, great mathematics, great philosophy, great religions, all are being slowly born again, even under the crushing influence of our rule. Let us lift off this carapace of greed and repression and hold out the hand of welcome and encouragement to the higher aspirations of this vast population. That England should herself take the first steps towards the complete emancipation of India would entitle her to an infinitely higher place in the world's esteem than a vain attempt to carry on for yet a few fatal years the harmful despotism of to-day.

* * *

4

1907 ONWARDS ›› JUGANTAR [NEW ERA]

Original: Bengali | Editor: Bhupendra Nath Dutt
4.1: Article: 'Away with Fear', 16 June 1907
4.2: Article: 'The Medicine of the Big Stick', 16 June 1907
4.3: Article: 'Hindu Heroism in the Punjab', 14 December 1907
4.4: Article: 'The Bengali's Bomb', 30 May 1908

JUGANTAR (ALSO SPELT AS *YUGANTAR*) WAS EDITED BY BHUPENDRA Nath Dutt, the brother of the famed religious preacher, Swami Vivekanand. The paper enjoyed a circulation of 7,000 in 1907. It was written in colloquial Bengali. In July 1907, Dutt was sentenced to one year's rigorous imprisonment by the Chief Presidency Magistrate of Calcutta for two articles published the previous month (both of which are reproduced in the following pages). The press was also ordered to be confiscated. On appeal to the High Court, his sentence was upheld but the confiscation of the press was set aside. A series of printers and publishers were prosecuted over the course of the next year and awarded between two and three years' rigorous imprisonment. The passage of the Newspapers (Incitement to Offences) Act of 1908 terminated the publication of the newspaper, and the Jugantar group shifted to leaflets thereafter. The historian Peter Heehs has remarked that repeated prosecutions of *Jugantar* had enhanced its circulation from 200 to 7,000, and then to 20,000 at the time of its closure.

* * *

4.1

16 JUNE 1907

'AWAY WITH FEAR'

In the course of conversation a respected pandit [Hindu priest] said the other day that this vast British Empire was a huge sham; that it was a house without a foundation or a garland strung without a thread; that though it glittered and looked so nice with its crimson hue, a slight pull or a little push would bring it down to fragments. That it does not fall is due simply to our foolishness. The tide of oppression has passed over us for century after century. Subjection for a thousand years has so bewildered us with fear that we cannot muster up enough courage even to come out of the privacy of our houses to see who is sitting to-day as king on the vacant throne. We see the high diadem from a distance and utter our prayers and take the name of God. Our King, too, seeing the opportunity, is aggravating our internal confusion by sometimes wielding the sceptre and sometimes smiling a forced smile. He and we have never become intimately acquainted with each other. A close look at the face of a ghost dispels all fear of it.

* * *

After looking at it from a distance for so long we, too, have at last come to suspect that the hands and feet of the ghost are not really so strong as its face is hideous; that the bugbear is not really so large as we have supposed it to be. What we ought to do now most of all therefore, is to give a little push to the bugbear and see what happens. In the Punjab scarcely was the bugbear touched with a finger when it leapt and jumped, mostly from fear and partly also from anger. What we want now is a number of men who will take the lead in giving a push and thus encourage the masses and infuse hope in the minds of those who are almost dead with fear and dread. It will not do to form a company with those who are stiff with fear. Mere words will not convince such men. They must be shown by deeds done before their eyes that the work is not impossible exactly to the extent that they think it to be, and that the arms of the English are not so long as to grasp India and keep it within their grasp against our wish. What is wanted therefore is a number of workers who will renounce every worldly thing and break off every worldly tie and plunge

Jugantar - *Emblem. Source: http://www.sriaurobindoinstitute.org/saioc/Sri_Aurobindo/yugantar_newspaper*

into the sea of duty; who will understand everything themselves and then make others understand; who will die themselves and deliver others from the fear of death; who will have neither home, nor son nor wife but will have only their Mother, the country of their birth, green with crops and well-watered. Will there not be found one in the whole of Bengal who is ready to respond to the Mother's call?

Once fear is dispelled the work will become easy and all the brag of the English will be of no avail.

* * *

4.2

16 JUNE 1907

'THE MEDICINE OF THE BIG STICK'

In Bengal we have cried ourselves hoarse during the last two years, and sent up the price of paper in the bazaar by using up quires upon quires in submitting petitions couched in the most correct and elegant language. But as the result of all this we have been fortunate enough to get nothing but thrusts of lathis, and partitioned Bengal remains parted. But in the Punjab a hue and cry was raised as soon as the water-rate was enhanced. The period of making representations and submitting petitions did not last more than two weeks. The people then applied the remedy which is always applied to fools. There were a few heads broken and a few houses were burnt down, and the authorities gave up the idea of enhancing the water-rate. The Colonisation Act, too, became inoperative. How wonderful is the remedy! The Kabuli medicine is indeed the best of medicines.

* * *

4.3

14 DECEMBER 1907

'HINDU HEROISM IN THE PUNJAB'

FOR THIS ARTICLE BAIKANTO CHANDRA ACHARJYA, THE PRINTER and publisher, who stated that he did not know who the author of this article was, was sentenced to two years' rigorous imprisonment and a fine of Rs. 1,000. Presidency Magistrate Douglas Kingsford (who was to become famous the next year as the proposed target of an assassination attempt) interpreted it as an attempt to incite Sikh soldiers to mutiny. By the time this article was published, the Sikh empire had been swallowed up by the British one, and Punjab was considered to be a province loyal to the British, and the pre-eminent centre for military recruitment. However, the article hailed back, in persuasive terms, to an earlier chapter in Punjab's history, before its annexation by the British.

* * *

In the middle of the 18th [19th] century, in seeking to measure strength with the highly powerful Sikh race on the field of battle, even the soldiers of the English race, who now brag of the strength of their sword, but are averse to fighting and are strong through the help of the swords of the Sikh and the Gurkha, were compelled to flee like a flock of sheep. The sharp whipping of the battle of Chillianwalla [January 1849, when British forces suffered heavy casualties against the forces of the Sikh empire in Punjab] the barbarous English are not even yet able to forget. The battlefields of Mudki, etc., still continue to float before the eyes of the people of India as so many proof [sic] of English defeat. If the Punjabi heroes of the land of the five rivers, released from the spell (which is now on them), again step forward to battle for the defence' of kine and Brahmins in India, the drunken drowsy eyes of this Western race will at once look out for a way of escape, flinging far off the sword of whose power the English brag in the pride of unreal strength. A country cannot be ruled by cannon and rifles; manliness and heroism too are wanted. In how many battles have the English, so far, been victorious? Yet the inhabitants of the Punjab, like gods under a curse, do not even now revive the memories of the past and step forward to defend their country.... Nevertheless, Bengalis, consider this – how long will a handful of cowardly English remain in India if the Sikh nation again takes its stand as it did in the days when Lord Gough and others, in their bovine ignorance of the art of war, were taught a lesson at Chillianwalla.

* * *

4.4

30 MAY 1908

'THE BENGALI'S BOMB'

THE PRINTER-PUBLISHER, BARINDRA NATH BANERJI, WAS SENTENCED to three years' rigorous imprisonment. This was the sixth prosecution of the *Jugantar* in just over one year.

* * *

Bengali boys have learnt to make bombs, but they have not yet learnt to throw them well. It is because they are yet unable to take proper aim and hit the mark that in the Muzaffarpur accident they killed persons other than him whom they intended to kill. It is only because their hands were not trained and their heads not sufficiently cool that two innocent ladies have had to die.... It is beyond the vision of the secret spies of the feringhi sirkar [foreign government] to see where, in some solitary room in the kitchen, brothers, sisters, mothers and daughters together are making and can make bombs. Even the extensive machinery and factories of England have to own themselves beaten by the way in which the Bengali can manufacture bombs, guns and cartridges. Let the unostentatious preparations for this great revolution be silently made and collected in every house. A handful of policemen and English soldiers will not be able to find them out. They will not be able to keep in check this extensive preparation for a great Kurukhetra [reference to the battlefield in the Mahabharata epic] by obstructing it. The inclination to make this preparation is due to the spirit of the age; it is a law of nature; it is the unobstructed awakening of the instinct of self-preservation of a sleeping race, persecuted, despised, and trampled underfoot for a long time. Two or four boys have been arrested to-day. Although Hem Chandra, Ullaskar and others [arrested Anusilan Samiti members] will never more be united with us in the field of action – we know indeed that they will never escape from the grim jaws of the English – thousands and thousands of Hem Chandras and Ullaskars have come up again and are standing in front. Hence there is no reason to despair. The soil of India is ever fertile with the blood of heroes.

* * *

5

1907 ONWARDS ›› BANDE MATARAM [HAIL, O MOTHER]

Original: English
5.1: Article reproduced from the *Jugantar* of 5 May 1907 in the 26 July 1907 issue of *Bande Mataram*
5.2: Article: 'Traitor in the Camp', 14 September 1908

BANDE MATARAM WAS A SISTER PUBLICATION, IN ENGLISH, OF *Jugantar* and occasionally reproduced articles from it. It was started by the Bengali nationalist Bipin Chandra Pal (1858–1932) in cooperation with Aurobindo Ghose (1872–1950), a Cambridge-educated nationalist who had spent his formative years in Britain, served as ideologue and mentor to an entire generation of revolutionaries, and was to attain renown later in life as a mystic. The title derived from a patriotic slogan mentioned in the famous historical novel *Anand Math* (Abode of Bliss), authored by novelist-intellectual-civil servant Bankim Chandra Chattopadhyay (1838–1894).

The Bengal government estimated *Bande Mataram*'s circulation to be about 6,000 in 1907, of which 2,400 copies were circulated to subscribers and 3,000–4,000 copies daily were sold in Calcutta. One such article, printed originally in *Jugantar* in May 1907, was re-published in *Bande Mataram* when the latter reported the case against *Jugantar* in its columns. During the prosecution proceedings, the defence held that the article was reproduced by way of a report on court proceedings. But the court held that *Bande Mataram* had reprinted 'the whole mass of seditious writing collected by the prosecution... with the actual intention of bringing the Government into hatred and contempt.' This article is reproduced.

* * *

5.1

26 JULY 1907

But it is useless to talk to you Englishmen in this strain. You are not a man, you are a demon, you are an "asura" [demon].... You are surely a demon, or otherwise you would not on the one hand have converted the millions of educated Indians into lambs and, on the other, would not have induced thousands of Musalmans in Eastern Bengal to forget themselves and engage in a quarrel with their brothers. Your Minto [Viceroy of India] and Hare [Lieutenant Governor of Eastern Bengal and Assam] are dangerous people who have no equal in the art of demoniac duplicity. Who calls you a tiger? Who calls you the British Lion? There are no tigers or lions in your country which contains only moles, jackals and dogs. In childhood we read only of these animals in your books and to-day in the field of politics, too, we are being acquainted with the self-same animals.

* * *

Bandê Mataram.

A Daily Organ of Indian Nationalism.

Bande Mataram. *Source: http://www.sriaurobindoinstitute.org/saioc/Sri_Aurobindo/bande_mataram_newspaper.*

5.2

14 SEPTEMBER 1908

'TRAITOR IN THE CAMP'

BANDE MATARAM WAS FAMOUSLY PROSECUTED FOR AN ARTICLE titled 'Traitor in the Camp', published on 14 September 1908. It referred to the 'Alipore Bomb Trial' and the assassination of two Englishwomen, Mrs and Ms Kennedy at Muzaffarpore [Muzaffarpur]. One of the accused in the case, Narendra Nath Gossain, turned informer and was killed by Kanai Lal Dutt in revenge. Dutt was tried and hanged for murder, and the article exalted him as a martyr who had killed a traitor. Less than a month after this article was published, after a successful prosecution, the printing press was forfeited and the declaration of the printer and published annulled under the Newspapers Act of 1908. In his judgment on the case, Chief Presidency Magistrate Thornhill at Calcutta stated that whether or not an article constituted an incitement to murder was dependent not on the content alone, but also on other factors, including the circumstances and the feeling existing at the time, the persons to whom the article was addressed, or by whom it would be read. In other words, there was no single objective criterion to decide what constituted 'incitement', and this left ample scope for judicial interpretation. In the opinion of the judge, Bengal, which had a large number of 'what may be termed discontented student class', who could read English, provided fertile ground for incitement. In fact, in most cases of this kind, the prosecution defined 'incitement to murder' in the widest possible terms, whereas the defence stressed on the ambiguity of the definition. In this case, Judge Thornhill ruled that the term 'any incitement' itself meant that the phrase was to be interpreted in the widest possible terms. Although in this case of this article the author had referred to the futility of using violence and bombs, Judge Thornhill held that:

> It is true that the last paragraph of the article contains a reference to the futility of using bombs as a means to bring about independence, but I cannot see now (sic) this cancels the encouragement or undoes the mischief preceding it.

A similar debate took place during the appeal hearing, when the defence argued that that article contained approbation in the sense of appreciation, and not incitement in the sense of urging. It also took the plea that even English newspapers such as the *Empire* and the *Englishman* had condemned Gossain, calling him a 'wretch'. While the central argument of the defence hinged on the fact that the article – far from advocating the use of bombs – referred to the futility of using bombs, the Advocate General, S.P. Sinha, had an interesting viewpoint. He argued that in fact the article constituted covert incitement, which was at par with direct incitement. Even the reference to bombs was present, said Sinha, because it was held that the use of bombs would be fruitless; had it been more effective, there would be no disapprobation. In other words, Sinha held that the article did not condemn the use of bombs because it was morally wrong, but merely because it was ineffective. In his judgment, Justice Holmwood of the Calcutta High Court finally held that the whole article was indirect or veiled incitement, and contained direct incitement to murder informers. He said that the European newspapers' views on the matter were of no consequence. He went on to say:

> We may point out that the incitement in this case addressed as it is to the youth of a peculiarly emotional and intellectually subtle race, is probably the most effective and dangerous form of incitement that could be addressed to them.... It deprecates isolated assassinations as useless but it implies that the wholesale removal of the bureaucracy would assist the cause of national independence.

The case of the *Bande Mataram* illustrates that when newspapers were prosecuted, it was not merely the content that was at the crux of the matter. The political situation, which was volatile in Bengal at this time following its partition in 1905, was also of great importance, as it provided the ground where the incitement would take root. In addition, as is clear from the comments of Justices Thornhill and Holmwood, the Bengali 'character' was also supposedly extremely susceptible to incitement.

The *Bande Mataram* case floundered on the inability of the prosecution to establish the identity of the editor conclusively. They held that Aurobindo Ghose was the editor; the defence held that there was no single editor but editorial staff. Well-known nationalist leader Bipin Chandra Pal had terminated his connection with the paper earlier and refused to give evidence. For this he was sentenced to six months' imprisonment. The government's case against Aurobindo Ghose thus failed. The printer and publisher, Apurba Krishna Bose, was sentenced to three months' rigorous imprisonment.

Excerpts from the article in question are reprinted on the following page:

* * *

From Jay Chand to Oomi Chand [12th and 18th century historical figures accused of collaborating with the Ghurids and the British respectively] is a far cry, but the Political history of our country for all those long centuries of indelible shame can be summarised and accounted for in the four short words "Traitor in the Camp". Reading down the pages of the annals of that interminable period of disgrace, you will hardly come across the account of a single movement towards emancipation that had not nursed in its bosom one or more vipers, named "Traitors" who, whilst remaining within the Camp in the seeming guise of loyal adherence, betrayed the object of their perjured allegiance at the season of fruition.

But need we stop at Oomi Chand? Are there not traitors in the land to-day who would sell their soul as readily for the paltry privilege of wearing a jewelled sabre, or for a ribbon to stick in their coat, or for a title to cover their base birth with? For it is in the blood of some of our countrymen, this accursed proneness to perfidy, and has been there, ever since the loss of our independence and Heaven alone knows when the last drop of it shall have been spilled or become sterile. And the no less singular feature of this ghastly thing is that through all these countless years it is always the person at whose instance he turned traitor who has punished the miserable miscreant, but the country could never find a single son to rise and avenge her on the hated monster by smiting him on the ground.

Now for the first time the current is turned. For the very first time a cause has produced a votary who has willingly sacrificed his life to visit on its betrayer his merited doom. Kanai has killed Narendra. No more shall the wretch of an Indian who kisses away the hands of his comrades reckon himself safe from the avenging hand. "The first of the avengers" History shall write of Kanai. And from the moment he fired the fatal shot the spaces of his country's heaven have been ringing with the echo of the voice "Beware of the traitor's fate."...

* * *

6

1907 ›› VIHARI [SUPREME ENJOYER/ KRISHNA]

Original: Marathi
Article: 'Explanation of Sedition', 26 August 1907

VIHARI WAS A MARATHI LANGUAGE WEEKLY PUBLISHED FROM Bombay. Vinayak Damodar Savarkar (for a biographical note, see chapter 15) had worked as a sub-editor on the staff of this paper, and his later writings on the events of 1857 as well as his reports from his time in London were also published in the weekly. In 1906 and 1907, two editors had been given warnings and had to deposit securities. For the article reprinted below, and another one published in September, the editor, Bhaskar Vishnu Phadke, was sentenced by the Bombay High Court to two years' simple imprisonment and asked to pay a fine of Rs. 300. The article offered a unique overturning of the conventional meaning of sedition, by accusing the British of sedition. It also relied on the readers' familiarity with the basics of Maratha history, and used historical personages – such as the reference to Ramdas and Shivaji (the latter a popularly venerated seventeenth-century Maratha ruler and the former believed to have been his mentor) and the 'Bhavani of Maharaja' (the goddess who was believed to have blessed Shivaji) – to rouse Indians to imitate them in the present.

* * *

26 AUGUST 1907

'EXPLANATION OF SEDITION'

Since the birth of the *swadeshi* agitation and the boycott movement nothing but sedition can be heard in India.... Anglo Indians may be thinking that India is smitten with the disorder of sedition, but this is a pure delusion. There is absolutely no sedition among Indians. The (very) use of the word sedition in connection with Indians is itself a mistake. If there had been a rule of the Indian people in India and if some of them had made an attempt to subvert it, then that (attempt) could have been called sedition. When there is no rule of the Indian people at all in India, how can there be sedition. If Feringee [foreign] writers and orators make use of the word sedition in the sense of hatred of English rule, then there is no meaning at all in it. For, who can have love for alien rule? What reason have the Indians to love British rule? If the Indians were to love British rule, it would mean that they love slavery. If anyone were to use the word sedition in such a sense that (the sentence) 'sedition is growing rampant in India' should mean that the love of Indians for slavery is becoming less, that they have begun to hate slavery (and) dependence, then such use of the word alone has some meaning and it is also true that this kind of sedition is growing rampant in India, But what is there improper in it? It is quite natural to have an aversion to slavery. He who does not feel abhorrence for slavery, is not a man but a brute....

The statement that we are disloyal towards the English is devoid of all meaning. From our point of view, if any one is disloyal, it is the English themselves. For, (it is) they (who) took our kingdom. Properly speaking, if any one is to be punished for sedition, it must be the English themselves, who have taken the kingdom of others and made them slaves. If there be no sedition in the English taking our kingdom, what kind of logic except the logic of pure selfishness can say that it is seditious on our part to cherish a desire of winning back our kingdom. That the English should raise an outcry of sedition is as villainous as (the act of) a cut-throat who complains that his victim does not allow his throat to be cut quietly. That there should be no sedition in India is in itself against nature. For the rulers to say that there is sedition in India is indirectly to declare that the Indians are unwilling to bend their necks to the slavery of others. If the rulers are using the word sedition in this very sense - and sedition cannot possibly have any other meaning here - we have no reason to feel sorry for it. On the contrary it is an honour to us. It (marks) the triumph of our patriotism and love of independence. It is a proof that we are not willing to spend our days in the slavery of others, that we are not beasts but living human beings impatiently panting for independence....

But when the desire for independence becomes intensified amongst the thirty crores of Indians and a Ramdas (capable of) giving an organized form to that desire and making it easy of accomplishment and (ready) to tell (the people) '(You) should take your kingdom by slaying (and) slaying; appears upon the scene, and a Shivaji (capable of) translating that exhortation into action is born, then it is evident that it would not take long for the Indians to raise the banner of independence....

O fiery patriots of young India, the night of servitude is now over and the dawn of the sun of independence has approached.... When (you) gird up (your) loins for independence, then the Bhavani of Maharaja will tell (you) what to do next. Betake yourself to it for protection. Then (you) need not be anxious about victory. Shouty victory to the goddess of independence! *Bande Mataram*!

* * *

7

1908 ›› KAL [TIME/ERA]

Original: Marathi
7.1: Article: 15 May 1908
7.2: Article: 18 December 1908

THIS WAS A MARATHI WEEKLY, WHICH WAS WARNED BY THE Government of Bombay several times since its commencement in 1898. The proprietor and editor, Shivram Mahadev Paranjape, was convicted by the Bombay High Court in July 1908. The jury had found the accused guilty under sections 124A as well as 153A of the Indian Penal Code, but nevertheless had recommended him to mercy, being of the opinion that the accused had been motivated by patriotism. Judge Dinshaw Davar nevertheless sentenced him to 19 months' rigorous imprisonment, which he considered a lenient sentence, given that the offence could be punished with transportation for life or a longer period of imprisonment.

The article covered several themes: racism against Indian officials, expression of the view that the Indian public was not opposed to 'bomb outrages', that Indian maharajas and Muslims' views did not represent those of other Indians, and a description of the aims of bomb-throwers.

* * *

7.1

15 MAY 1908

Why did Government reward so hastily the Police officers who arrested the accused implicated in the bomb outrages? The alleged offenders have yet to be arraigned and convicted before proper tribunals. More confessions, which are often made to escape Police torture, do not constitute conclusive evidence against the accused. What then can be the secret motive of this precipitate waste of public funds? Again, why are the European officers excluded and only natives rewarded? Is it not perhaps with a view to encouraging treachery, in regard to the unravelling of the still hidden details of the conspiracy? In other countries treachery is punished, but in India it is rewarded! The particular form of Government existing in India is perhaps responsible for this difference. Government should be careful how far to trust the meetings that are being held at various places to express indignation at the bomb outrage. We do not think the public at large is much on the side of Government, as only four such meetings have been held during the last fortnight. These public meetings are not worth a straw if they are engineered by Government officials. Even the Muzaffarpore meeting was held ten days after the outrage under the presidency of the Maharaja of Darbhanga. These Maharajas being mere puppets in the hands of Government, the importance of the meeting in the eyes of the people may be easily gauged. The Poona and the Behar [Bihar] Mahomedans have also expressed their indignation at the outrage; but Mahomedans are accustomed to express lip-sympathy towards Englishmen in order to gain their own ends.... People desire to get their rights. If these cannot be had by straightforward means, they are prepared to secure them by crooked devices. If the English do not conciliate the people by granting them *swarajya*, there will soon be a trial of strength. People are prepared to do anything for the sake of *swarajya* and they no longer sing the glories of British rule. They have no dread of British power. It is simply a question of sheer brute force. Bomb-throwing in India is different from bomb-throwing in Russia. Many of the Russians side with their Government against the bomb-throwers, but it is doubtful whether such sympathisers will be found in India. If, even in such circumstances, Russia got the Duma, *a fortiori* India is bound to get *swarajya*. It is quite unjustifiable to call the bomb-throwers in India anarchists. They do not desire that India should have no Government whatsoever. They do not advocate misrule. They merely want *swarajya*. Setting aside the question whether bomb-throwing is justifiable or not, Indians are not trying to promote disorder, but to obtain *swarajya*.

* * *

7.2

18 DECEMBER 1908

THE NEXT EDITOR, PURUSHOTTAM BAPUJI KHARE, WAS CONVICTED to six months' rigorous imprisonment and a fine of Rs.1,000 for the article below. The paper terminated publication after the Press Act of 1910 came into force. The article referred to the activities of revolutionaries in Bengal as well, appearing to disapprove of their activities, but in the end justifying them. This is a strategy to be found in many proscribed publications.

* * *

The English schemed to conquer India and succeeded in their attempts. The question of consolidating their conquests next stared them in the face and they were equal to the occasion. The Secretary of State for India appoints now-a-days fourth-rate Englishmen to the highest posts in the land, and they, too, are mere birds of passage. The people of India have now begun seriously to doubt whether the English desire to continue to rule over India at all. Otherwise it is difficult to account for all the absurd and reckless deeds committed by them recently in India. The cup of their sins is not only full but it is brimming over. We cannot help saying that the bureaucrats now in power are a set of dunces in politics. They do not care to ascertain the causes of discontent, but are prompt to advocate every measure of repression, and seem to be bent upon throttling every agitation started by the Indians. The English are by nature a kindly race. But their hands seem to be forced by circumstance. Apart from the isolated murders of individual Englishmen, the *Yugantar*, emerging at fitful intervals from its grave, indiscriminately howled for a general massacre of all European foreigners. The aims and objects of the Maniktolla conspirators were to subvert British rule. Their *modus operandi* was to murder European and Native officers and adverse witnesses and to commit dacoities to fill their war-chest. The Bengalees met in the temple of Kali and in front of her image tossed for the person who was to bomb the next victim. A lad of eighteen attacked Sir Andrew Fraser fearlessly in an open meeting. What will not youths, whose hearts are of stone and whose minds have become perverted, do? Government can pass whatever laws it wills. The only justification is that they are masters of the situation. Bosanquet says : — " Laws, strictly speaking, are only the conditions of civil association. The people which submits to the laws should be their author." When have the people of India given their consent to obey the laws passed by Englishmen? It is quite plain from all this how Englishmen pass laws and why Indians are found to break them. These are not laws, but mockeries of law.

* * *

8

1908 ›› KESARI

Original: Marathi | Author: B.G. Tilak
8.1: Article: 'The Country's Misfortune', 12 May 1908
8.2: Article: 'These Remedies Are Not Lasting', 9 June 1908

KESARI WAS A MARATHI WEEKLY STARTED BY BAL GANGADHAR Tilak (1856–1920) in 1880. In June 1897, he had been sentenced to 18 months' imprisonment for verses published in the journal. Six months of the sentence were remitted once Tilak agreed to certain conditions. It was described by James Ker in his confidential handbook as a weekly paper 'which expresses the most extreme views and enjoys the largest circulation of any vernacular organ in India.' He went on to comment that 'Its leading articles … contained enough ginger to make them palatable to the Indian public without too flagrantly offending the more sensitive taste of the Oriental Translator, and the legal advisors of Government.' In any case, the *Kesari* again came to the government's notice in 1908, when its circulation was estimated at 20,000 copies. Additionally, Tilak was in the sights of the government as well. In 1908, an official of the Government of Bombay termed him 'by far the ablest and most dangerous of the rebel party in this country', and further suggested that 'his complete overthrow will stagger that party and show to all waverers the strength of Government. It is not enough to imprison him when we can also suppress his newspaper.'

Tilak was arrested in June 1908 in connection with two articles, extracts from the first of which are reproduced in the following pages. Charges were framed under section 124A as well as 153A of the Indian Penal Code. None other than the to-be founder of Pakistan, Muhammad Ali Jinnah, appeared as his counsel during the bail hearing. Justice Davar, who tried his case in 1908, was – by an ironic coincidence – the same person who had defended him in the sedition case in 1897. During the course of his trial – where his address to the jury in his own defence lasted over twenty hours spread out over five days – Tilak used a number of arguments in his defence. He stated that his views were not novel, and had been mentioned in pro-British newspapers such as the *Pioneer* as well. He said that the translation of the phrase 'Obstinacy and perversity of the white official class' was a mistranslation. 'Perverseness' should have been substituted with 'stubbornness' and 'white official class' with 'English bureaucracy', thus changing the meaning. The phrase 'inebriated with the insolence of authority' should have been 'blinded with the intoxication of authority'. He said that even this phrase was not his own, but had been used by Burke when speaking of civil servants under the East India Company. With regard to the following sentence deemed objectionable – 'Even a cat shut up in a house rushes with vehemence upon the person who puts it there and tries to kill it,' – Tilak stated in court that he had intended to argue that Bengalis were better than cats and that if cats could stand at bay, it was possible Bengalis might be driven to desperation in some cases. Tilak also said that he did not ask for Swaraj all at once as he had used the word 'gradually'. He said that in his article he had shown the necessity of some reform in the administration, and that 'the bomb was a signal from which some lesson could be taken.' He also argued that Lord Morley had said in a speech at the Civil Service dinner that they could not govern India by mere repressive measures, and that the British public would not tolerate it. In other words, if that was the opinion of Lord Morley then it could not be seditious for him to say the same thing.

In contrast to Tilak's scepticism regarding the reliance on translations of the original articles, Judge Davar conveyed his faith in the accuracy of the translations done by a native-speaker of Marathi, Bhaskar Vishnu Joshi who was the First Assistant to the Oriental Translator (whom Tilak had extensively cross-examined in court) and asked the jury to think of the effect of the articles on the minds of readers who did not have the benefit of the author's verbal explanations. The context in which the articles were published, the first one only twelve days after the Alipore bomb outrage, was also considered significant by the judge.

The jury found Tilak guilty (by a majority of seven against two) and he was sentenced to three years' transportation for this article (plus three years' transportation and a fine of Rs. 1,000 for the second one). The sentences were to run one after the other. Later, the Government of Bombay commuted this to a simple imprisonment (at the Fort in Mandalay, Burma) and commuted the fine.

Tilak's conviction caused a furore; the *Tribune* reported that 'considerable consternation' was caused in Bombay when the verdict was declared, as 'all Deccani Hindus and several Parsees and Mahomedans closed their shops. All cloth markets and other markets were closed. The city presents appearance of general mourning today'. A meeting of sympathy was held in Calcutta and chaired by the eminent journalist Ramanananda Chatterjee, editor of the famous *Modern Review*. In Poona, the news created 'profound sensation'. Many shops were closed and the police had to take special precautions to prevent disorder. In the Mill district in Bombay, workers threw stones and shouted 'Tilak Maharaj ki Jai'. According to government estimates, as many as fifteen people were killed in the firing in the streets of Bombay in the last week of July.

Writing about the articles years later for his handbook, Ker stated that the articles could be read in two ways: 'either as a discussion of a purely hypothetical question, or as an encouragement to those who disapproved of the system of Government to go on using bombs till it was changed.'

* * *

वर्गणीचे दर. [illegible]

केसरी.

जाहिरातीचे दर. [illegible]

[illegible]

वर्ष १. पुणें:—मंगळवार तारीख ४ जानेवारी १८८१. अंक १,

आज मुंबई इलाख्यांत इतकीं मराठी वर्तमानपत्रें निघत असतां व या शहरांत ही तीन चार चालत असतां, नव्या वर्तमानपत्राची काय जरूर आहे हा विचार आमच्या वाचकांच्या मनांत येणारा आहे. वास्तव प्रथमतः या पत्राचा उद्देश लोकांस कळविणें अवश्य आहे.

वर्तमानपत्रांचा प्रचार पडल्यास आज पंचवीस वर्षें जरी होऊन गेलीं, व गेल्या दहापंधरा वर्षांत तर यांच्यांत जरी पुष्कळ सुधारणा झाली, तरी अद्याप वर्तमानपत्रकर्त्यांस आपणांवरची जबाबदारी पुरेपणीं कळू लागली आहे, किंवा लोकसुधारणेस आपल्या परिश्रमांनीं केवढें साहाय्य होणारें आहे याविषयीं त्यांचा पक्का समज झाला आहे, असें सामान्यतः पाहतां आढळणार नाहीं. दोन चार नामांकित वर्तमानपत्रांखेरीज बाकीच्यांची जर स्थिति पाहिली, तर वर्तमानपत्र म्हणजे जागोजागच्या बातम्या प्रसिद्ध करण्याचें साधन यापलीकडे वरील शब्दाचा अर्थ पत्रकर्त्यांच्या मनांत कधींही येत असलेसें वाटत नाहीं. बाकीकडे तर लहानसान गांवांतून सुद्धां वर्तमानपत्रें निघू लागलीं आहेत. छापखाना घालणें व पत्र काढणें हा एक व्यापारच बनल्यानें त्यास विद्येचा विशेष संस्कार नाहीं अशा मंडळीच्या हातीच [illegible] दोन [illegible] साधनें पडलेलीं बहुधा आढळतात. आतां येथें खरें आहे कीं, कोणत्याही तऱ्हेनें का होईना, वरील दोन साधनांची वृद्धि ही एकंदर देशास श्रेयस्करच आहे. [illegible] लोकांत वाचण्याचा प्रचार जरी होण्यास वरील साधनांचा उपयोग आहे. पण याच उद्योगांत वरच्या पेक्षां चांगली मंडळी पडली असतां लोककल्याणाचा मार्ग ज्यास्त खुला होणार आहे हें उघड आहे.

वर्तमानपत्रांचा मुख्यतः दोन प्रकारांनीं मोठा उपयोग आहे. एक हा कीं, त्यांनीं आपलें काम निःपक्षपातपणें व निर्भीडपणानें बजाविलें असतां सरकारी अधिकाऱ्यांवर मोठा दबदबा राहतो. [illegible] दिवस लागलेले असल्यानें व पॉलिसीची नजर [illegible] फिरत असल्यानें जो उपयोग होत असतो, तोच [illegible] वर्तमानपत्रकर्त्यांची लेखणी सदोदित चालू असल्यानें होत असतो. सरकारी अधिकाऱ्यांनीं आपापलीं कामें चोख रीतीनें चालविलीं असतां [illegible] किती कल्याण असतें हें कोणास सांगावयास नकोच. पण वरील चोखपणा राहण्यास त्यांचा सर्व कारभार जेव्हां लोकांच्या नजरेसमोर वरचेवर येत जाईल तेव्हां राहणार. सर्व गोष्टी सर्वांच्या समक्ष होत असल्या म्हणजे अर्थातच लांचलुचपत वगैरे जे अन्यायाचे प्रकार एरवीं होण्याचा संभव असतो ते पुष्कळ अंशीं नाहींसे होतात. जुन्या एतद्देशीय संस्थानांतून वरील प्रकार किती चालत असे, व अद्याप किती चालतो, हें क्षणभर लक्षांत आणलें असतां पत्रकर्त्यांची नजर लोकांस किती हितावह आहे हें कोणाच्याही लक्षांत आल्यावांचून राहणार नाहीं. विलायतेंत खुद्द महाराणी साहेबांपासून व मुख्य प्रधानापासून तों अगदीं छोट्या सरकारी कामगारापर्यंत सर्वांच्या कारभाराकडे लोकांची नजर वर्तमानपत्रांच्या द्वारें सारखी लागून राहिलेली असते, यामुळें कोणताही अन्याय प्रायः छपला जात नाहीं, व यामुळें तेथील लोक युरोपांतील इतर राष्ट्रांहून सुखी आहेत ही गोष्ट सर्व प्रसिद्धच आहे.

तर सरकारी अधिकारी आपापलीं कामें कोणकोणत्या तऱ्हेनें बजावतात याविषयीं केवळ निःपक्षपातबुद्धीनें व कोणाची भीड न बाळगतां मजकूर लिहिण्याचा आमचा इरादा आहे. अमुक अमुक गोष्ट आहे तेव्हां त्याच्या विरुद्ध कसें लिहावें, किंवा सरकारानें अमुक अमुक गोष्ट केली तर तिजवर चर्चा केली

Front page of *Kesari*, January 1881.

8.1

12 MAY 1908

'THE COUNTRY'S MISFORTUNE'

No one will fail to feel uneasiness and sorrow on seeing that India, a country which by its very nature is mild and peace-loving, has begun to be in the condition of European Russia... we did not think that the political situation in India would, in such a short time, reach its present stage, at least that the obstinacy and perversity of the white official class (bureaucracy) of our country would (so soon) inspire with utter disappointment the younger generation solicitous for the advancement of their country and impel them so soon to (follow) the path of rebellion. But the dispensations of God are extraordinary. It does not appear from the statements of the persons arrested in connection with the bomb explosion case at Muzafferpore, that the bomb was thrown through the hatred (felt) for some individual or simply owing to the action of some badmash madcap. Even Khudiram, the bomb-thrower himself feels sorry that two innocent ladies of Mr. Kennedy's family fell victims (to it) in place of Mr. Kingsford...

The young Bengali gentlemen, who perpetrated these terrible things, do not belong to the class of thieves or badmashes; had that been so they would not have made statements frankly to the Police as (they have done) now. Though the secret society of the young generation of Bengal may have been formed like (that of) the Russian rebels for the secret assassination of the authorities, it plainly appears from their statements that it has been formed not for the sake of self-interest but owing to the exasperation produced by the autocratic exercise of power by the unrestrained and powerful white official class. It is known to all that the mutinies and revolts of the nihilists, that frequently occur even in Russia, take place for this very reason, and looking (at the matter) from this point of view (one) is compelled to say that the same state of things, which has been brought about in Russia by the oppression of the official class composed of their own countrymen, has now been inaugurated in India in consequence of the oppression practiced by alien officers. There is none who is not aware that the might of the British Government is as vast and unlimited as that of the Russian Government. But rulers who exercise unrestricted power must always remember that there is also a limit to the patience of humanity. Since the partition of Bengal, the minds of the Bengalis have become most exasperated, and all their efforts to get the said partition cancelled by lawful means (have) proved fruitless, and it is known to the world that even Pandit Morley, or now Lord Morley, has given a flat refusal to their (request). Under these circumstances no one in the world, except the white officials, inebriated with the insolence of authority will think that not even a very few of the people of Bengal should become turn-headed and feel inclined to commit excesses. Experience shows that even a cat shut up in a house rushes with vehemence upon the person who confines (it there) and tries to kill him. That being the case, the Bengalis, no matter however powerless they might be thought to be, are human beings; and should not the official class have remembered that exactly like those of other men, the feelings of the Bengalis, (too), are liable to become fierce or mild as occasion demands? It is true that India having now been for many years under the sway of alien rulers the fire, spirit or vehemence natural to the Indian people have to a great extent cooled down; but under no circumstance can this vehemence or indignation descend to zero degree and freeze altogether. Old or experienced leaders can so far as they themselves are concerned, keep this indignation permanently within certain prescribed limits with the help of (their) experience or (mature) thought; but it is impossible for all the people of the country thus to keep their spirit, indignation or irritability always within such bounds, nay, it may even be said without hesitation that the inhabitants of the country in which it is possible for this feeling of indignation to always remain thus within prescribed bounds, are destined to remain perpetually in slavery....

But the experience gained from history, the growth of democratic public opinion in England, and the awakening caused throughout the whole continent of Asia by the rise of an oriental nation like Japan, have come in the way of the tyrannical policy of our whiter bureaucrats and imposed some restrictions on their imperial (autocratic) sway; However the desire of the people to obtain the right of *swarajya* is growing stronger and stronger. If they do not get rights by degrees, as desired by them, then some people at least out of the subject population, being filled with indignation or exasperation, will not fail to embark upon the commission of improper or horrible deeds recklessly.... 'As you sow, so you reap' is a well-known maxim. For rulers to tell their subjects "We shall practice whatever oppression we like, deport anyone we choose without trial, partition any province we like, stop any meeting we choose, or prosecute anyone we like for sedition and send him to jail; (but) you, on your part should silently endure all those things and should not allow your indignation, exasperation or vehemence to go beyond certain limits" is to show to the world that they do not know common human nature....

It is now plain that not only has the system of government in India become unpopular but also that the prayer made many times by the people for the reform of that system having been refused, even some educated people forgetting themselves in the heat of indignation have begun to embark upon the perpetration of improper deeds. Men of equable temperament and reason in the nation will not approve of such violence; nay, there is even a possibility that in consequence of such violence increased oppression will be practiced upon the people for some time (to come) instead of its being stopped. But a glance at the recent history of Russia will show that such excesses or acts of violence are not at all stopped by subjecting the people to increased oppression. It is true that in order to acquire political rights efforts are required to be made for several successive generations and those efforts, too are required to be made peacefully, steadily, persistently and constitutionally! But while such efforts are being made who will guarantee that no person whatever in society will go out of control? And as such guarantee cannot be given how would it be reasonable to say that all persons who put forth efforts for acquiring political rights are seditious? This is what we do not understand. Just as it is difficult to lay down a restriction that not even a tear or two must fall from the eyes of a man while his heart has become sorely afflicted by sorrow, in the same manner it is vain to expect that the unrestricted method of administration. under which India is being ruled over in a high-handed and reckless manner, should become only so far unbearable to the people that no one should become unduly exasperated and resort to excesses on that account....

There is no possibility of the structure of British rule giving way in consequence of the murder of high white officers. If one passes away a second will come in his place, if the second passes away a third will succeed, there is no one whatever so foolish as not to understand this. But Government should take this lesson from the Muzzafferpore affair that the minds of some (persons) out of the young generation have begun to turn towards violence on seeing that all peaceful agitation for the acquisition of political rights has failed, just as a deer attacks a hunter, totally regardless of its own life, after all means of protection have been exhausted. No sensible man will approve of this excess or sinful deed.... True statesmanship, it may be said, consists, indeed in not allowing these things to reach such an extreme or (critical) stage, and this is the very policy we are candidly and plainly suggesting to Government on the present occasion. We do not think that we have done the whole of our duty as subjects by humbly informing Government that the affair that occurred at Muzzafferpore was horrible and that we vehemently condemn or repudiate it. All heartily desire that such improper things should not take place and that none from among the subjects should have an occasion to resort to such extremes. But at such a time it must also be necessarily considered how far the ruling official class should, by utterly disregarding this desire of the subjects, try their patience to the uttermost [sic]; otherwise it will not be possible to maintain cordial relations between the rulers and the subjects and to carry on smoothly the business of either. We have already said above that the Muzzafferpore affair was not proper (and) that it was regrettable. But if the causes which gave rise to it remain permanent in future exactly as they are at present, then in our opinion it is not possible that such terrible occurrences will stop altogether; and it is for this very reason that we have on this very occasion suggested to Government the measures which should be adopted in order to put a stop altogether to such undesirable occurrences. The time has, through our misfortune, arrived when the party of "Nihilists," like that which has arisen in Russia, Germany, France and other countries, will now rise here. To avoid this contingency, to prevent the growth of this poisonous tree is altogether in the hands of Government. These abscesses affecting the country will never be permanently cured by oppression or by harsh measures. Reform of the administration is the only medicine to be administered internally for this disease; and if the official class does not make use of that medicine at this time then it must be considered a great misfortune of all of us. The Government official class may perhaps dislike this writing of ours but we cannot help it; for, as a poet has said, words both sweet and beneficial are hard to obtain. What we have said above is, in our opinion, true and reasonable and beneficial also to both the rulers and the subjects in the end...

* * *

8.2

9 JUNE 1908

'THESE REMEDIES ARE NOT LASTING'

IN THE ARTICLE BELOW, THE GOVERNMENT TOOK EXCEPTION TO the fact that Tilak explained that people could make bombs easily using a few chemicals as a factory was not required to make bombs. This was held to be an incitement to Indians to actually manufacture bombs.

* * *

From this week the Government of India have again entered upon a new policy of repression. The fiend of repression takes possession of the body of the Government of India after every five or ten years.... What does a policy of repression mean? Repression means not only stopping future growth but snipping off past growth also. To stop the future progress of those causes which have given birth to the nation in India, which have developed the nation and which have created the national fire for the rise of the nation, and to drag those (causes) backwards by pulling them by the leg is called a retrograde or repressive policy. Liberty of speech and liberty of the press give birth to a nation and nourish it. Seeing that these had begun to turn India into a nation, the official class had for many days entertained the desire to smash both of them; and they have gratified their ardent desire by taking advantage of the bomb in Bengal. Now question arises: will this repressive policy bring about that which is in the mind of the official? The first desire of the official class is that bombs should be stopped in India and that the mind of no one should feel inclined towards the manufacture or the throwing of bombs. That the authorities should entertain such a desire is natural and also laudable. But just as he who has to go towards the North goes to the South, or he who is bound for the East takes the way to the West, in the same manner the authorities have taken a path leading to the very opposite direction (of their goal).... The authorities have spread the false report that bombs of the Bengalis are subversive of society. There is as wide a difference between the bombs in Europe desiring to destroy society and the bombs in Bengal as between earth and heaven. There is an excess of patriotism at the root of the bombs in Bengal, while the bombs in Europe are the product of the hatred felt for selfish millionaires. The Bengalis are not anarchists but they have brought into use the weapon of the anarchists, that is all....

If common muskets and common swords be in the hands of the subjects, they can never equal the military strength (of Government). If there is nothing detrimental to the military strength (of Government) even in allowing the people to be with arms, then why did the English commit the great sin of castrating a nation? The answer to this question is that the manhood of the nation was slain by the Arms Act in order that the authority exercised even by petty officials from day to day should be unopposed and that the selfish administration might be carried on all right without any hitch (and) without granting the subjects any of the rights of *swarajya*! The English have not got even as much generosity as the Moghuls and they have not even as much military strength as the Moghuls. As compared with the imperial sway of the Moghuls, the English Empire in India is extremely weak and wanting in vigour from the point of view of military strength....

The bomb is not a thing like muskets or guns. Muskets and guns may be taken away from the subjects by means of the Arms Act; and the manufacture, too, of guns and muskets without the permission of Government, may be stopped: but is it possible to stop or to do away with the bomb by means of laws or the supervision of officials or the busy swarming of the detective police? The bomb has more the form of knowledge, it is a (kind of) witchcraft, it is a charm, an amulet. It has not much the features of a visible object manufactured in a big factory. Big factories are necessary for the bombs required by the military forces of Government, but not much (in the way of) material is necessary to prepare five or ten bombs required by violent, turn headed persons. Virendra's big factory of bombs consisted of one or two jars and five or ten bottles; and Government chemical experts are at present deposing that the factory was, from a scientific point of view, faultless like a Government bomb-factory. Should not Government pay attention to the true meaning of the accounts published in (the course of) the case of Virendra's conspiracy? Judging from the accounts published of this case, the formula of the bomb does not at all appear to be a lengthy one and (its) process also is very short indeed. The power of keeping the knowledge of this formula a secret from one who is turn-headed, has not now been left in the laws of Government. This knowledge is not a secret in Europe, America. Japan and other countries. In India it is still a secret knowledge. But when the number of turn-headed (persons) increases owing to the stringent enforcement of the policy of repression, what time will it take for the magical practices, the magical lore of Bengal to spread throughout India?... To speak in (the language of) hyperbole, this factory can be brought into existence in a trice and (also) broken up in a trice! Therefore, how can the nose-string of the law be put on these turn-headed wizards of the bomb?...

The object desired by Government cannot be accomplished by the Explosives Act, but, on the other hand, it will serve as an instrument in the hands of the police and the petty officials to persecute good men. This effort to impose a Prohibition upon the scientific knowledge about bombs and the materials (for making bombs) is vain. If bombs are to be stopped this is not the proper means (for it): Government should act in such a way that no turn-headed man should feel any necessity at all for (throwing) bombs. When do people who are engaged in political agitation become turn-headed? It is when young (political) agitators feel keen disappointment (by being convinced that their faculties, their strength and their self-sacrifice cannot be of any use in bringing about the welfare of their country in any other way than by acts of turn-headedness) that they become turn-headed. Government should never allow keen disappointment (to take hold) of (the minds of) those intelligent persons who have been awakened (to the necessity of) securing the rights of *swarajya*... The real and lasting means of stopping bombs consists in making a beginning to grant the important rights of *swarajya* (to the people). It is not possible for measures of repression to have a lasting (effect) in the present condition of the Western sciences and that of the people of India.

* * *

9

1908 ›› OH MARTYRS!

Original: English | Author: V.D. Savarkar | Leaflet

THE COMMEMORATION OF THE 50TH ANNIVERSARY OF THE revolt of 1857 at India House in London in 1908 was attended by 100 Indian students from Oxford, Cambridge and Edinburgh universities. Soon after, leaflets bearing this title were detected in India. The CID suspected it to be the work of 'Krishnavarma's men', printed in Paris and sent to India House to post into India, which was 'flooded' with the leaflet. Some copies were sent to a college in Madras, wrapped in a London newspaper. Krishnavarma denied authorship. The author was in fact Vinayak Savarkar (1883–1966). The historian John R. Pincince has suggested that after Savarkar read this essay out at India House on the function to commemorate the 50th anniversary of the events of 1857, it was sent to various people in India. One prominent recipient, who complained to the chief secretary of the Government of UP about it, was Madan Mohan Malaviya (1861–1946), associated both with the Indian National Congress and the Hindu Mahasabha (a Hindu nationalist organization of which Savarkar was later to serve as president). Malaviya called it 'a most seditious leaflet' and asked the government to stop the circulation of 'such poisonous matter'. Ironically, Malaviya's own writing was subject to banning less than twenty-five years later (see chapter 59).

The pamphlet was banned by five local governments (Bombay, Madras, Burma, Eastern Bengal and Assam, Central Provinces) under the provisions of the Press Act of 1910. It was described by the Criminal Intelligence Department as 'practically an incitement to repeat the mutiny of 1857.'

The complete pamphlet is reprinted in the following pages.

* * *

The battle of freedom once begun
And handed down from sire to son
Though often lost is ever won!!

To-day is the tenth of May! It was on this day, that in the ever memorable year of 1857, the first campaign of the War of Independence was opened by you, Oh Martyrs, on the battle-field of India. The Motherland, awakened to the sense of her degrading slavery, unsheathed her sword, burst forth from the shackles and struck the first blow for her liberty and for her honour. It was on this day that the war-cry 'Maro Feringhee Ko' [Kill the Foreigner] was raised by the throats of thousands. It was on this day that the sepoys of Meerut, having risen in a terrible uprising, marched down to Delhi, saw the waters of the Jamuna, glittering in the sunshine, caught one of those historical moments which close past epoch to introduce a new one, and 'had found, in a moment, a leader, a flag and a clause, and converted the mutiny into a national and a religious war.'

All honour be to you, oh Martyrs. For it was for the preservation of the honour of the race that you performed the fiery ordeal of a revolution when the religions of the land were threatened with a forcible and sinister conversion, when the hypocrite [sic] threw off his friendly garb and stood up into the naked heinousness of a perfidious foe breaking treaties, smashing crowns, forging chains and mocking all the while our merciful mother for the very honesty with which she believed the pretensions of the white liar, then you, oh Martyrs of 1857, awoke the mother, inspired the mother, and for the honour of the mother, rushed to the battlefield terrible and tremendous with the war-cry 'Maro Feringhee Ko' on your lips, and with the sacred mantra God and Hindusthan on your banner! Well did you do in rising. For otherwise, although your blood might have been spared, yet the stigma of servility would have been the deeper, one more link would have been added to the cursed chain of demoralizing patience, and the world would have again contemptuously pointed to our nation saying, 'She deserves slavery, she is happy in slavery.' For even in 1857, she did not raise even a finger to protect her interest and her honour!'

This day, therefore, we dedicate, oh Martyrs, to your inspiring memory! It was on this day that you raised a new flag to be upheld, you uttered a mission to be fulfilled, you saw a vision to be realized, you proclaimed a nation to be born!

We take up your cry, we revere your flag, we are determined to continue that fiery mission of 'away with the foreigner', which you uttered, amidst

OH MARTYRS!!

The battle of freedom once begun
And handed down from sire to son
Though often lost is ever won!!

To-day is the 10 th of May ! It was on this day, that, in the ever memorable year of 1857, the first campaign of the war of Independence was opened by you, oh martyrs, on the battlefields of India. The Motherland, awakened to the sense of her degrading slavery, unsheathed her sword, burst forth the shackles and struck the first blow for her liberty and for her honour. It was on this day that the warcry *Maro Firungee ko* was raised by the throats of thousands. It was on this day that the sepoys of Meerut having risen in a terrible uprising marched down to Delhi, saw the waters of the Jumna glittering in the sunshine, caught one of those historical moments whieh close past epoch to introduce a new one, and « had found, in a moment, a leader, a flag, and a cause, and converted the mutiny into a national and a religious war » ([1]).

All honour be to you, oh Martyrs ; for it was for the preservation of the honour of the race that you performed the fiery ordeal of a revolution, when the religious of the land were threatemed with a forcible and sinister conversion, when the hypocrite threw off his friendly garb and stood up into the naked heinousness of a perfidious foe breaking treaties, smashing crowns forging chains, and mocking all the while our merciful Mother for the very honesty with which she believed the pretensions of the white liar, then you, oh martyrs of 1857 awoke the Mother, inspired the Mother and for the Honour of the Mother, rushed to the battlefield, terrible and tremendous, with the warcry *Maro Firungee ko* on your lips, and with the sacred mantra « God and Hindustan » on your banner ! Well did you do in rising ! For otherwise although your blood might have been spared, yet the stigma of

([1]) Justin Mc Carthy " History of our own Times ", vol. III.

First page of the Oh Martyrs leaflet. Source: Home Political (Deposit), file 19, December 1908.

the prophetic thunderings of the Revolutionary war. Revolutionary, yes, it was a Revolutionary war. For the War of 1857 shall not cease till the revolution arrives, striking slavery into dust, elevating liberty to the throne. Whenever a people arises for its freedom, whenever that seed of liberty gets germinated in the blood of its fathers, whenever that seed of liberty gets germinated in the blood of its Martyrs, and whenever there remains at least one true son to avenge that blood of his fathers, there never can be an end

Allahabad 23rd August 1908.

My dear Mr: Hose,

I enclose a most seditious leaflet which I received yesterday with the English mail. Evidently it is a copy of the same to which His Honour referred in his speech on the political situation. I was going to tear and throw it away as I did not wish that it should fall into the hands of any person, and as I thought that it was not necessary to send it to Government as the contents of it are already known to them. But it struck me that I should yet in-from you that this incendiary pamphlet leaflet is still being mailed out to this country, so that the Government may take such further steps as it may deem proper to prevent the circulation of such poisonous matter.

Yours sincerely,

Sd. M.M.Malaviya

To

The Hon'ble Mr: J.W.Hose.

Letter by M.M. Malaviya to the Chief Secretary, Government of UP, complaining about the Oh Martyrs pamphlet. Source: Home Political (Deposit), file 19, December 1908.

to such a war as this. No, a revolutionary war knows no truce, save liberty or death. We, inspired by your memory, determine to continue the struggle you began in 1857, we refuse to acknowledge the armistice as a truce; we look upon the battles you fought as the battles of the first campaign—the defeat of which cannot be the defeat of the war. What? Shall the world say that India has accepted the defeat as the final one? That the blood of 1857 was shed in vain? That the sons of Ind [sic] betray their fathers' vows? No, by Hindusthan, no! The historical continuity of the Indian nation is not cut off. The war began on the 10th of May 1857 is not over on the 10th of May 1908, nor shall it ever cease till a 10th of May to come sees the destiny accomplished, sees the beautiful Ind [sic] crowned, either with the lustre of victory or with the halo of martyrdom.

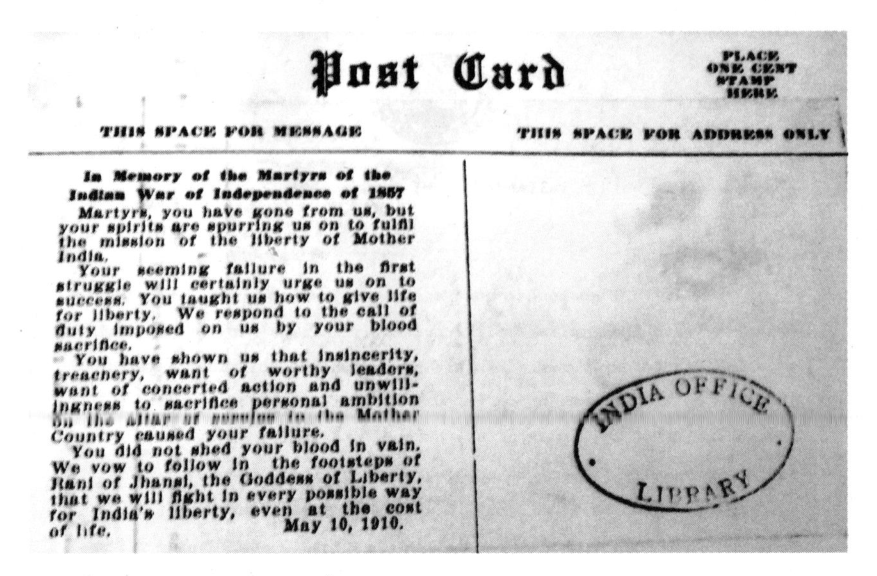

Post Card

PLACE ONE CENT STAMP HERE

THIS SPACE FOR MESSAGE | THIS SPACE FOR ADDRESS ONLY

In Memory of the Martyrs of the Indian War of Independence of 1857

Martyrs, you have gone from us, but your spirits are spurring us on to fulfil the mission of the liberty of Mother India.

Your seeming failure in the first struggle will certainly urge us on to success. You taught us how to give life for liberty. We respond to the call of duty imposed on us by your blood sacrifice.

You have shown us that insincerity, treachery, want of worthy leaders, want of concerted action and unwillingness to sacrifice personal ambition on the altar of [illegible] to the Mother Country caused your failure.

You did not shed your blood in vain. We vow to follow in the footsteps of Rani of Jhansi, the Goddess of Liberty, that we will fight in every possible way for India's liberty, even at the cost of life.

May 10, 1910.

1857 Commemoration Postcard.

But, O glorious Martyrs, in this pious struggle of your sons help. O help us by your inspiring presence! Torn in innumerable petty selves, we cannot realise the grand unity of the Mother. Whisper, then, unto us by what magic you caught the secret of Union. How the feringhee rule was shattered to pieces and the Swadeshi thrones were set up by the common consent of Hindus and Mahomedans. How in the higher love of the mother, united the difference of castes and creeds, how the venerated and venerable Bahadur Shah prohibited the killing of cows throughout India, how Shreemant Nanasahib [Nana Saheb, an ex-ruler and a leader of the revolt in North India] after the first salute of the thundering cannon to the emperor of Delhi, reserved for himself the second one! How you staggered the whole world by uniting under the banner of mother and forced your enemies to say 'Among the many lessons the Indian Mutiny conveys to the historian and administrator, none is of greater importance than the warning that it is possible to have a revolution in which Brahmins and Shudras, Mahomedans and Hindus were united against us and that it is not safe to suppose that the peace and stability of our dominion in any great measure depends on the continent being inhabited by different races with different religious systems, for they mutually understand each other and respect and take part in each other's modes and ways and doings. The mutiny reminds us that our dominions rest on a thin crust ever likely to be rent by titanic fires of social changes and revolutions.' Whisper unto us the nobility of such an alliance of Religion and Patriotism, the true religion whichever is on the side of patriotism, the true patriotism which secures the freedom of religion.

And give us the marvellous energy daring and secrecy with which you organized the mighty volcano; show us the volcanic magma that underlie the green thin crust on which the foe is to be kept lulled into a false security; tell us how the chapatti, that fiery Cross of India flew from village to village and from valley to valley, setting the whole intellect of the nation on fire by the very vagueness of its message and then let us hear the roaring thunder with which the volcano at last burst forth with an all shuttering force, rushing, smashing, burning and consuming into one continuous fiery flow of red-hot lava-flood! Within a month, regiment after regiment, prince after prince, city after city, sepoys, police, zemindars [landlords], Pundits, Moulvis [Muslim clerics], the multiple-headed Revolution sounded its tocsin and temples and mosques resounded with the cry 'Maro feringhee Ko' Away with the foreigners! MEERUT ROSE, Delhi rose, rose Benares, Agra, Patna, Lucknow, Allahabad, Jadagalpoor [Jagdalpur], Jhansi, Banda, Indore from Peshawar to Calcutta [Kolkata] and from the Narmada to the Himalayas, the volcano burst forth into a sudden, simultaneous and all consuming conflagration!!

And then, oh Martyrs, tell us the little as well as the great defects which you found out in our people in that great experiment of yours. But above all, point out that most ruinous, nay, the only material draw-back in the body of the nation which rendered all your efforts futile – the mean selfish blindness which refuses to see its way to join the nation's cause. Say that the only cause of the defeat of Hindusthan was Hindusthan herself, that shaking away the slumber of centuries, the mother rose to hit the foe, but while her right hand was striking the Feringhee dead, her left hand struck, alas, not the enemy, but her forehead! So she staggered and fell back into the inevitable swoon of 50 years.

50 years are past, but, oh restless spirits of 1857, we promise you with our hearts' blood that your Diamond Jubilee shall not pass without seeing your wishes fulfilled!! We have heard your voice and we gather courage from it. With limited means you sustained a war, not against tyranny alone, but against tyranny and treachery together. The Daub [Gangetic doab or plains] and Ayodhya making a united stand, waged a war, not only against the whole of the British power but against the rest of the India too; and yet you fought for three years and yet you had well-nigh snatched away the crown of Hindusthan and smashed the hollow existence of the alien rule. What an encouragement this! What the Duab [sic] and Ayodhya could do in a month, the simultaneous, sudden and determined rising of the whole of Hindusthan

can do in a day. This hope illumines our hearts and assures us of success. And so we allow that your Diamond Jubilee year 1917 shall not pass without seeing the resurging Ind [sic] making a triumphant entry into the world.

For, the bones of Bahadur Shah [the last Mughal emperor of India, exiled to Burma by the British] are crying vengeance from their grave! For, the blood of dauntless Laxmi [the Queen of Jhansi and a famous participant in the revolt] is boiling with indignation! For, the shahid [martyr] Peer Ali of Patna, when he was going to the gallows for having refused to divulge the secrets of the conspiracy whispered defiance to the Feringhee said in prophetic words 'You may hang me today, you may hang such as me everyday, but thousands will still rise in my place - your object will never be gained.'

Indians, these words must be fulfilled! Your blood, oh Martyrs, shall be avenged.

VANDE MATARAM

* * *

10

1908 ONWARDS » THE INDIAN SOCIOLOGIST

Original: English | Shyamji Krishnavarma
10.1: Article: August 1908
10.2: Article: 'Indian Martyrs' Memorial', December 1908
10.3: Article: July 1909
10.4: Article: October 1912
10.5: Article: November 1912
10.6: Article: 'A Freedom Loving Englishman's Sarcastic but True Version of British Rule in India: Holy Britain's Prayer', May 1913

THIS WAS A MONTHLY THAT WAS ISSUED BETWEEN 1905 AND 1914 by Shyamji Krishnavarma (1857–1930), mentor and patron of the first generation of Indian revolutionaries abroad, initially in London, where he set up India House and established scholarships for Indian students. Krishnavarma's biographer Harald Fischer-Tiné comments on the global circulation of this monthly, with up to 1,000 copies being circulated to 'virtually every place on Earth with an Indian minority community.' He also points out the political content of the monthly which, despite its name, did not contain scholarly sociological articles. The Sea Customs Act was used in 1907 to prohibit its import into India, but copies continued to be smuggled in via the post.

After the assassination of Sir Curzon Wyllie in London by Madan Lal Dhingra (more about which in chapter 12), the *Indian Sociologist* came under the scanner for words of approbation (see 10.3 below). Even as Krishnavarma escaped from prosecution on account of his migration to Paris, two consecutive English printers of the journal were sentenced to jail.

* * *

10.1

AUGUST 1908

As to the ethics of dynamite, it may be laid down in a general way that where the people have political power there is no need for the use of explosives. It only promotes reaction. But where the people are utterly defenceless, both politically and militarily, then one may look on the bomb or any other weapon as legitimate. Its employment then becomes merely a question of expediency.

* * *

THE

INDIAN SOCIOLOGIST

AN ORGAN OF FREEDOM, AND OF POLITICAL, SOCIAL, AND RELIGIOUS REFORM.

"EVERY MAN IS FREE TO DO THAT WHICH HE WILLS, PROVIDED HE INFRINGES NOT THE EQUAL FREEDOM OF ANY OTHER MAN."—*Herbert Spencer, Principles of Ethics, Section 272.*

"RESISTANCE TO AGGRESSION IS NOT SIMPLY JUSTIFIABLE BUT IMPERATIVE. NON-RESISTANCE HURTS BOTH ALTRUISM AND EGOISM."—*The Study of Sociology, Chap. 8.*

Edited by SHYAMAJI KRISHNAVARMA, M.A. (Oxon.).

Vol. II.—No. 1.] LONDON, JANUARY, 1906. One Penny, Monthly.

All Literary Communications, Orders for the Indian Sociologist, and Money, Postal Orders, or Cheques may be sent to Shyamaji Krishnavarma, 9, Queen's Wood Avenue, Highgate, London, N.

A Specimen copy of the Indian Sociologist will be sent *gratis* to all who apply to Shyamaji Krishnavarma.

THE Rt. Hon. JOHN MORLEY AND HOPES OF POLITICAL FREEDOM FOR INDIA.

In the first number of the "Indian Sociologist" which appeared in January, 1905, we stated that Mr. John Morley, amongst others, had co-operated in [illegible] with Mr. Herbert Spencer in doing something towards checking the aggressive tendencies displayed by England all over the world. We then little thought that in less than twelve months the coadjutor of the great philosopher would be the official head of the greatest bureaucratic and aggressive administration the world has ever seen. The sincere respect we entertain for Mr. John Morley on account of his powerful advocacy of political freedom and of the rights of the oppressed is best shown by an incident which may be mentioned here without impropriety. In the early part of 1904 the University of Oxford accepted an offer made by the Editor of this journal for founding a Lectureship to honour the memory of Mr. Herbert Spencer. Knowing that the eminent thinker held a high opinion of his friend Mr. John Morley, the Editor, as a member of the Board of Management, submitted to the other members that Mr. John Morley would be the most appropriate first Lecturer. The Board adopted the suggestion and unanimously requested Mr. Morley, through the Vice-Chancellor, to be the first "Herbert Spencer Lecturer." He was however reluctantly obliged to decline the proposal. We know that other engagements of various kinds being very pressing prevented Mr. Morley from accepting the invitation, although he fully appreciated the honour that was done to him by the Board of electors.

Holding as we do that the government of one country by another is pernicious, it does not very much signify to us who is at the head of the Indian administration. However sympathetic and well-meaning a Secretary of State for India may be, he cannot, without the consent of Parliament, change the system of bleeding to death which must go on so long as the English domination endures.

We hope that both in the interests of England and India Mr. John Morley as a thinker, statesman and lover of freedom and justice will do all he can towards abolishing "the cunning despotism which uses native soldiers to maintain and extend native subjection" to quote the words of his late lamented friend Mr. Herbert Spencer.

INDIANS' ADMISSION INTO BRITISH PARLIAMENT RETARDS INDIA'S PROGRESS.

The Investor's Review of 18th, November 1905, publishes a scheme for the formation of "United States of India" alluded to in the October number of the "Indian Sociologist." The Editor scouts the idea of Mr. Gokhale who would like to see at least six men elected by the natives of India and sent to England to represent them in the British Parliament. It is gratifying to observe that the Editor of *The Investor's Review*, with his usual acumen and foresight, makes the following pertinent remarks:—

"Under existing conditions such men would have no weight whatever. They would be voted a nuisance, and relegated to the same position as the far more numerous Nationalist representatives of Ireland."

We strongly recommend the leaders of the Indian National Congress, who supported Resolution IX (a) passed at the Bombay session in 1905, to ponder over the weighty words just quoted and we beg their friends in this country to desist from wasting the resources of India on a few Indians' admission into the British Parliament. Such admission may perhaps pander to personal vanity or self-glorification but can never promote the true interests of India. Moreover, the admission of Indians into the British Parliament will afford an argument against a representative form of government in India in as much as the people of this country will naturally say that India needs no Home Rule or Self-Government since it is already represented in the House of Commons. It is evident therefore that Indians who stand for parliamentary honours really retard India's progress towards freedom and independence.

Above: Stamp issued in 1989.
Left: Indian Sociologist, *January 1906 issue.*

10.2

DECEMBER 1908

'INDIAN MARTYRS' MEMORIAL'

The four young Indians who have been done to death, three of them having been hanged, by the British Government for attempting to promote their country's cause by braving all risks present instances of absolute unselfishness and thus offer an object lesson to their fellow-countrymen. Their deed which the enemies of India have called "crime " must be regarded as "patriotism" and "virtue" by all Indians who really love their country, and we think that some sort of Indian Martyrs' Memorial should be raised out of respect to their memory. We offer for this purpose the sum of Rs. 5,000 and propose that a part of this donation should be placed at the disposal of their parents, as a token of gratitude, for such uses as they may deem best and that the balance should be spent in scholarships for the education and training of four young Indians who, regardless of any personal gain, may be willing to devote all their time and energy for the regeneration of their country. The proposed scholarships shall bear the names of the four martyrs, viz., Profulla Chaki, Khudiram Bose, Kanailal Dutt and Satyendra Nath Bose. We further propose that some monument should be erected at "India House" 65, Cromwell Avenue, Highgate, London, N., which may take the form of a tablet giving a succinct account of their deeds of daring and self-devotion.

* * *

10.3

JULY 1909

At the risk of alienating the sympathies and good opinion of almost all our old friends and acquaintances in England and some of our past helpmates in India, we repeat that political assassination is not murder. It is thus clear that both International Law and Ethics support our contention with regard to the right and duty of individuals or nations to use force for obtaining freedom in general and for liberating themselves from oppressive alien rule in particular, it being quite immaterial in what form that force is employed.

* * *

10.4

OCTOBER 1912

The world is ignorant of the plunder of India and of the slaughter of her sons, because the plunder and slaughter are carried on systematically and scientifically and because the world does not investigate. The facts, were they published, would be much more frightful and staggering than the Putumayo or Congo atrocities. It would be a revelation to the civilised world, and countries that are now indifferent would quickly lose their apathy and demand just reparation of England....

Over-taxation causes poverty and poverty causes crime and crime leads to the gallows. Poverty, too, causes famine and hunger, and famine leads to the grave. Poverty is the cause of insanitation and diseases, and disease ploughs through whole districts like an evil spirit cutting short millions of lives. But the worst disease of all, plague, is introduced. This disease quickly spreads amongst the poorest classes, those who are dying of starvation and whose surroundings are insanitary. It blazes furiously like a prairie fire through the whole country leaving death and ruin behind, and everything that was beautiful before its introduction is barren and desolate after it has passed....

On first entering the country the English treated the natives no better than the natives of the Putumayo [area in Peru notorious for ill-treatment of rubber plantation labour] have been lately treated; but their methods are now almost scientific and they can slay millions, (as indeed they do) without firing a shot or unsheathing a sword, by this refined up-to-date method. This system of wholesale extermination carried on daily in India is more revolting than any incident that history has yet recorded. Sir Walter Strickland who has travelled much in the East, points out in his " Extinction of Mankind" that the object of England in making the death roll so alarmingly high is the extermination of the Hindus, a race that is physically and mentally superior to the English.

* * *

10.5

NOVEMBER 1912

The loyalty of the Sikhs was one of the main causes of the failure of the Mutiny [the revolt of 1857]. Another rebellion would be just as futile as long as any considerable section of the native troops remains loyal. Enlistment must be discountenanced by all Indian patriots, thus shall the number of native soldiers diminish year by year. If they could be altogether detached from the enemy, India's march towards freedom would be a promenade. The force thus detached from John Bull's fighting assets would more than suffice to turn the balance of strength on the side of justice. The Indian Nationalists might consider the following suggestions as to how the unity of Indians of all creeds might be achieved, so that they could form themselves into one powerful league, with which to wrest their common rights from the despot...

(1) Prevent, whenever possible, all Indians from entering the army or police force, which like all government posts must be boycotted.

(2) Spread patriotic literature widely amongst the native soldiery, and try to convert them to become true Indians.

* * *

10.6

MAY 1913

'A FREEDOM LOVING ENGLISHMAN'S SARCASTIC BUT TRUE VERSION OF BRITISH RULE IN INDIA: HOLY BRITAIN'S PRAYER'

THE CID THOUGHT THIS SATIRICAL SKIT, WRITTEN AS THE BRITISH people's report to God about India, to be the work of Sir Walter Strickland (1851–1938). Strickland was a British aristocrat who had the best education possible in England: schooling at Harrow, followed by stints at Christ Church, Oxford, and Trinity College, Cambridge. By 1912 he had turned against the British establishment and wrote of the English in India as 'infamous, bestial and obscene thieves, murderers, liars and worse....' The CID came to know that after hearing of the death of Madan Lal Dhingra (executed for assassinating a British official in 1909; see chapter 12), Strickland sent a wreath to Shyamji Krishnavarma, and a letter advising Indians to 'beat the English till the blood ran out of their pores.'

* * *

Instead of gratitude we have received hatred and contumely, and now, Oh Lord! our condition is parlous. 'Precarious and not at all permanent.' Oh Lord! Moreover, many of these firebrands from hell are still at large. Dhingra, Thou Thyself hast dealt with ere this; Savarkar is safe in our holy, merciful, Christ-like keeping, but the execrable Krishnavarma is beyond our reach spreading his damnable doctrines broadcast and even contaminating some of Thy white saints themselves. Thy flock, Oh Father, is in imminent peril; danger clouds threaten to obscure the sun of our peace, for lo! our charges no longer 'beseech' us. Their tone of utterance is now no longer plaintive but severely menacing. They speak saying: — 'Too long, have we begged ye (sic) white-livered, black-hearted, red-handed hypocrites and cut-throats to desist from spoiling our fair land, murdering and plundering our fathers and brothers, ravishing our wives, and debauching our daughters. We shall beg to ye (sic) no longer, but think not ye have crushed us. One day, not far distant, we shall speak to ye (sic) again, assuredly; but our mouths shall be iron mouths, our tongues shall be tongues of lurid flame and the message we shall deliver shall be a message of lead and steel and ye shall carry it to your anthropomorphic God in your own worthless carcasses. Be warned? And now Oh Lord! answer us we beseech Thee. What must we do to be saved?

* * *

11

1908 ONWARDS >> FREE HINDUSTHAN

Original: English | Author: Taraknath Das
11.1: Article: October 1908
11.2: Article: 'The Awakening of the Sikhs', September–October 1909

TARAKNATH DAS (1884–1958) WENT FROM INDIA TO JAPAN, AND then enrolled as a student at California's Berkeley University. He was to earn three degrees, including a doctorate, from American universities, and sought German help for anti-British activities during the First World War. He served as the manager of this paper, which was first published in April 1908. Das was also an associate of Har Dayal of the Hindustan Ghadr Party (see chapters 19 and 23). The paper terminated publication due to the intervention of United States' authorities. The CID considered this paper to be an imitation of the *Indian Sociologist*, 'conducted with much less ability'.

* * *

11.1

OCTOBER 1908

We all know that the national uprising of 1857 would have been successful in throwing off the foreign yoke if our own people and the Nepalese [Gurkha soldiers] had not engaged in helping the tyrants. Let us remember that the British Government required a force of 200,000 (two hundred thousand) to oppress the national rising and of this force there were only 40,000 Europeans and of the rest 80,000 were Gurkhas [Nepalese soldiers of the British Indian army] and 80,000 Sikhs and other troops. The Nepalese first took the fort of Lucknow from the Sepoys and so gave the death blow to the national aspiration in 1857. Now the problem before us is to see whether the native troops of the British Government which number over 200,000 will again join hands with the tyrants or not. We believe not, if work could be carried on in giving the idea of the benefits of independence among the native troops. At least we have seen the Sikhs refuse to fire upon the Punjabee peasants at Lahore and at Rawalpindi during the riots of 1907. To work among the native troops is not a very difficult matter, because they are already discontented owing to unjust treatment by the British Government; they are underpaid, underfed and badly treated....

It is not a very hard task if we go to work earnestly. Compare our possibility of success with the English. The English do not read or write 'Devnagari' [the script in which Hindi is written.] which the Nepalese do as we do. The Nepalese are Hindus and the Nepalese were bitter enemies of England some time ago. The only thing we have to do is to preach the sense of Hindu honour among the Nepalese, to stimulate their National desire to get a place among international powers.

* * *

11.2

SEPTEMBER-OCTOBER 1909

'THE AWAKENING OF THE SIKHS'

They refuse to wear medals and titles of slavery.

The Sikh soldiery is known as the backbone of the British Empire in India. It is gratifying to know that the Sikhs are awakening to the sense that they are nothing better than slaves, and are serving the British Government to put our mother country in perpetual slavery. The religion of the Sikhs is to help the downtrodden and crush tyrants. On October 3rd, 1909, a very interesting incident took place in the Sikh Temple of Vancouver, B. C. [British Columbia], Canada. One Sardar Natha Singh stood up before the assembly and humbly pleaded for the deplorable condition of our countrymen in India and other parts of the world, especially in the British colonies. In conclusion he presented a resolution to the following effect:

> "Resolved that no member of the Executive Committee of the Sikh Temple should wear any kind of medals, buttons, uniforms or insignia which may signify that the position of the party wearing the article is nothing but a slave to the British supremacy."

He cleverly argued that the medals they wore signify that they fought for the British as mercenaries against the cause of our fellow-countrymen, or some free people. The medals acquired by serving in the British army ought to be regarded as medals of slavery. The audience solemnly and unanimously accepted the proposal. Sardar Gharib Singh, a member of the committee of the Sikh Temple, and formerly sepoy 2760 in the Fourteenth Sikh Regiment, who went to China during the Boxer trouble and acquired a medal for chivalry, took off his medal and declared that he should not wear any medal or uniform acknowledging supremacy of the British. Later on Sardar Bhag Singh, the Secretary of the Khalsa Divan, who served in the Tenth Bengal Lancer Regiment for over five years, made a bonfire with his certificate of honourable discharge. The above incidents are a few of the many genuine proofs of the awakening of the

Sikhs. Coming in contact with free people and institutions of free nations, some of the Sikhs, though labourers in the North American Continent, have assimilated the idea of liberty and trampled the medals of slavery. There is in this a lesson for the so-called educated people of India and their moderate leaders.

* * *

12
1909 ›› MADAN LAL DHINGRA'S STATEMENT

Original: English | Leaflet

THE CID BELIEVED THAT THIS NOTE, FOUND IN MADAN LAL Dhingra's (1883–1909) pocket at the time of his arrest for assassinating Sir Curzon Wyllie in London, was drafted by V.D. Savarkar and not by Dhingra. It was printed as a leaflet and sent from India House in London to India by post, prompting three local governments (Bombay, Burma Central Provinces, Eastern Bengal and Assam) to ban it under the provisions of the Press Act of 1910. This leaflet was referred to as the 'Challenge Document' in official correspondence, since its writer challenged the British government to prove that this was not Dhingra's statement. It was described as a 'defence of anarchism'. The complete statement is reprinted below and the following page.

* * *

I admit that the other day I attempted to shed English blood intentionally and of purpose, as an humble protest against the inhuman transportations and hangings of Indian youth.

In this attempt I consulted none but my own conscience; conspired with none but my own duty.

I believe that a nation unwillingly held down by foreign bayonets is in a perpetual state of war. Since open battle is rendered impossible I attacked by surprise – since cannon could not be had I drew forth and fired a revolver.

As a Hindu I feel that the slavery of my nation is an insult to my God. Her cause is the cause of freedom. Her service is the service of Sri Krishna. Neither rich nor able, a poor son like myself can offer nothing but his blood on the altar of Mother's deliverance and so I rejoice at the prospect of my martyrdom.

The only lesson required in India is to learn how to die and the only way to teach it is by dying alone.

The soul is immortal and if every one of my countrymen takes at least two lives of Englishmen before his body falls the Mother's salvation is a day's work.

This war ceases not only with the independence of India alone, it shall continue as long as the English and Hindu races exist in this world.

Until our country is free Sri Krishna [from the Hindu scripture the Bhagawad Gita] stands exhorting "if killed you attain the heaven; if successful you win the earth."

It is my fervent prayer - May I be reborn of the same mother and may I redie [sic] in the same sacred cause till my mission is done and she stands free—for the good of humanity and to the glory of God.

* * *

13

1909 ›› SONAR BHARAT [GOLDEN INDIA]

Original: Bengali | Author: Swamadas Mukhopadhyaya
Poem: 'Keeping Awake in the Dead of Night! Suggested by the memory of the battle between the Gods and the Asuras [Demons]'

IN NOVEMBER 1908, THE BENGALI NEWSPAPER *SONAR BHARAT* published a poem by Syamadas Mukhopadhyaya. The poem was translated and discussed, after which the Government of Bengal proposed confiscation of the press under the provisions of the Newspapers (Incitements to Offences) Act of 1908. After the order of confiscation was issued in early 1909, the proprietor of the Sulav Hitaishi Press, N.C. Sarkar, pleaded in his mercy petition that he was an uneducated man and hence unable to understand the content of the poem. He had published it under the impression that it was merely a hymn to the Goddess Kali. However, when the District Magistrate of Howrah, H.T.S. Forrest, analysed the poem, he stated that the poem compared India to a cremation ground, stressed that India had been cast into a distressing state by demons, that there was a unique opportunity for slaying them, that all Hindus must unite, and that the demons were already panic stricken. He further said that the lawyer representing the proprietor had admitted that such references were foreign to the spirit in which hymns to Kali were found in the ancient texts or modern compositions. Given the context, the District Magistrate concluded that English residents were being referred to in the poem. He added that the poem was of little or no literary merit. The poem is a good illustration of the strategy of using familiar religious imagery in new ways, even though the invocation to the goddess failed to prevent the press from being forfeited. Excerpts from the sixteen-stanza poem are reproduced below.

* * *

'KEEPING AWAKE IN THE DEAD OF NIGHT!'

Suggested by the memory of the battle between the Gods and the Asuras [Demons]

Stanza 1
The night of the new moon is enveloped in terrific gloom,
The cremation-ground of India is to-day full of horrors;
Why (are you) unconscious in sleep, O people of India?
This is the proper time for Sava-Sadhan [Meditation while sitting on a corpse, in the Tantric tradition].

Stanza 4
In the sky of India the sun of Pratipada [first day after the full or new moon]
Destroying the mass of darkness with the rays of Aruna [sun/dawn]
Will certainly, brothers, rise before long,
Lighting the whole (literally, the ten directions) of India.

Stanza 6
See how the Goddess with dishevelled hair is dancing to-day,
Frequently shakes her sword which is in (her) hand,
As if the Mother after killing the entire race of demons,
Will swim in a sea of blood.

Stanza 7
The Mother is very thirsty for blood,
A fight with demons (is to take place) to-day after a long time;
That desire will be satisfied to-day with the blood of demons,
Hence (her) terrific tongue is lolling.

Stanza 16
Listen there on all sides the cry of victory is rising,
The Earth is trembling at the shout of India's victory.
Hearing that shout of victory the demons are shuddering with fear,
Awake, O people of India, why are (you) under the influence of sleep?

* * *

14

1909 ›› KARMAYOGIN [SAGE]

Original: English | Author: Aurobindo Ghose
Article: 'To My Countrymen', 25 December 1909

THIS WAS A WEEKLY MAGAZINE STARTED BY AUROBINDO GHOSE in June 1909. A single copy was available for two annas, and subscription could be had for five rupees. Peter Heehs has recounted the story of how the first issue itself reached Viceroy Minto within a fortnight of its publication. The letter 'To My Countrymen' published in the 31 July 1909 issue gave the Government of Bengal an opportunity to prosecute Ghose. By that time he was in Pondicherry, a French territory, and therefore it was difficult for the British Government to arrest or prosecute him. Instead, they prosecuted the printer, Monmohan Nath Ghose, who was sentenced to six months' rigorous imprisonment under charges of sedition. The officiating Chief Presidency Magistrate at Calcutta, D. Swinhoe, held the article to be seditious because it 'imputes repression, dishonesty, partiality and base motives to the government in its administration of this country and appeals to the people of India to abandon moderate methods and to join the nationalist and with their aid coerce the Government and compel it to alter its present policy of which the writer strongly disapproves.' The conviction was set aside in October by the High Court upon appeal.

Aurobindo Ghose began the article with a criticism of 'moderate politics', exemplified by Gopal Krishna Gokhale (1866–1915) and Pherozeshah Mehta (1845–1915). Excerpts are reprinted in the following pages.

* * *

25 DECEMBER 1909

'TO MY COUNTRYMEN'

...The period of waiting is over. We have two things made clear to us, first, that the future of the nation is in our hands, and, secondly, that from the Moderate party we can expect no cordial co-operation in building it. Whatever we do, we must do ourselves, in our own strength and courage. Let us then take up the work God has given us, like courageous, steadfast and patriotic men willing to sacrifice greatly and venture greatly because the mission also is great. If there are any unnerved by the fear of repression, let them stand aside. If there are any who think that by flattering Anglo-India or coquetting with English Liberalism they can dispense with the need of effort and the inevitability of peril, let them stand aside. If there are any who are ready to be satisfied with mean gains or unsubstantial concessions, let them stand aside. But all who deserve the name of Nationalists, must now come forward and take up their burden.

The fear of the law is for those who break the law. Our aims are great and honourable, free from stain or reproach, our methods are peaceful, though resolute and strenuous. We shall not break the law and, therefore, we need not fear the law. But if a corrupt police, unscrupulous officials or a partial judiciary make use of the honourable publicity of our political methods to harass the men who stand in front by illegal ukases [a decree issued by the Russian Tsar], suborned and perjured evidence or unjust decisions, shall we shrink from the toll that we have to pay on our march to freedom? Shall we cower behind a petty secrecy or a dishonourable inactivity? We must have our associations, our organisations, our means of propaganda, and, if these are suppressed by arbitrary proclamations, we shall have done our duty by our motherland and not on us will rest any responsibility for the madness which crushes down open and lawful political activity in order to give a desperate and sullen nation into the hands of those fiercely enthusiastic and unscrupulous forces that have arisen among us inside and outside India. So long as any loophole is left for peaceful effort, we will not renounce the struggle. If the conditions are made difficult and almost impossible, can they be worse than those our countrymen have to contend against in the Transvaal? Or shall we, the flower of Indian culture and education, show less capacity and self-devotion than the coolies and shopkeepers who are there rejoicing to suffer for the honour of their nation and the welfare of their community?

REGISTERED NO. C532.

SUBSCRIPTION RUPEES 5.

KARMAYOGIN

SINGLE COPY ANNAS 2.

A WEEKLY REVIEW

OF

National Religion, Literature, Science, Philosophy, &c.,

Vol. I. | SATURDAY 6th NOVEMBER 1909. | No. 18.

Contributors:—Sj. Aurobindo Ghose and others

OFFICE:—14 SHAM BAZAR STREET,
CALCUTTA.

Karmayogin. *Source: http://www.sriaurobindoinstitute.org/saioc/Sri_Aurobindo/karmayogin_newspaper.*

What is it for which we strive? The perfect self-fulfilment of India and the independence which is the condition of self-fulfilment are our ultimate goal. In the meanwhile such imperfect self-development and such incomplete self-government as are possible in less favourable circumstances, must be attained as a preliminary to the more distant realisation. What we seek is to evolve self-government either through our own institutions or through those provided for us by the law of the land. No such evolution is possible by the latter means without some measure of administrative control. We demand, therefore, not the monstrous and misbegotten scheme which has just been brought into being, but a measure of reform based upon those democratic principles which are ignored in Lord Morley's Reforms,— a literate electorate without distinction of creed, nationality or caste, freedom of election unhampered by exclusory clauses, an effective voice in legislation and finance and some check upon an arbitrary executive. We demand also the gradual devolution of executive government out of the hands of the bureaucracy into those of the people. Until these demands are granted, we shall use the pressure of that refusal of co-operation which is termed passive resistance. We shall exercise that pressure within the limits allowed us by the law, but apart from that limitation the extent to which we shall use it, depends on expediency and the amount of resistance we have to overcome.

On our own side we have great and pressing problems to solve. National education languishes for want of moral stimulus, financial support, and emancipated brains keen and bold enough to grapple with the difficulties that hamper its organisation and progress. The movement of arbitration, successful in its inception, has been dropped as a result of repression. The Swadeshi-Boycott movement still moves by its own impetus, but its forward march has no longer the rapidity and organised irresistibility of forceful purpose which once swept it forward. Social problems are pressing upon us which we can no longer ignore. We must take up the organisation of knowledge in our country, neglected throughout the last century. We must free our social and economic development from the incubus of the litigious resort to the ruinously expensive British Courts. We must once more seek to push forward the movement toward economic self-sufficiency, industrial independence.

These are the objects for which we have to organise the national strength of India. On us falls the burden, in us alone there is the moral ardour, faith and readiness for sacrifice which can attempt and go far to accomplish the task. But the first requisite is the organisation of the Nationalist party. I invite that party in all the great centres of the country to take up the work and assist the leaders who will shortly meet to consider steps for the initiation of Nationalist activity. It is desirable to establish a Nationalist Council and hold a meeting of the body in March or April of the next year. It is necessary also to establish Nationalist Associations throughout the country. When we have done this, we shall be able to formulate our programme and assume our proper place in the political life of India.

* * *

15

1909 ›› THE FIRST INDIAN WAR OF INDEPENDENCE

Original: Marathi/English | Author: V.D. Savarkar
15.1: Book Excerpt: 'Author's Introduction'
15.2: Book Excerpt: Chapter 1 – 'Swadharma and Swaraj'

VINAYAK DAMODAR SAVARKAR (1883–1966) WAS A VOTARY OF THE idea than only an armed struggle could free India from British rule. He went on to become an influential ideologue of Hindu nationalism, and president of the Hindu Mahasabha; he remains a divisive figure in India today. He wrote this book while he was studying in England and living at India House.

Informed about the publication of a pamphlet or book on the Indian Mutiny by Savarkar by Scotland Yard in November 1908, the Government of India's machinery started whirring. Anticipating it to be a 'most objectionable book', the decision was to intercept it in the post, examine it, and then prohibit it under the Sea Customs Act. However, a problem arose. Notifications under the latter were to be published in the Gazette of India and were therefore in the public eye and could cause a lot of publicity. C.J. Stevenson-Moore, the director of Criminal Intelligence noted in this context that 'Seditious literature is no less deleterious than cocaine but the existing restrictions to its consumption are very insufficient.' At this point, possession of a prohibited publication was in itself difficult to punish by law. In January 1909, the Government of India instructed the Director General of Post Office to intercept and deliver to the director of Criminal Intelligence a 'postal article' if they found it circulating. The article was described as 'A book or pamphlet in Marathi on the subject of the Indian Mutiny, by V.D. Savarkar, which is reported as being printed in Germany.'

According to CID official James Ker, the book was sent into India 'under various disguises', the most common being a false cover bearing the title 'The Posthumous Papers of the Pickwick Club.' CID informants had reported that Savarkar had stated at the 'mutiny' celebrations in India House in 1908 that as Indians had been treated with utmost cruelty, they were justified in taking revenge.

Several historians and political scientists have recently engaged in an assessment of Savarkar's writing and ideology (see Further Reading section at the end of this book). Janaki Bakhle has argued that 'the word itself became evidence of a crime' in the eyes of the colonial state; sedition was difficult to control and therefore dangerous. She calls Savarkar a 'rhetorical revolutionary'. Megha Kumar has persuasively argued that this book is quite different from Savarkar's later works and career, in which he displayed undisguised animosity towards Muslims. She highlights arguments in this book for collective and united Hindu and Muslim action against the British, and notes Savarkar's appreciation of the fact that loyalty to Islam was very much compatible with loyalty to India.

The publisher's note in the first edition of 1909 declared that the book had originally been written in an Indian vernacular, and had been translated into English so that 'the whole of the Indian nation' could read about the events it described. The task, in their view, was to change the perception of the Indian participants of the events of 1857 from 'madmen and villains' to heroes. Savarkar prefaced his book with a list of thirty-five books he had consulted – all by English authors listed by name.

In an essay titled 'The Proscription and Censorship of Books' written in 1929, Jawaharlal Nehru, with characteristic generosity towards political opponents, had this to say about the book:

> It is a brilliant book though it suffers from prolixity and want of balance occasionally. I had occasion to read it in Europe and I have often felt that a new edition, more concise and with many of the oratorical flights left out, would be an ideal corrective to the British propaganda about the events of 1857. But I'm afraid we shall have to wait for this till Swaraj comes.

Excerpts from the original edition are reprinted on the following pages.

* * *

15.1

BOOK EXCERPT

AUTHOR'S INTRODUCTION

The nation that has no consciousness of its past has no future. Equally true it is that a nation must develop its capacity not only of claiming a past but also of knowing how to use it for the furtherance of its future. The nation ought to be the master and not the slave of its own history. For, it is absolutely unwise to try to do certain things now irrespective of special considerations, simply because they had been once acted in the past. The feeling of hatred against the Mahomedans was just and necessary in the times of Shivaji—but, such a feeling would be unjust and foolish if nursed now, simply because it was the dominant feeling of the Hindus then.

* * *

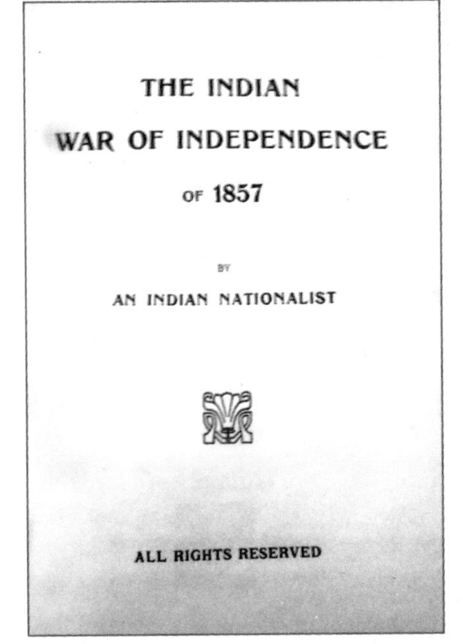

Cover, Indian War of Independence, *1909.*

Publicity material issued by Bande Mataram *of Geneva*

15.2

BOOK EXCERPT: CHAPTER 1

SWADHARMA AND SWARAJ

The fear of greased cartridges and the annexation of Oudh were only temporary and accidental causes. To turn these to real causes would never help us in understanding the real spirit of the revolution. If we were to take them as the real moving causes, it would mean that, without these, the revolution would not have taken place—that without the rumour of greased cartridges and without the annexation of Oudh, the revolution would not have been there. It would be impossible to find a theory more foolish and more deceptive. If there had been no fear of the cartridges, the principle underlying that fear would have cropped up in some other form and produced a revolution just the same. Even if Oudh had not been annexed, the principle of annexation would have manifested itself in the destruction of some other kingdom. The real causes of the French Revolution were not simply the high prices of grain, the Bastille, the King's leaving Paris, or the feasts. These might explain some incidents of the revolution but not the revolution as a whole. The kidnapping of Sita was only the incidental cause of the fight between Rama and Ravana. The real causes were deeper and more inward.

What, then, were the real causes and motives of this revolution? What were they that they could make thousands of heroes unsheath their swords and flash them on the battlefield? What were they that had the power to brighten up pale and rusty crowns and raise from the dust abased flags? What were they that for them, men by the thousands willingly poured their blood year after year? What were they that moulvies [Muslim clerics] preached them, learned Brahmins blessed them, that for their success prayers went up to Heaven from the mosques of Delhi and the temples of Benares?

These great principles were Swadharma [One's own faith/religion/duty] and Swaraj. In the thundering roar of 'Din, Din,' [Arabic word for faith/religion] which rose to protect religion, when there were evident signs of a cunning, dangerous, and destructive attack on religion dearer than life, and in the terrific blows dealt at the chain of slavery with the holy desire of acquiring Swaraj, when it was evident that chains of political slavery had been put round them and their God-given liberty wrested away by subtle tricks—in these two lies the root-principle of the revolutionary war. In what

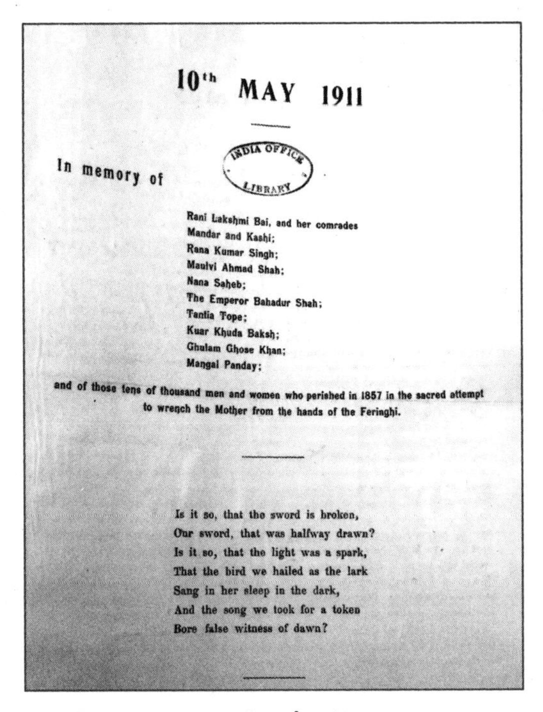
10th MAY 1911

In memory of

Rani Lakshmi Bai, and her comrades
Mandar and Kashi;
Rana Kumar Singh;
Maulvi Ahmad Shah;
Nana Saheb;
The Emperor Bahadur Shah;
Tantia Tope;
Kuar Khuda Baksh;
Ghulam Ghose Khan;
Mangal Panday;

and of those tens of thousand men and women who perished in 1857 in the sacred attempt to wrench the Mother from the hands of the Feringhi.

Is it so, that the sword is broken,
Our sword, that was halfway drawn?
Is it so, that the light was a spark,
That the bird we hailed as the lark
Sang in her sleep in the dark,
And the song we took for a token
Bore false witness of dawn?

1857 Commemoration Circular.

other history is the principle of love of one's religion and love of one's country manifested more nobly than in ours? However, much foreign and partial historians might have tried to paint our glorious land in dark colours, so long as the name of Chitore [Chittor] has not been erased from the pages of our history, so long as the names of Pratapaditya and Guru Govind Singh [17th century Bengali ruler and 18th century Sikh martyr, both of whom were engaged in conflict with the Mughals] are there, so long the principles or Swadharma and Swaraj will be embedded in the bone and marrow of all the sons of Hindusthan! They might be darkened for a time by the mist of slavery—even the sun has its clouds—but very soon the strong light of these selfsame principles pierces through the mist and chases it away. Never before were there such a number of causes for the universal spreading of these traditional and noble principles as there were in 1857. These particular reasons revived most wonderfully the slightly unconscious feelings of Hindusthan, and the people began to prepare for the fight for Swadharma and Swaraj. In his proclamation of the establishment of Swaraj, the Emperor of Delhi says, "Oh, you sons of Hindusthan, if we make up our mind, we can destroy the enemy in no time! We will destroy the enemy and will release from dread our religion and our country, dearer to us than life itself!" What is holier in this world than such a Revolutionary War, a war for the noble principles propounded in this sentence, Release from dread our religion and our country, dearer to us than life itself? The seed of the Revolution of 1857 is in this holy and inspiring idea, clear and explicit, propounded from the throne of Delhi, THE PROTECTION OF RELIGION AND COUNTRY. In the Proclamation issued at Bareilly, he says: "Hindus and Mahomedans of India! Arise! Brethren, arise! Of all the gifts of God, the most gracious is that of Swaraj. Will the oppressive demon who has robbed us of it by deceit be able to keep it away from us for ever? Can such an act against the will of God stand for ever? No, no. The English have committed so many atrocities that the cup of their sins is already full. To add to it, they have got now the wicked desire to destroy our holy religion! Are you going to remain idle even now? God does not wish that you should remain so; for he has inspired in the hearts of Hindus and Mahomedans the desire to turn the English out of our country. And by the grace of God, and your valour, they will soon be so completely defeated that in this our Hindusthan, there will not remain even the least trace of them! In this our army, the differences of small and great shall be forgotten, and equality shall be the rule; for, all who draw the sword in this holy war for the defence of religion are equally glorious. They are brethren, there is no rank among them. Therefore, I again say to all my Hindu brethren, 'Arise and jump into the battlefield for this divinely ordained and supreme duty!'" The man who, after seeing such magnificent utterances by the Revolutionary leaders, does not understand its principles is, as we said, either a fool or a knave. What stronger evidence is needed to prove that Indian warriors drew their swords at the time for Swadharma and Swaraj, feeling it the duty of every man to fight for the rights given to man by God? These proclamations issued at different times and places during the war make it unnecessary to dilate more on its principles. These proclamations were not issued by non-entities, but they were orders issued from adorable and powerful thrones. They were burning expressions of the agitated feelings of the time. In these the real heart of the nation had spoken out, when at the time of war, there was no occasion to conceal real sentiments through pressure or fear. This tremendous, heroic shout 'Swadharma and Swaraj' proclaims to the world the character of the Revolution in which 'all who draw the sword are equally glorious'.

* * *

16
1910 ›› HIND SWARAJ/INDIAN HOME RULE

Original: Gujarati/English | Author: M.K. Gandhi
16.1: Book Excerpt: Chapter XIV – 'How Can India Become Free?'
16.2: Book Excerpt: Chapter XVII – 'Passive Resistance'
16.3: Book Excerpt: Chapter XX – 'Conclusion'

WRITTEN ON BOARD A SHIP IN TEN DAYS, *HIND SWARAJ* IS A profoundly influential book. While he was in London, Mohandas Karamchand Gandhi had interacted with the 'extremists', who believed in violent and anarchist methods to end British rule in India. The book was written in Gujarati, in the form of a dialogue between two Indians subscribing to different viewpoints. It was first serialized in two parts in *Indian Opinion*, a weekly journal edited by Gandhi, and then published in booklet form. It was banned by the Government of Bombay in 1910 for being anti-British and seditious. Despite the ban, several editions of the work were published subsequently in their English translation (by Gandhi himself). Unlike his contemporaries, Gandhi chose not to accept Swaraj in terms of political self-government alone but gave it a moral dimension, by interpreting it as 'self-rule' or self-restraint (and not as absence from all restraint) in a much broader sense. Gandhi relied on the works of Western critics of Western civilization – Tolstoy, Emerson, Ruskin and Thoreau among others. However, *Hind Swaraj* was equally critical of Indians: 'The English have not taken India; we have given it to them. They are not in India because of their strength, but because we keep them.'

In April 1910, soon after the Government of Bombay had banned the book, Gandhi wrote to the Government of India with an English translation of his book (which, a government official conceded, was very similar to that made by the Gujarati interpreter to the Madras High Court). Gandhi requested that the Gujarati copies that were confiscated be returned to him. Having examined the English translation, government officials were convinced afresh of the need to confiscate even its English version. The director of Criminal Intelligence, C.R. Cleveland, was in favour of proscribing the English version as it was likely to be read all over India, unlike the Gujarati version.

In July 1910, the Government of India therefore forbade the 'importation into India of the booklet titled *Indian Home Rule* by M.K. Gandhi of Johannesburg, South Africa'. The Criminal Intelligence Department noted that:

> This book is undoubtedly revolutionary; it is in the form of a dialogue between the "Editor" and the "Reader" ingeniously constructed so that the editor always appears to be on the side of moderation as compared with the reader who is carried away by his feelings.

The book was un-banned by the Central Government in 1939, at the request of the Congress-run Government of UP.

Excerpts from three chapters are reprinted on the following pages.

* * *

16.1

BOOK EXCERPT: CHAPTER XIV

HOW CAN INDIA BECOME FREE?

Reader: I appreciate your views about civilisation. I will have to think over them. I cannot take in all at once. What, then, holding the views you do, would you suggest for freeing India?

Editor: I do not expect my views to be accepted all of a sudden. My duty is to place them before readers like yourself. Time can be trusted to do the rest. We have already examined the conditions for freeing India, but we have done so indirectly; we will now do so directly. It is a world known maxim that the removal of the cause of a disease results in the removal of the disease itself. Similarly, if the cause of India's slavery be removed, India can become free.

Reader: If Indian civilisation is, as you say, the best of all, how do you account for India's slavery?

Editor: This civilisation is unquestionably the best, but it is to be observed that all civilisations have been on their trial. That civilization which is permanent outlives it. Because the sons of India were found wanting, its civilisation has been placed in jeopardy. But its strength is to be seen in its ability to survive the shock. Moreover, the whole of India is not touched. Those alone who have been affected by western civilization have become enslaved. We measure the universe by our own miserable foot-rule. When we are slaves, we think that the whole universe is enslaved. Because we are in an abject condition, we think that the whole of India is in that condition. As a matter of fact, it is not so, but it is as well to impute our slavery to the whole of India. But if we bear in mind the above fact, we can see that, if we become free, India is free. And in this thought you have a definition of Swaraj. It is Swaraj when we learn to rule ourselves. It is, therefore, in the palm of our hands. Do not consider this Swaraj to be like a dream. Here there is no idea of sitting still. The Swaraj that I wish to picture before you and me is such that, after we have once realised it, we will endeavour to the end of our lifetime to persuade others to do likewise. But such Swaraj has to be experienced by each one for himself. One drowning man will never save another. Slaves ourselves, it would be a mere pretension to think of freeing others. Now you will have seen that it is not necessary for us to have as our goal the expulsion of the English. If the English become Indianised, we can accommodate them. If they wish to remain in India along with their civilisation, there is no room for them. It lies with us to bring about such a state of things.

* * *

16.2

BOOK EXCERPT: CHAPTER XVII

PASSIVE RESISTANCE

Reader: According to what you say, it is plain that instances of this kind of passive resistance are not to be found in history. It is necessary to understand this passive resistance more fully. It will be better, therefore, if you enlarge upon it.

Editor: Passive resistance is a method of securing rights by personal suffering; it is the reverse of resistance by arms. When I refuse to do a thing that is repugnant to my conscience, I use soul-force. For instance, the government of the day has passed a law which is applicable to me. I do not like it. If, by using violence, I force the government to repeal the law, I am employing what may be termed body-force. If I do not obey the law, and accept the penalty for its breach, I use soul-force. It involves sacrifice of self...

Reader: You would then disregard laws - this is rank disloyalty. We have always been considered a law-abiding nation. You seem to be going even beyond the extremists. They say that we must obey the laws that have been passed, but that, if the laws be bad, we must drive out the lawgivers even by force.

Editor: Whether I go beyond them or whether I do not is a matter of no consequence to either of us. We simply want to find out what is right, and to act accordingly. The real meaning of the statement that we are a law-abiding nation is that we are passive resisters. When we do not like certain laws, we do not break the heads of law-givers, but we suffer and do not submit to the laws. That we should obey laws whether good or bad is a new-fangled notion. There was no such thing in former days. The people disregarded those laws they did not like, and suffered the penalties for their breach. It is contrary to our manhood, if we obey laws repugnant to our conscience. Such teaching is opposed to religion, and means slavery. If the government were to ask us to go about without any clothing, should we do so? If I were a passive resister, I would say to them that I would have nothing to do with their law. But we have so forgotten ourselves and become so compliant, that we do not mind any degrading law.

A man who has realised his manhood, who fears only God, will fear no one else. Man-made laws are not necessarily binding on him. Even the government do not expect any such thing from us. They do not say: 'You must do such and such a thing' but they say: 'If you do not do it, we will punish you.' We are sunk so low, that we fancy that it is our duty and our religion to do what the law lays down. If man will only realise that it is unmanly to obey laws that are unjust, no man's tyranny will enslave him. This is the key to self-rule or home-rule.

It is a superstition and an ungodly thing to believe that an act of a majority binds a minority. Many examples can be given in which acts of majorities will be found to have been wrong, and those of minorities to have been right. All reforms owe their origin to the initiation of minorities in opposition to majorities. If among a band of robbers, a knowledge of robbing is obligatory, is a pious man to accept the obligation? So long as the superstition that men should obey unjust laws exists, so long will their slavery exist. And a passive resister alone can remove such a superstition.

To use brute force, to use gunpowder is contrary to passive resistance, for it means that we want our opponent to do by force that which we desire but he does not. And, if such a use of force is justifiable, surely he is entitled to do likewise by us. And so we should never come to an agreement. We may simply fancy, like the blind horse moving in a circle round a mill, that we are making progress. Those who believe that they are not bound to obey laws which are repugnant to their conscience have only the remedy of passive resistance open to them. Any other must lead to disaster.

* * *

16.3

BOOK EXCERPT: CHAPTER XX

CONCLUSION

Reader: What, then, would you say to the English?

Editor: To them I would respectfully say: 'I admit you are my rulers. It is not necessary to debate the question whether you hold India by the sword or by my consent. I have no objection to your remaining in my country, but, although you are the rulers, you will have to remain as servants of the people. It is not we who have to do as you wish, but it is you who have to do as we wish. You may keep the riches that you have drained away from this land, but you may not drain riches henceforth. Your function will be, if you so wish, to police India; you must abandon the idea of deriving any commercial benefit from us. We hold the civilisation that you support, to be the reverse of civilisation. We consider our civilisation to be far superior to yours. If you realise this truth, it will be to your advantage; and, if you do not, according to your own proverb, you should only live in our country in the same manner as we do. You must not do anything that is contrary to our religions. It is your duty as rulers that, for the sake of the Hindus, you should eschew beef, and for the sake of the Mahomedans, you should avoid bacon and ham. We have hitherto said nothing, because we have been cowed down, but you need not consider that you have not hurt our feelings by your conduct. We are not expressing our sentiments either through base selfishness or fear, but because it is our duty now to speak out boldly. We consider your schools and law courts to be useless. We want our own ancient schools and courts to be restored. The common language of India is not English but Hindi.

You should, therefore, learn it. We can hold communication with you only in our national language.

We cannot tolerate the idea of your spending money on railways and the military. We see no occasion for either. You may fear Russia; we do not. When she comes we will look after her. If you are with us, we will then receive her jointly. We do not need any European cloth. We will manage with articles produced and manufactured at home. You may not keep one eye on Manchester, and the other on India. We can work together only if our interests are identical.

This has not been said to you in arrogance. You have great military resources. Your naval power is matchless. If we wanted to fight with you on your own ground, we should be unable to do so; but, if the above submissions be not acceptable to you, we cease to play the ruled. You may, if you like, cut us to pieces. You may shatter us at the cannon's mouth. If you act contrary to our will, we will not help you, and, without our help, we know that you cannot move one step forward....

* * *

17
1910 ›› 'MOTHER, FAREWELL' – POEM ON DHOTI [WAISTCLOTH]

Original: Bengali
Poem: 'Mother, Farewell'

IN 1910, S.K. MAHAPATRA, DEPUTY SUPERINTENDENT OF THE Criminal Intelligence Department, noticed a strange kind of dhoti [waistcloth] being sold by boys and women in Calcutta, then the capital of British India. The dhoti, a five-yard long piece of clothing priced at four rupees, had a 'seditious and inflammatory' Bengali poem printed on its border. After some deliberation about the technical meaning of what might or might not be considered a 'document', the Government of India directed three local governments (Bengal, Central Provinces, and Eastern Bengal and Assam) to ban this dhoti. It was taken to be a document under Section 2(b) of the Indian Press Act and duly proscribed on the grounds that it contained incitements to violence and a tendency to excite disaffection against the government. The complete poem is reproduced here.

* * *

MOTHER, FAREWELL

I shall go to the gallows with a smile.
The people of India will see this.
One bomb can kill a man.
There are a lakh of bombs in our homes.
Mother, what can the English do? If I come back.
Do not forget, Mother,
Your foolish child Khudiram.
See that I get your sacred feet at the end.
When shall I call you again "Mother" with the ease of my mind?
Mother, do not keep this sinner in another country.
It is written that you have 36 crores of sons and daughters.

Mother, Khudiram's name vanishes now.
He is now turned to dust.
If I have to rise again
See that, Mother, I sit on your lap again.
In this kingdom of Bhisma [patriarch-statesman in the Mahabharata], who else is there like you?
You are unparalleled Mother.
When shall I depart from this world with a shout of Bande Mataram?
This is the saying of Bhabataran [first name, likely to be the author's],
Farewell, Mother.
I shall go to the gallows with a smile.
The people of India will see this.
One bomb can kill a man.
There are a lakh of bombs in our homes.
Mother what can the English do?

* * *

18

1910 ›› THE METHODS OF THE INDIAN POLICE IN THE 20th CENTURY

Original: English | Author: Frederick Mackarness
18.1: Pamphlet: Excerpts from Government Reports
18.2: Pamphlet: Excerpt from the Proceedings of the House of Commons

THE IMPORT OF THIS PAMPHLET, WRITTEN BY FREDERICK Mackarness, a barrister, county court judge and Member of the British Parliament (1854–1920) was prohibited under the Sea Customs Act in August 1910. Additionally, eight local government also banned it under the Indian Press Act.

The Criminal Intelligence Department observed that the pamphlet was seditious since it 'suggests that the torture of prisoners by the police is the rule rather than the exception in India, that Government is well aware of this and connives at it or at least takes no measures to stop it. The arguments are supported by garbled quotations from government reports and the judgments of the courts in a few cases.' In his telegram to the Secretary of State for India in London, the Viceroy, Lord Minto, mentioned that:

> Apparently it is stated that the details are taken from official reports, but no mention is made of the fact that such brutalities are rare, are invariably punished when detected, and are committed by Indian subordinates without knowledge of European superior officers. If the contents of the pamphlet are such as are described by the Anglo-Indian press, I consider it most inexpedient that its importation into and circulation in India should be permitted.

In the preface, Mackarness mentioned that he had sourced all the evidence he cited from official sources including the report of the police commission, and statements by judges (based on cases of police brutality from Bengal, Madras, Punjab and UP) and British Members of Parliament. This made his book even more credible, and, therefore, more damaging. As he put it,

I venture to ask any dispassionate person whether it does not reveal a state of things not only sufficient to justify discontent in those who suffer under it, but one that is thoroughly discreditable to the British administration in India.

This pamphlet was re-published by the Hindustan Ghadr Party, San Francisco, and in that edition the appendix contained several news reports of abuse of police power in different parts of India.

* * *

THE METHODS

OF

THE INDIAN POLICE

IN THE

20TH CENTURY

Here is the story of what the police did to the woman, in the very words of the official "Resolution": **Gulab Bano (the woman) made a statement to the following effect: "I was hung to the roof by the police (Superintendent and two Head Constables) . . . during the investigation, with a rope in my legs, and a baton smeared with green chillies was thrust up my anal opening."—See page 17.**

PUBLISHED BY

THE HINDUSTAN GADAR OFFICE

SAN FRANCISCO

Cover, The Methods of the Indian Police in the 20th Century.

18.1

EXCERPTS FROM GOVERNMENT REPORTS

EXCERPT FROM THE REPORT OF THE POLICE COMMISSION appointed by Viceroy Curzon and headed by Sir Andrew Fraser, then the Lieutenant Governor of Bengal (1902; report presented to the Parliament in 1905).

* * *

(CURZON COMMISSION, P. 16)

The Commission regret to have to report that they have the strongest evidence of the corruption and inefficiency of the great mass of investigating officers of higher grades. The forms of this corruption are very numerous. It manifests itself in every stage of the work of the police station. The police officer may levy a fee or receive a present for every duty he performs. More money is extorted as the investigation proceeds. The station-house officer will sometimes hush up a case in payment of his terms. He will receive presents from their parties and their witnesses: he will levy illicit fees from shop keepers and others for services rendered, or to obviate vexatious espionage. The illicit gains in some police stations in Bengal in connection with alluvial lands are almost incredible.

* * *

(CURZON COMMISSION, P. 17)

Another very serious ground of complaint against them is the unnecessary severity with which they often discharge their duties.... A body of police comes down to the village, and is quartered in it for several days. The principal residents have to dance attendance on the police all day long and for days together. Sometimes all the villagers are compelled to be in attendance, and inquiries degrading in their character are conducted *coram populo*. Suspects and innocent persons are bullied and threatened into giving information they are supposed to possess. The police officer, owing to want of detective ability or to indolence, directs his efforts to procure confessions by improper inducements, by threats, and by moral pressure. *It is easy, under the conditions of Indian society, to exercise strong pressure and great cruelty without having recourse to such physical violence as leaves its traces on the body of the victim.... What wonder is it that the people are said to dread the police, and to do all they can to avoid any connection with a police investigation! Deliberate association with criminals in their gains, and deliberately false charges against innocent persons on the ground of private spite or village faction, deliberate torture of suspected persons, and other most flagrant abuses occur occasionally.*

* * *

(CURZON COMMISSION, P. 21)

The Commission have the strongest evidence that the police force is, as a whole, regarded as far from efficient, and is stigmatized as corrupt and oppressive.... Honorable exceptions and mitigating circumstances can not efface the general impression created by the evidence recorded. There can be no doubt that the police force throughout the country is in a most unsatisfactory condition, that abuses are common everywhere, this involves great injury to the people and discredit to the government, and that radical reforms are urgently necessary.

* * *

18.2

EXCERPT FROM THE PROCEEDINGS OF THE HOUSE OF COMMONS

Mr. Mackarness asked the Under Secretary for India whether the Secretary of State's attention had been called to the Report. of Mr. Halliday, Commissioner of Police in Calcutta, and whether it was the fact that in the course of the last year 1 sergeant, 4 head constables, and 65 constables were dismissed from the service, of whom 2 head constables and 15 constables were dismissed for taking bribes; that 1 head constable and 7 constables were judicially convicted of crime; that 1 head constable and 22 constables were dismissed for illegal acts; and that, in addition, over 500 inspectors, sub-inspectors, sergeants, head constables, and constables were punished departmentally for various offences?

* * *

(HANSARD, FOR 27TH JULY, 1909)

Master of Elibank: "The number of punishments inflicted appear to show that the responsible officers are exercising proper supervision. *That being so, the Secretary of State deprecates inquiries, which may have the effect of lowering in the public estimation a body of men which is loyally doing its best in difficult circumstances, and upon which the public must rely for their security*"

* * *

(HANSARD, 4TH NOVEMBER, 1909)

The Master of Elibank: "The percentage of constables unable to read and write in the police forces of the three provinces is as follows:

Bengal -- 65 per cent; Bombay -- 48 per cent; Madras -- 8 per cent

* * *

19

1910 ›› THE SOCIAL CONQUEST OF THE HINDU RACE

Original: English | Author: Har Dayal | Pamphlet

HAR DAYAL (1884–1939) WAS A MENTEE OF SHYAMJI KRISHNAVARMA who was able to cross class divides; as an academic at Berkeley in California, he was able to reach out to many working-class Indian migrants in the United States and Canada (who by 1910 numbered about 30,000 in all) and involved them in his radical vision of India's future. Although he is better known for authoring and disseminating literature on behalf of the Hindustan Ghadr (Mutiny) party, this pamphlet bore his name as author.

This ten-page pamphlet was banned by the Sea Customs Act as well as by five provinces (Bombay, Burma, Eastern Bengal and Assam, Central Provinces and North-West Frontier Province). In the assessment of the Criminal Intelligence Department, the pamphlet was seditious because:

> The writer seeks to show that British supremacy in India is based on the control of almost all the social activities of the subject race by the rulers. He does not discuss the methods by which this "social conquest" should be resisted, but he implies that Indians should put an end to this "serfdom and perpetual bondage."

Har Dayal spoke of the 'moral drain' by which rulers both acquired as well as demonstrated their social superiority on a day-to-day basis. He made use of a fascinating analogy to describe Indian acquiescence to British domination: that of the so-called lower castes' acquiescence to so-called upper castes' domination. Excerpts are reprinted on the following pages.

* * *

THE SOCIAL CONQUEST OF THE HINDU RACE

By HAR DAYAL

POLITICAL dominion is never permanent unless it is based on a social conquest of the subject race. The social conquest must, in the nature of things, follow the political subjugation of one race by another. Political power is acquired by means of military superiority and skill in diplomacy; it is also maintained by the same means. But the social conquest is a slower process; it cannot be accomplished with the help of maxim guns and disciplined armies. Even Alexander or Chengiz Khan could not effect a social conquest of other nations by the use of force alone. Force can crush the organised physical strength of a weak people. It can demolish the forts, and scatter the armies, of an inferior race, but it can never enable the conquerors to obtain control over the hearts and minds of their subjects. The sword is worse than useless for the rulers when they set about the task of conquering their subjects socially. It actually mars the success of the enterprise. It must be sheathed in the scabbard: it must be put away out of sight for the moment.

The necessity of a social conquest as a means of consolidating and perpetuating the political conquest can be understood by all who know the conditions under which alone a strong nation can establish and maintain its rule over other peoples. No nation can lose its birthright of independence until it has been so demoralised through avarice, luxury and indolence as to forget the virtues of national pride and self-respect, religious enthusiasm and the sense of individual responsibility for the social welfare. The decay of the moral calibre of a nation paves the way for foreign domination which, in turn, accelerates the process of decline by its very existence. Professor Seeley says that subjection to a foreign rule is one of the most potent causes of moral deterioration. Thus moral decrepitude is both the cause and the effect of foreign rule, just as fever attacks the man whose system has been weakened by intemperance or unhealthy living and at the same time renders him more unfit to resist disease and physical decay.

The social conquest is an essential part of the political conquest, because the latter can never be stable and enduring if the manly qualities of the subject race are not impaired. If the conquered people manage to keep alive their self-respect and dignity through centuries of foreign political supremacy, they are sure to enter into their inheritance of independence some day. Sooner or later, the unsubdued heart and mind of the sturdy race will seek its outward sign and symbol, its embodiment in the world of fact, *viz*., a national state. The great duty of a subject people consists in guarding the Promethean spark of national pride and

Lala Har Dayal

self-respect, lest it should be extinguished by the demoralising influences that emanate from foreign rule. The natural almost inevitable effect of foreign domination is the gradual loss of the virtues which distinguish free men from slaves. The extinction of these requisites of national existence proclaims the death of the nation. The social conquest is necessary for killing the soul of the nation. National pride is the greatest asset of a fallen race. Conquerors will always teach us that we are an inferior people: their laws and their methods

72—10

Social Conquest of the Hindu Race.

Political dominion is never permanent unless it is based on a social conquest of the subject race. The social conquest must, in the nature of things, follow the political subjugation of one race by another. Political power is acquired by means of military superiority and skill in diplomacy; it is also maintained by the same means. But the social conquest is a slower process; it cannot be accomplished with the help of maxim guns and disciplined armies. Even Alexander or Chengiz Khan could not effect a social conquest of other nations by the use of force alone. Force can crush the organized physical strength of a weak people. It can demolish the forts, and scatter the armies, of an inferior race, but it can never enable the conquerors to obtain control over the hearts and minds of their subjects. The sword is worse than useless for the rulers when they set about the task of conquering their subjects socially. It actually mars the success of the enterprise. It must be sheathed in the scabbard: it must be put away out of sight for the moment....

The social conquest is the process which increases this Moral Drain by giving the ruler opportunities of acquiring and asserting social superiority in every-day life over the conquered people. If they exercise merely political dominion, assess taxes and correct them, enact laws and execute them, they can be can be conquerors and legislators, tax-gatherers and constables but they can never be masters of their subjects. Something more than military occupation and political sovereignty is required in order to render their position impregnable, and make them the real and undisputed rulers of the people. Dominion is acquired by the sword, but it is generally preserved and perpetuated by other means. As time goes by, the sword is superseded by more efficient, weapons, which are not so terrible to behold, but which are more fatal to the national life of the subject race than the keenest Toledo blade. Force can defeat and conquer: it cannot crush. It can bind. it cannot make one bend. Political conquest, binds the subject race: it does not make it bend. How to achieve the latter result is the great problem which confronts the conquering race.

Let us take an example. It is believed that the Pariahs [Paraiyan; a caste considered 'untouchable'] of Southern India are the descendants of the aboriginal inhabitants who were conquered by the Aryans. It is also known that the number of Aryans who colonised Southern India was very small compared with that of the Aborigines. The Aryans were more Vigorous, and were united among themselves and possessed better weapons. They went and defeated the forces of the dark chiefs who could not plan and organise and who sometimes joined the enemies of their race through short-sighted selfishness. The Brahmans settled in the land. So far everything is plain. A nation has been conquered in battle by another nation which is numerically weaker but morally and physically stronger than it. But then how has it come to pass that the Pariah of the Deccan prostrates himself before the Brahman in the street and voluntarily stands aside as the latter approaches him? There is now no law requiring the Pariah to demean himself in this way. He cannot be punished by British courts of law if he refuses to compromise his self-respect by this saluting it representative of the race which conquered his nation. The Brahman is not armed with weapons : he is generally a weak scholar, whom the Pariah could easily beat in a hand-to-hand encounter. And yet we behold the curious spectacle of hundreds of Pariahs, possessing fine physical stamina, bowing to a single

Brahman in the street even in the twentieth century when there is no law requiring them to do so....

Thus we have only to ask and answer the question. How did the astute Brahmans of old secure for themselves a permanent position of predominance in the South? We must understand the Brahman's polity in those ancient times, if we desire to fathom the significance of British policy in India in the twentieth century. History repeats itself, and our own wisdom of five thousand years ago is today employed against us by another race....

How does the social conquest of the Hindus by the British people proceed? Are the three factors of success present in this case?

(a) *The control of all activities* —School and Colleges for general knowledge, Medical Colleges, Law Colleges, Hospitals, Post Offices, Pipes for water, etc., etc.

(b) *A common platform for social intercourse on terms of inequality* —Legislative Councils, Schools and Colleges, Durbars. Courts, Municipalities, District Boards, Occasional Public Meetings, etc., etc.

(c) *A class of men ready to avail themselves of social intercourse, on terms of inequality* – The landed gentry, the "English-educated" classes, etc., etc....

The attempt of Mrs. Besant [Annie Besant, 1847-1943; British-born founder of the Indian Home Rule League] and other Europeans to control and guide Hindu religious life, represents the last phase of the Social Conquest which was inaugurated with the establishment of schools and colleges, hospitals and dispensaries.

After the social conquest, serfdom and perpetual bondage. Those who assist in the process reduce themselves to the position of Pariahs. The military and political leadership of the nation has already passed from the Kshatriya to the Briton: will he also succeed to the social leadership which has been the privilege of the Brahman and the *rishi*? If the social conquest is completed, there is no hope for our nation. The evil effects of the process which has only begun are already visible. These must be counteracted in order to prepare the way for political regeneration. On this occasion, I do not propose to discuss the methods of resisting this social conquest. I only ask Hindu India the great question, "Shall the Briton be your Brahman?"

* * *

20

1910 ›› THE TALVAR [THE SWORD]

Original: English
20.1: Article: 'The Nasik Double Murder', January 1910
20.2: Article: April–May 1910

THE FIRST ISSUE, DATED NOVEMBER 1909, MENTIONED BERLIN, but it was printed in Rotterdam. The CID considered it to be the work of Indian Communist Virendranath Chattopadhyay (1880–1937), using the alias Signor Alfieri. It was banned both by local governments, as well as under the Sea Customs Act. In its February issue, the following appeal was printed just below the header, with Madame Cama mentioned as the person to whom orders and payments had to be made:

> AN APPEAL: As the enemy has prohibited the circulation of this paper in Hindusthan, every reader is earnestly requested to help in its circulation as much as he possibly can.

Madame Bhikaiji Cama (1861–1936) was a wealthy Parsi (Indian Zoroastrian) heiress who, from her European bases after 1902, became a locus of revolutionary networks ranging from the India House group in London till the Yugantar Ashram group in San Francisco. She funded and composed revolutionary publications and arranged for their transmission around the globe. She participated in the International Socialist Congress in Stuttgart in Germany, and her activities were closely monitored by intelligence authorities.

* * *

Single Copy: Six pence.
Annual Subscription: Five shillings
Strictly in advance.

THE TALVAR

Ghazion men bu rahegi jab talak iman ki.
Tab to London tak chalegi tegh Hindusthan ki.
EMPEROR BAHADUR SHAH.

AN ORGAN OF INDIAN INDEPENDENCE

Vol. I. | BERLIN, 20th, February 1910. | No. 4.

AN APPEAL: As the enemy has prohibited the circulation of this paper in Hindusthan, every reader is earnestly requested to help in its circulation as much as he possibly can. All remittances and communications to be sent to Madame B. R. CAMA, Poste Restante, Bureau de Poste, Rue Montaigne, PARIS, who has kindly consented to receive orders and payments on our behalf.

The Responsibilities of the Religious Leaders of Hindusthan.

If there is any country in the world more than any other, in which the relation between religion and politics is organic and vital, that country is Hindusthan. It is here that society was evolved and consolidated not on the pirnciples of selfish individualism and the contrat social but on the basis of passionate self-sacrifice and unflinching renunciation.

The Vitality of Our Nation.

But the brilliant milleniums of history that saw the evolution : consolidation of Hindu society un the guiding genius of the Brahn and the rishi, the milleniums tnat gave humanity the sublimest productions of the mind and the most transcendent achievements of the soul, had hardly come to an end, when, attracted by the dazzling lustre of the wealth of Hindusthan, invader after invader brought his murderous hosts to attempt its conquest and subjugation. Darius the Persian established a nominal satrapy in the extreme northwest corner; Alexander the Greek succeeded for a while in overcoming by force of arms a small fraction of the same unfortunate province but the Greeks were beaten and repulsed by the Hindu Nation under Chandragupta. Mahmud of Ghazni brought his contingent of iconoclasts but though he harassed he did not conquer. Muhammad Ghori followed and founded a dynasty. Timur swept over the valley of the Ganges and committed the wildest havoc. Babar the Mongol ne and established an Empire produced great rulers. Nadir ravaged towns and villages turned with enormous booty. But all these waves of destruction beat in vain against the impregnable rock of Hindu Nationalism. The Brahman organized, the Ksha- riya fought and died, and all ranks f the Hindu nation were up in ms against these warriors whose ly function in this world has been bring misery and ruin to large ses of humanity. And it is a surprising proof of the vitality of the Indian nation that notwithstan

[...]

all these thousands of years. Ancient Egypt has gone the way of all flesh; so have the Assyrians, the Babylonians, the Medes, the Persians, the Greeks, the Romans and the Phoenicians. Hindusthan alone has survived the shock of aggression and the ravages of time. Hindusthan, more than any other land, has been the tramping ground of the armies of the world; yet Hindusthan alone of all countries has defied them to break through her solidarity, or to alter the spirit, the strength, and the individuality of her mental and moral, her social and religious life. This admirable continuity of the life and vitality of the nation is mainly the result of the wonderful organization of our society. But we have latterly, in the true spirit of slaves, accepted the verdict of our enemies as to our life and history and ideals. And it has become the fashion among our "enlightened" and spiritless countrymen to join Christian missionaries and Firinghi tyrants in decrying and denouncing the caste system. But that social and religious system of life has been the salvation of Hindusthan. We do not wish to pose here as reactionary advocates of that institution in all its harshness and rigour. We believe that the darkest pages in our national history are the record of the Brahman's treatment of the Pariah and the Chandal, and his many acts of insolence and arrogance towards the lower castes.

The Patriotic Traditions of the Brahman.

But when all the worst faults of human beings have been laid at his door, the indisputable fact still remains that to the Brahman Hindusthan owes both her glory and her salvation. There never has been a time in our history when the Brahman has not identified him-

[...]

threatened by the robbers, the murderers, the vandals of alien lands, the soul of the Brahman, trembling with passion at the thought of impending danger to the Mother, arose to organise the might of the nation to repel the foreign intruder. Restlessly patriotic, knowing no higher ambition than the service of people, aspiring to no higher ho in this world than the intelle and spiritual leadership of toiling millions of our land, li the simplest, the purest, the not life of any yet invented by n the Brahman has been the li embodiment and representative the highest ambitions and asp tions of Hindusthan. No hierarchical council or organisation has ever been created to enforce his supremacy and protect his power in society. No pope, no college of cardinals, no ordained priesthood, no magnificence of ceremonial, no enforcing of dogmas not understanded of the people. The Brahman by his very birth is the inheritor, the repository, the propagator of the highest and noblest ideals and aspirations of our country. He is the teacher, the guide, the leader of the people. He, above all other individuals in society, is responsible, in every act and detail of his life, for the honour and independence and glory of Hindusthan. To him the masses have always looked for

The Talvar, *20 February 1910.*

20.1

JANUARY 1910

'THE NASIK DOUBLE MURDER'

The city of Nasik would have been false to her traditions and title as a Dharmakshetra [blessed land] if she had failed to send forth a Dharmavira [virtuous warrior] at the present crisis of our national existence. Both Sri Ram and Dharmasiri [title denoting honour] Sri Ramdas, the great master and the great disciple, have stored up their Tapas-tej [radiance borne of austere spiritual practices] in that holy place and it is without much surprise that we learn, today that Nasik has claimed the honour of being the first city in India to successfully strike down an alien foe.

The Rana of Udaipur, overwhelmed by the defeat and disgrace of the Hindu race, invoked the tutelary deity of Chitore and implored her to show him how he could prevent the downfall of the nation. It is said in the Rajput annals that the goddess Kali appeared to him in a dream and shrieked ominously, 'Main bhuki hun!' [Hungry am I and blood I want!] Even so, ever since the martyrdom of Chapekar and Ranade, Kali the Terrible has been shrieking aloud in all directions of Hind, 'Main bhuki hun! Main bhuki hun!' Jackson is the first victim that the War-goddess has claimed, and Kanare the Martyr devotee who purchased it at the cost of his own life.

* * *

20.2

APRIL–MAY 1910

Alas, what a pathetic sight it is to see the descendants of Sri Ram and Sri Krishna, Arjun and Bhim, the Ghazis and the Akalis, Nana Saheb and Khan Bahadur tremble before a puny race of shop-keepers, because, forsooth, these are armed with modern guns and cannon, and we are not! Where is our heroism, where is our love of fighting gone? Have we lost our resource and faith in ourselves and the greatness of our destiny? Have we become so blind that we do not see the large quantity of arms that is still in the country available to us and the immense possibilities of increasing the same.

* * *

NOTIFICATIONS.

Nagpur, the 10th June 1910.

No. 1352.—Whereas the Local Government of the Central Provinces has received reliable information that the issue, dated the 20th February 1910, of a newspaper entitled "The Talvar—an organ of Indian independence," contains words which have a tendency to incite to acts of violence and to bring into hatred and contempt His Majesty and the Government established by law in British India and to excite disaffection towards His Majesty and the said Government, and whereas the said Local Government is of opinion that immediate action should be taken with respect to the said issue of the said newspaper under the Indian Press Act, 1910 (I of 1910), in order to prevent the dissemination by its means of matter the publication of which is punishable under Section 124-A of the Indian Penal Code, the said Local Government, acting under the powers vested in it by Section 12 (1) of the said Act, hereby declares all copies of the said issue of the said newspaper, wherever found in the Central Provinces, to be forfeited to His Majesty.

No. 1353.—Whereas the Local Government of the Central Provinces has received reliable information that the issue, dated the 20th February 1910, of a newspaper entitled "The Talvar—an organ of Indian independence," contains words which have a tendency to incite to acts of violence and to bring into hatred and contempt His Majesty and the Government established by law in British India and Berar and to excite disaffection towards His Majesty and the said Government, and whereas the said Local Government is of opinion that immediate action should be taken with respect to the said issue of the said newspaper under the Indian Press Act, 1910 (I of 1910), as applied to Berar, in order to prevent the dissemination by its means of matter the publication of which is punishable under Section 124-A of the Indian Penal Code, the said Local Government, acting under the powers vested in it by Section 12 (1) of the said Act, hereby declares all copies of the said issue of the said newspaper, wherever found in Berar, to be forfeited to His Majesty.

B. P. STANDEN,
Chief Secretary to the Chief Commissioner,
Central Provinces.

'ress, Nagpur—20-6-10—15.

Government of Central Provinces' notification banning The Talvar.

PART II: 1911-1920

21

1911 ›› BANDE MATARAM (GENEVA)

Original: English | Editor: Bhikaiji Cama
21.1: Article: April 1911
21.2: Article: January 1913

THE FIRST ISSUE APPEARED IN SEPTEMBER 1909 AND MADAME Bhikaiji Cama was mentioned as the corresponding person. According to information with the CID, thousand copies of each issue were published between January and August 1910. The CID believed that Madame Cama in Paris was its editor, but that it was printed in Rotterdam and sent by her to India as well as to Indians in other countries.

* * *

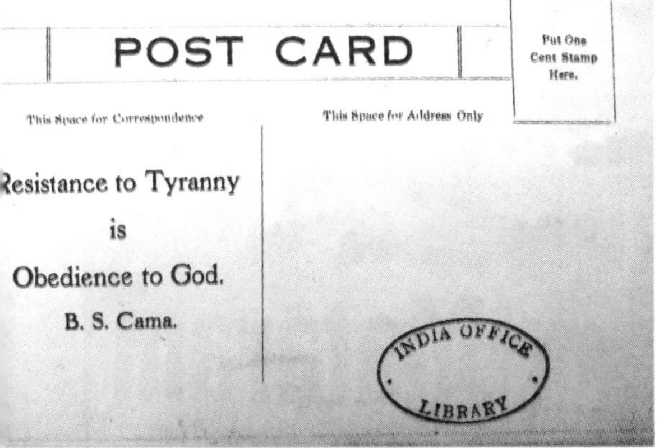

oscribed postcard featuring Madame Cama, Front.

Proscribed postcard featuring Madame Cama, Reverse.

21.1

APRIL 1911

Dealing with villains like these, an Indian must throw to the winds all the ordinary rules of warfare. The Englishman is a snake and he must be thrashed and mauled and killed wherever he is found. With gentlemen we can be gentlemen, but not with rogues and scoundrels. It is no infamy if an Indian pupil shoots down his English professor, if an Indian clerk shoots down his English superior, if an Indian barrister shoots down the English Judge and an Indian patient shoots down an English doctor. In a meeting or in a bungalow, on the railway or in a carriage, in a shop or in a church, in a garden or at a fair, wherever an opportunity comes, Englishmen ought to be killed. No distinction should be made between officers and private people. The great Nana Sahib [prominent leader of the revolt of 1857] understood this, and our friends the Bengalis have also begun to understand. Blessed be their efforts! Long be their arms! Now indeed we may say to the Englishman, "Don't shout till you are out of the wood."

* * *

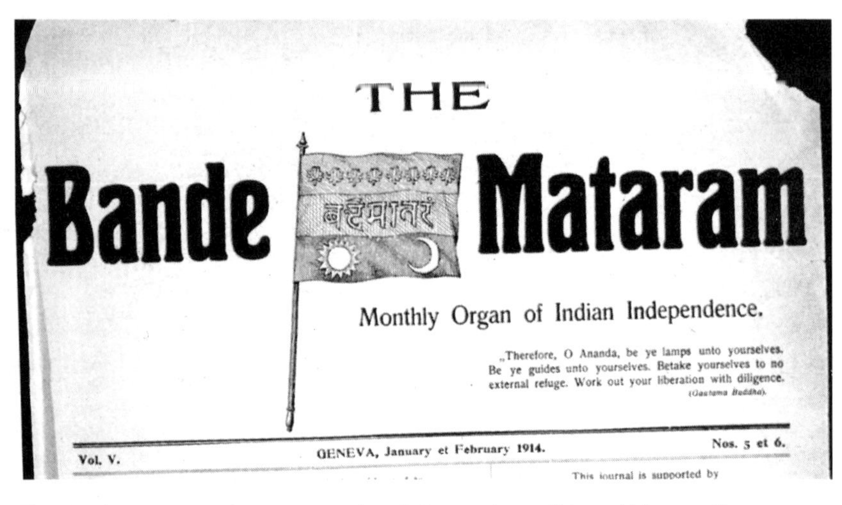

THE

Bande Mataram

Monthly Organ of Indian Independence.

„Therefore, O Ananda, be ye lamps unto yourselves. Be ye guides unto yourselves. Betake yourselves to no external refuge. Work out your liberation with diligence.
(Gautama Buddha).

Vol. V. GENEVA, January et February 1914. Nos. 5 et 6.

This journal is supported by

The Bande Mataram, *Geneva, Masthead. Source: https://digital.library.villanova.edu/Item/vudl:145643#?c=&m=&s=&cv=&xywh=-4434%2C-292%2C12761%2C5826*

PHOTOGRAPH OF MADAME BHIKHAIJI RUSTOM K. R. CAMA.

Taken about October 1907.

Specimen of Madame Cama's handwriting.

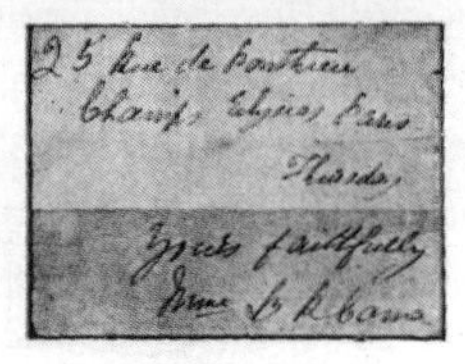

Madame Bhikaiji Cama's photo and handwriting sample in her chargesheet file maintained by the Government of India. Source: Home Political B (Proceedings), file 61, August 1913.

SECRET.

CRIMINAL INTELLIGENCE OFFICE.

HISTORY SHEET OF MADAME BHIKHAIJI RUSTOM K. R. CAMA.

Madame **Cama** was born about 1875, the daughter of **Sorabji Framji Patel** of Bombay. Her husband is the son of **K. R. Cama**, the Parsi reformer, and is a well-to-do solicitor at Bombay. Madame Cama received her early education at the Alexandra Parsi Girls' School, Bombay, and speaks several languages fluently. According to her own account she has been in Europe since about 1902, spending about a year each in Germany, Scotland, Paris and London.

2. In August 1907, Madame Cama attended the **International Socialist Congress at Stuttgart, Germany,** in the company of **Sardarsinghji Rewabhai Rana,** the well-known Paris seditionary, and at the meeting of this body on August 22nd she made a speech, "for the dumb millions of Hindustan, who are undergoing terrible tyranny under the English Capitalists and the British Government." She said 35 million pounds were taken annually from India to England without return, and in consequence people in India died of poverty at the rate of half a million every month. At the close of her speech she unfolded the Indian National flag, a tricolour in green, yellow and red, with the words "Bande Mataram" on the middle band, and bearing emblems to represent the Hindus, Muhammadans, Buddhists, and Parsis. She implored them to read **Comrade Hyndman's** paper on the impoverishment of India, and again waving the flag before them she said she had every hope of seeing the republic of India established in her lifetime. **Madame Cama** and **S. R. Rana** attended this Congress as delegates from the **Paris Indian Society,** and according to the Indian Congress organ, **India,** "they were not entitled to membership of the Congress, but were admitted by the courtesy of the British section, to whom **Mrs. Cama** desires to tender her thanks."

3. The following appeared in the "**Indian Sociologist**" for September 1907 :—

"We announce with great pleasure that at the instance of **Mrs. Bhikhaiji Rustom K. R. Cama,** with whose name our readers are familiar, some Indian ladies residing in Paris have offered a lectureship

S25Cr

History Sheet of Madame Cama. Source: Home Political B (Proceedings), file 61, August 1913.

21.2

THIS AND OTHER BANNED PUBLICATIONS MADE MUCH OF THE 'bomb outrage': an unsuccessful attempt on the life of the then Viceroy, Lord Hardinge (1858–1944, in office 1910–1916) in 1913, shortly after the capital of British India shifted from Calcutta [Kolkata] to Delhi.

* * *

JANUARY 1913

The enemy entered formally Delhi on the 23rd December, 1912, but under what an omen? A bomb was thrown on the Viceroy Lord Hardinge, as he was marching through the historical Chandni Chowk on an elephant supplied by the lackey of Faridkot. His Jemadar [low ranking military official] who held the gold umbrella over his head was killed instantaneously, but the Viceroy escaped, though he was severely wounded in the scapula! The Hindusthani Revolutionaries have nothing whatever to do with his wound being fatal or not, as they are not bloodthirsty hounds like the British!

This bomb-throwing was just to announce to the whole world that the English Government is discarded, and verily, whenever there is an opportunity the Revolutionaries are sure to show their mind, spirit and principle in Hindusthan!

There is one point of satisfaction still greater and more hopeful than ever, i.e., not a single soul has yet betrayed the hands which manufactured and used the machine, and therein lies the success of it.

* * *

22

1913 ›› OATH OF ABHINAV BHARAT [YOUNG INDIA SOCIETY]

Original: English | Postcard

THE YOUNG INDIA SOCIETY WAS AN UNDERGROUND POLITICAL organization in London that counted Indian students among its members. Postcards were sent to India in 1913 with this oath printed on one side, and a photograph of Savarkar and an advertisement for his book on the revolt of 1857 (also banned; discussed in chapter 15) printed on the other.

* * *

In the name of God,
In the name of Bharat Mata.
In the name of all the Martyrs that have shed their blood for Bharat Mata.
By the Love, innate in all men and women, that I bear to the land of my birth, wherein the sacred ashes of my forefathers, and which is the cradle of my children.
By the tears of Hindi Mothers for their children whom the Foreigner has enslaved, imprisoned, tortured, and killed.
I ....convinced that without Absolute Political Independence or *Swarajya* my country can never rise to the exalted position among the nations of the earth which is Her due.
And convinced also that *Swarajya* can never be attained except by the waging of a bloody and relentless war against the Foreigner.
Solemnly and sincerely swear that I shall from this moment do everything in my power to fight for Independence and place the Lotus Crown of *Swarajya* on the head of my Mother;
And with this object, I join the *Abhinav Bharat,* the revolutionary Society of all Hindusthan, and swear that I shall ever be true and faithful to this my solemn Oath, and that I shall obey the orders of this body.
If I betray the whole or any part of this solemn Oath, or if I betray this body or any other body working with a similar object,
May I be doomed to the fate of a perjurer!

23
1913 ›› THE GHADR [MUTINY]

Original: Punjabi (Gurmukhi)/Gujarati/Urdu
23.1: Article: 8 November 1913
23.2: Article: 23 December 1913

THE TITLE MEANT MUTINY, A REFERENCE TO THE EVENTS OF 1857. The first issue appeared in November 1913 and was published in San Francisco. The paper described itself as 'the enemy of the British Raj' and was started as a weekly paper in Urdu and Gurmukhi by Har Dayal (see chapter 19). By 1914, a Gujarati edition had also appeared. The CID believed that copies were sent to Canada, from where they were posted to India. Copies also came to India from places as far apart as Nairobi, Hong Kong, Shanghai and Bangkok.

It was dispatched by post from the US and Canada. The British intercepted 215 packets – envelopes with different handwriting, containing copies in Bombay, in January 1914. All envelopes were addressed to people in Punjab, including to Indian Army personnel.

The Sea Customs Act had prohibited its import in December 1913. Har Dayal had claimed in a speech the previous month that many copies had reached India. The CID (Ker) also conceded that even after the SCA notification, many copies escaped interception and a few were handed over by recipients. Copies were also sent via Europe and even China by Indians living in those places. In mid-1915, the CID estimated that 3,000 copies were posted from San Francisco to the Federated Malay States, Dutch East Indies and Siam.

In March 1914, Har Dayal was arrested by the United States' authorities. A new Gujarati edition was started in May 1914. In 1915, it began appearing in Hindi.

* * *

15

PROCEEDINGS OF THE

HOME DEPARTMENT, JANUARY 1914.

Prohibition under section 19 of the Sea Customs Act, 1878 (VIII of 1878), of the importation into British India of any copy of an Urdu paper entitled the *Ghadr* (Mutiny). [Pro. nos. 42-43.

PROHIBITION UNDER SECTION 19 OF THE SEA CUSTOMS ACT, 1878 (VIII OF 1878), OF THE IMPORTATION INTO BRITISH INDIA OF ANY COPY OF AN URDU PAPER ENTITLED THE *GHADR* (MUTINY) PUBLISHED BY THE *YUGANTAR ASHRAM* OF SAN FRANCISCO, U. S. A.

No. 212-C., dated Delhi, the 22nd December 1913. Pro. no. 42.

Notification by the Government of India, Department of Commerce and Industry.

In exercise of the power conferred by section 19 of the Sea Customs Act, 1878 (VIII of 1878), the Governor-General in Council is pleased to prohibit the bringing by sea or by land into British India of any copy of an Urdu paper called, the *Ghadr* (Mutiny) published by the *Yugantar Ashram* of San Francisco, United States of America.

No. 213-214-C.

Endorsed by the Government of India, Department of Commerce and Industry.

Copy forwarded to the Home Department and to the Director-General of Posts and Telegraphs for information.

No. 55-C., dated Delhi, the 5th January 1914. Pro. no. 43.

Endorsed by the Government of India, Home Department.

Commerce and Industry Department notification dated the 22nd December 1913.

Copy forwarded to the Director, Criminal Intelligence, for information.

Sea Customs Notification banning The Ghadr *from entry into India.*

23.1

8 NOVEMBER 1913

What dear readers, is your duty?...

It is that you should help us with your body, mind and wealth in achieving success. It is not sufficient that a few men should exert themselves. This great work can be accomplished only through labour and sacrifice on the part of all.

Your first duty is regularly to remit money to us. Thousands of copies of this paper should be published .... so that the enemy may be frightened and may forthwith begin to pack up.

Your second duty is to read the paper carefully, to remember the things published in it and as far as possible not to destroy it.

Your third duty is to make others read the paper.

Your fourth duty consists in sending the paper to India by placing it in a cover or otherwise.

Your fifth duty is to prepare to fight and die in the rising. Independence will not come by reading newspapers and causing them to be read. Look out for the time when the rising will take place and you will slay the enemy.

* * *

Amsterdam,
Oct. 25, 1915.

Dear Comrade,

I am well and busy and sad. Can you send me some earnest and sincere comrades, men and women, who would like to help our Indian revolutionary movement in some way or other? I need the co-operation of very earnest comrades. Perhaps you can find them in New York or at Paterson. They should be real fighters, I.W.W's. or anarchists. Our Indian Party will make all necessary arrangements.

If some comrades wish to come, they should come to Holland. We have a centre in Amsterdam and Dutch comrades are working with us. If some comrades are ready to come, please telegraph me in some feminine name from New York to the following address:-

Israel Aaronson,
C/o Madame Kercher,
116, Oude Scheveningseweg,
Scheveningen. (Holland).

My assumed name is "Israel Aaronson." Kindly don't telegraph in your own name. The word "Yes" will suffice. The Rotterdam-America Line will receive instructions from us here to give tickets etc. to as many persons as you recommend. All financial arrangements will be made by our Party.

News from India is good. We have lost (?) some very brave comrades in the recent skirmishes.

It would be better if you could intimate in your telegram how many comrades wish to come. For instance, put the number in some sentence. I shall understand, e.g. Five months' holiday coming, etc. etc.

The need for the services of comrades is urgent. Please do come to our help. We are fighting against heavy odds.

With love and respect,

Yours for the fight,

HAR DAYAL.

P.S.

Kindly be very careful in keeping everything secret and confidential.

THE BALANCE SHEET
(Bilan, Compte Rendu)
OF BRITISH RULE IN INDIA
(Translated from the "Hindustan-Gadar")

SOME MAIN ITEMS

(1). Englishmen drain from India and take to England every year 50 crores of rupees (167 million dollars); consequently the Hindus have become so poor that the daily average income per capita is only 5 pices (2½ cents).

(2). The land tax is more than 65 per cent of the net produce.

(3). The expenditure on the education of
240 million persons is.......... 7¾ crores of rupees ($25,000,000)
on sanitation...................... 2 " " (6,000,000)
but on the army.................. 29½ " " (97,000,000)

(4). Under British rule, the famines are ever on the increase, and in the last ten years twenty million men, women and children have died of starvation.

(5). From the plague have occurred, during the sixteen years past, eight million deaths, and the death rate during the last thirty years has steadily increased from 24 per mille up to 34 per mille.

(6). Means are employed to spread disunion and disorder in the native states and to increase British influence there.

(7). Englishmen are not punished for murdering Hindus and for insulting Hindu women.

(8). From money taken from the Hindus aid is given to English Christian priests.

(9). Attempt is always made to create enmity between people of different religious denominations.

(10). The arts and crafts (industries) of India have been destroyed for England's benefit.

(11). Employing India's money, and sacrificing the lives of the Hindus (as soldiers), China, Afghanistan, Burmah, Egypt and Persia have been conquered.

PUBLISHED BY
THE HINDUSTAN-GADAR OFFICE
1324 Valencia Street
San Francisco, Cal., U. S. A.

Intercepted letter from Har Dayal to a Comrade, 25 October 1915. Source: Home Political (KWI) file 9/V, 1932.
Right: Balance Sheet of British Rule, issued by the Ghadr Party in 1915.

23.2

23 DECEMBER 1913

We appear to-day for the first time in our yellow apparel because in the history of India this garb is associated with the memory of martyrs, and heroes. We send out to-day a message and a prophecy about Mutiny in letters of bold on this coloured paper. To day this heroic paper, in the glory of its new garb, loudly conveys this message to you—Brethren do you also don your yellow garments, and leaving aside all material comforts and luxuries begin to fight with the British Government. Burn to ashes your weakness of spirit in the fire of bravery, throw away from to-day your old dress which is saturated with servility, and putting on yellow apparel become men by bathing in the sacred river of heroism. Wash away the filth of ages, and come into the temple of freedom to make an offering of your life. Here no offering less than one's life is accepted. Every devoted son of his Motherland who reads this newspaper is charged with the duty of becoming a soldier of revolution. He should enlist in the regiment of Mutiny; he should be spared to fight. He should dream of revolt; he should wait with eager expectancy for the day of rebellion.

* * *

24
1913 ›› YUGANTAR CIRCULAR [NEW INDIA CIRCULAR]

Original: English | Circular

ISSUED BY THE HINDUSTAN GHADR PARTY IN 1913, THE CIRCULAR was sent to India in February 1913, but the previous month itself CID had information that a pamphlet had been prepared by Har Dayal on the significance of the bomb and sent by him to Shyamji Krishnavarma in Paris. Madame Cama was believed to have 1,500 copies of it with her for circulation. The original pamphlet was in English.

The pamphlet contained a paragraph severely criticizing moderate Indian politicians, comparing them to dogs who had been thrown bones by the British.

* * *

THE DELHI BOMB

This is the name that we propose to give to this epoch-making, thought-provoking, far-resounding bomb of December 23, 1912. One may say that it is one of the sweetest and loveliest bombs that have exploded in India since the great day on which Khudi Ram Bose first ushered in a new era in the history of India, more than four years ago. Indeed this bomb is one of the most serviceable and successful bombs in the History of Freedom all over the world. Delhi has redeemed her ancient fame. She has spoken, and the world has heard and the tyrant has heard too! And we, the devoted soldiers of freedom in the country or abroad, have also heard the message....

And why do we rejoice with a great joy over the broken *howdah* and prostrate form of the tyrant on this memorable day? Why do our eyes fill with tears of gladness and our hearts feel the stirrings of a mighty purpose? What lesson should our young men and women learn from this thunder-peal of Freedom?

Yugantar Circular.

The Delhi Bomb.

This is the name that we propose to give to this epoch-making, thought-provoking, far-resounding bomb of December 23, 1912. One may say that it is one of the sweetest and loveliest bombs that have exploded in India since the great day on which Khudi Ram Bose first ushered a new era in the history of India, more than four years ago. Indeed this bomb is one of the most serviceable and succesful bombs in the History of Freedom all over the world. Delhi has redeemed her ancient fame. She has spoken, and the world has heard and the tyrant has heard too! And, we the devoted soldiers of freedom in the country or abroad, have also heard the message.

Hail! All hail! Bomb of December 23, 1912! Harbinger of hope and courage, dear re-awakener of slumbering souls, thou hast come just in time: not a moment too soon. Thou wast indeed overdue.

And why do we rejoice with a great joy over the broken *howdah* and prostrate form of the tyrant on this memorable day? Why do our eyes fill with tears of gladness and our hearts feel the stirrings of a mighty purpose? What lesson should our young men and women learn from this thunder-peal of Freedom?

This bomb marks the definite revival of the Revolutionary movement after the short interval of inactivity that has been recently noticeable. The repressive measures that have been taken by the government during four years have deprived us of some of our best comrades, but left their indomitable spirit and unbounded faith with us. The government in a panic did its work: our journals and newspapers were suppressed: our brave men were imprisoned and condemned to a living grave; our faithful fighters for the cause were exiled and persecuted. All India was hushed into silence. The Revolutionary spirit seemed crushed. The tyrants were happy: the hirelings in Calcutta felt safe in their seats.

Then the tyrants looked ahead. They saw that a new era had begun. They decided to conciliate the people by offering " reforms " and " concessions ". Jobs were created for " educated parasites "; councils were enlarged and expanded for the benefit of ambitious politicians and lawyers. These futile and deceptive measures served to rally the " moderates " to the side of the government, as dogs are silenced with a bone thrown among them.

And, to crown all, the tyrants wished to assert their prestige and power by imitating the old Oriental rulers of the country. The British must step into the shoes of the Grand Mogul. They must build fine palaces for themselves and surround themselves with pageants and courts in order to impress the " imagination " of the people. That is the great thing if you want to rule India — the " imagination " of the people must be touched. That was what Lord Curzon was after.

Yugantar *Circular.*

This bomb marks the definite revival of the Revolutionary movement after the short interval of inactivity that has been recently noticeable. The repressive measures that have been taken by the Government during four years have deprived us of some of our best comrades, but left their indomitable spirit and unbounded faith with us. The government in a panic did its work: our journals and newspapers were suppressed; our brave men were imprisoned and condemned to a living grave; our faithful fighters for the cause were exiled and persecuted. All India was hushed into silence. The Revolutionary spirit seemed crushed. The tyrants were happy; the hirelings in Calcutta felt safe in their seats.

Then the tyrants looked ahead. They saw that a new era had begun. They decided to conciliate the people by offering "reforms" and "concessions". Jobs were created for "educated parasites"; councils were enlarged and expanded for the benefit of ambitious politicians and lawyers. These futile and deceptive measures served to rally the "moderates" to the side of the government, as dogs are silenced with a bone thrown among them....

Finally, the jaded King of England was trotted out to Delhi in the winter of 1911 to impress the grandeur of the "Empire" on the minds of the assembled hosts of Hindusthan. The great "Durbar" in which the money of the people was squandered on debauched kings and queens and princes and princesses, was intended to mark the final culmination of the empire-building process in India. It was also meant to proclaim to the whole world that the Revolutionary spirit was conquered and tamed. The decrepit King George cried from the balcony of the Delhi palace "Lo! the work of Khudi Ram Bose is now undone." But the spirit of Revolution willed otherwise.

Many were the wishes and prayers that surged in the hearts of all lovers of Freedom in those dark days of shame. How we yearned for the news of the assassination of the blessed "Emperor" from day to day! The entire thought-power of all the good men and women of India was then concentrated on this one idea. As the "Durbar" ended without the desired consummation, we were sad and gloomy. Our Durbar had not been celebrated. The bomb was not there and no "Imperial Durbar" can be complete without the bomb. How loyal we seem to be—we the Revolutionists cannot be absent from a Durbar! Strange, is it not?

A year passed. The pride of the tyrants was not gratified. They must imitate the Moghuls in all respects. It was unworthy of an august person like the Viceroy of India to enter Delhi without pomp and ceremony! He must celebrate the event with becoming splendour. And then why should he be left behind Curzon of Kedleston? Curzon had ridden an elephant; why not

Hardinge? And how can the Empire be consolidated and defended without the elephant? So the Viceroy must make an "Imperial" entry into Delhi!....

Who can describe the moral power of the bomb? It is concentrated moral dynamite. When the strong and the cunning in the pride of their power parade their glory before their helpless victims, when the rich and the haughty set themselves on a pedestal and ask their slaves to fall down before them and worship them, when the wicked ones of the earth seem exalted to the sky and nothing appears to withstand their might, then, in that dark hour, for the glory of humanity, comes the bomb, which lays the tyrant in the dust. It tells all the cowering slaves that he who sits enthroned as a god is a mere man like them. Then, in that hour of shame, the bomb preaches, the eternal truth of human equality and sends proud Emperors and Viceroys from the palace and the *howdah* to the grave and the hospital. Then, in that tense moment when human nature is ashamed of itself, the bomb declares the vanity of power and pomp, and redeems us from our own baseness. How great we all feel when someone does a heroic deed! We share in his moral power; we rejoice in his assertion of human equality and dignity.

Deep down in the human heart, like a diamond in a mine, lies hidden the yearning for justice, equality and brotherhood. We do not even know it ourselves, but it is there all the same. And that is why we instinctively honour those who make war on inequality and injustice by any means in their power—the pen, the tongue, the sword, the gun, the strike, and last but not the least, the Bomb....

Comrades of the Revolution in India, be up and doing. Organize your propaganda anew at home and abroad. Take new vows of service and sacrifice. Lo! The bomb has spoken. Let the young men and women of Hindusthan answer.

BANDE MATARAM

* * *

25

1914 ›› GHADR DI GOONJ [THE ECHO OF MUTINY]

Original: Punjabi (Gurmukhi)
25.1: Poem: No. 4
25.2: Poem: No. 18 – 'The Oath of a Sepoy'

PUBLISHED BY THE YUGANTAR ASHRAM IN SAN FRANCISCO, THIS pamphlet was advertised in the newspaper *Ghadr*, and a copy was sent to Indian authorities by the superintendent of police at Shanghai. It had a collection of twenty-five poems, and 10,000 copies had been printed. The poems had also appeared in the *Ghadr* periodical. Described by the director of Criminal Intelligence, C.R. Cleveland, as 'highly seditious', it was prohibited under the Sea Customs Act as well as proscribed under the Indian Press Act of 1910.

* * *

25.1

POEM NO. 4

Young and old, awake from your foolish sleep! You have slept for ages, turn over, Brothers, and be on your guard.
Open your eyes, the flies are swarming over your face.
Seize a fan, Brothers, and take strength to use it.
The plank on which you are standing is about to fall.
Give up looking for support, and stand on your own feet....

Look to every side, Beloved, and be upon your guard against the fire of tyranny, which is burning rapidly and is approaching you.
Arise quickly lest you die, otherwise you will perish and cause others to die.
Cease your cowardice, and become men and heroes.
Establish secret Societies, to obtain your own Government.
Become the friends of (ie, unite with or follow the example of) the Marhattas, and Bengalis.
First deal with the traitors of your country, and then bestride the bodies of your enemies....

Bind the symbol of Martyrdom on your wrists.
Be brave and kill, or die yourselves in the fight.
Hindus, Sikhs, Mussalmans, act quick and each assist the other.
Drink the blood of the Christian Kafirs; when you have had your all you will find relief.
Drive out the faithless Feringhis, and rule Hindusthan yourselves.

* * *

25.2

POEM NO. 18 - 'THE OATH OF A SEPOY'

The hour has come, why do you not awake, oh Hindu and Mussalman brothers, from your sound sleep?
The wickedness of the oppressive English race is very great. They are robbing India,
Brothers.
They are a greedy and illigitimate [sic] spawn. They never cease from their treachery,
Brothers.
Taxes are levied on hand-mills and looms, and still you continue to hold your tongues,
Brothers.
You spend your strength in quarrels over religion, and you pay no attention to the state of your country,
Brothers.
Oh, Foolish ones, have you noticed nothing at all? You are quarrelling, over the Vedas and Koran,
Brothers.
Your quarrels are the ruin of your country. You understand nothing in your ignorance,
Brothers.
Your temples and mosques are being demolished, what has become of your religion and faith,
Brothers.
You are prohibited from touching the flesh of cow and pig but the white men eat them daily,
Brothers....
Hasten and prepare for mutiny. The precious time is passing quickly,
Brothers.
Fight for the sake of your country, do not fear at all,
It is a glorious thing to die fighting,
Brothers.
Hindus are bound by oath on the Vedas and Granth, and Mussalmans by oath on the Koran to fight against the Feringhis, Whoever fails is a shameless son of the Devil, Brothers.

26

1914 ›› SHABASH [KUDOS]

Original: Urdu | Leaflet

A BOX CONTAINING COPIES OF THIS LEAFLET IN ENVELOPES WAS sent by the Yugantar Ashram in San Francisco to Madame Cama in Paris. The envelopes already bore addresses of recipients in India, and Madame Cama was supposed to send them to England to be stamped and then dispatched from there to India. After the box was confiscated by French Customs authorities, the CID carried out an experiment to test the efficacy of the confiscation mechanism in India. They posted five copies to India to addresses on the envelopes. C.R. Cleveland, the director of Criminal Intelligence, reported with some pride that all five were intercepted by local authorities, leading the Punjab government to ban the pamphlet under the Indian Press Act of 1910. Cleveland deemed the pamphlet to be 'frankly anarchical as well as revolutionary'. He referred to its frontispiece (a picture of the Tree of Liberty) and to the caption below it, which stated, 'Price per copy…An Englishman's Head'.

The pamphlet was also proscribed under the Sea Customs Act as it was feared that once the Yugantar Ashram realized what happened to the Paris consignment, they might have sent copies directly to India, as they did with issues of the *Ghadr*. The latter was posted by Indians residing in USA, Canada, China and elsewhere, directly to their contacts in India so as to avoid detection.

Excerpts from the pamphlet are reprinted on the following pages. The pamphlet contained a striking and undisguised indictment of the methods of moderate politicians, and assessed the 'method of the bomb and the pistol' to be the only efficacious one.

* * *

…. How should we put life into a dead nation? How should we wake up a nation that is asleep? How is the fear of the overawed to be removed? How are slaves to become free? We reply, "By means of the bomb". We shall prove that the bold man, who converted the ceremonial procession of the Viceroy into a funeral on that day of last year, was not only the lion of the lions and the brave of the brave, but a sage and a deep philosopher....

Men of the Congress party, such as Gokhale, Lajpatrai and others, are undignified cowards and are misleading the nation, because they entertain the absurd notion that the English Government will become alarmed at mere talk or will be cajoled by flattery, humility and praise into granting us freedom, and abating their tyranny. The whole history of the world, however, gives evidence that no oppressive Government has ever been induced by mere flattery to grant justice and freedom to its subjects. In countries possessing a democratic Government the laws can no doubt be amended by the unanimous opinion of the people; but where the rule is in the hands of a few scoundrels, as is in India and Russia, the tyrannical rulers introduce no useful reforms without being forced. In India during the last thirty years the leaders of the Congress have been flattering and begging the Government to repeal the various oppressive and unjust laws. But what has been the result? Nothing.

In the year 1907 the Indians adopted the policy of chastising Government officers personally. The firing of a few pistols and the throwing of a few bombs have created consternation in the Government camp. Every one from the Governor General down to the humblest European soldier is in mortal terror of a bomb being thrown or a shot being fired from the corner of a gate or a wall, in a railway carriage or from behind a bush. Whenever the Viceroy now goes on tour to a Native State, the branches of all the trees on the roads are lopped off for fear lest the message of death may suddenly be delivered and end the existence of His Excellency....

The best reason for the pursuance of the bomb and pistol policy is that there is no more efficacious way of dealing with the situation. There is no better instrument than the bomb. The roar of the bomb represents the voice of the united-nations. Who does not understand this? The Madrasi and the Bengali, the Punjabi and the Pathan, the educated and the uneducated—all understand the meaning of the bomb. How are we to convey the message of freedom to the Sikhs, the Gurkhas, and the Pathans in the Indian Army? These people are, in the first place, uneducated, and, secondly, they are confined in cantonments where it is difficult to approach them. But the tyrant himself gave us the opportunity. On the 28th December, 1912, the Alibaba of the English thieves, the Viceroy of India, mounted an elephant and started in a procession through the 8 streets of Delhi. Both sides of the road were lined with thousands of Indian soldiers. Rajas, Maharajas and hundreds of thousands of men, women and children were assembled to testify to the

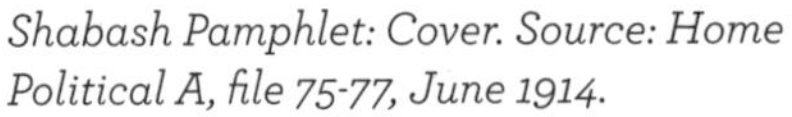

Shabash Pamphlet: Cover. Source: Home Political A, file 75-77, June 1914.

Shabash Pamphlet: Tree of Liberty. Source: Home Political A, file 75-77, June 1914.

grandeur of the Government on every side. But the hidden lightning of revolution was also present, ready to demolish the seven-storied tower of the pride of the mischievous. The bomb demonstrated to the Sikhs, Pathans, Gurkhas, Rajas and Maharajas in three seconds that the British kingdom in India was about to come to an end. The bomb in question was a national warning, by beat of drum, to the brave men of India to gird up their loins and come out into the field of battle. It was the voice of the goddess of liberty crying, "You that are prepared to sacrifice your lives, be up and doing." Who did not hear that cry? The existence of the bomb proves that oppression prevails in the country. In short, the use of the bomb and the pistol is the most effective weapon of the political sermon....

In Asiatic countries the appearance of the bomb is the advance guard of complete liberty. The reader will know that the first lesson of warfare that Doctor Sun Yat Sen learnt was the manufacture of the bomb. It is not twenty years since the said doctor introduced the bomb into China, in consequence of which a republican Government was established in China long ago. In India the great warrior Hem Chandra Das established the first college of bomb literature in Bengal in 1907. He, as it were, planted the flag-staff of liberty in the country on that day. Since then the national warlike party has won many battles. Last year at Delhi the battle of Plassey was revenged and the slightest doubt that was left about the brave people of Northern India taking their proper share in the battle for freedom was totally removed. Delhi has been the battlefield of many a kingdom and the warrior that was defeated there was ruined. The English have lost the first trick and suffered defeat at the outset.

All these are signs of our liberty. Germany and other European nations are determined to break the British Empire into pieces and will not rest till they have accomplished their object. We shall not be surprised if a telegram is suddenly received one day that ruinous war has broken out between Germany and England. Shall we let that opportunity slip out of our hands? No, never. Germany itself is anxiously waiting for an opportunity to begin war with the English in India and to crush them in Europe.

We present this gift to-day on the anniversary of the bomb to all Indians with the prayer that they may spill their own blood or that of the Europeans in India, even as our pen has spilt ink on the paper. You should either die or be put to death after killing. Do not sit idle in your homes. The bread of servitude is bitter. Death is a thousand times better than a life of servitude. Then, O young men and women I do not remain hidden in your holes like so many worms, but come out and kill the Englishmen and their servants and supporters who are scoundrels. Life is short and death is hanging over your heads. Opportunities will not occur over and over again. Seek to perform some great deed before you pass away. Crores of persons are born and die daily, but blessed is the birth of the man who punishes an oppressor. Blessed is the death of the man who suffers martyrdom for the sake of freedom. Remember the Persian saying, "Birth for martyrdom." Make up your mind that you will not die of disease, or accident or old age, like ordinary men, but will die after killing an oppressor. Sooner or later you must die. Then why should you not do some good before dying?

During this period of calamity, there is nothing more useful for India than the bomb. It is the bomb that frightens the Government into conceding rights to the people. The chief thing is to frighten the Government. Under the whip of fright the Government will reduce the taxes, will spend more money on the protection of health, and will abstain from interference with reforms in Native States. Whatever freedom is left in the Native States will be maintained by virtue of the bomb, for then the Government will not interfere much in the internal affairs of the Native States. The fear of the bomb will induce lazy and intemperate Rajas to discharge their duties properly. The bomb is the messenger of mutiny, and the fear of mutiny is the weapon for correcting the Government, while a general mutiny will be the means of its total annihilation. Without the bomb, slavery and poverty would have gone on increasing in India in the twentieth century, and there would have been no limit to oppression. But a voice proclaims from Paris now that the oppression is about to come to an end, for the bomb, the benefactor and protector of the poor, has been brought across the seas; bow down to it in worship and sing its praise.

* * *

27
1915 ›› A FEW FACTS ABOUT BRITISH RULE IN INDIA

Original: English | Pamphlet

THIS PAMPHLET WAS ISSUED BY THE HINDUSTAN GHADR OFFICE in San Francisco. Excerpts are reprinted below and on the following pages. Issued in the middle of a World War in which over a million Indians were to fight on behalf of Britain, for British ends, this pamphlet derived its power from the nationality of the authorities it cited: all British.

* * *

There is no truth in the assertion made by British newspapers that India is loyal to the British or sympathizes with their cause. India is from one end to another Dis-Affected. The country is seething with anti-British revolutionary ferment.

Why does India hate the British?

The answer follows.

Editor HINDUSTAN GADAR.

JUNE, 1915.

MR. ALFRED WEBB (late M. P.), who has studied the subject with care, says: "In charges for the India office (in London); for recruiting (in Great Britain, for soldiers to serve in India); for civil and military pensions (to men now living in England, who were formerly in the Indian service); for pay and allowances on furloughs (to men on visits to England); for private remittances and consignments (from India to England); from interest on Indian debt (paid to parties in England): and for interest on railways and other works (paid to shareholders in England), there is annually drawn from India, and spent in the United Kingdom, a sum calculated at from £25,000,000 to £30,000,000. (Between $125,000,000 and $150,000, 000.)"

Taxation in British India, as observed by impartial British writers: "The present condition of affairs undoubtedly renders the struggle for existence a hard one, as may be realized when it is considered that a

Bulletin No. 1

201

A Few Facts
About British Rule
in India

Published from
THE HINDUSTAN GADAR OFFICE
1324 Valencia Street
San Francisco
U. S. A.

Cover, A Few Facts About British Rule in India, *Hindustan Ghadr Office.*

vast population of India not only from the inevitable droughts which so frequently occur, BUT ALSO FROM A NARROW AND SHORTSIGHTED IMPERIAL POLICY WHICH PLACES EVERY OBSTACLE IN THE WAY OF INDUSTRIAL DEVELOPMENT AND IMPOSES HEAVY TANES ON THE STRUGGLING PEOPLE. According to various authorities Russia's demand upon land owners in her Central Asia possessions are not so exacting as ours in India. FOR THE BRITISH GOVERNMENT INSISTS ON A FIFTH OF THE PRODUCE, MAKING NO ALLOWANCE FOR GOOD OR BAD YEARS, WHILE RUSSIA IS SAID TO ASK ONLY A TENTH AND ALLOW FOR VARLATION OF PRODUCTION." (Pages 135-36, Russia Against India," by Sin ARCHIBALD R. COLQUHOUN, Gold Medalist Royal Geographical Society.)

TAXATION

The British policy of bleeding Indian people: "The injury is exaggerated in the case of India where so much of the revenue is exported without a direct equivalent. As India must be bled, the lancet should be directed to the parts where the blood is congested, or, at least, sufficient, not to those already feeble for the want of it." (LORD SALISBURY.).

INDIAN FINANCE

"In replying to a question of mine in April last (1907) Mr. Morley (now Lord) stated that 50 per cent of the net assets is the ordinary standard of assessment of land revenue alone throughout India. Net assets mean the annual profit after paying the cost of cultivation, the income, in fact, of the farmer. So we have it admitted that the normal land tax is 10 shillings in the pound. The word "alone" needs explanation. It means that the farmer has besides his land tax many other rates and taxes to pay for roads, police. irrigation, public works, etc. Mr. Morley's answer suggested that 50 per cent is the higher limit of land tax throughout India; so a few days later I questioned him definitely in regard to the Central Provinces, giving date and number of the government of India's order. The reply I received runs thus: 'The rule at present in force in the Central Provinces is that the assessment should not be less than 50 per cent and should not exceed 60 per cent, but in exceptional cases, if the existing assessment has hitherto exceeded 65 per cent and been paid without difficulty, it is provided that the assessment shall be fixed at 65 per cent.' It, therefore, appears that 50 per cent is the lower limit and it may be 65 per cent if it can be paid without difficulty. We are always assured that the land tax is light and paid without difficulty, which, perhaps, explains the fact that in the Central Provinces over a million people disappeared or died of starvation between 1894-1901, as admitted in the census report of the late years." ("The Causes of the Present Discontent in India" by C. J. O'DONNELL, M. P.)

IRRIGATION TAX.

We beg to quote a few lines to prove the real motive of the British Government about the so-called benevolent irrigation work in India:

"The capital of $35,000,000 invested in the Punjab canals yielded in 1905-07 the large net profit of 10% per cent, whilst in the case of the Chenab canal it rose to the extraordinary and unhealthy figure of nearly 22 per cent."

* * *

28

1915 ›› BRITISH RULE IN INDIA, CONDEMNED BY THE BRITISH THEMSELVES

Original: English | Pamphlet

THIS WAS PUBLISHED BY THE INDIAN NATIONAL PARTY IN LONDON in 1915. The pamphlet began by summarizing the history of the British connection with India and ended with an unfavourable comparison of the British empire in India with Russian despotism.

* * *

India is ruled for the benefit of Great Britain and the former country is aptly called the "milch-cow" of England. Those who are acquainted with the history of the British occupation of India, know it well that England's chief motive in going to India was plunder and she has never lost sight of it. England's unbounden [sic] prosperity owes its origin to her connection with India, and it has largely been maintained—disguisedly—from the same source, from the middle of the eighteenth century up to the present time. "Possibly since the world began, no investment has ever yielded the profit reaped from the Indian plunder." And this plunder made the English industrial supremacy possible.

But what has been the result of this alien occupation of India? The world does not know much about it and the British prevent the facts being known, while they eulogise their own rule that it is

"All for love and nothing for reward."

The apologists of the British rule spare no pains in portraying the former Native rule in the blackest characters while they are in ecstacies [sic] over their own. But in discerning the true state of affairs, those who have no prejudice to warp their judgment, will come to a different conclusion. It will be evident to them that India is ruled for the benefit of the British, and the British alone. No extenuating efforts can disprove the fact that England suppresses all attempts of the Indian people to progress, no partisan spirit can deny the fact that the sources of India's fabulous "wealth" have dried up and the country is racked with perennial famines, no naked eyes can be blind to the fact that India is the most poverty-stricken country in the world. In spite of the vauntings of the British that their rule is providential and a blessing to India they stand self-condemned. Some of their politicians have made no secret of their policies in India. Thus a British-Indian statesman, Mr. William Thackeray, said: "But in India, that haughty spirit, independence, and deep thought, which the possession of great wealth sometimes gives, ought to be suppressed. They are directly adverse to our power and interest. We do not want generals, statesmen and legislators; we want industrious husbandmen." Another British statesman of greater fame, the Marquis of Salisbury, while Secretary of State for India, uttered: "As India must be bled, the lancet should be directed to the parts where the blood is congested, or at least sufficient, not to those which are already feeble for the want of it." Also another writer as early as 1792 has said: "The primary object of Great Britain, let it be acknowledged, was rather to discover what could be obtained from her Asiatic subjects, than how they could be benefited." These utterances are the true index of British policy and they clearly expose the fact that the British policy is to exploit and plunder India, which country is bleeding to death by this drainage of her wealth. The result of this drain is summed up by Mr. H. Hyndman in these pungent words: "India is becoming feebler and feebler. The very life-blood of the great multitude under our rule is slowly yet ever faster ebbing away."

To the casual visitor and the globetrotter and to those who are fed with the stories of British apologists, this part of Indian life is kept unknown, the misery and the sufferings of India are carefully hidden from their gaze and a screen is drawn between their eyes and Hindustan, which country is a "Terra incognita" to them. Because, as has been well observed by William Digby, there are two countries, situated in the land between the mountains which constitute the roof of the world and the eight degree north of the equator and bounded east and west by Chinese territory and the Afghan Kingdom. That land called India is divided into :- Anglosthan, the land specially ruled by the English, in which English investments have been made, and by which a fair show and reality of prosperity are ensured, Hindusthan, practically all India fifty miles from each side of the railway lines except the tea, coffee, indigo, and jute plantations and not including the Feudatory States. Anglosthan is the region to which the roseate statements in the viceregal and State Secretary's speeches refer. All that is eulogistic in Indian Welfare Blue Books apply only to Anglosthan, and this land is the theme of the praises of panegyrists of the

BRITISH RULE IN INDIA

CONDEMNED BY THE BRITISH THEMSELVES

LONDON 1915
PUBLISHED BY THE INDIAN NATIONAL PARTY

Cover, British Rule in India: Condemned by the British Themselves.

British rule in India. But behind the screen is Hindusthan, the land where over three hundred millions of people live, and what do we find there?

In that unfortunate land there is more preventable suffering, more hunger, more insufficiently clothed bodies, more stunted intellects, more wasted lives, more disappointed men. In that unhappy country, as the result of the British occupation, there is chronic famine the appalling list of which is quoted below from the various famine commissions in their respective reports.

FAMINES:

In the last thirty years of the eighteenth century, 1769-1800....4 cases.
In the first half of the nineteenth century, 1802-38....12 cases.
In the second half of the nineteenth century, 1854-1908.... 35 cases.

And death from famine only during the nineteenth century is over *thirty two millions*! Mr. William Digby in his "Prosperous British India" says that the loss of life by war in all world during 107 years (1793-1900) is five millions while the loss of life by famine in India during ten years (1891-1900) is nineteen millions! While according to the calculations of some British statisticians there are ninety millions of continually hungry people in British India at the beginning of the twentieth century! The truth of this appalling misrule and misery of the people is evident to every unbiassed person. It does not require a searching enquiry to find out, that India enchained by a people who crept in the land in the darkness of her nights, and whom her magnanimity had tolerated in the days of her power, is bereft of all mental and material advancement and is lying stagnant for over a century! To India is denied all the cheerfulness of life and all the hopes and ambitions that make life worth living. As a result of this slavery life in India has lost its interestingness; as if the Indian's destiny is to be born and rot on the Indian soil! Why? Because India has been converted into a great slave empire of Great Britain.....

Yes, India is an unfortunate country on account of its life-blood being sucked by the British vampires. The starving millions bound hand and foot are groaning under the tyrannical fetters. They ask the world to lift the veil thrown over Hindustan by hypocritical England and discover the real situation. They appeal to the conscience of the civilized world to hear their case, that British misrule has ruined India and that they want to make themselves free from the hated yoke. Their case is a just one and humanity will have to blush in shame if it does not lend its ears to the cries of three hundred millions of people. India stands at the bar of Humanity and pleads her case, she calls witnesses from the enemy's camp to substantiate her charges, for even in perfidious Albion there have been some men in every decade, though their numbers are very few, who have raised their voices in protest or confessed the truth otherwise. The damaging evidence of these men who have exposed the true nature of the British rule in India, and some of whom have dared to say that former Native rule was more conducive to the happiness of the people than British rule, is published here to prove that the British occupation of India has been a curse and Great Britain stands condemned by her own tribunal.

* * *

29
1916 ONWARDS ›› YOUNG INDIA

Original: English | Author: Lajpat Rai
29.1: Book Excerpt: Chapter VIII – The Future | 'An Interpretation and a History of the Nationalist Movement from Within, 1916'
29.2: Book Excerpt: 'An Open Letter to the Right Honourable David Lloyd George, Prime Minister of Great Britain, 1917'

IN ADDITION TO BEING A LEADING LAWYER OF PUNJAB PROVINCE, Lala Lajpat Rai (1865–1928) was also a philanthropist, engaged in journalism, and was active both in the Congress movement (serving as its president in 1920) as well as in the Arya Samaj (a conservative Hindu reform organisation), including in the latter's educational institutions. In 1907, he was deported to Burma as a 'state prisoner' for causing 'internal commotion'. Upon his release, he lived in and made several trips to Great Britain and the USA, conveying his views on India's future to audiences there. He founded the Indian Home Rule League of America in 1917. His death in November 1928 was attributed to a violent assault on him by a senior British police officer, James Scott, a fortnight prior, during the course of a political demonstration. As we shall see in subsequent chapters, the desire to avenge his death acted as catalyst for most significant revolutionary activities in the coming years. He is also mentioned in chapters 26, 52, 56 and 57 of this anthology; the reference in chapter 26 is far from positive.

* * *

29.1

YOUNG INDIA

YOUNG INDIA WAS PUBLISHED IN NEW YORK IN 1916 WITH A foreword by American missionary Jabez T. Sunderland (whose own book, titled *India in Bondage*, was to be banned in 1928. Its second edition the next year was published in London with a foreword by J.C. Wedgwood, a British Member of Parliament. This too was banned). The Government of India stated in the House of Commons that they believed the publication to have been financed by German agents in the United States; given that Germany was at war with Great Britain in these years, this was a rather serious allegation. These editions were proscribed using the Sea Customs Act (preventing import) and the Indian Press Act of 1910 (prohibiting republication of extracts in Indian publications). However, the Government of India conceded that since the book had been reviewed in the Indian press before the ban was imposed, it was likely that several copies had already been circulating in the country. In his review of this 250-page book in July 1917, the director of Criminal Intelligence termed it 'probably the most damning indictment of the loyalty of the Indian politician that has ever been written'. The first section of the book consisted of a summary of Indian history before the coming of the British, with an emphasis of traditions of self-governing. The book also described the various strands of nationalist activity current in India in the day, classifying nationalists into 'extremists', 'advocates of organized rebellion', 'terrorists', 'advocates of constructive nationalism' (within which he included himself and the Arya Samaj) and 'moderates'. Excerpts from one chapter are reprinted below.

* * *

CHAPTER VIII

'THE FUTURE'

...There is a great deal of exaggeration about the immobility of Indian people. There may be millions in India who are as unaffected by modern conditions of life and modern ideas as they were fifty years ago, but then there are millions who have consciously awakened. Their strength is not to be judged by the attendance at Congresses and conferences or other public meetings

DADABHAI NAOROJI

YOUNG INDIA

AN INTERPRETATION AND A HISTORY OF THE NATIONALIST MOVEMENT FROM WITHIN

LAJPAT RAI

FOREWORD BY J. T. SUNDERLAND

ILLUSTRATED

NEW YORK
B. W. HUEBSCH
1917

Young India. *Front cover, 1916*

or demonstrations, nor by the circulation of newspapers or books. Popular demonstrations organised in honour of popular leaders, and the increase in the circulation of newspapers give indications of a great change in Indian life, but the actual change is even much greater. Read the poetry of the country or its prose, read the rough versifyings of the half-educated or even uneducated men and women (including some who are even illiterate), listen to the talk in the village park or square or other meeting places, see the games which the children of rustics and the poorest classes play, attend to the patterings of children, examine the popular songs or the music that is now in demand, then you will see how deeply nationalism has pervaded Indian life and what a strong hold it has gained in the thoughts of the people. No foreigner can realise that; only an Indian can properly understand it. Examine the vernacular press — the most sober and the most loyal papers, and underlying the expressions of deepest loyalty, you would assuredly come across genuine tears of blood, shed for the misfortune of the country, its decline, its present wretched and miserable condition. From the Indian press we hear a never ceasing lamentation. Listen to the utterances of the most wanton chief, and the most callous millionaire, bring him out from his isolation or retirement, put him on the public platform, and you will notice a vein of nationalism in his thoughts and in his words. But if you can know what he talks in private to friends from whom he keeps no secrets, you will see and notice a great deal more. The writer has not so far met a single Indian of any class — he has met

Indians of all classes and of all shades of opinions, educated, uneducated, prince and peasant, moderate and extremist, loyalist and seditionist, — who was genuinely sorry at the outbreak of this war. A number of Indians are fighting at the front. They are sincerely loyal and true to their oath of allegiance. They would leave nothing undone to win, but in their heart of hearts lurks something which in moments of reflection or when they are off duty, reminds them of the wrongs which they and their countrymen are suffering at the hands of England. Nationalism is no longer confined to the classes. It promises to become a universal cult. It is permeating the masses. Only those Indians realise it who mix with the people and do not derive their knowledge from works written by Englishmen or by other arm-chair politicians. No foreigner, however kind and sympathetic, however great his knowledge of the language of the country, can ever realise it fully. Even the dancing girls are affected by it. They will sing political or national songs if you so wish. Even the wandering minstrel with his rude, one-stringed instrument, knows the song that is likely to bring him help.

Nationalism Fertilised by Blood of Martyrs

No amount of repression or espionage can stop it. No amount of official terrorism and no devices, invented or followed to inculcate loyalty, can stop or check the flow of the new feeling of patriotism and nationalism which is being constantly fed by the sentences of death and transportation that the British courts are passing on beardless youths. The Government can not help it. They must punish the offender and the criminal. They must hunt up the seditionist. They would not be a government if they would do otherwise, but India is now in that stage and Indian nationalism is in that condition when repression, death sentences, and imprisonments are more beneficial to it than otherwise. The more it is repressed and suppressed, the more this spirit grows and spreads. It is a seed that is richly fertilised by the blood of martyrs. The people do not argue, they do not reason, they do not analyse; they feel that good, well-connected, healthy, beautiful boys are dying in the country's cause and to get a redress of the country's wrongs. When a bomb is thrown, the people genuinely condemn the bomb thrower, are sincere in their detestation, but when he is hanged or transported, they are sorry for him. Their original abhorrence changes into sympathy and then into love. They are martyrs of the national cause. They may be misguided, even mad, but they are martyrs all the same. The moralist and the legalist and the loyalist and the constitutionalist, all condemn their deeds, but the doers themselves, they adore, and their names they enshrine in their hearts

Nationalism has come to Stay

...one thing seems to be assured and certain, that Indian nationalism can neither be killed nor suppressed by repression, nor by minor concessions. Nationalism has come to stay and will stay. What will be the upshot is only known to the Gods. England may win or lose in the great war in which she is engaged. Indian nationalism will gain in either case. We need not consider how India will fare if England loses. She may come under Mohammedan domination, or the Germans may take possession of her; the English would be gone and then India would enter upon a new life. India does not want it. She will resist it with all her strength. But if it comes she can't help it and Great Britain would be responsible for having brought it. In case, however, England wins, as she is likely to, the Indian nationalism will still gain. There will be a demand for political advance, for a change in the political status of the country and in its relations towards England and her colonies. From what we know of English temper, of English political machinery, of English political methods, of English ways and of English history, that demand is sure to be refused. Some minor, petty concessions may be made, but they would be disproportionate to the sacrifices of men and money that India is making in the war. They will not satisfy the country. Disaffection and discontent will grow and that is the kind of food on which nationalism thrives and prospers. So long as there are Curzons, Macdonnels, and Sydenhams in the English Parliament. Indian nationalism will not starve for want of congenial food. And we have no reason to think that these dignitaries of the British Government are likely to disappear.

Curzons, Macdonnels, Sydenhams, responsible for Bombs and Revolvers

These persons are directly responsible for the appearance of bombs and revolvers in Indian political life. The young men who use them are mere tools of circumstances. If any persons deserve to be hanged for the use of these destructive machines by Indian nationalists, it is they. It is a pity that while the latter are dying by tens on the scaffold, the former should be free to carry on their propaganda of racial discrimination, racial hatred, and social preferment. But the ways of Providence are inscrutable. It is perhaps some higher dispensation that is using these miserable Junkers for its own purposes. Indians have faith in Providence and they believe that what is happening is for the best. The Indians are a chivalrous people; they will not disturb England as long as she is engaged with Germany. The struggle after the war might, however, be even more bitter and more sustained.

* * *

29.2

BOOK EXCERPT

'AN OPEN LETTER TO THE RIGHT HONOURABLE DAVID LLOYD GEORGE, PRIME MINISTER OF GREAT BRITAIN, 1917'

THIS SIXTY-TWO-PAGE LETTER WAS PUBLISHED IN NEW YORK IN 1917. Rai was living in exile in the United States at the time. Rai first spoke of the tragic life of a political exile, forced to leave his homeland to speak the truth, since press and penal laws in India would not allow him to speak freely. He then criticized the raising of a war loan in India of $500,000,000 (then equivalent to Rs. 150 crores, or £100,000,000) and the increase of duty on cotton imports to facilitate the same. This loan was termed a 'free gift' of India to Great Britain. Rai peppered his letter with extracts from various British newspapers such as the *Manchester Guardian* which too had criticized this loan. Rai also reprinted various wages from the Government of India's own report of 1915 to show the pitiable condition of India's labourers. Rai also criticized the terms of the Indian Press Act of 1910. Excerpts are reprinted below and on the following pages.

* * *

...The Indians are very easily satisfied. They abhor bloodshed. They do not like revolution. They will gladly remain in the Empire, if permitted to do so on terms of self-respect and honor. Their needs are few. Their life is simple. They care more for spiritual values than for worldly goods. They envy nobody's property. They have no ambition to start on a career of exploitation. All they want is to be let to live and think as they will. At present they are let *to exist*, but not to live. More than 100 million are insufficiently fed. At least 60 millions do not get two meals a day. More than 80% of the boys receive no schooling, and more than 90% of the girls. They work and toil and sweat primarily in the interests of the British capitalist and secondarily in the interests of his Indian colleague. The latter only gets the leavings of the former. The ships, the railways, the leading banking houses, the big insurance offices, the tea plantations, one-half of the cotton mills, about all the woollen mills, most of the paper mills, all jute mills are owned by the former; a few by the latter. The profits of agriculture are divided between your Government and the big landlords. The pressure on land has reduced the size of the ryots' holdings, while the number of mouths requiring food and the number of bodies requiring clothing has increased....

Mr. Lloyd George, you and your colleagues in the Government of Great Britain, say that in fighting the Germans you are fighting the battle of Democracy, to make the world safe from autocracy and militarism, that you are fighting for rights of small nations, and for the domination of right over might. The United States has joined the war for the same reason. I have seen numerous recruiting posters exhibited in New York City exhorting young Americans to enlist in the army "to make the world safe" for Democracy. I have not the slightest doubt of the sincerity of the American professions because their international record is so far clean. Vide their record in Cuba and the Philippines. Can we say the same for Great Britain? I am afraid not, so long at least, as you continue to deny self-government to India, the second of the two biggest democracies of the world. Here is a nation of 315 million human beings (or say several nations, if you wish, as your publicists are so fond of repeating *ad nauseam* that India is not a nation) whom you are governing by the force of might, without their consent, and on absolutely despotic lines; whom you deny freedom of speech, freedom of association and freedom of education; whom you tax without their consent and then spend those taxes outside of their country, and in providing luxuries to your representatives in India or in bribing such Indians as uphold you in your possessions. I have no doubt that you are sincere in your denunciation of German militarism. For myself I have no use for Czars and Kaisers, Emperors and Sultans, and I dare say that you, too, have none. Thus I am in full sympathy with your efforts to exterminate the race of Kaisers. So far you are right. But an Indian cannot help smiling rather cynically when he hears you saying that you are waging the war to make the world safe for democracy. Your conduct in India and in Egypt, and in Persia belies your protestations....

Mr. David Lloyd George, I have addressed this letter to you, because at this moment you seem to be the only British statesman possessed of imagination. Exercise your imagination, sir, a little and save India for the Empire; win the gratitude and blessings of a fifth of the human race—of a people who were one of the first pioneers of civilization in the world, who laid the foundations of culture, which you profess to be so very anxious to save. Remember that the Indians were rich, prosperous, free, self-governing, civilized and great, both in peace and war, when not only Britain but even "Greece and Rome were nursing the tenants of the wilderness." The Indians have lost their freedom because they oppressed the people under them and as surely as night follows day, the British will lose all that makes them great to-day, if they continue to oppress and exploit the subject races within their Empire. The world cannot be safe for democracy unless India is self-governed. Nor can there be any lasting peace in the world, so long as India and China are not strong enough to protect themselves.

* * *

PART III: 1921-1930

CONTEXT NOTE

GANDHI'S RETURN TO INDIA IN 1915 RESULTED IN NEW KIND OF politics: radical in its ability to draw Indian masses – men and women, urban and rural, privileged and under-privileged – from all parts of the country towards public demonstrations and expressions of discontent with colonial rule. The Non-Cooperation campaign (1920–1922) was explained to rural peasants both by elite nationalists (for example by Motilal Nehru) as well as by anonymous authors using dramatic metaphors and easily intelligible references and themes. Many of the chapters in this section pertain to such campaigns for boycott: of tax payments, and of courts and other colonial institutions.

In August 1925, four armed revolutionaries – Ashfaqullah Khan (1900–1927), Roshan Singh (1892 1927), Rajendra Lahiri (1901–1927) and Ram Prasad Bismil (1897–1927) – robbed a train near Lucknow; the case came to be known as the Kakori conspiracy case, and they were executed at its culmination. Bismil popularized a poem written a few years earlier by a poet who shared his nom de plume – Bismil Azimabadi. This poem, reprinted in chapter 43 in this section, has inspired generations, become embedded in Indian popular culture, and its first couplet is instantly recognizable to many even today.

Ideas, ideals and ideologies are translated to local conditions even as they are transmitted from the metropolis to the colony, or from the world to the homeland. Communist literature has begun circulating in India at the end of the First World War and after the Bolsehvik Revolution of 1917; the Communist Party of India was founded in 1925. Indian Communists in Moscow and Berlin played an important role in the dissemination of such literature and their counterparts in India amplified its appeal, often by indigenizing or 'vernacularizing' them in terms that their audience could understand. This section contains examples of the rendering of Communist ideals and aims in local and very vivid idioms. The 1920s was a decade of well-publicized prosecutions of Indian as well as non-Indian Communists in three trials: the Peshawar conspiracy case (1922), the Kanpur conspiracy case (1924) and the Meerut conspiracy case (1929). In 1932, a General Communist Notification was issued by the Government of

India banning all literature issued by the Comintern (Communist International) automatically (that is, without any need for separate notifications for each item).

By the end of the 1920s, two streams of nationalist activity were the most prominent – the Congress movement, with emphasis on non-violence under Gandhi's leadership, and the revolutionary movement, best exemplified by the heroic activities of members of the Hindustan Socialist Republican Association (HSRA). Recent scholarship by Kama Maclean, Christopher Moffat and Neeti Nair has effectively shown the linkages between these two streams, despite differences of opinion regarding methods, and public disagreements expressed on the podium and in print. Several key events form the framework of reference for banned publications from this period. the assassination of Assistant Superintendent of Police John Saunders by Bhagat Singh (1907–1931) and Shivaram Rajguru (1908–1931) on 17 **December 1927** in order to avenge the death of Lajpat Rai; the lobbing of two bombs inside the Central Legislative Assembly in Delhi (8 April 1929) by Bhagat Singh and Batukeshwar Dutt (1910–1965); the Lahore session of the Congress where the Purna Swaraj (Complete Independence) resolution was passed (December 1929); and the attempt by HSRA members to assassinate no less than Viceroy Irwin himself by bombing his train (on 23 December 1929).

The next two years were also eventful, and these sensational events inspired publicists (and activated censors) enormously for years to come. Gandhi launched the Civil Disobedience movement on 12 March 1930, and in less than a year, on 5 March 1931 brought the viceroy to the negotiating table and signed a pact (known as the Gandhi-Irwin pact) with him. (The movement continued till 1934.) A few days prior to the pact, Chandrashekhar Azad (1906–1931), member of the HSRA, who was wanted by the police for his role in the Kakori train robbery as well as for the killing of a police official, was surrounded by the police in a public park in Allahabad on 27 February 1931, where he died. On 23 March 1931, Bhagat Singh, Shivaram Rajguru and Sukhdev Thapar (1907–1931) were hanged for the killing of J.P. Saunders. The deaths of these young revolutionaries electrified the country and volumes can be filled with the texts (as well as the banned literature) composed and circulated for years afterward, in all parts of India, about their life, work, and manner of death. Included in this section are excerpts from two biographies of Azad and Bhagat Singh, respectively, as well as poems and writings that remembered these revolutionaries in the genre of 'martyrology'.

30
1921 ›› ASAHYOG [NON-COOPERATION]

Original: Hindi | Leaflet

THIS HINDI LEAFLET WAS AUTHORED BY 'KRISHNA' (DESCRIBED as a 'non-cooperator'), and printed at the Chandra Prabha Press in Benaras [Varanasi]. It – as well as its translations – were declared forfeit by the Government of UP in May 1921 under the terms of the Indian Press Act of 1910. The excerpt reprinted on the following page refers to a variety of themes that were to be repeated in other banned texts: reminders of landmark events (of oppression, or resistance), a call for communal amity and a reminder of the power of the many over the few.

* * *

No. 951/VIII—252.
NOTIFICATION.
POLICE DEPARTMENT.
Dated Naini Tal, the 11th May, 1921.
MISCELLANEOUS.

In exercise of the powers conferred by sub-section (1) of section 12 of the Indian Press Act, 1910 (I of 1910), the Governor in Council hereby declares to be forfeited to His Majesty all copies, wherever found, of the leaflet in Hindi, or of its translation, entitled "*Asahyog*" (Non-co-operation), written by one Krishna, a non-co-operator, and printed at the Chandra Prabha Press, Benares, in-as-much as the said leaflet contains matter of the nature described in clause *(c)* of sub-section (1) of section 4 of the said Act.

By order of the Governor in Council,
G. B. LAMBERT,
Chief Secy. to Govt., United Provinces.

Notification banning Asahyog.

If people do not non-co-operate the Government will not change its policy. If the Government is not driven out every city will have a Jallianwala Bagh of its own. We shall subdue the enemy with the weapons of non-co-operation. It matters little if we have no sword and gun. These jails will be broken and others shall have to be constructed. They cannot accommodate the whole nation. The prison walls will be enamoured of those patriotic Indians who are confined in jail. We are mad, let us be put into our chains; there would be no such rattle in the gold ornaments. Our native land cannot be fruitful till it is watered with our blood. The Hindus and Muhammadans are so much united that there will be no mere distinction between the Brahmanical thread (*zunar*) and the rosary (*tasbih*). We shall destroy this Government which does not sympathise with us in our afflictions.

* * *

31

1921 ›› BANDE MATARAM SUCHANA [PATRIOTIC NOTICE]

Original: Hindi | Leaflet

THIS LEAFLET IN HINDI WAS FORFEITED BY THE GOVERNMENT OF UP under the provisions of the Indian Press Act of 1910. As per the information with the government, it was written by a 'Hanuman' and published in Benaras [Varanasi]. An excerpt is reprinted on the following page. The reference to 'unmanly' conduct or conduct similar to eunuchs is an all too common motif in such texts, employed to motivate men to join the anti-colonial movement,

No. 935/VIII—253.

NOTIFICATION.

POLICE DEPARTMENT.

Dated Naini Tal, the 11th May, 1921.

MISCELLANEOUS.

In exercise of the powers conferred by sub-section (1) of section 12 of the Indian Press Act, 1910 (I of 1910), the Governor in Council hereby declares to be forfeited to His Majesty all copies, wherever found, of the leaflet in Hindi, or of its translation, entitled "*Bande Matram-Suchana*" (Reminder), written by one Hanuman and printed at the Art Press, Kundigar Tola, Benares, in-as-much as the said leaflet contains matter of the nature described in clause *(c)* of sub-section (1) of section 4 of the said Act.

By order of the Governor in Council,

G. B. LAMBERT,

Chief Secy. to Govt., United Provinces.

Notification banning Bande Mataram Suchana.

but also revealing the writers' understanding of gender norms a hundred years ago. References to the Ramayana, a living text and tradition known even to the unlettered, are used to great effect. After all, everyone knows that the Ramayana ends with the victory of Ram.

* * *

Brethren it is easy to get *swaraj*; but the condition is that the Hindus and Muslims should unite.

Oh the inhabitants of Ghazipur why you have been keeping silence like slices of dead bodies, the neighbouring districts are advancing and are firm in their rights and are seeing you with hatred; you are it is sure to die one day, then why you are dying like eunuchs (*hijra*) on a *charpai* (bed). Why don't you enlist yourself in the peaceful righteous battle and die like brave heroes for your country and nation, after a few days you will see that the garland of victory will be in your neck. Remember it is sure that Janki [Sita] will be carried back from Lanka (Ceylon) and Ravan [references to the antagonist in the Ramayana] will surely be defeated, and it is certain Ram Raj [righteous rule, as in the reign of King Ram] would prevail. How will you show your face if you do not come forward at such a moment, keep the prestige of Ghazipur; be firm so that the world may not get opportunity of saying that the inhabitants of Ghazipur want that their mothers, sisters, wives and daughters should be insulted, made naked, spitted in their mouths and the men may be flogged on the buttocks with canes and hunters by the English.

One cannot be free if he is not tortured and one who is tortured is sure to be free.

* * *

32

1921 ›› BHARTIYON KO CHITWANI [SIC] [WARNING TO INDIANS]

Original: Hindi | Leaflet
Poem: 32.1
Poem: 32.2

FORFEITED UNDER THE INDIAN PRESS ACT OF 1910, THIS LEAFLET in Hindi was written by a student from Benaras [Varanasi], Kanhaiya Lal, and published at the Bharat Press. Two of the offending poems were translated and included with the official notification by the Government of UP. The first one repeatedly used the term 'satyagraha'/soul force, indicating the percolation of Gandhian ideals among publicists of the period. The second poem recounted events at the Jallianwala Bagh in 1919 with great passion and pathos.

No. 1329/VIII—297.
NOTIFICATION.
POLICE DEPARTMENT.
Dated Naini Tal, the 15th June, 1921.
MISCELLANEOUS.

IN exercise of the powers conferred by sub-section (1) of section 12 of the Indian Press Act, 1910 (I of 1910), the Governor in Council hereby declares to be forfeited to His Majesty all copies, wherever found, of the leaflet in Hindi, or of its translation, entitled "*Bhartion ko chitwani*" (Warning to Indians), written by Kanhaiya Lal, a student of Benares, and printed at the Bharat Press, Chaitganj, Benares, inasmuch as the said leaflet contains matter of the nature described in clause *(c)* of sub-section (1) of section 4 of the said Act.

By order of the Governor in Council,
G. B. LAMBERT,
Chief Secy. to Govt., United Provinces.

Notification banning Bhartiyon ko Chitwani.

32.1

POEM

O Indians do now some work. Get rid of your lethargy and increase your ability.

Thieves entered in the night and created a great row.

Turn them out by your soul force [or Satyagraha, a term popularized by Gandhi].

This sacred land has become polluted. It is in bondage.

Set it free.

You are sons of lions. Do away with all doubts. I would die for *Bharat*, make this a firm determination (in your mind).

Destroy at once by your soul force the terrible repressive power above you.

Work at spinning wheel, establish panchayats and prove it that by doing this you will be independent.

* * *

32.2

POEM

(You) caused me to die of weeping.

Dyer! you killed the helpless by bullets. What wrong had they done to you that you worried the life out of them?

What for, O tyrant, did you send for these machine guns and why did you show us the days on which you opened fire on us?

I have no strength in my body to recount all the incidents.

You thought it just to spill our blood.

You made thousands of widows in the Punjab. There were already so many (perhaps because of war) and you made many more.

Widows are weeping and crying. O sinful Europeans why have you killed our husbands like rebels.

O oppressive Dyer mothers are crying 'Oh you made my child to lie on sand and killed him.'

Shame you called a six months old child a rebel. You did not take pity and killed him by a lance.

If that child was a rebel O Lord Krishna make all children rebels very moment of conception ...

* * *

33

1921 ›› FIRANGIYON [FOREIGNERS]

Original: Hindi | Pamphlet
Poem by Manoranjan Prasad

THE GOVERNMENT OF UP DECLARED THIS PAMPHLET AND ITS translations forfeit in June 1921. The editor, Ganga Mahesh Shukla, addressed his countrymen in the preface, and thanked the publisher for printing this poem initially published in the journal *Patliputra*, in the form of a pamphlet. Its printer and publisher (Babu Sri Prasad Maheshwari and Babu Sheo Charan Lal Gupta) were from the Chintamani Press in Farukkhabad. Such pamphlets therefore amplified the message published in more expensive and less accessible journals. The poem, rhythmic even in translation, simplified sophisticated economic theories and arguments of Drain of Wealth (from India to Britain) in language and metaphors that could be appreciated by all. Reference to heroes, both epic and historic, was intended to resonate with the audience of this poem.

* * *

The beautiful and charming land of the *Bharat* (India) has to-day been turned into a crematory, O *Firangi* (Englishman)!
The produce of the soil, wealth, population, strength and wisdom have all been ruined and no trace is left of any of them, O *Firangi!*
The country, which only a few days ago, produced lakhs of maunds of grain and paddy, there, to-day, O *Firangi*, sits the *kisan* weeping and wailing, his forehead resting on his hand.
O Lord! What sins did we commit that our condition has come to this?
Famine visits the land every moment and seven hundred lakhs of people eat but one meal a day.
The little that remained in the country, you carried away, O *Firangi*, across the seas.
At home, the people are dying of hunger: the wheat is taken away to foreign lands, such, O *Firangi*, are the dealings of the world!

Where the people ate to their satisfaction and possessed immense fortunes, there, O *Firangi,* we see poverty-stricken people, whithersoever we turn our eyes.
Trade and commerce have all been ruined, O *Firangi.*
Alas! we have to depend upon foreigners for every trifling thing:
We have to clothes ourselves with the cloth that is imported from foreign countries.
If to-day, we cease to get cloth from foreign countries, we will have to live naked.
O *Firangi,* you take (raw) cotton from us at a cheap rate, make it into cloth and sell it (dearly).
In this manner, O *Firangi,* you have robbed Bharat of her wealth and taken it away to foreign countries.
Forty crores of rupees of India pass annually to foreign hands.
If the present condition continues for sometime more, *Bharat* will be utterly ruined, O *Firangi!*
We have lost all sense of *izzat* and utter words to please the *Firangi.*
We flatter the *Sahib* night and day and lick the foot of the foreigner.
Where there were brave men like Rana Pratab [sic] Singh and Surtan [16th century Rajput rulers], who would rather lose their life than break their word or bow their head, the people of that very country have become so degraded, O *Firangi,* that they lick the feet of the foreigner!
They injure their own brethren to seek the pleasure of their officers. Bravery has gone and cowards inhabit the land which produced warriors like Arjun. Bhim, Dron, Bhisham and Karan [epic heroes from the Mahabharata].
For what sinful deeds has our condition come to this?
The country has lost all wealth, strength, wisdom and learning and has become quite destitute. In spite of its extreme poverty, you have enhanced the burden of taxes, O *Firangi*!
O *Firangi*! You have imposed taxes on everything. You levy (even) salt tax and coolie tax.
You have made such laws, O *Firangi,* that we do not possess even the nominal Independence.
You have closed our hands, gagged our mouths and slackened our business.
You have broken everything and made us sit (idle).
Alas! When we recall the events of the Punjab [1919], O *Firangi,* our hearts are rent asunder.
On the breasts of the *Bharat* flows the blood of her own sons, O *Firangi,*

Her cupid-like little sons have suffered torture and given up their lives.
All the old men have died; the young and the brave are also dead, O *Firangi*.
Those that were like the resting-stick to the aged mother have been snatched away from her.
The husband who was the soul of his beloved wife has been separated from her. You did not feel shame, O *Firangi*, in taking the honour of the ladies of the house.
You painted the body of the Sadhu [ascetic] with lime and made him stand nude before the prostitute. You treated us as if we were worse than brutes and you made us crawl on the belly, O *Firangi*.
Bharat (India) was in sore trouble, people came to such a pass and the country Cried 'alas Bisham' with pain. Even then, O *Firangi*, you did not award any punishment to your butcher officer [Col. Dyer]!
Brothers, beware! And guard yourselves from the Firangi. And leave the path of sin O *Firangi*! Give up evil methods and work on good ones and God will help you, O *Firangi*.
Cancel cruel laws, abolish taxes and give *swaraj* to *Bharat*. Else – I tell you the truth – your atrocities will prove ruinous, O *Firangi*!

MANORANJAN PRASAD

* * *

34

1921 ›› A MESSAGE TO KISANS [PEASANTS]

Original: Hindi | Pamphlet | Author: Motilal Nehru

FAMED LAWYER, AUTHOR OF THE NEHRU REPORT OF 1928 proposing a constitutional scheme for India's future, and father of India's first Prime Minister Jawaharlal Nehru, Motilal Nehru (1861–1931) issued this two-page pamphlet in his capacity as the president of the United Provinces' Kisan Sabha [Peasants' Association]. It was published by the Allahabad Law Printing Press. Nehru persuasively quoted Gandhi to suggest that Swaraj was only six months away, referred to jails as 'holy places' and gave peasants a simple list of dos and don'ts to follow. The appeal of this message is palpable and effective even a hundred years after it was made. The message is reprinted in full.

* * *

KISANS are in great trouble in these days. They are being tyrannized over in many ways. The servants and *karindas* [employees] of zamindars tyrannize over them. The police and Government officers are threatening them and giving them trouble. It was recently declared by the Government that it did not desire to prevent kisans from establishing *sabhas* [associations] for the purpose of securing their rights and removing their afflictions, but it would prevent the formation of *sabhas* for committing riots or other objectionable acts. It is well-known that no *Kisan Sabha* has till to-day been established for plundering people, committing riots and doing other illegal acts and wherever plundering and killing took place it was not the work of any *sabha*. Yet kisans are being freely prosecuted and punished. In all the four districts of Oudh (Partabgarh [Pratapgarh], Sultanpur, Rael Bareli and Fyzabad [Faizabad]) the Government has passed a law according to which all the *sabhas* have to be closed. Taking advantage of this legislation, the police have in many villages *chalaned* [fined] the *panches, sar panches* [village headmen], presidents and secretaries, and these respectable and patriotic kisans have been made to furnish securities and execute recognizances or

GOVERNMENT, UNITED PROVINCES.

MISCELLANEOUS.

POLICE DEPARTMENT.

The 6th May, 1921.

No. 899/VIII.—In exercise of the power conferred by sub-section (12) of the Indian Press Act, 1910 (I of 1910), the Governor in Council hereby declares to be forfeited to His Majesty all copies, wherever found, of the leaflet in Hindi or of its translation entitled *Kisanon ko sandesa* (message to the *Kisans*), written by Pandit Moti Lal Nehru, President of the United Provinces *Kisan Sabha*, inasmuch as the said leaflet contains matter of the nature described in clause (c) of sub-section (1) of section 4 of the said Act.

Notification banning A Message to Kisans

punished in some other way without any fault. All this is done to terrify the kisans and to break up their *sabhas*. What are the kisans to do under these circumstances. The remedy is known to the whole country. There can be no other remedy except getting self-government. It is now to be considered by what means it can be obtained. If people are terrified and dare not come out of their houses, they can not obtain swaraj. It is, therefore, necessary to leave off all fear and act according to the following instructions of Mr. Gandhi :-

(1) They should enlist in the Indian National Congress.

(2) Arrangements should be made for spinning yarn in every house.

(3) People should have their quarrels settled by *panchayats* [village assemblies] and should not go to English law courts.

(4) They should subscribe as much money as they can to the *Swaraj* Fund.

(5) Hindus, Muhammadans, Brahmans, Kshatriyas, Kurmis and Pasis [castes] should all have unity among them.

No meeting should be held in the four districts where a law has been passed prohibiting the holding of meetings. But the five instructions given above should be peacefully followed in every house in those districts. There ought to be no fear of any one in doing these things and if a man is prosecuted under a false charge and punished, he should cheerfully accept the punishment.

It is certain that the kisans have undertaken a huge task. They have started on a long and arduous journey and shall have to bear many hardships if they want to put an end to their sufferings. There can be no success without penance. They should bear whatever tyranny and hardships they are subjected to. This is the penance that will lead to *swaraj*. It is of the greatest importance that all kisans should remain in the path of righteousness, never telling a lie, or plundering, killing or abusing any one. They should not use force. Ours is a religious war. We should not do any unrighteous act and should always try to maintain peace. However much we may be tyrannized over by our enemy we should not commit any sin.

Kisans have up to now been working with great zeal. They have formed *sabhas* and have clearly shown how united they are and what strength they possess. The British Government knew that if the kisans were united and became fearless they would soon obtain *swaraj*. Owing to this fear it wanted to break up their *sabhas* and prosecuted them, but thanks to God the kisans have not been terrified by all this. On the other hand they have been doing their business with greater vigour. The Government devised various means to terrify them. Babu Ram Chandra [Fiji-returned Indian leader who organized peasants in UP] was prosecuted and punished. But the meetings continued to be held. Now the Government has passed a new law in the four districts of Oudh and has got all the *sabhas* closed. This is a defeat of the Government. The kisans should rejoice over it, and remaining firm on the path of righteousness, should serve their community and the country.

The time for that penance and sacrifice has now come without which no pure act can be accomplished. Mahatma Gandhi says that *swaraj* will be obtained in six months. We should all remember God and become a soldier of the army of Mahatma Gandhi and liberate our country once more by means of this religious war. No one should have any fear of being sent to jail. The jail where Tilak Maharaj, Mahatma Gandhi, Maulanas Shaukat Ali and Muhammad Ali [leaders of the Khilafat movement, initiated in 1919 to protest against the treatment of the Ottoman Caliph; allied with the Non-Cooperation movement] have been confined is a holy place and those who go there for the sake of the country are very fortunate. What can the Government officers and the police people do when there is no fear of jail and how can they tyrannize over the people.

News is being received from every direction about people being prosecuted under false accusations. There can be no hope of justice being done in such cases. What the police say will be accepted by the court, however many the defence witnesses. For this reason kisans should not waste their money by employing vakils [lawyers]. They should state the true facts and if they like they can produce true witnesses and then let the court do what it pleases. It is not good to furnish securities and give recognizances. This shows that the man is afraid of going to jail. One should cheerfully go to jail instead of giving securities and recognizances. This will bring victory to kisans and defeat to Government. Kisans! this is the time when your strength is being put to test. If you show your courage now, trusting in God, you shall succeed. Those kisans who have gone to jail and who are being subjected to other hardships are to be congratulated. Their sacrifice will bring *swaraj*.

Kisan brothers! If you act according to the instructions given above, then only will you be the true disciples of Mahatma Gandhi and make the words of Mahatmaji true by certainly obtaining *swaraj*.

MOTI LAL NEHRU,
President, United Provinces Kisan Sabha.

* * *

35

1921 ›› MITRA MANOG [FRIEND'S LOVE]

Original: Hindi | Author: Jagat Narayan Sharma
35.1: Poem: 'A Poem on Dyer'
35.2: Poem: 'Hearts' Fire'
35.3: Poem: 'Soul Force'
35.4: Poem: 'Fear'

THIS BOOK OF SONGS AND VERSES WAS FORFEITED BY THE Government of UP in May 1921 under the Indian Press Act of 1910. Its translations were also declared forfeit. It was written by Jagat Narayan Sharma of Farukkhabad, whose nom de plume was 'mitra' or friend. Some of the poems in a section of the book titled 'Murder Section' were considered to be 'exciting' in the review by the government official that accompanied the notification. The last section of the book contained poems on the theme of Hindu-Muslim unity, praise of Tilak and thoughts on the Mahabharat and Ramayana. Excerpts from some of the poems that were thought to be inflammatory are reprinted on the following pages.

* * *

35.1

'A POEM ON DYER'

Thousand curses on such vicious Dyer, the blood-thirsty of the Punjab and Hindustan.
O cruel Dyer, you did not take the least pity! We were left restless at every attack of yours, O tyrant!
The snow of cruelty will surely rust, as it bears the blot of our blood.
Be ashamed of this cowardly attack. You ordered firing on the subjects and on unarmed people.
In history thy misdeeds will ever remain a blot to the British Government.
Nothing would be unjust and wrong if wrath be let loose on thy power of action.
Cool sighs have faced the bullets and tears are shed at the shower of fire!

* * *

35.2

'HEARTS' FIRE'

Wonder! why thine tongue was not burnt while giving order for firing.
If Kaiser [the German emperor in the First World War] is guilty of Europe's blood then Dyer is accused for the massacre in the Punjab.
Why should you not be punished for your crimes when you exceeded Kaiser in cruelties.

* * *

35.3

'SOUL FORCE'

We will proclaim to the world the bullets we got in return for our sacrifices.
It is known that Indians are blacks but we will blacken the faces of India's enemy.
We will give up our lives in serving our country.

* * *

35.4

'FEAR'

O tongue, stop, else it shall be cut and (you) will be cut to pieces by Dyer's sword!

If anything except flattering will be said the order of externment will be the result.

If you wish good of your fellowmen you shall be considered a rebel.

If even you thought of freedom the machine guns will be sent for as was done in Amritsar. If you oppose Rowlatt Act, Martial Law will be declared.

Never accept what your leaders say. If you do it, double barrelled guns will be aimed at your chest. If you join the National Assembly, you shall be punished in the manner of Jallianwala Bagh.

If you even sighed at your brothers' blood you shall be brought enchained before the Martial Law Committee.

If you are for truth, you shall be troubled in every way.

* * *

36

1923 ›› HAMARA HAKO AND HAMARA DESH [OUR RIGHTS AND OUR COUNTRY]

Original: Gujarati
36.1: Hamara Hako
  36.1.1: Song
  36.1.2: Song: 'We shall call you to account'
36.2: Hamara Desh
  36.2.1: Song: 'Hamara Desh'
  36.2.2: Song 9: 'Darkness without justice'

KESHAVLAL GOKALDAS SHAH OF BROACH WAS THE PUBLISHER and seller of pamphlets deemed to contain seditious songs, and the manager of Gujrat Sahitya Mandir. One such pamphlet was banned in 1922. The following year, two more came to the attention of the Government of Bombay: Hamara Hako and Hamara Desh. Both contained songs in Gujarati. The former was printed in Ahmedabad and the latter in Bhavnagar. The Government of Bombay deemed the following poems and songs objectionable. Consequently, in June 1923, they were banned by notifications for 'containing seditious matter'. The notification as well as review of the leaflets with translations was then circulated to all provincial governments. Additionally, Keshavlal was ordered to undergo one year's simple imprisonment as he did not furnish security (as a guarantee of good behaviour in the future).

* * *

36.1

HAMARA HAKO

36.1.1

'SONG'

O' you oppressors why do you harass us! Fear God and act as moral men
O' you blind arrogant men, look before you leap; fear God because you will be called to account by Him. O' you oppressors...
Youth is fleeting, then why are you unnecessarily puffed up; fear God and keep to the path of virtue. O' you oppressors...
You are slaying the slain and burning those who are already burnt;
You trample those who are already trodden down; fear God. O' You oppressors...
What do you care whether we starve or our bodies suffer pain, as long as you can fill up your stomachs; fear God, O' you oppressors...
In the course of our earthly life, we have been doing virtuous deeds but you have gone mad with self-interest; fear God.
I conjure [sic] you to do all what you can and to do your worst; fear God. O' you oppressors...

* * *

36.1.2

'WE SHALL CALL YOU TO ACCOUNT'

We shall ask you to account for our rights which you have usurped to-day.

You have been making merry (at our cost) and we know it; we shall call you to account for our rights.

You consumed away our well-stocked granaries and emptied the treasury and you did not fulfil your promises; we shall call you to account.

Our guardians entrusted us to your care, thinking that you were good and simple hearted but you render no account and so we shall call you to account.

You are thoroughly vicious and you are forward (lit. bold) in debauchery; you broke your promises; we shall call you to account.

You misappropriated and carried away all our property and we shall call you to account.

You sat upon us although we fed you; why should you not return to us what you took away; we shall call you to account.

You have grown stout and plump by feeding on our grain (produce of our country); yet you don't feel grateful; we shall call you to account.

If you care for your own good, listen to what we say; I am serious; we shall call you to account.

K. G. Shah, Seth, says, we will fight you to the bitter end; we shall no more undergo your forced labour; we shall call you to account.

* * *

36.2

1923

HAMARA DESH

36.2.1

'HAMARA DESH'

Questions arise in (my) mind on seeing the plight of 'Bharat' [India]
How to achieve the freedom of the Motherland from her state of dependence
Question with a calm mind the soul which is enshrined in the heart and fearlessly demand an answer about the present rotten (lit. hollow) state of affairs.
What is the remedy? When the guardian becomes the destroyer, when hedges rush to devour their creepers and when the parents harass their children.
How is it possible to co-operate with a Government who broke its promises, who having given pledges of the inviolability to Khilafat [The Ottoman caliphate], forgot all about them?
The Punjab has suffered fresh atrocities, a recollection of which sets one's blood boiling; when those who took innocent lives, are seen stalking about the land triumphantly
Under the tyrant's regime of men like Dyer and O' Dwyer where justice and self respect become extinct, the true Indians will not live
The lion, although dying of starvation, will never eat grass;
Likewise lion-like sons of Bharat will not crave for co-operation with the tyrannical.
After centuries of long sufferings, we have realized our correct situation to-day; even the enjoyment of heavenly bliss under the auspices of the unjust is hell-like.
Honours and medals are snares to catch us; even the best of us were deceived but now our eyes are opened;
The country in ruined by the selfish: they are the people who are traitors to the country; their thoughts, their words and their deeds are at variance.
Those who consider themselves happy under the protection of the tyrant are the abettors and enemies of the motherland

Though their hearts are lacerated and their feelings are injured still they cannot tell the truth! *(refers apparently to the Moderate party)*
I wonder how people still don't understand the precious instrument of non-co operation
Those who are themselves prisoners, how could they release us; only those who are free can give us freedom
The blind cannot see the right path and those who have eyes can avert danger;
The call of Mother Bharat to Hindus and Musalmans is to become one;
India will win victory (only) through the training of self-sacrifice.
Take Gandhiji as your leader and love non-co-operation
Take a vow to-day to sacrifice your body, soul and money.

* * *

36.2.2

'DARKNESS WITHOUT JUSTICE'

O' British ! there is darkness to-day because there is no justice
You like the Moderates; the Untruth is bitter as salt is saltish; O' British...
When the ladder of Reforms was raised, the Great Gandhiji thundered out and the heart became sore; O' British...
You speak sweet things but you part with nothing: such I find is always your heart; O' British...
You committed great atrocities in the Punjab thinking as if you had drunk nectar (as if you had never to die); Do you think it was any good: O' British...
You have spread discontent in India by meddling with Khilafat and having things in your own way; O' British...
Be wise and tell the truth and open your heart clean and say what virtues if [sic] yours may I recollect? O' British...
You claim descent from Queen Victoria the learned, (but) on all sides I see oppression; O' British...
You have eaten us and eaten us till nothing is left and you entertain no fear in exercising oppressions and still you are bankrupt; O' British...
You crush those who speak out the truth and you restrain others; A hundred maunds [unit of weight] of oil is being burnt and still there is darkness; O' British...
To-day I see you breaking your promises to Turkey; Now I'm quite tired of you; O' British...
Where should we go to complain and to what side should we turn to get justice?
Manu [ancient Indian law-giver/ the poet referring to himself] says there is bankruptcy of justice; O' British...

* * *

37

1924 ›› SATYABHAKTA, BHARATIYA SAMYAVADI DAL [THE INDIAN COMMUNIST PARTY]

Original: Hindi | Leaflet

THIS WAS AN INFORMATION SHEET, PUBLISHED AS A LEAFLET IN Kanpur in *c.* 1924 at the Shakti Press. The publisher's name was listed as Satya Bhakt (literally, 'Devotee of Truth'). The historian Charu Gupta has recently discussed Satyabhakta's (1897–1985) career as an activist, publicist and committed 'vernacular Communist' who combined a deep commitment to Communist ideals with his faith in Hindu beliefs. In this he was quite different from other Communist leaders such as M.N. Roy (1887–1954) with whom he shared an antagonistic relationship. The entire leaflet is reprinted here. It outlined the aims and methods of the party, explained why Communism was the need of the hour and also stated how it differed from other political parties. The leaflet ended with an application form for membership.

* * *

INDIA is beset on all sides with suffering of all sorts at the present juncture. Men who can be called really prosperous can hardly be found. The condition of the peasants and workers had better be left unsaid. They start work at 6 in the morning and continue to toil hard till 5 or 6 in the evening. In return for all this they got only bare bread. All of them do not get even pulse and vegetable. Many have to content themselves with sauce of salt and pepper. Under such circumstances it is idle to talk of butter, milk, fruits and other health-giving food stuffs. The condition of the middle classes or those whom we call well dressed or high class people is in no way better. They conceal the hunger of their stomachs by polishing their faces. They have nothing to eat in their homes, they cannot find any job, still they cannot extend the hand of beggary before any person or undertake any menial or manual work; for if they do so they lose their honour. So they have only their honour to treasure but they have nothing to eat.

On all sides there is a holocaust in which all are one by one being consumed. But no one thinks of means to save himself from it. Famine, dearness, disease, quarrels and riots are ruining the populace. But no one is thinking of devising means to combat them. People only blame their God or their luck and keep quiet. There is no dearth of leaders, politicians, religious divines and social reformers and numerous societies of sorts and leaders are showing the path to the people. But many of these paths will rather aggravate the malady. Many of the guides knowingly mislead the people into a gulf in order to fill their stomachs.

The Indian Communist Party had been formed to save people from these false guides and to point out means to them to chalk out their own paths. The Indian Communist Party unlike other parties does not ask the public to follow in their footsteps in the hope of being relieved from all sufferings. It rather says that no single party or organisation can relieve the people of all their sufferings. These sufferings will go only when all the people unite and stand on their own legs and strive for their salvation. Therefore the Indian Communist Party does not propose to set up any separate organisation but to concentrate all its energies in organising and awakening the people.

The main object of the Indian Communist Party is to level those terrible differences which are standing between the rich and the poor, and the high and the low in India at present. Therefore all who love equality and do not like that they alone should enjoy comfort but that its blessings should go to all should undoubtedly join this party. Only those who feed in leisure by cheating and robbing others will keep aloof from it. Otherwise all who make money by the sweat of their brow and do not prefer to live on ill-gotten gains will find the principles of this agitation to be the *best* specially poor peasants, labourers, clerks, petty Government officials, school masters, railway employees, postal hands, orderlies, police constables, press employees, students, *ekka* and *tonga* drivers, *thelawalas*, petty tradesmen and others who earn from the sweat of their brow ought surely to become members of this party, because it alone can secure redress of their wrongs.

I would now describe in brief the objects, principles and rules of the Indian Communist Party. These rules have been improvised for the preliminary stage. When the membership becomes sufficiently large new rules will be framed by the will of the majority.

THE FINAL GOAL OF THE INDIAN COMMUNIST PARTY.

The present social organisation and Government of India should be so changed that all the sources of production and distribution (such as land, factories, mines, railways, telegraphs, merchant marine, etc.) may come under the possession of the general public and they may become the masters thereof. This work should be accomplished in such a manner that all may take part in it and benefit from it.

PROGRAMME.

Peasants, workers, and middle class people (educated people and employees) should be organised and enduring relations should be cemented between the peasants and workers.

METHODS.

1. To share the daily difficulties of the peasants and workers, to help them and thus to win their confidence.
2. To make peasants and workers themselves the leaders of the peasants and workers' movements.
3. To distribute Communistic pamphlets, newspapers, and tracts.
4. To create among the people a zest for reading Communist books and papers and to start at various places libraries with this end in view.
5. To foster such relations between workers in employment and out of employment so that they may help each other.
6. To agitate among peasants and workers and to enlist them in the Indian Communist Party.

THE PRINCIPLES OF THE INDIAN COMMUNIST PARTY.

1. At present all the sources of wealth in India (like land, factories, mines, telegraphs, railways, merchant marine, etc.) are in the possession of a few capitalists or the so-called owners. The result is that the remainder of the population which toils to produce all things becomes the slave of these capitalists.
2. Because of this two classes have been created in the country which are diametrically different from each other, one class consists of those capitalists who do no work and produce nothing but are still usurping the position of masters of everything. The second class consists of those persons who toil day and night to produce all things but are able to retain nothing. Therefore there is constant conflict between these classes.
3. The conflict will cease only when the workers are freed from the serfdom

of the capitalists. The only way to effect this is to take all sources of production and distribution (such as land, factory, mines, railways, merchant marine, etc.) from the hands of the capitalists and make them the property of the people at large. They should also manage them.

4. It is a law of social expansion that workers always become victorious in the end, and then all other classes are absorbed by them. Therefore the victory of the workers means the conclusion of the sufferings of all classes of men and women.
5. Workers can gain such a victory or free themselves from slavery only by their own efforts.
6. At present Government and its armed forces always try to defend the wealth and the rights of the capitalists. The capitalists only gain this wealth by despoiling the workers. It is therefore the duty of the workers to organise themselves openly. In this way they will control the imperial council, the provincial councils, district boards, municipalities and other organisations which rule the country. When this takes place all those official councils, government servants, soldiers and policemen, etc., who at the present moment cause great suffering to the people will become the means of relieving the suffering. Then with the help of these an end will be put to injustices and high-handednesses of the selfish people.
7. It is a well known fact that every political party strives for the welfare of its supporters. It is also well known that the working class is the largest class. It is so numerous that the entire capitalist class is like a drop before it. Therefore whenever there is a conflict between the capitalists and the working class more regard should be always shown to the latter.
8. Therefore the Indian Communist Party definitely proposes either to suppress or absorb all organisations that are overtly or covertly acting for the capitalist class. It is now the paramount duty of all the workers to gather under the banner of the Indian Communist Party and to stand by it till the last. When all workers work unitedly then all those present day laws which deprive the worker of the fruits of his labour can be amended, plenty will take place of want, all distinctions of high and low will be levelled, and all will be treated on equal terms and in place of slavery the banner of freedom will begin to wave.

OTHER RULES.

Every person of 18 years who believes in the above-mentioned objects and principles can become a member of the Indian Communist party by paying an annual subscription of annas 8. At places where a large number of

(2)

(5) Our party holds that, as in the order of social evolution the working class is the last class to achieve its freedom the emancipation of the working class will involve the emancipation of all mankind without the distinction of race and sects.

(6) Our party holds that this emancipation must be the work of the working class itself.

(7) Our party holds that the present Zamindari system is the sole cause of all the miseries of the Indian peasants and so long as it exists there is no hope of improving their condition. Therefore the zamindari system must be [illegible]shed at once, and peasants should be deemed as the rightful masters of th[illegible] of their labour.

(8) Our party holds that, as the machinary of the Govt., including the armed forces of the nation exists only to conserve the monopoly by the capitalist class, of the wealth taken from the workers, the working class must organise consciously and politically for the conquest of the powers of Government, national, provincial and local, in order that this machinary, including these forces, may be converted from an instrument of oppression into the agent of emancipation and the overthrow of buearocratic and capitalistic privileges.

(9) Our party holds that, as political parties are but the expression of class interests, and as the working class is the biggest of all classes, so much so that all sections of the master class put together will, comparatively, look infinitesmal, the interest of all the other classes must be superseded by the interest of the working [illegible]

(10) Our party holds that the workers of all countries of the world are suffering from the same unjustice at the hands of the capitalists, and that their interests are one and the same, it is therefore, necessary for their salvation to unite and act harmoniously.

(11) The Indian Communist Party, therefore, enters the field of political action determined to supersede or envelope, all such parties whether alleged or avowedly capitalist and calls upon all the members of the working class of this country to muster under its banner to the end, that a speedy termination may be wrought to the system which deprives them of the fruits of their labour, and that poverty may give place to comfort, privileges to equality and slavery to freedom.

S. Satya Bhakta
Secretary
THE INDIAN COMMUNIST PARTY, CAWNPORE.

Printed at the Brahman Press Cawnpore & published by S. Satya Bhakta at the Indian Communist Party's Office, Cawnpore.

The Indian Communist Party.

(हिन्दुस्तानी साम्यवादी दल)

I ______________________

aged.... agree with the aims and objects of the Indian Communist Party, declare to become a member of the party, and herewith forward annas eight a[s] membership fee for a year. I shall try my best to follow and propogate its aims [and] objects.

Signature (member)

Date ______________ 192 ______________

Full address with occupation. ______________________

____

Signature (secretary)

____

Pamphlet and Membership form, Indian Communist Party

members are enlisted a committee or branch will be formed. There should be at least one hundred workers or 30 peasants or 16 educated men on the rolls to permit of the opening of a branch. Members who undertake to carry out any item of the programme of the Indian Communist Party will become members of the Executive Committee. Selected branches will also have the right to send representatives to the Executive. All correspondence should be addressed to:

The Secretary, Indian Communist Party,
C/o Socialist Bookshop, Cawnpore.

NOTE-The Indian Communist Party fund has been established with a view to carry on the work and the agitation of the Indian Communist Party. I have the fullest confidence that gentle men enlisting as members will besides paying their annual subscriptions contribute to this fund a sum not less than a rupee as their means and desires dictate. Those who cannot enlist as members for any reason can help in this work by contributing to this fund. Members should bear in mind that the work cannot be properly carried on without making the fund a success. Therefore they should themselves pay subscriptions as well as try to collect subscriptions from others. (Persons enlisting as members should fill in their names, etc. in the following form and return it):

INDIAN COMMUNIST PARTY.

I ______________________, age __________, agree with the objects and principles of the Indian Communist Party. I am willing to become a member of this party and am remitting the sum of annas eight as annual subscription thereof. I will try as far as possible to observe and propagate the ideals and principles of this body.

Date______________________

Signature of member______________
Full address____________________
Occupation ____________________

Signature of Secretary.____________

* * *

38

1925 ›› SWADESH: VIJAY ANK [MOTHERLAND: VICTORY SPECIAL ISSUE]

Original: Hindi | Editor: Pandit Bechan Sharma Ugrai
Poem: 'Victory' by Pandit Ram Charit Upadhya

IN FEBRUARY 1925, THE GOVERNMENT OF UP BANNED, UNDER section 124A, the special 'Vijay Ank' [Victory Special Issue] of the *Swadesh* newspaper of Gorakhpur, printed in Benaras [Varanasi] at the Saraswati Press owned by the famous writer Premchand (1880–1936). The printer and publisher, Dasrath Prasad Dwivedi, was sentenced to two years' rigorous imprisonment and a fine of fifty rupees. Justice Stuart of the Allahabad High Court dismissed his appeal, expressing his full faith in the translating abilities of Pandit Sheo Chandra Misra, an official translator with sixteen years' experience. While dismissing the appeal, the judge also commented on the fact that the issue was published at the time of the Hindu festival of Dusshera (connected to the epic hero Ram, also the subject of the poem 'Victory', reprinted here). He also mentioned that the Chauri-Chaura incident (in 1922, when the burning of a police station by nationalist agitators caused the death of twenty-two Indian policemen) had happened in Gorakhpur, from where *Swadesh* was also issued.

The editor of this edition, Pandit Bechan Sharma Ugra (1900–1967), went on to publish his very controversial collection of short stories titled *Chaklet*, on the theme of homosexuality, in 1927. When a warrant for his arrest was issued in connection with the case, he escaped to Bombay [Mumbai]. He was to recall in his memoirs how he was arrested after five months, and then sentenced to nine months' rigorous imprisonment in connection with this case.

The first page of the newspaper carried a poem by Anoop Sharma titled 'Future Revolution'. The poem ended with the rather violent exhortation: 'The spear of the love of Gandhi will pierce through the head of the enemies and their hearts will be rent asunder into pieces.' The historian Shahid Amin has demonstrated how Gandhi's message was adopted, adapted and changed – to the point of becoming unrecognizable – by recipients to reflect their understanding of political realities, objectives and methods. Another poem from the same issue is reprinted on the following page.

* * *

'VICTORY'

There may be shouts of victory once more.
O Ram, the time-limit is approaching, you may ponder deeply.
Assume a wonderful re-incarnation this time suited to the occasion.
They were the demons of the Treta age [mythical time cycle]. These are of the Iron age.
Ram, this time you will not have to cross the ocean.
Demons swarm in this very place, relieve the land of its burden.
What terrible atrocity remained undone in India?
O Lord! forthwith sound the twang of your bow along with your angry shout. Those who are generous towards demons are traitors to the country.
Ram, we rely on you, emancipate the country. What reform can be made by mere words? Listen to the gist of the prayer.
Again fondle India by destroying the enemy.

* * *

39

1927 ›› SAINIK [SOLDIER]

Original: Hindi | Author: Munishwar Prasad Avasthi
Article: 'Bomb Party ka Itihasa', 31 August 1927

AUTHORED BY MUNISHWAR PRASAD AVASTHI, THIS WAS AN article first published in *Sainik*, a weekly Hindi newspaper from Agra. It was banned, by name, just under a month later, by the Government of UP in 1927 after being deemed seditious. The order was signed by the Chief Secretary of UP, Jagdish Prasad. The article aimed to educate people living in North India about the inspirational activities of Bengali revolutionaries. It also explained the connections between nationalism and communalism, and how one shifted to the other.

* * *

31 AUGUST 1927

HISTORY OF THE BOMB PARTY

During the days of the swadeshi movement the idea of nationalism arose, as a result of which the boycott movement began. The idea of "my country's right or wrong" gradually began to take hold of the people. The element of orthodox Hindus predominated at that time in the party. Therefore the wave of nationalism gradually diverted itself into the channels of Arya Samaj and the orthodoxy of the Hindus, that is to say, nationalism changed into communalism. The comments made by Sir Valentine Chirol in his book "India(n) Unrest" are not untrue.

Even now, as in the past, there are a number of orthodox Hindus in this movement. Many Brahmo Samajists take part in our activities, and, strange to say, they too gradually separated from Brahmo Samaj and became more and more attached to Arya Samaj or orthodox Hinduism.

At the outset we had Muslim boys also among us, but afterwards their

GOVERNMENT OF THE UNITED PROVINCES.
No. 6411/VIII—717.
POLICE DEPARTMENT.

Dated September 28, 1927.

NOTIFICATION.
MISCELLANEOUS.

IN exercise of the powers conferred by section 99-A of the Code of Criminal Procedure, 1898 (Act V of 1898), as amended by the Press Law Repeal and Amendment Act, 1922 (Act XIV of 1922), the Governor in Council hereby declares to be forfeited to His Majesty all copies, wherever found, of the issue dated August 31, 1927, of the *Sainik*, a Hindi weekly newspaper of Agra, which contains an article entitled "Bomb party ka itihasa" (History of the Bomb party), inasmuch as the said article, in the opinion of the local Government, contains seditious matter the publication of which is punishable under section 124-A, Indian Penal Code.

By order of the Governor in Council,
JAGDISH PRASAD,
Chief Secy. to Govt., United Provinces.

Notification banning Bomb Party ka Itihasa, Sainik.

recruitment was stopped. Some time later it was decided to organize them, but either on account of mutual mistrust or some other reason, their interest in the work abated, and, moreover, recruiting from among them slackened. Musalmans are not yet prepared for revolution. Brahmo Samajists are losing interest in it. They objected to revolutionaries propagating Hinduism. This resulted in a dearth of men other than those of the orthodox Hindu class.

The revolutionary movement of Bengal assumed a religious role. The revolutionaries were ever ready to sacrifice themselves, their property, their dear ones and their lives for the revolution, like fanatics blinded by religion, who are prepared to sacrifice their all for their ideals and convictions. The achievements of a handful of revolutionaries astonished, not only Bengal, but the whole of India. The only reason that can be ascribed to this is their enormous sacrifices.

The first party was much harassed on account of its ideals and convictions and had to undergo many inhuman atrocities. Many of them were exiled, sent to Andamans, interned in jail and put to the gallows. Most of those of us who were in foreign countries were imprisoned and the rest are still suffering the penalty of banishment. But, in spite of all this, the second party came forward.

Bengalis are said to be a race of cowards. But when the situation demanded they were among the heroes. With an ideal before them, they can be persuaded to make untold sacrifices. All of us have heard the story of the two heroes Prafulla and Khudi Ram Bose. But there is no scarcity of such heroes in Bengal....

The courage, achievements, patience and heroism of these educated youths a unparalleled in the history of the world. Had these heroes the opportunity of being on the battlefield, their victory would have undoubtedly impressed the world with its laudable effect.

In the Bomb party of Bengal there were indefatigable heroes bearing such good characters that with proper military training every one of them would have become a Napoleon.

* * *

40
1928 ›› CHAND: PHANSI ANK [THE MOON: HANGING/EXECUTION SPECIAL ISSUE]

Original: Hindi
40.1: Editorial Foreword By Chatur Sen Sastri
40.2: Poem: 'From the Scaffold' by Shobha Ram Sewak
40.3: Article: 'The Sentence of Hanging' by Rai Saheb Har Vilas Sarda

CHAND WAS A HINDI MAGAZINE PUBLISHED FROM ALLAHABAD since 1922. Its special issue of November 1928, termed the Phansi Ank (Hanging/ Execution Special Issue), was forfeited under section 124A in December 1928 by the Government of UP.

The magazine was edited by litteratcur Chatur Sen Sastri and published by Ramrakh Singh Saigal of the Fine Art Printing Cottage, Allahabad. This special issue contained 323 pages of densely packed fiction and non-fiction articles. The latter included profiles of more than fifty Indian revolutionaries, many written by Bhagat Singh, who was to become India's most famous and best-remembered revolutionary martyr in the coming years. Text was interspersed with illustrations from famous episodes in world and Indian history: Christ on the Cross (bearing the caption: Thrilling Scene of Great Man Jesus's Capital Punishment), Leonardo da Vinci's painting of Christ, the seventeenth-century Sikh martyr Arjun Dev, Joan of Arc (the caption indicating that she was burnt alive for the crime of patriotism), scenes from the French revolution and so on. There were articles on Sanskrit literature (mention of capital punishment therein), Roman law and punishments in Elizabethan England. In addition to satirical short plays (one a conversation between Yama, the Hindu god of death, and a lawyer), there were also learned deliberations on the Indian penal code by Indian lawyers and judges.

The issue also carried four pages of endorsement and praise, in English and Hindi, from prominent newspapers such as *Amrita Bazar Patrika*, *Bombay Chronicle* and *Tribune*. Individual endorsements of the journal included those of the Dewan [prime minister] of Patiala state, from Indian ICS officials, and from the nationalist leader and poet Sarojini Naidu (1879–1949), who wished for the journal: 'May your "Moon" always wax and never wane in beauty and splendour....'

The historian Avinash Kumar has documented how the magazine's popularity exploded in the aftermath of this notorious and banned special issue: its circulation figures grew from 3,000 to 15,000 in the one year after this issue was published. The banned issue was sold in the black market and made its proprietor wealthy. Kumar has also commented on the fact that this issue did not discuss the Congress-led movement against colonialism; Gandhi himself received only passing mention.

* * *

40.1

Foreword by Chatur Sen Sastri

A TRANSLATION OF EXCERPTS FROM THE FOREWORD ACCOMPANIED the notification. Since the issue was released on the Hindu festival of lights, Diwali, celebrated on a moonless night, it made much of light and darkness as metaphors for slavery and independence.

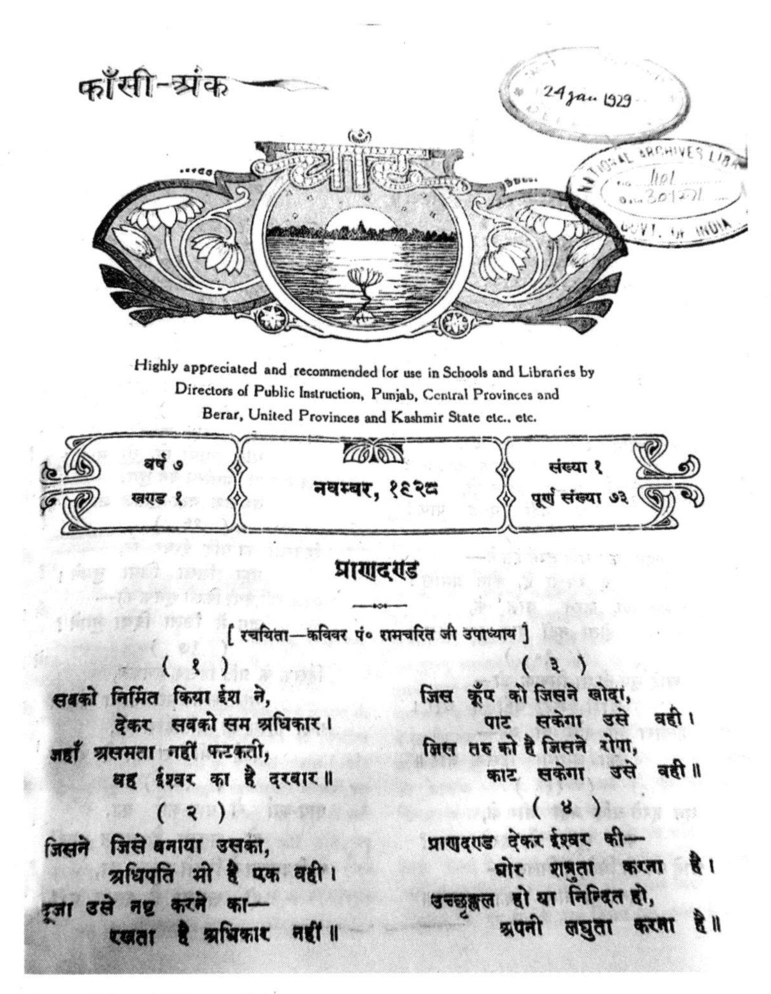

फाँसी-अंक

Highly appreciated and recommended for use in Schools and Libraries by Directors of Public Instruction, Punjab, Central Provinces and Berar, United Provinces and Kashmir State etc., etc.

वर्ष ७ खण्ड १ | नवम्बर, १९२८ | संख्या १ पूर्ण संख्या ७२

प्राणदण्ड

[रचयिता—कविवर पं० रामचरित जी उपाध्याय]

(१)

सबको निर्मित किया ईश ने,
देकर सबको सम अधिकार।
जहाँ असमता नहीं फटकती,
वह ईश्वर का है दरबार॥

(२)

जिसने जिसे बनाया उसका,
अधिपति भी है एक वही।
दूजा उसे नष्ट करने का—
रखता है अधिकार नहीं॥

(३)

जिस कूँप को जिसने खोदा,
पाट सकेगा उसे वही।
जिस तरु को है जिसने रोपा,
काट सकेगा उसे वही॥

(४)

प्राणदण्ड देकर ईश्वर की—
घोर शत्रुता करना है।
उच्छृङ्खल हो या निन्दित हो,
अपनी लघुता करना है॥

Cover, Chand, *Phansi Ank*.

Look upon this *Phansi Ank* as the dark night of *Diwali*. Behold how in it the lights of the immolated ones of the twentieth century are flickering and also see how at places flaming fire is blazing forth and how in the midst of all the waking light, Lady Death, beautifully bedecked is dancing unreservedly. Adore her, O men and women of unfortunate India, divorced from sovereignty rights, power and authority as they are; she is your household goddess—this Lady Death of imperishable youth, this great goddess of destruction. Love her, cultivate her acquaintance and wed her. Then you will see that no sooner does she become the red star of your bosom instead of being a noose round your neck your thousands of years old slavery vanishes into nothingness... The day is near. Let a few months or a few years pass by. There comes the hurricane of a great revolution which will not allow India to light the *Diwali* lights for many fifty years. But after that the lights which will be lighted will not be the mean earthen ones. They will be of precious stones and will be lighted by the goddess of Royalty with her own hands.

* * *

GOVERNMENT, UNITED PROVINCES.

No. 3774/VIII—100.

POLICE DEPARTMENT.

***Dated December* 10, 1928.**

NOTIFICATION.

(MISCELLANEOUS.)

IN exercise of the power conferred by section 99-A of the Code of Criminal Procedure (Act V of 1898), the Governor in Council hereby declares to be forfeited to His Majesty every copy of the special *Phansi Ank* (Capital Punishment) number of the Hindi *Chand* magazine issued in November, 1928, edited by Sri Chatur Sen Shastri and printed and published by R. Saigal at the Fine Art Printing Cottage, 28, Elgin Road, Allahabad, on the ground that the said number contains matter the publication of which is punishable under section 124-A of the Indian Penal Code.

By order of the Governor in Council,

JAGDISH PRASAD,

Chief Secy. to Govt., United Provinces.

Ban Notification, Chand Phansi Ank.

40.2

'FROM THE SCAFFOLD'

In the eyes of the country I was a devoted lover of the feet of the Mother,
In the opinion of the traitors to the country I was simply a wretched man.
In the eyes of those who died for the mother I was a selfless man,
To the autocrats if I was anything I was a rebel.
I shall break the bonds of the mother, this was the one constant thought,
Or I shall die for the mother's honour, this was my pride.
I was longing in life for the boon of execution,
I shall be born again in India, this thought rose up in the heart.
When did those who are intoxicated with the love of country yield through fear of the gallows
Which powers have been able to shake these heroes from their resolve?
When government becomes weak through excessive high-handedness,
Then the world looks with amazement on the complete victory of the sacrifices.
Nation-edifices were built with the blood of brave martyrs,
The fortune lamps of Royal dynasties went out by their becoming oppressors.
Those countries did not remain under subjection for a minute and secured blessings,
Which dedicated their lives at the feet of the mother.
I depart, O mother, grant me this boon, that I may be born in India again,
Not once but a hundred times, O mother, may I die for thy freedom.

* * *

40.3

'THE SENTENCE OF HANGING'

Rai Saheb Har Vilas Sarda
MLA [Member of the Legislative Assembly] and Retired Judge

THE AUTHOR WAS TO BECOME FAMOUS THE NEXT YEAR FOR THE so-called Sarda Act (The Child Marriage Restraint Act). His illustrious career and reputation gave his words immense weight and added to the prestige of the special issue and the journal more generally. I have translated excerpts from this article.

* * *

Humans have been given life by God, and as per true justice, only he is entitled to take it back. No other creature has the right to take life, because nobody except God has the power to grant life. To sentence a criminal to death is correct neither from the point of view of justice, nor from that of enlightened actions. A death sentence is only given to murderers, those engaging in conspiracy, revolution or sedition. In the military, cowardice, running away from battle or leaking military secrets attracts this penalty.... When a person murders another then he is animated by feelings of extreme rage and mental stress. That time his humanity gets destroyed. In other words, at that time neither does he have a sense of right and wrong nor is he in his right mind... at the time when he commits murder his mental state is totally different from that of a person who, sitting in a court of justice, deliberates on the matter in a peaceful environment, and with full faculties intact, gives the punishment of death sentence.

If a person animated by patriotism and love for country, animated by public interest opposes the oppressor, and spreads sedition after being animated by noble thoughts of independence, or blows the conch of revolution, or declares war against unjust rulers, then the person will be said to be following his duty and high principles, and is not a criminal. Then how can anyone, keeping justice and fairness in mind, term it correct to sentence that person to hanging? How can depriving such a person of life further public interest or public service?....

The sentence of hanging begins with the intention of taking revenge.... If a person commits a crime then to commit another crime to punish him is not judicious. This is why wise people have always sought to end capital punishment. In the present situation as well it is necessary to amend this penalty appropriately by generating public interest in this matter.

* * *

41

1930 ›› KRANTI KA SINGHANAD [WAR-CRY OF REVOLUTION]

Original: Hindi
41.1: Poem: 'The Desire of a National Flower'
41.2: Poem: 'Do As You Like'
41.3: Poem: 'Non-Co-operation'

THIS HINDI PAMPHLET WAS BANNED BY THE GOVERNMENT OF UP in 1930 under section 124A. It was published by Pandit Ganga Sahaya Chaube of the Rashtriya Sahitya Pracharak Mandal [National Literature Propagation Society], Kanpur. The official review that accompanied the translations of 'objectionable poems' from the pamphlet called them 'sufficiently inciting' as the pamphlet 'exhorts people to suffer tyranny, court imprisonment and death in the cause of the country, to put an end to oppression, to sacrifice their lives and be ready for war.' One of the poems printed in this pamphlet was 'Yearnings of Bismil', banned in its Urdu avatar as well (see chapter 43). The metaphors of flower, garden and gardener were shared by Hindi and Urdu both, which by this decade were already cleaved apart by votaries of linguistic purity.

* * *

41.1

'THE DESIRE OF A NATIONAL FLOWER'

I do not desire to be strung in the ornaments of a fairy;
Not do I desire to be put in the garland round the neck of the beloved.
O gardener, my only desire is that you should pluck and throw me on the road
Along which several heroes pass to offer their heads in the cause of the country.

* * *

41.2

'DO AS YOU LIKE'

Pick up flowers, so that your desires may not remain unfulfilled;
And this garden of India may not continue to be prosperous.
This is not a garden which becomes desolate and barren by plucking flowers;
Pick up flowers, so that there may not remain any obligation of love.
Throw us into jails and gag our mouths.
Pick up flowers, so that none may remain to sacrifice himself for the country.
Exploit India with fraud and deceit;
(So that) nothing may remain for her to subsist on.
Pick up flowers, so that your desires may not remain unfulfilled.

* * *

41.3

'NON-CO-OPERATION'

The activities of the Government will not change
If the nation will not be ready for non-co-operation.
There will be a Jallianwala Bagh in every city
If this Government will not be removed from this country.
Until we water it with our blood
The crop of our country O friends will not thrive.
We are mad men, give us the shackles of iron;
The ornaments of gold will not produce such a rattle.
The Hindus and Muslims have united.

* * *

42

1930 ›› CONGRESS PUSHPANJALI [FLORAL OFFERING]

Original: Urdu | Poem

THIS URDU PAMPHLET, PUBLISHED BY THE FARUQI PRESS IN Saharanpur, was banned by the Government of UP in 1930 under section 124A of the Indian Penal Code. Its editor was mentioned as 'Bharti' [Indian]. The notification was signed by an Indian, Jagdish Prasad, Chief Secretary to the Government of UP. This evocative poem urged women to use spinning wheels, popularized by Gandhi as simple symbols of self-reliance, as 'guns'.

* * *

Ply the spinning wheel, O my mothers!
Save the prestige of the country.
Since you have left off plying the spinning wheel, the enemies have surrounded us;
Save us from their clutches.
O my mothers! ply the spinning wheel;
All the factories of Manchester are robbing us to fill their coffers;
Keep the money from their pockets..
O my mothers! ply the spinning wheels.
You have filled the purses of the enemies and they are making rifles and ammunition from the money.
Use your spinning wheels as guns.
O my mothers! ply the spinning wheel.
What tyranny have they perpetuated in the Punjab;
They have dropped bombs from the aeroplanes.
Take up the shields of *khaddar* [hand-woven cloth popularized by Gandhi].
O my mothers! ply the spinning wheel.

* * *

43

1930 ›› INQULAB KI LAHR [REVOLUTIONARY WAVE]

Original: Urdu | Poem
43.1: Poem
43.2: Poem
43.3: Poem: 'If Bhagat Singh and Dutt Die'
43.4: Poem

THIS URDU PAMPHLET, PUBLISHED BY THE FARUQI PRESS IN Saharanpur, was banned by the Government of UP in 1930 under section 124A of the Indian Penal Code. Its editor was mentioned as 'S.P.' The first of several (translated) poems that accompanied the notification mentioned its author as 'Ram Prasad Bismil, martyr of the Kakori case'. This erroneous attribution persists in contemporary India as well. The poem – Sarfaroshi ki Tamanna/The Desire of Sacrificing Our Heads – was written by Bismil Azimabadi (1901–1978), a landlord-poet from Bihar in 1921, and popularized by Ram Prasad Bismil (1897–1927), executed in 1927 for his participation in the Kakori conspiracy case two years prior. Some of the couplets were reprinted in this pamphlet. It retains its power and popularity thanks to its frequent usage in films, demonstrations and poetry recitals.

* * *

43.1

The desire of sacrificing our heads is in our hearts;
Let us see how much power the murderer's arms possess.
O traveller on the path of love do not tarry on the way;
For the joy of wandering in the desert is realized only at the end of the journey.
Let the time come and we will show thee, O sky;
At present what can we say about our intentions?
O martyr for the cause of the country and the nation let us die for thy sentiment;
The fame of thy sacrifices has reached the assembly of the rivals.
He has none of former ambitions or the thronging of desires;
Now Bismil only desires to be destroyed.

* * *

43.2

There are still many drunkards who are prepared to die;
Many stories have still to be written with our blood.
It does not end with Bhagat Singh and [Batukeshwar] Dutt only.
There are still many moths in India the flame of freedom.
Their sacrifices can never be useless.
There are still many mad men who will come to the place of slaughter to have their heads severed.
O tyrant, it does not matter if one or two are broken;
For there are still many goblets for Indian drunkards to drink from.
Their orders had been torn to pieces in two days only;
Their officers were much annoyed at their own doing.
A time will come when India will be at the height of success.
Spring will return as soon as we have our own gardener.
We will punish the gatherer of flowers for despoiling the garden.
Let the time come when both the earth and the sky will be our own.
Fairs will be held on the pyres of the martyrs every year and the names of those who die for the country will be perpetuated.

* * *

43.3

'IF BHAGAT SINGH AND DUTT DIE'

Leave off thy harsh treatment. O tyrant ruler;
In this way the pangs of heart will become incurable.
[Batukeshwar] Dutt, Bhagat Singh and [Jatindranath] Dass are the pride of the country;
Their lives will make the tree of freedom bloom forth.
If thou dost not hear the cries of the oppressed:
Do not think that God also will remain deaf.

Thou art proud of the fact that nothing can be done against thee;
And it does not matter if they die in the jail.
Remember, their sacrifice will cost thee dear;
And the Day of Judgement will come to India.
They will die of hunger and thirst;
O tyrant, thy jail will become Karbala [the site of an epic 7th century Battle, considered sacred by Shia Muslims].

Thy prestige will be destroyed because of this;
And thy head will be bent before other nations.
Their death will teach the lesson of martyrdom to the country:
And every child in India will come to know of pains.
Tyrants will dig their own deaths;
And unjustifiable tyranny will disappear from earth....
O tyrant, we will destroy the very existence of thy tyranny;
Whatever we say we will prove by doing it.

When the fire of our heart flares up in prayers, We will draw a deep sigh and burn thee.
Do not consider our weeping to be useless;
We will cause rivers to flow out when we begin to weep.
The hardships of the jail are nothing for us;
We will go even to the gallows for the sake of the country.
Our poverty should have serious consequences;
We shall destroy all signs of thee when we begin to curse.

There was a secret in our remaining still up till now;
We have now decided to fight and will show thee that we can do it.
If the goddess of Liberty asks for a sacrificial offering,
We shall consider it good fortune to offer our heads.

* * *

43.4

The master of the curved bow [Ram of the Ramayana] has been reincarnated.
The people of India will bring about the day of resurrection;
The followers of Veda and Quran have become so united.
They will break off all relations and rule for themselves;
While the whole world will look helplessly in their faces.
The revolving sky will upset everything in a minute;
And the bearers of titles and flags will be in the grave.
Such winds are blowing that they cannot be checked now;
Dwellers the realm of fancy should therefore remain quiet.
Gandhi has wakened now and all the pain and sorrows will be destroyed;
The master of the curved how has now been reincarnated.
Be careful, O Agha [Sir]! the people are becoming angry;
The owners of houses and palaces will be homeless now.

* * *

44

1930 ›› JAWAHARLAL NEHRU, THE EIGHT DAYS' INTERLUDE

Original: English
44.1: Excerpts from a speech
44.2: Statement made by Pandit Jawaharlal Nehru at his Trial at the Naini Central Jail on 24 October 1930

PUBLISHED BY THE JAWAHAR PRESS IN DELHI, THIS TWENTY-TWO-page booklet was issued after Jawaharlal Nehru's arrest in October 1930. The cover bore his portrait and a statement in his handwriting – 'Success often comes to those who dare and act; it seldom goes to the timid', bearing the date 29 December 1929. The book included a timeline of his activities from 11 October 1930, when he was released from prison, till 19 October when he was arrested again. In this whirlwind week, Nehru had visited Mussoorie, Dehradun and Lucknow, and addressed dozens of public meetings. The booklet consisted of statements issued to the press by him, on the boycott of foreign cloth and khadi, his message to people in the North-West Frontier Province, letters that he wrote in his capacity as Congress president, and a report (with excerpts) quoted from his speech at Allahabad on 12 October. The excerpts were translated from Hindi and published in this booklet with prefatory comments. Nehru spent nine years of his life in prison.

* * *

44.1

12 OCTOBER 1930

EXCERPTS FROM A SPEECH

THE BOOKLET REPRINTED EXCERPTS FROM A SPEECH MADE AT Allahabad at a public meeting on 12 October 1930. The first four paragraphs were reported in the first-person, and the last was a report of Nehru's words in the third person. Nehru gave the speech in Hindi at a public park. He had received information from the All India Congress Committee office that 40,000-50,000 people had been imprisoned for participating in the Civil Disobedience movement.

* * *

The success of our movement could well be gauged by the number and variety of the ordinances which are produced with regularity in the factories of Simla [the summer capital of British India]. The fact that this ordinance is the severest of all is in itself a sign that the British Government in India is getting in a bad way.

Indeed, the time had come when from the point of view of the British government every one of us should be a rebel. It is clear that India, big as it is, is not big enough to contain both the Indian people and the British. One of the two has to go and there can be little doubt as to which this is going to be.

The Congress to-day is the Indian people including every major and minor community. The Congress is not even Mahatma Gandhi, great as he is. When the Indian people decide otherwise, they can put an end to our movement or carry it on in any other form. It is because the Indian people have entrusted us with this duty and made us take a pledge and carry it out that we cannot be false to our pledge and our people.

If Lord Irwin or any of his colleagues want to know what the Indian people think, why do they not come down from their mountain tops and go to the bazaars and the fields and the factories, and watch the lathi charges, the atrocities on women and old men and children and the firing. No, they have chosen the other path of shutting their eyes to truth, suppressing it and deliberately preventing it from spreading by various ordinances and the like and then making a hysterical reference in praise of the police and the military. But we do not complain.

But let there be no mistake about it. Whether he [Nehru] agreed with him or not, his [Nehru's] heart was full of admiration for the courage and self-sacrifice of a man like Bhagat Singh. Courage of the Bhagat Singh type was exceedingly rare. If the Viceroy expects us to refrain from admiring this wonderful courage and the high purpose behind it, he is mistaken. Let him ask his own heart what he would have felt of Bhagat Singh had been an Englishman and acted for England.

* * *

44.2

STATEMENT MADE BY PANDIT JAWAHARLAL NEHRU AT HIS TRIAL AT THE NAINI CENTRAL JAIL ON 24 OCTOBER 1930

THIS WRITTEN STATEMENT WAS ISSUED BY NEHRU WHEN HE WAS charged with sedition, with instigating Indians not to pay taxes, and with offences under the Indian Salt Act.

* * *

For the fifth time I have been arrested and charged with various crimes by the officials of the British Government. For the fifth time, I have no doubt, I shall be convicted. I have so far taken no part in this trial and I desire to take none. But I wish to say a few words so that those who are trying me to-day and my own people, who have honoured me beyond measure, may have some glimpse of what I have in my heart.

I am charged with sedition and with the spreading of disaffection against the British Government. Eight and a half years ago I was charged with a similar offence and I stated then that sedition against the present government in India had become the creed of the Indian people, and to preach and practise disaffection against the evil which it represents had become their chief occupation, for the Indian people had come to realise that there could be no freedom for them, no lessening of the terrible exploitation which had crushed the life out of millions, till British rule was removed from India. Since this realization came upon me in all its tragic intensity, I have had no other profession, no other business, no other aim than to fight British imperialism and to drive it from India.

On the first day of this year the National Congress finally resolved to achieve the independence of India, and on the 26th of January the Indian people pledged themselves in their millions to put an end to British rule in India. They declared the age-long right of a people to subvert any government which had misgoverned and crushed them, and they charged the British Government with having exploited them ruthlessly and done them almost irreparable injury politically, economically, culturally, and spiritually. Since that pledge was taken, there can be no willing submission of any Indian to British authority, no recognition by him of British rule and if a few of us side with the enemy or parley with him while the fight in in progress, it is a terrible measure of the spiritual injury caused by British rule making them kiss the rod that smites them and hug the very chains that bind. Some of these misguided and erring countrymen of ours have chosen to desert the motherland in her hour of need and talk of compromises with British imperialism, but the country has chosen another path under the guidance and inspiration of our great leader, and that path it will pursue till success comes to it. There can be no compromise between freedom and slavery, and between truth and falsehood. We realise that the price of freedom is blood and suffering--the blood of our own countrymen and the suffering of the noblest in the land--and that price we shall pay in full measure.

Already the world is witness to the sacrifice and suffering of our people at the altar of freedom, to the wonderful courage of our women and to the indomitable spirit of our brave peasantry. Strong in the faith with which our leader has inspired them, with confidence in themselves and in their great cause, they have willingly set aside their material pleasures and belongings, and written a stirring and a shining chapter in India's long history. And the world has also seen how our peaceful struggle is sought to be crushed by frightfulness and methods of barbarism which have earned for the British Government in India a comparison with the Huns of old. Unlike the Huns, however, they have added insult to deep injury and have sought, after the manner of their kind, to cover their deeds of frightfulness with cloak of piety and sanctimoniousness. Fearful of exposure they have sought to suppress truth in every way. Those whom the gods wished to destroy they first drive mad, and all the mad deeds which the British Government has done in India during the last seven months – desperate devices of a tottering empire are visible emblems of the crash to come.

We have no quarrel with English people much less with the English worker. Like us he has himself been the victim of imperialism, and it is against this imperialism that we fight. With it there can be no compromise. To this imperialism or to England we own [sic] no allegiance, and the flag of England in India is an insult to every Indian. The British Government today is an enemy for us, a foreign usurping power holding on to India with the help of their army of occupation. My allegiance is to the Indian people only and to no king or foreign government. I am a servant of the Indian people and I recognise no other master.

The end of our struggle approaches and the British Empire will soon go the way of all the Empires of old. The strangling and the degradation of India has gone on long enough. It will be tolerated no longer, and let England and the world take notice that the people of India are prepared to be friends with all who meet them frankly as equals and do not interfere with their freedom. But they will be no friends with such as seek to interfere with their liberties or to exploit the peasant or the worker. Nor will they tolerate in future the humbug and hypocricy [sic] which has been doled out to them in such ample measure by England.

To the Indian people I cannot express my gratitude sufficiently for their confidence and affection. It has been the greatest joy in my life to serve in this glorious struggle and to do my little bit for the cause. I pray that my countrymen and country women will carry on the good fight unceasingly till success crowns their effort and we realise the India of our dreams.

LONG LIVE FREE INDIA!

Central Prison, Naini
October 24th, 1930.

JAWAHARLAL NEHRU

* * *

45

1930 ›› VIDYARTHIYON! [STUDENTS!]

Original: Hindi | Pamphlet

THIS PAMPHLET WAS ISSUED BY SHAMBHU NARAYAN DIXIT OF the Satyagraha Board, Farukkhabad and published by Agarwal Press, Kanpur in 1930. The entire pamphlet is reprinted here. Students were an important constituency in the late colonial period: revolutionaries courted them, the colonial state wanted to protect them from 'irresponsible' ideas, and anti-colonial mass movements needed their support to succeed. In a persuasive as well as imperative tone, the pamphlet appealed to the sense of honour of Indian students and taunted them (i.e. male students) with examples (not to be emulated) of eunuchs and bookworms, since 'even women' were on the field. I have translated it to English.

* * *

Mahatma Gandhi started the war of liberty on 8 April. It has been a whole three months since the Satyagraha movement was started, but we want to ask how much help you rendered this war for liberty! Aren't you ashamed by the enslavement of the country? Mahatma Gandhi, Jawaharlal Nehru, Patel, Motilal ji, don't the sacrifices of such people hurt your hearts. Swaraj, liberty, independence – do these country-wide slogans not enrage you? Mahatma Gandhi has clearly stated that he will either return with Swaraj, or my [his] dead body will be found floating on the ocean. This is the last statement made by that saint of truth that you should understand. Since then this oppressive government has carried out terrifying injustices in India, have carried out dictatorial measures in Dharsana, Bombay, Sholapur and Peshawar, carried out dark acts, treated women and children in an evil manner, heartlessly used whips, sticks and batons on them, crushed them under horses – don't these terrible events make your blood boil. Wherever in the world there have been battles for liberty, students have risked their lives to please the goddess of liberty. We believe that our Indian students are not cowards and eunuchs, such that during a dark period in which even our women are in the battle-field, they will remain bookworms and like [unclear] run away with fright from the battlefield. The resolution of complete independence had been passed only due to your insistence, and due to faith in you. Long-live Revolution [*Inqulab Zindabad*], Destruction of Imperialism [*Samrajyavad ka Naash*] - these heart-rending slogans given by hard-working youth - where have they gone? Were they only screaming machines. If not, then we pray that that the time has come that they [the youth] immediately abandon colleges and come and join in the battle-field. It is the highest duty of the youth to sacrifice themselves in the fight for independence under the Congress flag. That youth does not deserve to be called one whose heart is not aflame with the fire of patriotism. We urge all youth to offer their sacrifices to the Satyagraha movement. After abandoning colleges they will have to participate in the movement.

* * *

46

1930 ›› PARWANA [MOTH OF THE FLAME]

Original: Urdu
46.1: Excerpt from the Introduction
46.2: Letter no. 5554 of the Indian Republican Army stationed at Lucknow from (Major) Nur-ud-din, Officer Commanding, Indian Republican Army, Lucknow

IN FEBRUARY 1930, THE GOVERNMENT OF UP FORFEITED AN URDU pamphlet titled 'Parwana'. It was a collection of letters written to the Urdu newspaper *Mashriq* (Gorakhpur) and was edited by Muhammad Qurban Warsi, who had also written an introduction to the letters. The editor's introduction, as well as all the letters, criticized Congress policies and leaders in the harshest of terms, either by allusion, or by name, for negotiating with the British government on constitutional progress. It accused Congress leaders of inciting revolutionaries, who then made tremendous sacrifices. The editor's introduction to the letters employed a verse from the fourteenth-century Persian poet Hafez Shirazi to signal the futility of expecting loyalty from some people.

The view that the Congress was antagonistic to revolutionaries is one that has persisted to this day, and was certainly also current in the 1930s among some circles. Recent scholarship has, however, pointed out to overlaps and cooperation between these two streams (see context note to Part III of this anthology).

* * *

46.1

EXCERPT FROM THE INTRODUCTION

...This time or this period, which is hiding the world under its skirts, is a time of examination. Poor India is also passing through this period of test. This has been acknowledged by the Viceroy in his declaration and it is owing to his being impressed by the peculiar unrest and persistence in demands of this age that he wants to make such changes in the system of Indian Government as may make it adapted to the condition of the time and bring rest to hearts and quiet to politics. On the one hand is the Government and on the other a party of selfish, cowardly, shallow-hearted and hypocritical so-called leaders, who by their own shouting, have made themselves known as the representatives of the crores of ignorant, poor and weak common people. This showy party has incited the simple-hearted and enthusiastic young men to come to the front, where they may have to use the bombs and pistols, and from where they may go to the gallows and get long periods of imprisonment as their share.

Now that there is hope of getting something in exchange for these sacrifices and bloody presents, these loud-shouting leaders have left behind these dead and imprisoned unknown people and, like a criminal worshipping a tyrant Governor, have fallen at the feet of the Government in the hope of sitting on the thrones of governorship and attaining prominence in the legislative bodies. This, therefore, is a critical time both for the country and the Government. There is the danger that these selfish and cowardly people and so-called leaders will be taken by the Government for the true representatives of the people, be given high posts, and the changes in the Government of India may be made in the interest of their capitalistic advancement, while the crores of people inhabiting the villages are forgotten. Whatever changes the Government makes, it should always keep in view the welfare and happiness of the largest number of people. The Government should keep in view the real trouble in India and should think over the internal causes of disease. We are passing through the most important period of the present unrest and agitation. We should take those things with us which may help us during the onward march. At this time we must find out the true feelings, the true demands and the true internal facts.

These few letters are being collected today so that by reading them the people may be warned and may know that the shining glowworm of the freedom which they took for the burning candle of nationalism and around which they were falling dead like moths, has upon the approach of the dawn proved to be nothing more than an insect... These letters are like the telescopes which enable the ship to know the dangers ahead and to find out its way... At the end I wish to say that after reading these letters you should think over for yourself about the picture of Indian politics presented here and discover the illusion created by a few persons which hides a large amount of show, worship of self-interest and egotism.

O! thou who spendest nights and days with the hair
and the face of the friend;
Leisure is thine, for thou spendest pleasant mornings and evenings.
O! Hafiz, the habit of the beautiful ones is tyranny and oppression,
Who art thou that expectest faithfulness from this group?

* * *

46.2

LETTER NO. 5554 OF THE INDIAN REPUBLICAN ARMY STATIONED AT LUCKNOW

FROM (MAJOR) NUR-UD-DIN, OFFICER COMMANDING, INDIAN REPUBLICAN ARMY

To -- The Editor, the Mashriq, Gorakhpur

Sir, -- Young brothers! lovers of the motherland! Has not the time come when you should wake up and destroy your deluded leaders? If the time has not come, when shall it come? When you wake up and open your eyes you will be completely surrounded by the burning fire. For God's sakes be warned and kill these slavery-loving, moderate-thinking, cowardly leaders. These people have become absolutely useless. The English ghost has taken possession of their mind. They have never tried with a sincere heart to win freedom. They think slavery to be freedom and are contented with it. Their only criterion of freedom is that Indians should get a few high posts. They have always agitated for such trifles and have never tried to break the iron cage but have rather tried to strengthen it thinking it to be their nest. Ghalib says -

"My efforts are an example of an imprisoned bird's gathering of straws in the cage for building a nest."

These people have always given us the lesson of slavery until a young party (of which we also have the honour of membership) appeared, and had the attaining of complete independence as its aim. These people cared neither for their lives nor for their wealth and children but were always accustomed to proclaiming the truth loudly and fearlessly. As soon as this party came to the notice of these traitorous and reactionary leaders they began to burn with envy and anger and were much disturbed by the fact that the period of their leadership was to end now.... The leader of this party, Gandhi, spat poison against us on every occasion.... Our real aim is complete independence only. We are in love with it and can love nothing else...

* * *

47

1930 ›› PHILOSOPHY OF THE BOMB

Original: English | Pamphlet

THIS FAMOUS PAMPHLET WAS WRITTEN AS A RESPONSE TO Gandhi's criticism of revolutionaries' methods; it was written by Bhagwati Charan Vohra and distributed by members of the Hindustan Socialist Republican Association (HSRA) from January 1930 onwards. The historian Kama Maclean has recently revealed its pattern of distribution – much like bombs, the pamphlet was thrown into crowds; it was posted on walls and left abandoned for curious onlookers to pick up. In startling prose, the author demolished the stark, clear and water-tight opposition between 'violence' and 'non-violence' that then existed in both the official as well as the public imagination. Excerpts are reprinted here.

* * *

PHILOSOPHY OF THE BOMB

...It is hoped that this article will help the general public to know the revolutionaries as they are and will prevent it from taking them for what interested and ignorant persons would have them believe it to be.

VIOLENCE OR NON-VIOLENCE.

Let us, first of all, take up the question of violence and non-violence. We think that the use of these terms, in itself, is a grave injustice to either party for they express the ideals of neither of them correctly. Violence is physical force applied for committing injustice, and that is certainly not what the revolutionaries stand for. On the other hand, what generally goes by the name of non-violence is in reality the theory of soul force, as applied to the attainment of personal and national rights through courting suffering and hoping thus to finally convert your opponent to your point of view, When a revolutionary believes certain things to be his right, he asks for them, pleads for them, argues for them, wills to attain them with all the soul-force at his command, stands the greatest amount of suffering for them, is always prepared to make the highest sacrifice for their attainment, and also backs his efforts with all the physical force he is capable of. You may coin what other word you like to describe his methods, but you can not call it violence, because that would constitute an outrage on the dictionary meaning of that word. Satyagraha is insistance [sic] upon Truth. Why press, for the acceptance of Truth, by soul-force alone? Why not add physical force also to it? While the revolutionaries stand for winning independece [sic] by all the forces, physical as well as moral, at their command, the adocates [sic] of soul-force would like to ban the use of physical-force. The question really, therefore, is not whether you will have violence or non-violence, but whether you will have soulforce plus physical force or soul-force alone....

TERRORISM

The revelutionaries [sic] already see the advent of the revolution in the restlessness of youth, in its desire to break free from the mental bondage and religious superstitions that hold them. As the youth will get more and more saturated with the psychology of revolution, it will come to have a clearer realisation of national bondage and a growing, intense, unquenchable, thirst

The Hindustan Socialist Republican Association.

Manifesto.

THE PHILOSOPHY OF THE BOMB.

INTRODUCTRY.

Recent events, particularly the congress resolution on the attempt to blow up the Viceregal Special on the 23rd December 1929, and Gandhi's subsequent writings in 'Young India', clearly show that the Indian National Congress, in conjunction with Gandhi, has launched a crusade against the revolutionaries. A great amount of public criticism, both from the press and the platform, has been made against them. It is a pity that they have allalong been, either deliberately or due to sheer ignorance,misrepresented and misunderstood. The revolutionaries do not shun criticism and public scrutiny of their ideals, or actions.They rather welcome these as chances of making those understand, who have a genuine desire to do so, the basic principles of the revolutionary movment and the high and noble ideals that are a perennial source of inspiration and strength to it. It is hoped that this article will help the general public to know the revolutionaries as they are and will prevent it from taking them for what interested and ignorant persons would have it believe them to be.

VIOLENCE OR NON-VIOLENCE.

Let us, first of all, take up the question of violence and non-violence. We think that the use of these terms, in itself, is a grave injustice to either party for they express the ideals of neither of them correctly. Violence is physical force applied for committing injustice, and that is certainly not what the revolutionaries stand for. On the other hand, what generally goes by the name of non-violence is in reality the theory of soul-force, as applied to the attainment of personal and national rights through courting suffering and hoping thus to finally convert your opponent to your point of view. When a revolutionary believes certain things to be his right, he asks for them, pleads for them, argues for them, wills to attain them with all the soul-force at his command, stands the greatest amount of suffering for them, is always prepared to make the highest sacrifice for their attainment, and also backs his efforts with all the physical force he is capable of. You may coin what other word you like to describe his methods, but you can not call it violence, because that would constitute an outrage on the dictionary meaning of that word. Satyagraha is insistance upon Truth. Why press, for the acceptance of Truth, by soul-force alone? Why not add physical force also to it? While the revolutionaries stand for winning independece by all the forces, physical as well as moral, at their command, the adocates of soul-force would like to ban the use of physical-force. The question really, therefore, is not whether you will have violence or non-violence, but whether you will have soulforce plus physical force or soul-force alone.

OUR IDEAL.

The revolutionaries believe that the deliverance of their country will come through Revolution. The Revolution they are constantly working and hoping for, will not only express itself in the form of an armed conflict between the foreign government and its supporters and the people, it will also usher in a New Social Order. The revolution will ring the death knell of Capitalism and class distinctions and privillages. It will bring joy and prosperity to the starving millions who are sweating today under the terrible yoke of both foreign and Indian exploitation. It will bring the nation into its own. It will give birth to a new State—a new social order. Above all it will establish the Dictatorship of the Ploritariat and will for ever banish social parasites from the seat of political power.

TERRORISM.

The revolutionaries already see the advent of the revolutionin the restlessness of youth, in its desire to break free from the mental bondage and religious superstitions that hold them. As the youth will get more and more saturated with the psychology of revolution, it will come to have a clearer realisation of national bondage and a growing, intense, unquenchable, thirst for freedom. It will grow, this feeling of bondage, this insatiable desire for freedom, till, in their righteous anger, the infuriated youth will begin to kill the oppressors. Thus has Terrorism been born in the country. It is a phase, a necessary, an inevitable phase of the revolution. Terrorism is not the complete Revolution and the Revolution is not complete without Terrorism. This thesis can be supported by an analyis of any and every revolution in history. Terrorism instills fear in the hearts of the oppressors, it brings hopes of revenge and redemption to the oppressed masses, it gives courage and self confidence to the wavering, it shatters the spell of the superiority of the ruling class and raises the status of the subject race in the eyes of the world, because it is the most convincing proof of a nation's hunger for Freedom. Here in India, as in other countries in the past, Terrorism will develop into the Revolution and the Revolution into Independence, social, political and economic.

REVOLUTIONARY METHODS.

This then, is what the revolutionaries believe in; this is what they hope to accomplish for their country. They are doing it both openly and secretly and in their own way. The experience of a century-long and world-wide struggle, between the masses and the governing class, is their guide to their goal and the methods they are following have never been known to have failed.

Philosophy of the Bomb, HSRA Manifesto.

for freedom. It will grow, this feeling of bondage, this insatiable desire for freedom, till, in their righteous anger, the infuriated youth will begin to kill the oppressors. Thus has Terrorism been born in the country. It is a phase, a necessary, an inevitable phase of the revolution. Terrorism is not the complete Revolution and the Revolution is not complete without Terrorism. This thesis can be supported by an analysis of any and every revolution in history. Terrorism instills fear in the hearts of the oppressors, it brings hopes of revenge and redemption to the oppressed masses, it gives courage and self confidence to the wavering, it shatters the spell of the superiority of the ruling class and raises the status of the subject race in the eyes of the world, because it is the most convincing proof of a nation's hunger for Freedom. Here in India, as in other countries in the past, Terrorism will develop into the Revolution and the Revolution into Independence, social, political and economic.

* * *

PART IV: 1931-1940

&

PART V: 1941-1947

CONTEXT NOTE

THE COLONIAL STATE ATTEMPTED A DIFFICULT BALANCING ACT in the 1930s; it attempted constitutional reform with a view to allying with moderate nationalists, and at the same time dealt firmly with challenges to its authority, most dramatically during the Civil Disobedience movement (**1930–31**), which, as we have seen, commenced with the Salt Satyagraha in March 1930. By November of that year, almost 30,000 Indians were in jail for political reasons. About half were released immediately after the signing of the Gandhi-Irwin pact of March 1931.

Amidst ardent hopes and rumours of the commutation of their death sentences, the execution of three young and hugely popular revolutionaries – Bhagat Singh, Rajguru and Sukhdev – on 23 March **1931** provoked a wave of sympathy and immense anger from all parts of India. The material on these revolutionary-martyrs that was banned is enough to – and has – filled books all by itself (see also context note to Part III of this anthology).

Even as 'terrorist crimes' and assassination of government officials increased in the aftermath of the executions, the Government of India passed Emergency Ordinances, some impacting the press by giving officials enhanced powers of effecting seizures and imposing bans. Simultaneously, the impatience of many Indians with slower methods of negotiations with the British meant that revolutionary methods and approaches remained an attractive source of inspiration for many Indians. The Government of India Act of **1935** provided for elections to the provincial legislatures as part of provincial autonomy, and between **1937** and **1939** the Congress formed governments in seven out of the eleven provinces of British India. These Congress ministries resigned at the outbreak of the Second World War as a protest against India's inclusion in the war without a process of consultation.

Over 100,000 Indians were jailed for political activities in **1942** in the aftermath of the Quit India movement, launched by the Congress leadership in

August 1942 in the middle of the Second World War. Even as ordinary Indians took to the streets in violent as well as non-violent protests, Indian political leadership subscribing to different ideologies engaged in correspondence with the viceroy and provincial governors, placing their views on record. Two such examples, published as books, were banned: that of Gandhi (chapter 74) and Syama Prasad Mookerjee (chapter 72). The bans came a little too late, however, as excerpts had already been printed in newspapers. At the same time, critiques of colonial rule in India that were rooted in economic arguments were bolstered during war-time with arguments in favour of allowing Indians to decide their future course of action without reference to British aims and objectives. In February 1946, the Royal Indian Navy Mutiny, with an estimated 20,000 Indian participants from naval ships and shore establishments dotted all over coastal India, rattled the confidence of the colonial state. In this event we see – jumping from the page to the real world – many of the themes that were discussed in banned texts in the previous four decades: Indians' ardent desire for communal amity, racial and class equality, and a steely determination to shape their own future.

* * *

48
1931 ›› SHRI CHANDRA SHEKHAR AZAD KI JEEVANI [A BIOGRAPHY OF MR CHANDRA SHEKHAR AZAD]

Original: Hindi | Author: Baldev Prasad Sharma
Book Excerpt: Chapter 28 – 'Encounter with the Police in Allahabad and Life-Sacrifice'

THIS WAS PRINTED AT THE ADARSH PUSTAK BHANDAR, BENARAS [Varanasi] as part of a 'Pocket Book Biography' series. Reprinted below are excerpts from the last dramatic chapter, which I have translated into English. These books – inexpensive and written in accessible style – were considered dangerous by the state on account of their popularity and mass reach.

* * *

On 27 February at around 10 am two revolutionaries [Azad and Sukhdev Raj] had an encounter with police personnel in Allahabad's Alfred park. The result of this was the attainment of martyrdom of the famed revolutionary Pandit Chandrashekhar Azad....

The Superintendent [CID; John Nott-Bower] stopped his motor and asked the people something from a distance of about 10 yards. Both got their pistols our and started firing. The Superintendent saw them do this and fired before they could fire. But some people say that Azad was the first to fire. The Superintendent sahib says that perhaps his bullet hit Azad's feet. Because he could not rise. The Superintendent's second bullet probably hit his [Azad's] body. His companion got up rapidly, fired, and ran away. Till this time one Superintendent and two constables constantly fired bullets at them. The Superintendent was loading his pistol. At this time, Azad fired at his left arm. The pistol fell on the ground. Then he [the Superintendent] hid behind a tree. Azad too crawled behind a nearby tree. At this time Thakur Visheshwar Singh (Deputy Superintendent CID) reached behind a shrub about 40-50 yards away and fired towards Azad. Azad fired and the bullet hit Visheshwar Singh's face.

Superintendent sahib got injured on his arm. That is why he could not shoot. But Azad was constantly firing. In the end, Azad lay supine. It is said that he shot himself because of lack of ammunition/ missing a shot ['goli chook jaana' in the original could reference either possibility.]

By this time a crowd had gathered at some distance. At that point some unknown person (we have got to know that it was a constable) reached there with his weapon. Superintendent Sahib suspected that perhaps Azad was fooling the police. He asked the unknown person to fire at the dead Azad. That person did so. Then the Superintendent believed for sure that Azad was dead. Then he approached Azad. By this time other police personnel had also reached the site. They found 448 notes and some rupees with Azad.

16 bullets and 22 empty cartridges were found there. After this the body was sent for post-mortem. Members of the public asked for the government's permission to bury the body, but the body was not given. It is said that the public was told by officials that the body would be buried in Daraganj but in the end it was buried in Rasoolabad.

Some people say that there was not one but two people with Azad. The police had been following them since Benaras [Varanasi]. At the time of the shooting, there was only one person with Azad. Azad had purposely removed that person from there. He said that I will go to the mouth of death. You run away.

It is said that at the time of the incident a student was going on a bicycle. An unknown person showed him a pistol and asked him to hand over the bicycle. The police is following me. That boy was terrified and disembarked and the unknown man disappeared with the bicycle.

The CID Superintendent Mr Blunden [it is not clear who exactly is referenced here since the CID Superintendent was Nott-Bower] himself praised the spiritedness of Azad. He said that he had rarely come across such a true marksman. Especially in such tense circumstances. Especially when bullets were rained down upon him from three sides. He also accepted that if the first bullet had not pieced his [Azad's] thigh then not a single police officer would have returned alive. Because Mr Nott-Bower's hand was already useless. He said that Azad was a famous leader, perhaps the commander in chief, of the revolutionary group.

An eyewitness said that the tree behind which Azad sacrificed his life was laden with flowers and many visitors had written 'Azad park' on many places on the tree. The place where his blood fell. It is said that college students have taken away that soil.

* * *

49

1931 ›› CULT OF VIOLENCE

Original: English | Pamphlet

THIS THIRTEEN-PAGE PAMPHLET WAS PROBABLY PUBLISHED IN 1931/1932 and did not bear any information about the author or publisher. Gerald Barrier interpreted it as an 'attack on non-violence'. This pamphlet was a thinly veiled attack on Gandhi, ironically referred to as 'Great Man', for the Gandhi-Irwin pact in the context of the execution of young and hugely popular revolutionaries (see the previous two context notes in this anthology). The irony of censorship is that the colonial state's desire to stem the circulation of a document inciting violence also meant that cracks within various segments of the national movement were also hidden from sight of the Indian public.

It began with a verse from Shelley's Mask of Anarchy (also quoted in Nehru's *Glimpses of World History*).

* * *

Cult of Violence
War for War.
and Peace for Peace.

And at length when ye complain
With a murmur weak and vain
'Tis to see the Tyrant's crew
Ride over your wives and you—
Blood is on the grass like dew.

In the world's history of revolutions cult of Violence has been the only means to bring about success, peace and happiness to the weak, poor and oppressed. The philosophical study and interpretation of the word confirms its importance and effecacy [sic] not as a general principle of revolutions, but in everyday life of a human being, in a nation and even in Nature....

Be Aware!

ntence of GENERAL BHAGAT SINGH result in slaughter of British Officers.

Wake up! Wake up! O! youths of India, sons of BHARATMATA. Time has come! Make an end of British Beauracracy. The Punjab is clamouring for BHAGAT SINGH. Will Bengal go unrevenged? Don't forget! your Beloved BINAY! Every drop of BHAGAT'S Blood will produce thousands and thousands of BHAGAT SINGH.

Let not your SARDAR. The Light of Freedom be hanged up, before you lay your IRON HANDS on TEGART and············to quench the thirst of—

"Bharatmata"

Long live Bhagat Singh.

Commander-in-chief
Indian revolutionary Party
(Atishi-chakkar)
Calcutta (B. B. Branch)

Leaflet banned by the Government of Bengal in February 1931. Source: Home Political (Proceedings), file 114, 1932.

Beware of the cult that harbours cowardice and hypocrisy in its fold. Beware of the capitalists who suck poor peoples blood.

Let not the British soldiers come with boyanets [sic] at your doors ere you think of extricating yourself from their meshes. Raise all what is left with you. Unite hands and press forward. Live a free man or die the death of a martyrs. Remember the day in Jalianwala [sic] Peshawar and Sholapur, the sad fate of the martyrs. Remember tha [sic] day when people laughed and the Greatman [sic] with a smiling face signed the bloody documents of 'Truce' at a time when our young comrades, Bhagat Singh, Rajguru and Sukhdev were wreathing with agony of death on the scaffold. A 'Truce' was signed with the cordial shaking of hands at the cost of three brave Patriots. Such was the spirit of Patriotism that was exhibited.

NOTIFICATION.

No. 3722P.—27th February 1931.—In exercise of the power conferred by section 99A of the Code of Criminal Procedure, 1898 (Act V of 1898), the Governor in Council hereby declares to be forfeited to His Majesty all copies, wherever found, of a leaflet in English commencing with the words "Be aware" and ending with the words "(Atishi-Chakker) Calcutta (B. B. Branch)", on the ground that the said leaflet contains matter which brings or attempts to bring into hatred or contempt and excites or attempts to excite disaffection towards the Government established by law in British India, the publication of which is punishable under section 124A of the Indian Penal Code.

R. N. Reid,

Chief Secy. to the Govt. of Bengal (offg.).

Ban Notification. Source: Home Political (Proceedings), file 114, 1932.

Surely amids merriment of the Hypocrites and even on the smiling face of the Great man there was written in bold and bloody letters -"A Traitor." They all felt it. He felt it too. They sold us for a piece of bread which was thrown towards them and for nothing else.

Forward-Forward O, ye Comrades and resort to *Bombs* and *Pistols*. Gird on thy sword and rush to fame and laurels. Make every foe your target and death your motto. Let those who may court starvation misery and death come in your fold. Let every corner of the Indian soil be the grave of martyrs or the haven of a Free Nation. Let every citizen be a rebel and every hut a rebel's shelter. Let every drop of Indian blood be paid with streams of English blood.

Revolt! Revolt, and thou shalt reach the goal.
"LONG, LIVE REVOLUTION."

* * *

50

1931 ›› INQULAB ZINDABAD [LONG LIVE REVOLUTION]

Original: English | Pamphlet
Poem

THIS PAMPHLET, WITH AN URDU TITLE THAT HAD BY NOW BECOME a popular revolutionary slogan, vividly captured the mood of extreme anger after the execution of Bhagat Singh, Rajguru and Sukhdev.

* * *

THEY ARE ALL THIRSTY. THEY WANT BLOOD

Bhagat Singh, Rajguru and Sukhdev they are not with us. They have been murdered -- murdered by the exploiters and paid agent of British capitalist. In their prime of life they have been forced to leave this world to make the capitalists comfortable. Why were they illegally and brutally murdered? Because they exposed the true character of the British Imperialism to the world, they tried to show the naked and treacherous picture of the mock parliament of India. They tried to give voice to the voiceless oppressed, starved millions of their country. They tried to do away with the exploiters. Youth of the country cannot tolerate more and so they revolted against the enemies of India. Like the Punjab, Bengal also paid the penalty. Bengal lost many of her brave and worthy sons. Remember our brave comrades Benoy Krishna, Bimal and Anuja Sen Gupta [Bengali revolutionaries who had been executed or died during their missions.] What did they do? They have taken the extreme vengeance [sic] and fought bravely to the last blood. The country was thirsty for and they quenched her thirst. Non-violence [sic] will not help in any way. We want blood for blood. We rejoice at their extreme sacrifice. History tells that freedom was conquered by bloodshed in the past and the same should be repeated in our present struggle.

Inqulab Zindabad.

THEY ARE ALL THIRSTY.

THEY WANT BLOOD

Inqulab Zindabad.

Push their ideas of revolution among the mass. Collect arms and explosives. Be up with them. Silence the autro cities [sic; atrocities] of the dogs. Kill indiscriminately the enemies of freedom, the betrayers and the traitors. And make them to know that India is not for Imperialism.

LONG LIVE OUR RED COMRADES.

* * *

51

1931 ›› LAGAN BAND KAR DO [STOP PAYING TAXES]

Original: Hindi | Leaflet

THIS WAS A ONE-PAGE LEAFLET IN HINDI ISSUED BY THE UNITED Provinces' Congress Committee in 1931. As with publicity material from the early 1920s, it explained the aims of the Congress movement in very simple terms, and urged landlords and peasants to work together (in keeping with the idea that class antagonisms among Indians could wait to be resolved till after the defeat of the British). I have translated it into English.

* * *

Why is the Congress fighting with this government?

Because this [government] is sucking the peasants, making them impoverished and enslaved.

By stealing from the peasants it is giving income to the British and people who welcome them, to waste as their salaries.

This has become an excuse to monopolize trade and take India's wealth abroad.

Under the pretext of establishing peace, women are being dishonoured. Innocent children are being oppressed. Innocent children, preservers of peace, are being subject to cruelty. Taking the pretext of fines and taxes, each house is being looted.

The extent of the terrible oppression is such that few countries in the history of the world can match them. The police has established a self-willed raj.

This is peaceful raj!! Compared to this, even Ravan Raj [the antagonist in the popular Hindu epic Ramayana] will appear as Ram Raj!

This is why, peasants, beware!

What should each peasant and zamindar do in order to defeat this government?

No peasant or zamindar should give even one pice [smallest denomination of money] as tax or land revenue.

Whatever troubles you have to suffer—endure beatings, taste bullets or lose everything—accept this with happiness and bravery.

The government indulges in its revelry on the basis of our money. The way to finish it off is to deprive it of money.

This is why, whether in the form of land revenue or in any other form do not pay any kind of tax to the government.

To give this demonic government tax or to help it in any respect is to assist in evil-doing.

Stand with the thousands of brothers and sisters who are filling the jails and meditating there, and help them bring Swaraj closer.

Do not pay taxes so matter what problems you face!

CHAIRMAN
United Provinces Congress Committee

* * *

52

1931 ›› MAN MOH LIA LANGOTI WALE HAS HAS KE [THE MAN CLAD IN LOIN-CLOTH WON OUR HEART WITH A SMILING FACE]

Original: Punjabi (Urdu) | Pamphlet

THIS WAS A PAMPHLET IN PUNJABI LANGUAGE IN THE URDU SCRIPT. It was edited by Hans Raj 'Safri' and printed at the Arjan Press in Amritsar. It was declared forfeit by the Government of Punjab in June 1931. Though the title referred to Gandhi, who had adopted the loin-cloth as his uniform by this time, the poem went on to discuss several traumatic events and important martyrs of the anti-colonial movement from 1919 onwards. It also suggested measures that ordinary Indians could take to challenge colonial rule. One verse is reprinted here.

* * *

The man clad in loin-cloth has won our heart with smiles.
(He) has permeated us with the blood of freedom.
The mother-Bharat is weeping bitterly.
She is making herself miserable by weeping.
The alien does not at all take pity.
He strikes with violence.
The Indians are dying of starvation.
(But) the aliens are enjoying themselves.
Young men are rotting in jails.
Handsome young men, after getting implicated.
Gandhi, Malaviya [Madan Mohan] and Patel [Vallabhbhai]. They are playing a strange game.
They say, 'O, brethren! Fill each and every jail laughing.
Master Mota Singh, the leader, [1888-1960; Punjabi revolutionary leader imprisoned several times]

The Commander-in-Chief of young men,
The old lion and a friend of India,
He was bound tightly.
O, brethren! If you want swaraj "Don't forget my request.
Work the spinning-wheel in every home.
This is what I tell you."
Further I will relate the story of what befell us,
(They) killed the nation's real gems.
The handsome Lajpat (Rai) who was brave (lit. young) like a lion.
The dishonest people beat the lion.
He received blows (lit. marks) from *lathis*.
On the day on which he died of *lathi*-blows
Every child and every old man of India wept.
Tears began to trickle from eyes.
Handsome Rajpal, the Chief
He was the Jathedar [cleric/leader] of Bharat Bal (Sabba).
He was thrown into the tank.
They fired bullets at Peshawar, [23 April 1930; killing of estimated 400 unarmed protestors]
Killed Hindu and Mussalman brethren,
Put the unarmed people to death.
They caught several innocent youths and put them in jails
They fettered them tightly.
Those who preserve the honour of the country are not un
nerved by death,
They put the nooses round their necks laughing.
Bhagat Singh the handsome leader
(And) Rajguru and Sukh Dev his two friends
The national generals, were stung to death
Ah! The enemies brought their enmity into play.
After powdering the salt they sprinkled it on the wounds.
They shot an arrow right into the liver.
The lamp of India has been extinguished,
The green garden has become desolate.
The brand of separation has been stamped on India's forehead.
If you (Government) show a little compassion to them
(And) had not hanged them,
You would have been honoured by the whole world,
The Jallianwala (Bagh) has not been forgotten

(Where) blood ran in a stream.
O Indians! come to your senses even now, O Young saplings of Bharat Mata
Place (your) heads on your palms laughing, O brethren.
O brethren! If you want to take revenge,
Do not use foreign cloth at all,
Work the spinning-wheels,
Fire the balls of thread
Put off the collar of slavery from your necks.
O Safri (the poet) this is the only remedy for removing the stigma of slavery,
Raise your voice in a chorus

* * *

53
1931 ›› SARDAR BHAGAT SINGH – A SHORT LIFE SKETCH

Original: English | Author: Jitendra Nath Sanyal
53.1: Book Excerpt: Chapter VI – 'The Saunders Murder'
53.2: Book Excerpt: Chapter VIII – 'The Assembly Bomb Outrage'
53.3: Book Excerpt: Chapter XIII – 'The Executions'

THIS BOOK, WRITTEN BY AN ASSOCIATE OF BHAGAT SINGH, WAS priced at two rupees. The first edition was of 1,000 copies and was printed at the Fine Art Printing Cottage, Allahabad – the publisher-printer of the banned journal *Chand* (to which Bhagat Singh had been an important contributor; see chapter 40). It was published in May 1931, two months after Bhagat Singh's execution. Excerpts from three of the most dramatic chapters in this book are reprinted here.

The scholar Chaman Lal who has collected and popularized Bhagat Singh's writings, credits Bhagat Singh and his associates with changing the vocabulary – and therefore the underlying assumptions – of anti-colonial nationalism in India. The replacement of the slogan 'Bande Mataram' with 'Inqulab Zindabad' is, to his mind, a change at the level of consciousness, as a slogan steeped in religious values was replaced by one speaking of revolutionary values.

Bhagat Singh came from a family that simultaneously housed loyalists as well as opponents of the British Raj. His visit to the Jallianwala Bagh at the age of twelve changed his life. Another turning point came with his dissatisfaction with Gandhian methods after the termination of the Non-Cooperation movement in 1922. An avid reader, he also wrote for *Pratap* and *Arjun* (in Hindi) and the socialist journal *Kirti* (in Punjabi and Urdu).

* * *

Banned Bhagat Singh Martyrology Poster.

53.1

'THE SAUNDERS MURDER'

No sooner had Bhagat Singh and his party left the D.A.V. [Dayanand Anglo Vedic] College Boarding House [after the murder of Saunders], the police appeared on the scene in full force, surrounded the boarding house, began to search every nook and corner, and blocked all exits and entrances. Not only that. Strong police force was posted on all roads leading in and out of Lahore, the railway stations became full of C.I.D. men, and all young men leaving Lahore were carefully scrutinized. But the three young men [Bhagat Singh, Rajguru and Azad] frustrated all the attempts of the police and safely got away from Lahore.

The stratagem that Bhagat Singh adopted was as clever as it was bold. He dressed up as a young government official, adopted a big official name, put labels of that name on his trunks and portmanteux, and in the company of a beautiful lady, entrained a first class compartment at the Central Railway Station in the face of those very C.I.D. officials who were specially deputed to arrest the assassin of Mr Saunders. He had a fully dressed orderly in the person of Rajguru, with the inevitable tiffin-carrier in his hand; of course, all were fully armed for any emergency.

Chandra Shekhar Azad adopted a simple method. He got up a pilgrim-party for Muttra [Mathura], with old ladies and gentlemen, and in the capacity of a Brahmin Pandit in an orthodox style, escorted them, -- and himself -- out of Lahore!

* * *

53.2

'THE ASSEMBLY BOMB OUTRAGE'

On the eighth of April, 1929, the royal city of Delhi witnessed one of the most colourful spectacles that it is ever destined to see, when two representatives of the Hindusthan [sic] Socialist Republican Association entered unnoticed the Assembly Chamber and threw two bombs towards the seats occupied by Government Officials. With deafening noise the bombs exploded and covered the room with dense smoke. The benches near which the bombs fell were broken to pieces, and a portion of the floor was also hollowed out. But, except for a few minor scratches, no one received any injury.

The scene presented by the Assembly Chamber immediately after the explosions beggars descriptions. There was a rush towards the adjoining room where gallant members fled as if pursued by the very devil. It was reported that even the lavatories were not free from these gentlemen who sought refuge in every nook and corner of the building.

Amidst these mirthful scenes a few members remained unnerved, foremost amongst whom were Pandit Moti Lal Nehru, Pandit Madan Mohan Malaviya and as truth must be spoken, Sir James Crerar [Home Member of the Viceroy's Executive Council]. The visitors' gallery also presented a deserted appearance. But lo! towards these official benches, midway between the central gate and the ladies' gallery could be seen two young men, undaunted and calm, as if diving deep into a vision of the future! They are the two historic figures, Sardar Bhagat Singh and Sj. Batukeshwar Dutt....

We want to emphasize here the fact that there was ample opportunity for both of them to make good their escape, if they so desired. It was part of a deliberate plan that they calmly surrendered to the police and thereby consciously and willingly offered themselves for that terrible penalty which was inevitable after the commission of an act of that nature.

* * *

Banned Bhagat Singh Writing Pad.

53.3

CHAPTER XIII

'THE EXECUTIONS'

From early in the morning on Tuesday, the 24th March, there was seen to be great commotion among the people in numerous towns all over the length and breadth of India. The news spread like wild fire that Sardar Bhagat Singh and his two comrades had been executed. All the morning newspapers came out with glaring headlines, some with black borders, announcing the news to the people. It was found out that Sardar Bhagat Singh, Sj. Shivaram Rajguru and Sj. Sukhdeva were hanged to death in the Lahore Central Jail at 7.33 pm, on Monday, the 23rd March. Loud shouts of "Long Live Revolution" were heard from inside the jail fifteen minutes before and after the executions.

The manner of death was full of that bravery and tranquility which were Bhagat Singh's own since his childhood. While mounting the scaffold with his two comrades who were as unperturbed as Bhagat Singh himself, Sardarji addressed the European Deputy Commissioner who was present to witness the executions, and said with a smile on his face -- "Well Mr. Magistrate, you are fortunate to be able to-day to see how Indian revolutionaries can embrace death with pleasure for the sake of their supreme ideal."

As soon as the Privy Council had failed, a powerful and well-organized movement was started to get the sentences commuted. Though the public may not be aware of it, Mahatma Gandhi made a sincere attempt to save them from gallows. Young men and women took a leading part in organising demonstrations to impress upon the Government that the hangings would have very bad effect on the people of India. Never in the history of British India had there been such a widespread and genuine demand for the commutation of the sentences. Even in England the movement was gaining ground. It was stated that even the Viceroy had felt the influence of the public opinion in this matter. This was exactly as Bhagat Singh desired.

Then the truce, which was regarded by the young party as nothing but surrender, came in; the Congress leaders suddenly suspended the mass-movement; the Government heaved a sigh of relief and then--calmly carried out the death sentences. Yes, this was exactly as Bhagat Singh desired. Was Providence also siding with Bhagat Singh in his efforts to score the last glorious point over his adversaries?

As we have stated, the hangings and the subsequent events fully justified the expectations of Sardar Bhagat Singh and others. Sardar Bhagat Singh hanged has proved much more useful for the younger party than Bhagat Singh alive. As Pt. Jawahar Lal so beautifully expressed -- "...... But there will also be pride in him who is no more. And when England speaks to us and talks of settlement, there will be the corpse of Bhagat Singh between us lest we forget, lest we forget!"

In a last letter to his younger brother Kultar Singh, whom he dearly loved, he wrote --"In the light of dawn, who can withstand destiny? What harm even if the whole world stands against us? ... Dear friends, the days of my life have come to an end. Like a flame of candle in the morning, I disappear before the light of the dawn. Our faith and our ideas will stir the whole world like a spark of lightening. What harm, if this handful of dust is destroyed!"

* * *

54

1931 ›› SHAHID-E-WATAN [MARTYRS OF THE HOMELAND]

Original: Hindi | Booklet
Poem

IN MAY 1931, THE GOVERNMENT OF BENGAL DECLARED FORFEIT this Hindi booklet published in Calcutta. The poem reprinted here reserved its wrath not for the British, but at Indians who collaborated with them.

* * *

O traders of Calcutta, give up ruining yourselves.
Give up importing cloth from England.
Either give up foreign cloth or give up calling yourselves Hindu
Give up getting your nose cut with your own hands.
Come into field if you have got any manliness.
Give up running away, hiding your face
Or putting your tails between the legs.
Of what use if you become a Knight or a Rai Bahadur [an honorary title]
Give up being called a Mir Jafer or Jaichand. [18th century and 12th century historical figures accused of collaborating with the British and Ghurids respectively]
If you cannot do then do not cause any harm
and do not put thorns on our path
Even now nothing spoilt do not allow yourselves to be picketted.
Give up getting the honour to your mothers, sisters and daughters
being sallied [sic].
Give up getting yourselves spat at, clapped at, barked at, at every door
Give up blackening the faces of your men folks.
This is the desire of "Bharatendu" that welfare lies in consenting
And not on passing knives over the necks of your brethren.

* * *

Mr. Raj Guru, S. Bhagat Singh and Mr. Sukh Deva hanged
सर्दार भगत सिंह और उसके मित्रों की फांसी
Arorbans Press, Lahore.
No. 1302

Banned Martyrology poster.

55

1931 ›› VIRLAP

Original: Punjabi (Gurmukhi)
55.1: Dialogue between Bhagat Singh and [Batukeshwar] Dutt
55.2: Dialogue between Mother India and Bhagat Singh

THIS WAS A PUNJABI PAMPHLET BANNED BY THE GOVERNMENT OF Punjab in 1931 for being seditious. The pamphlet was written by 'Comrade' Amar Nath Ahluwalia, p resident of the Nau Jawan Bharat Sabha [an organization to which Bhagat Singh and Azad had also belonged], Ferozepur City. It was printed at the Sanatan Dharam Steam Press, Lahore.

* * *

55.1

DIALOGUE BETWEEN BHAGAT SINGH AND [BATUKESHWAR] DUTT

Dutt - How are you doing, Bhagat Singh?
Bhagat Singh - My blood increased by a seer when I heard of my impending execution.
Dutt - O brother! Your separation has wounded my heart.
Bhagat Singh - O my beloved Dutt! Don't weep I shall send for you soon.
Dutt - O Bhagat Singh! I will die weeping for you.
Bhagat Singh - O my dear Dutt! Accept my last salutation.

* * *

भगत सिंह और उसके साथी स्वर्ग में लेजाए जा रहे है
Bhagat Singh & his companions being carried to paradise
No. 1304.

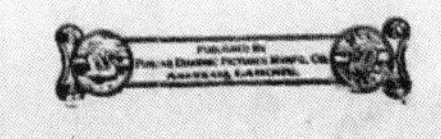

ارورڈ بنچ پریس انارکلی لاہور بلاک بنانے اور چھاپنے والے

Banned Martyrology poster.

55.2

DIALOGUE BETWEEN MOTHER INDIA AND BHAGAT SINGH

Mother India - When my "Moon" [a term of affection] disappears, darkness will spread all over the world, O people!

Bhagat Singh - O mother! This "Moon" of yours will illumine the whole world.

Bhagat Singh - We will swing on the gallows as people do in swings in the rainy season.

Mother India - O son! Your sacrifice will cast asunder my bonds.

Bhagat Singh - I mother! Let me sleep in peace, do not wake me up now.

Mother India - O son! Your execution will break the chains of India.

Bhagat Singh - I will be reborn a lakh of times for the liberation of India.

Mother India - O people! I bred and brought up the lion but (Lord) Irwin put him in a cage.

Bhagat Singh - O mother! When your lion roars the whole of England will shake. Let one lion die and lakhs of lions will take birth in his place.

* * *

56

1931 ›› BHAGAT SINGH KIRTANAMRUTAM [BHAGAT SINGH: SWEET HYMNS]

Original: Tamil | Author: V. Nataraja Pillai
Book Excerpt

EXTRACTS FROM THIS TAMIL BOOK WERE INCLUDED IN A DOSSIER prepared by the Government of India to indicate the kind of books and articles that were published all over India in 1931, which were either prosecuted or for which warnings were issued. Kama Maclean has included this among her list of literature that claimed that Bhagat Singh was innocent of the charge of political assassination.

* * *

...When (an) unparalleled (crowd of) people gathered under the leadership of Lajpat (Rai) for the purpose of discarding, without welcoming, the Simon Commission that arrived at the beautiful (city of) Lahore, in the year (19) 28, a white Sergeant assaulted Lajpat deeming it to be a proper opportunity and Lajpat, the virtuous soul, lost (his) life consequence. Bhagat Singh, the great hero of the Punjab, who was grieved and moved very much by this, cried aloud shedding tears and threw a bomb on the exalted Indian Legislative Assembly, having understood the real policy of Englishmen. As he was arrested and held responsible for the serious (crime of) murder, having been deemed to be the person that killed the simpleton, Saunders, whose end was ordained by Brahma, he renounced his life on earth in a tender age and disappeared....

In spite of the great Mahatma having sent a letter to the godly Irwin, gone to him on an errand like Krishna and interviewed him in person for (the purpose of) getting (them) acquitted of the charge of murder, the black-hearted man refused to grant (the request) and, as decided (by him), issued orders for the hanging of the three persons, who were not afraid of even the God of Death. Thereupon, owing to (their) broad outlook, they ascended the gallows and cheerfully kissed the treacherous rope, wishing prosperity for the Empire....

Martyrology poster banned in April 1931. Source: Home Political file 116, 1932.

Is there (a person) on earth like Sirdar Bhagat Singh!... He was the son of Sirdar Krishna Singh; he was a great person that did not care for his own interest. He was an excellent and virtuous person who gave up his life for (his) motherland. He was fortunate in having acquired now the name of the hero of the Punjab. He was a highly devoted son of Goddess Bharata.

He is a martyr who gave up his life for the land of Bharata. He was a shrewd person who was not afraid of the Court, confinement in the cruel prison and the firing of the gun on (him). He was a bold person that stood foremost in the intensity of the thirst for liberty in the world. He was a beautiful person who promoted the war of revolution with perseverance and in a valiant manner.

As Lala Lajpat, who was the leader at Lahore, was hit hard on his chest by a white, he departed (from the world) quickly so that the celestial world

NOTIFICATION.

No. 8084P.—22nd April 1931.—In exercise of the power conferred by section 99A of the Code of Criminal Procedure, 1898 (Act V of 1898), the Governor in Council hereby declares to be forfeited to His Majesty all copies, wherever found, of a picture of Sardar Bhagat Singh, Rajguru and Sukdeva with a heading "Tin Sahid" (Three Martyrs), on the ground that the said picture contains matter which brings or attempts to bring into hatred or contempt and excites or attempts to excite disaffection towards the Government established by law in British India, the publication of which is punishable under section 124A of the Indian Penal Code.

R. N. Reid,

Chief Secy. to the Govt. of Bengal (offg.).

Ban Notification. Source: Home Political file 116, 1932.

might prosper and (Bhagat) Singh pondered over (this) false dealing and felt enraged.

Setting (his) heart on living only after getting rid of the unjust cruelty perpetrated under the English rule, he threw a bomb on the exalted Indian Legislative Assembly and thereby became guilty of a serious crime.

...They conducted false cases (against him) on the ground that he killed Saunders who got bewildered, and arrested the illustrious Sukhdev and Rajguru as well.

Even the excellent persons, who administer justice on righteous lines, charged the patriotic heroes, that resembled the Trinity, with the serious crime of murder and inconsistently passed a sentence of hanging. (These are) cruel persons of the Kali age [a mythological dark era]. Is this creditable?

* * *

57

1932 ›› SENTHAMIL DESIYA GEETHAM [PURE TAMIL PATRIOTIC SONGS]

Original: Tamil | Author: T.K. Durai Rajan
Book Excerpt

THIS WAS A TAMIL BOOK AUTHORED BY T.K. DURAI RAJAN IN 1932. The author as well as the keeper of the press, P.R. Appadurai Mudaliyar (Saravanabhava Press, Madras) and the publisher, Venkatakrisha Mudaliyar, were all prosecuted under section 124A, even though they were not considered by the Government of Madras to be of 'more than provincial importance'. As was often the case, the translator was a native speaker – C.N. Saravana Mudaliyar, Tamil translator to Government. The pan-Indian appeal of revolutionaries did much to cement ideas of national belonging, a sentiment which the British had claimed Indians lacked.

* * *

Is it not enough that (we) have become enslaved to foreigners? Should there be a quarrel about the wearing of khaddar cloth?

(This is) a tyrannical government. In this, poverty is increasing beyond bounds and plenitude is disappearing....

They killed the three lions among patriots and left (the people) in excessive grief. (They killed the three lions and) made the people of the world feel greatly agitated, roar and shed tears and our loving devotees suffer much with mental anguish. (They killed the three lions and) thereby made (their) parents agonize, the people of the vast world weep aloud and the learned persons feel greatly agitated and anxious and stand with tears in (their) eyes.

Our Bhagat Singh, who had an undaunted mind, felt greatly agitated on learning that Lal Lajpat, the victorious lion of the Punjab, died only because he was beaten with a lathi by the merciless and wretched Police so as to make him die and threw a bomb in the Legislative Assembly which confers no benefit. In view of this offence, they sentenced (him) to transportation for life and, confining (him)in prison on that day in a cruel manner, hatched a big conspiracy.

The rude and highly fraudulent Police accused our Rajguru, Bhagat Singh and Sukhdev, the valiant persons, who had resolved to sacrifice their lives solely for the country, of having murdered two persons and the unjust and cruel demons hanged the princes, refusing even the prayer of the faultless saint Gandhi.

Which is the law that warrants (one) being charged with an offence without (any) evidence? Does (this) become the glorious British rule? Is (it) proper for the government to do so?

The whites, who practice fraud and who are highway robbers, (killed the three lions)....

Why, is this misery suffered not yet sufficient? Is the harm caused by the cruel wretches inconsiderable? Should there be a quarrel about the wearing of khaddar cloth? Will not the words uttered by Gandhi, the supernal person having mystic powers, enter (your) ears?

He is a bold person that entered prison which is a place of penance. He is a hero that performed penance there at all times.

O highly courageous sons of Mother Bharata! O friends of India! Why should (we) feel sorely distressed on earth, in spite of (our) having been born as heroes that win victory in the war?

Is it not enough that (we) have remained in bondage for so many days? Could (we) not attain happiness by realizing at least hereafter the significance of the words of the saint Gandhi, who is Deemed to be a supernal person having mystic powers, and wearing pure khaddar dress, which will secure victory. If we remain dispirited, the western wretches will make us suffer much misery on earth.

Not a little is the trouble caused by hypocrites. In order to estimate its extent, realise the significance of the elegant words of Durairajan of Tanjore and give up seeking the help of those that are guilty of the five heinous sins....

He (Mr. Gandhi) is an incarnation that has appeared for getting rid of the bondage of our Indians, who fear that they have no other support. He is a highly renowned and glorious person that has achieved victory in securing harmony by fearlessly going to prison and following the principle of non-violence.

He asked our motherland, which is drooping and pining, to take to spinning in order to attain happiness. If (we) turn the hand spinning-wheel (we) may secure self-government which is our government.

* * *

58
1932 ›› BRITISH ADALAT BAHISHKAR DIVAS [BRITISH COURTS' BOYCOTT DAY]

Original: Hindi | Poster

THIS ONE-PAGE HINDI POSTER, ISSUED BY SATYAGRAHA SANGRAM Benaras, was banned in 1932 by the Government of UP as it was deemed to be seditious, since it questioned the very basis of rule of law on which colonial rule claimed to rest. I have translated it into English.

* * *

22 October 1932
Saturday
British Courts' Boycott Day

Courts are one of the tricks which the bureaucrats have used to suck the blood of the country. The whole country knows very well that nothing happens in these courts except injustice and oppression. These courts house deceit and lies. Lakhs and Crores of our brothers have been caught in the trap of these courts, have lost every penny that they had, and have now been reduced to begging. If you have any intelligence at all, curse these vampire-like courts and sort out your internal family conflicts within the family. If you are not able to sort out your internal conflicts, ask the elderly to form *panchayats* and sort out these matters. You will save money, not face any problems, and keep your honour intact as well. Establish panchayats in every village and never make the mistake of going to courts. Eliminate from society as well as from the body-politic the poison of the games of courts.

Leader
Satyagraha Revolution,
Kashi [Varanasi]

* * *

59

1932 ›› PANDIT M.M. MALAVIYA'S STATEMENT ON REPRESSION IN INDIA UPTO APRIL 20, 1932

Original: English | Booklet

THIS THIRTEEN-PAGE BOOKLET WAS PUBLISHED BY PANDIT Govind Malaviya, Secretary to Madan Mohan Malaviya. Malaviya (1861–1946), was associated both with the Indian National Congress and the Hindu Mahasabha, and had founded the Banaras Hindu University in 1916. Malaviya stated that he had compiled a summary of government repression of the Civil Disobedience movement till April 1932. As his source he had used reports published in 'the most prominent newspapers of the country which are being published under a rigid censorship of news'. His summary was credible because it 'presents the picture as it has been appearing in the public press with the tacit permission of the Government.' Malaviya further stated that any news that could not be confirmed be omitted from his account, and the estimates it gave were 'quite conservative'. The period it covered was 1 January 1932 till 20 April 1932. The numbers as well as descriptions of harassment of anti-colonialists were indeed provocative.

* * *

In the very nature of things, it [the summary] cannot be exhaustive nor can it convey to the reader a full idea of the brutality, the meanness and the revolting nature of the acts of repression which Government agencies and officials are inflicting upon the men and women of my country under the unholy protection of the Ordinances now in force in India.

TOTAL ARRESTS

During this period, according to reports published in newspapers, arrests made all over the country in connection with the Civil Disobedience movement total 66,646 which includes 5,325 women and many children...

anyone familiar with the conditions in India today will readily agree that arrests all over the country may safely be assumed to be over 80,000.

PAROLE ORDERS

372 persons including editors, lawyers, doctors, professors, merchants and respectable wealthy citizens were arrested and then released on parole with orders asking them to submit to humiliating conditions which generally required them to report themselves at the police station every day....These orders brought ridicule upon and disgust against the Government in the public mind...

FLAG SATYAGRAHA

There have been 496 reported cases of flag satyagraha in different parts of the country where people were arrested merely because they wanted to hoist, display or honour the National Flag. On many such occasions the police have made lathi-charges injuring several persons. An innocent thing like the tri-colour Indian National Flag has become to the Government officials what a red rag appears to a bull and they have gone about suppressing it with the stupid tenacity of the same animal. Inspite of this, the flag is flying in numberless places in the country.

JAILS PACKED

Inspite of all these arrests, every type of activity under the Civil Disobedience movement in continuing and people in an endless stream are offering themselves for arrests...Temporary camp jails have been set up. But all this has not sufficed to cope with the rush of incoming political prisoners.

TREATMENT IN JAILS

Widely respected persons, well-to-do citizens habituated all their lives to ease and luxury have been put in the C class like ordinary felons.*...the treatment meted out to them should be a blot upon any civilized government... But the worst treatment has been given to women prisoners. They are ill-treated and harassed. In one case a group of twelve of them in a lock up was severely beaten with lathis, kicks and fists and some of them were stripped naked....

FIRING

Besides these lathi charges there have been at least 29 cases in different parts of the country where fire was opened upon unarmed and unresisting people. If an impartial enquiry were to be made, I believe that in almost every one of these cases it would be proved that the firing was unjustifiable and uncalled for, and was the outcome of a vindictive desire to punish the people for their defiance of authority and to strike terror in their hearts....

HOUSE SEARCHES

633 cases are reported where houses of individuals have been searched, in many cases on the flimsiest grounds...

CONFISCATIONS

There have been 102 cases where properties have been attached for participation in the Civil Disobedience movement...

FINES

It appears to be the general policy of the government to impose heavy fines on persons who are convicted in connexion with the movement... In some cases fines of Rs.10,000/- were inflicted. In a recent case a fine of Rs.20,000/- has been imposed.

PRESS GAGS

On the top of all of this, the public press has been gagged as it had never been gagged before. 163 cases have been reported where newspapers and public presses have been interfered with by orders for confiscations, demands for securities and consequent closing down of the presses, warning, searches, and arrests of editors, printers or keepers....

ACTS OF REPRESSION

...Students have been expelled from educational institutions and magistrates have awarded stripes to boys of tender age... Women pickets have been caned, and, as a milder measure, drenched with dirty water. Political prisoners have been kept chained in groups. Men pickets have been rendered unconscious by beating....

PART PLAYED BY WOMEN

...Almost every important centre has had women presidents or dictators of local Congress Committees. The present Acting President of the All-India Working Congress Committee is a lady. Women have been conducting the movement almost everywhere and have borne the brunt of it with magnificent courage and fortitude. Young girls and old ladies who have never before come out of their houses to join any cause however important or sacred, have thrown off their veils in large numbers and have walked into the active ranks of the workers of the Civil Disobedience Movement. They have exposed and are exposing themselves to inconveniences, indignities and suffering with a cheerfulness which extorts admiration.

MUSLIM PARTICIPATION

The propaganda that Musalmans as a whole have kept aloof from the movement is not to be accepted without qualification. During these three months, the All India Congress Working Committee has had two Musalmans as Acting Presidents. More than one province have had Musalmans as their Provincial dictators, while many towns and villages have had Musalmans as local dictators. The total number of arrests mentioned above includes several thousand Musalmans, and while it is true that they have largely kept away from the movement, a considerable section of them have stood shoulder to shoulder with the Congress.

DETERMINATION OF THE PEOPLE

...All the repressive policy of the Government has not succeeded in cowing them down. It has failed in its avowed object of crushing the Congress... If proof were needed, these three months have furnished it that it is the Congress alone which can speak in the name of the country and that no settlement or reform can have any chance of success in India unless it is accepted by the Congress.

*[*After the fatal hunger strike of Jatin Das in Lahore Central Prison, a system of classification of prisoners was introduced. Prisoners of 'higher status and habits' were placed in A and B classes. Ordinary convicted felons were category C. Those who were involved in offences involving moral turpitude or violence were classed as B. Malaviya stated that of the 80,000 only a few hundred were in A or B, despite assurances given by the Home Member.]*

* * *

60

1932 ›› RASHTRA KO RASHTRAPATI KA SANDESH [THE PRESIDENT'S ADDRESS TO THE NATION]

Original: Hindi | Author: C. Rajagopalachari | Pamphlet

THIS TWO-PAGE PAMPHLET WAS THE HINDI VERSION OF AN ENGLISH pamphlet that had already been banned a week prior. It was banned by the Government of UP for being seditious. C. Rajagopalachari (1878–1972) – later to be independent India's only Indian governor general, and still later a critic of the Congress party after independence – issued this in his capacity as president of the Congress during Gandhi's absence on account of being jailed. The statement's power lay in his ability to convince ordinary Indians to contribute in a variety of practical ways to the nationalist cause. I have translated it into English.

* * *

...Those who believe that it is not possible for them to enter the battlefield as soldiers, I want to tell you that in one sense the key lies in your hands. I appeal to you to help us from your present location. I want to explain your tasks to you in five points.

1. Do not be afraid. Do not worry about the tasks that you do because of the orders of your conscience.
2. Protect the honour of the Congress. Help the smallest of Congress workers with compassion. To refuse them will be utter cowardice and hazardous for social unity.
3. Carry out a campaign for Swadeshi and Prohibition [avoiding intoxicants] among people. This kind of service is your right and is completely different from the political fight. There is no need to stop one for the sake of the other.
4. Do not buy a shred of foreign cloth. Nobody can force you to buy British goods even if you are a clerk in a government office. Stop using things for which you do not find Swadeshi equivalents.

4. Use khadi instead of other kinds of cloth. Stop using fine cloth under all circumstances.
5. Do not use imported cosmetics. The price that shopkeepers charge you for these goes to the government in the form of toll/tax.

* * *

61

1932 ›› A WORD TO COLLEGE AND UNIVERSITY STUDENTS

Original: English | Author: Sampurnanand | Pamphlet

THE GOVERNMENT OF UP HELD THIS PAMPHLET TO BE SEDITIOUS and banned it. Sampurnanand (1891–1969) was a votary of Hindi (versus Urdu) propagation and cultural revivalism; he was a Congress Socialist who went on to serve as education minister in the Congress-run Government of UP in 1937. A teacher himself, he went to have an illustrious career in independent India, serving as the chief minister of UP (now Uttar Pradcsh) and governor of Rajasthan. In contrast to the other appeal to students published in this anthology (see chapter 45), Sampurnanand calmly summarized hundreds of years of Indian history in order to make his case. He suggested a range of options to students so that they could become part of the movement that was sweeping India at the time. The pamphlet is reprinted in full.

* * *

Gentlemen,

I believe I need not offer you an apology for encroaching upon your time and attention with this letter, although no one regrets more than myself that it should have been necessary for me to write it.

You know the present political state of the country and the stages which have led up to it, Taking advantage of the temporary and inevitable chaos which conditioned the breakup of the Moghal Empire, the British established their rule in the country and for the first time in its long and chequered history, subjected it to a foreign domination which has lasted for over a century. We have been hypnotised through a systematic course of false and misinterpreted history into believing that for the last one thousand years India has been under the heel of foreigners. But this is false. There have been foreign conquerors and ruling dynasties of foreign origin but the Slaves, Khiljis, Tughlaqs, Lodis and Moghals became a truly Indian as the Rajputs,

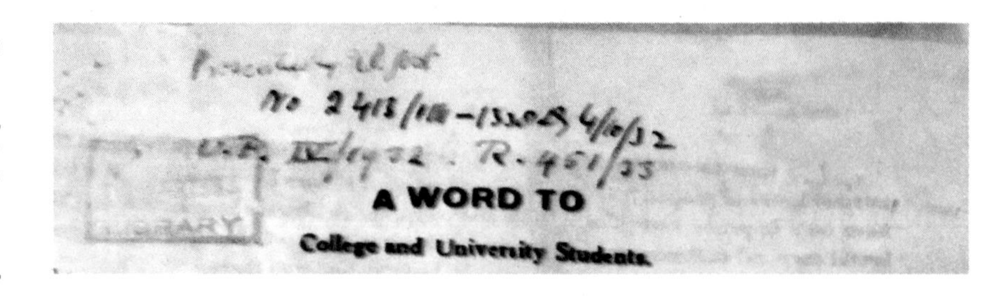
A WORD TO

College and University Students.

the Sikhs and the Mahrattas indisputably are. India has no more been under continuous foreign rule than England under her Norman and Stuart kings and the rulers of the Houses of Orange and Hanover. But all the resources of the State have been mobilized with a view to convince Indians of their own utter incapacity for self-government and the miserable state of the country before the fortunate advent of the British and, unfortunately, the attempt has met with remarkable success. Every device, educational and political, was adopted that could be trusted to prevent a sentiment of national solidarity from growing among us. Hindus and Muslims were set by the ears and every effort was done to reduce India to a mere geographical expression.

But, in the face of all these adverse circumstances, the country has proved itself sound at heart. It has not acquiesced in its servitude and has always struggled to gain its liberty. 1857 and 1921 are important landmarks in our history, not so much for what they achieved but for what they attempted. The memories of 1931 are green in the mind of the youngest amongst you. You know how the truce was undermined and then broken by the Government, how the ordinances were forged in a period of profound peace and how Lord Willingdon [Viceroy after Lord Irwin], by his impertinent refusal to see Mahatmaji [Gandhi], precipitated the present struggle, for which the Government had carefully prepared themselves. You know how they thought they would be able to crush the movement within a fortnight and you know how signally they have failed. The struggle has now gone on for over nine months and the end is not yet in sight. There have been lathi charges and firings. Men and women, in their thousands, have courted imprisonment and cheerfully borne the terrible losses of property which the realization of fines has entailed. We who have been in prison know the terrible hardship, the deliberate humiliation and the brutal corporal sufferings which political prisoners, many of them persons of good social standing and education like yourself, have to undergo there.

Does all this leave you cold? Are the sufferings and indignities heaped upon your country men and country women of no concern to you? Does it not strike you that the threat of the Government to crash the Congress is really a threat to crush you, for the Congress is a symbol for all that is manly and self-reliant, all that refuses to kow-tow to the foreigner, in Indian life. You are preparing yourselves for one career or another, but is any career, howsoever lucrative, worth much when you are a slave, when the greatest amongst us is nothing but dirt under the feet of the lowliest among Englishmen. Does not your education teach you to rise above considerations of mere self? Others, men and women, are working for the country's liberation. Will not you? You have youth and education -- Yours is the privilege and the duty to fight for your liberty. You know what young men in other countries have done and are doing. What explanation will you offer at the bar of world opinion to-day, and of posterity to morrow, for your supineness at this juncture. Do you not realize that, even if we fail?

'Tis better to have loved and lost
Than never to have loved at all.

Does not your reading of history give you faith in the ultimate victory of our righteous cause?

There are a number of ways in which you can serve. We want men, men of your calibre, as volunteers and organisers. We want money, the sinews of war. And there is one little sacrifice, negative in nature but of vast potentiality, which all can make. You can give up the use of foreign cloth and of British goods -- stationery, perfumery, toilet requisites, bicycles, motor cycles, cigars and cigarettes, cutlery and articles of food like biscuits, preserved fruits and the like. The giving up of these things may involve some little discomfort but surely you will not grudge this. We live in stirring times, as the Acting President of the Congress recently observed. Such opportunities of service as these times offer are rare in the history of nations. Those who avail themselves of them are thrice blessed.

Will you not join the ranks to-day and do what lies in your power -- and I am sure there is no one who can not be of some service -- to further our cause?

SAMPURNANAND
Acting President,
Hind Provincial Congress Committee.

* * *

62

1932 ›› WATAN DE LAL [RUBIES OF THE HOMELAND]

Original: Punjabi (Gurmukhi script) | Author: Kavi Panchhiji | Pamphlet

THIS WAS A PUNJABI PAMPHLET WRITTEN BY KAVI PANCHHI JI OF Sialkot; the publisher was Lahore-based and the pamphlet was printed at the Sanatan Dharam Steam Press, Lahore. It was forfeited by the Government of Punjab in April 1931, for contravening section 124A of the Indian Penal Code. All documents containing its copies, extracts, reprints and translations were also declared forfeit.

* * *

Those who have sacrificed themselves for their country do not absolutely fear death. Raj Guru, Bhagat (Singh) and Sukh Dev went to the gallows willingly. By becoming dear ones of the country they sacrificed themselves for the sake of their country. They bore lakhs of hardships, they stepped forward to die. Many heroes have been seen in India who placed their heads on the palms of their hands. They are staunch to their religion, and die willingly. Those who believe in death have tied the Gana (a sacred thread tied round the wrist of bridegroom at the time of marriage) of death on their wrists (or) wearing the dress of a martyr ride on the mare of death.... The sons of mother India (Bharat Mata) played their part well. They make a true bargain. On the day when they were sent to the gallows none of the three were afraid. Those who have learnt the Lesson of freedom put their heads on the palms of their hands. The first said that it was his turn (to go to the gallows). The second said that he was already standing ready. The third raised shouts four times. They went to the gallows smiling. Before breathing their last, they in order to show to the tyrant, went to the gallows with a smile saying that he should tighten the noose as much as possible because the fate could not be altered. They uttered there [sic] words before dying which awakened sleepy India. They sang the song of mother India (and therefore) all the people praise

Mr. Raj Guru, S. Bhagat Singh and Mr. Sukh Deva hanged
Arorbans Press Lahore.
No 1302

Martyrology poster banned in April 1931. Source: Home Political file 116, 1932.

them. What an act of oppression has been committed, for which the public shed tears profusely. Our light has been extinguished. The clouds of wrath are rising. The tyrants after practising great oppression and killing innocent people are deceiving the injured hearts. Have you noticed their new piece of work? They burnt the dead bodies on the banks of the river Sutlej after cutting them into pieces. They introduce new systems. The tyrants have committed a crime. They have killed them by trickery.

They were sent to the gallows but the dead bodies were not returned. The mother of Bhagat Singh says that his parents are dying of grief. The executioners will die of themselves; the public is in mourning for them. The sister says weeping, O brother! You have left me after striking an arrow of separation. O brother! You have pierced my liver. Hearts are palpitating. No sooner did Bhagat Singh's younger brother see the letter, than he felt a burning feeling in his heart (and cried) that although he was alive his feelings were dead because of his being sorrowful for his brother. Your oppression has reached its zenith. India is tired of you. You should leave India now because the Indians do not fear you.

NOTIFICATION.

No. 8750P.—30th April 1931.—In exercise of the power conferred by section 99A of the Code of Criminal Procedure, 1898 (Act V of 1898), the Governor in Council hereby declares to be forfeited to His Majesty all copies, wherever found, of a picture portraying Rajguru, Bhagat Singh and Sukdeva on a triple gallows with nooses round their necks and two European officers in uniform on either side, on the ground that the said picture contains matter which brings or attempts to bring into hatred or contempt and excites or attempts to excite disaffection towards the Government established by law in British India, the publication of which is punishable under section 124A of the Indian Penal Code.

R. N. Reid,

Chief Secy. to the Govt. of Bengal (offg.).

B. G. Press—1931-32—1454G—600.

Ban Notification. Source: Home Political file 116, 1932.

* * *

63

1934 ›› ZULMI SARKAR [DESPOTIC GOVERNMENT]

Original: Hindi | Pamphlet
63.1: Poem No. 1
63.2: Poem No. 2

THIS HINDI PAMPHLET WAS PUBLISHED IN PESHAWAR IN 1934. THE author was listed as 'ek jail pravasi' (a resident of jail). The definition of Aman Sabhas was given in the official translation itself. While the first poem, claimed to be written by someone who had been to jail, rebelliously defied the claims of British authority, the second one chastised the British and questioned their claims to legitimacy in every possible way.

* * *

63.1

POEM NO. 1

We shall show you our valour by offering our head to the motherland,
We shall break repressive laws and kick them aside.
If you are proud of your Police and the Captains of the Army,
They will also deceive you at the very eleventh hour.
We shall fill the jails or get them locked,
We shall take our meals only after turning you out of India,
You may stop the newspapers and Telegraphic connections,
Or you may start Aman Sabhas (Associations to counteract N. C. O. or C. D.
[Non Cooperation or Civil Disobedience)
but this battle will not be stopped.
Tell us what more you can do!
We shall get you out from Surat [the site of the East India Company's first factory in the 17th century] with your bag and baggage,
Where you have entered first, the same gate you will have to pass by.
We shall show to the world by making India independent.
We shall hoist the National Flag with the help of Gandhi's army.

--One who was jailed.

* * *

63.2

POEM NO. 2

1. Oh! This is a tyrant Government, don't allow it to remain any longer.
2. We won the German war [First World War] by giving men and money, And in return we got the Rowlatt Bill and the Jalianwalabagh as rewards.
3. Lalaji [Lajpat Rai] was belaboured with lathi and ultimately was done to death, He was the greatest amongst men and the soul of India.
4. Who imprisoned even the President of the Nation [M.M. Malaviya, Congress President in 1933], And who could also chastise Sen Gupta [Nellie; an Englishwoman who served as Congress President] and Babu Subash [Bose].
5. He, who is the best of mankind and the Crown of India, Such Mahatma Gandhi was also imprisoned without consideration.
6. The thieves and dacoits may carry on their plundering raids with immunity But the patriots of the country are arrested and made the victims of lathis and gunshots.
7. Who ordered firing on the unarmed crowd, Hundreds were killed at Peshawar [1930] by gunshots.
8. Which is belabouring the whole of Indian subject, And is bent upon to enforce despotism.
9. By ruining our trade we have been enslaved, We are being looted in broad daylight by the imposition of several kinds of taxes.
10. Our spinning wheels are broken, thumbs chopped off, and we have been made poor, They have massed a lot at the cost of India.
11. We have been weakened by creating dissensions and thus rendered helpless, Under the shelter of justice they have made their trade prosperous.
12. The wood may rot and the grass may be burnt, But this rogue will not allow us to use the same without payment.
13. Seventy-five lakhs of cows are being slaughtered every year [this was an emotive issues for some Hindus, who considered cows sacred], See, how this land, depending solely on agriculture, is going to dogs.

14. Oh! there was a time once, when streams of milk and ghee used to flow here,
    But now cocogem [hydrogenated oil from vegetables] and vegetable are used in abundance.
15. They ride in motors and make merry themselves in bungalows,
    While crores are dying here for want of food, clothes and shade.
16. It is held to be an offence to touch even the God-gifted salt and the jungle,
    We are not treated even as insects and are kicked.
17. The mode of expression of mind, the pen and the mouth, are locked,
    Oh! this monkey has rendered India worst [sic] than the jails.
18. High posts have been reserved for the English as if it were their hereditary right.
    We, the sons of India, are called blackmen and coolies.
19. Gur, cotton, wheat and grain is exported by them,
    And in exchange they dupe us by giving us iron, needles and toys, etc.
20. Howsoever non-violent we may be, they repress us,
    We are being belaboured with lathis mercilessly.
21. Being the descendants of Guru Govind, Pratap and Shivaji [legendary historic heroes from North, North West and West India, respectively],
    Say how long we, of a warrior class, should bear beating like helpless?
22. Enough of tolerance! the culminating point of forbearance has reached,
    Oh! wise men, why are you sitting silent?
    Fie on us, who prefer to live like eunuchs!
23. Give up liquor, break down the bottles and break the laws,
    Stop all co-operation, they will be perplexed.
24. No one should purchase even the foreign rags,
    Oh! sons of India, be independent and dauntless.
25. Your ancestors are looking at you with hopeful sight,
    Such times seldom come.
26. Get up! either, make it independent and let the fame of India be known,
    Or for its sake sacrifice your body, wealth and life.
27 Death is doomed and all will be left here,
    Why then Sunder, you should miss the opportunity?

* * *

64
1935 ›› CONGRESS SOCIALIST PARTY MANIFESTO

Original: English and other languages | Pamphlet

THIS TWO-PAGE PAMPHLET LISTED JAYAPRAKASH NARAYAN OF Kashi [Varanasi] as the publisher. Jayaprakash/Jai Prakash Narayan (1902–1979), or JP, as he came to be called in independent India, was a political theorist, activist and one of the founders of the Congress Socialist Party. This was formed, initially within the Congress, in opposition to communal (religion-based) parties and elements, and had both alliances and ruptures with the Communist Party of India. After Independence, JP became a popular campaigner for land redistribution and against corruption. He was imprisoned during the colonial period as well as in 1975 during the Emergency, both times for the same reason: being an outspoken critic of the government.

This manifesto, effective because of its simplicity as well as for its clearly stated goals, was declared forfeit by the Government of Bihar and Orissa for contravening section 124A and 153A of the Indian Penal Code. The entire manifesto is reprinted here.

* * *

WHAT AND WHOM DO WE STAND FOR?

We stand for a Society in which only those who work -- with their brains or hands, in the fields or the factories-shall enjoy the fruits of their labour.

We do not want a Society in which a few oppress and exploit the many. We do not want a Society of landlords and capitalists and Princes.

We stand for the destruction of these classes. We want that society should consist of a single class-the class of the workman.

We stand for a scientifically ordered and planned society, with social welfare as its basic objective, free from exploitation, and greed, oppression and ignorance, poverty and unemployment, social and economic injustice, and inequality.

We stand for the abolition of private ownership of productive wealth -- lands, forests, mines, mills, banks, etc. We want these to be owned by the whole people and worked entirely for their benefit. Wealth is socially created and most be socially owned and consumed.

We stand for the poor, the exploited, the downtrodden the rackrented peasant, the peasant who groans under debts, the worker who scarcely gets enough to live, the white collar slaves— the *babus*.

We stand for bread for all, for comfort, for a rising standard of living.

We wish that the poorest of the poor in the country should have enough to live decently, a clean and cultured home, clothes, books, means of amusement and recreation.

We wish that every adult should find gainful occupation or maintenance for himself; every child should be able to get full education; social amenities should be equally available to every one.

To make all this possible, we want freedom of India from British suzerainty and the transference of power to the Indian masses, in a Workers and Peasants Republic.

Till this is done, there shall be for us no burying of the hatchet, no truce, no retreat.

All India Congress Socialist Party.

* * *

65
1935 ›› RAVIPATI KAMESWARA RAO, ROUND TABLE ROYABHARAM [THE ROUND TABLE NEGOTIATIONS]

Original: Telugu | Book Excerpt

THE GOVERNMENT OF MADRAS BANNED THIS BOOK IN MARCH 1935 under the terms of the Indian Press Act of 1931. The use of several metaphors and proverbs by the author made his message both vivid and persuasive. He described for his readers in very simple terms concepts such as the social contract and the operation of colonial difference, whereby the colony and the metropolis were subject to different norms and laws. Excerpts are reprinted here.

* * *

It is our part to give sixty crores (of rupees); but, it is the British people's part to enjoy the fruit thereof. It is our part to earn money by hard labour; but it is the White Dorais' [masters'] part to loot (it). It is our part to suffer hardships in jails; but it is Englishmen's part to live in palaces. It is our part to bear terrible lathi charges; but it is their (the British people's) part to make ordinances. Unless they (the British) thus have the full military authority in their hands, how can their part be realized? Is not the adage that the cock which has been accustomed to eat always would got [sic] upon the top of the house and begin to crow, true?....

Whosoever may tender any number of counsels, would this British Government try to lend its ear to them and consider them? In the past, did Duryodhana heed the advice of persons like Bhishma [Characters from the epic Mahabharata]? Did Ravana heed the words of Vibheeshana (his brother) [characters from the epic Ramayana]?....

The system of Government must always be such as would please the people, Otherwise, it cannot last long. This (consummation) has become impossible under the administration of foreigners. It could never have been like this, if the Government had belonged to Indians. Would be (the Britisher) punish relentlessly in this fashion his countrymen and brethren? Would he not find out their wishes in a friendly manner and full them?....

... Would an elephant in rut yield to good words without a severe stab of the goad being administered to it? Unless the powerful cobra is bound by a spell, would it not fall (upon people) unfurling its hood and hissing? How can a rheumatic patient be cured of his trouble except by the administration of brands with red hot iron? Similarly would this British Government which has been ruling in defiance of 35 croree of people ever become humble and yield except by means of Satyagraha?

* * *

66
1935 ›› SILVER JUBILEE

Original: Urdu | Poster

THE GOVERNMENT OF PUNJAB BANNED THIS CYCLOSTYLED poster in Urdu. The complete text of the poster is reprinted here. Colonial rule in India rested on pomp and show, signalled most grandly by grand durbars in the late nineteenth and early twentieth century. Events significant in the reigns of the royal family in Britain were celebrated in India. This poster, issued by the Communist Party of India in Punjab, listed a catalogue of the sins of the colonial state in a sarcastic tone. It overturned the colonial state's definition of loyalty. To celebrate the silver jubilee of an unjust king was to be disloyal to one's own country.

* * *

Silver Jubilee of the King Emperor – the King Emperor under whose orders hundreds of innocent and unarmed Indians were made targets of machine-guns in Jallianwala Bagh, the King Emperor under whose orders the tyrannical and bloody Dyer, who brought the machine guns into action in the Jallianwala Bagh, was granted a pension of £100 a year, the King Emperor under whose orders lakhs of people were confined into jails in 1920-22, lakhs of children were ruined, and modesty of lakhs of women was outraged, because they cherished love for their Motherland. Silver Jubilee of the King under whose orders Indians were governed by the sword and gun from 1922 to 1929, and every person who raised a voice of protest against it was put to death. Silver Jubilee of the King under whose orders Bhagat Singh, Raj Guru and Sukhdev were hanged and their associates were sent to the Andamans and sentenced to long terms of imprisonment simply for the reason that they loved their country. Silver Jubilee of the King under whose orders hundreds of youths were hanged in other parts of the country and thousands were sent to the Andamans and lakhs were still rotting in jails because they loved their country. Silver Jubilee of the King under whose orders lakhs of young men are still rotting in jails without any fault. Silver

Jubilee of the King who, by means of the Communal Award, has divided the country into small communal groups and has, thereby, tried to crush the national movement for ever. Silver Jubilee of the King under whose orders unarmed crowds were fired at in Karachi. Silver Jubilee of the King because of whome [sic] lakhs of widows are mourning their husbands' death, lakhs of mothers are feeling restless on account of their sons and lakhs of orphans are weeping for their parents and shaking the heaven with their sighs. Silver Jubilee of the King in whose reign crores of labourers are living the life of animals inspite of their having been born in the house of human-beings and crores of peasants are yearning for bread inspite of producing food-stuff for the whole world. Silver Jubilee of the King in whose reign patriotism is considered to be a great sin and treachery to the Motherland a benevolent act. Silver Jubilee of the King Emperor in whose reign devastation and destruction are rampant every where and who has ruined all the Indians. Can any one celebrate the Silver Jubilee of the King Emperor, who can indulge in merry-making on such occasions, except the traitors and enemies of the country? Those who do not raise their voice against these celebrations are also traitors and toadies no matter whether they be Congressites. We wish to avenge the Jallianwala Bagh (tragedy) and (the execution of) Bhagat Singh and (the firing at) Karachi.

Inqilab. Inqilab. Inqilab.

Be ready for revenge. O youths of India! The day is near and the cup of sins is now full to the brim. Shout "Silver Jubilee Boycott", "King Emperor Murdabad", "Hindustan Zindabad", "Mazdur Kisan Zindabad" "Inqilab Zindabad", "Communist Party of India Zindabad."

COMMUNIST PARTY OF INDIA,
Punjab Branch

* * *

67
1936 ›› TWO TELUGU BOOKS

Original: Telugu
67.1: Book Excerpt: *Trotsky Jeevitamu* [Trotsky's Life]
67.2: Poems from Karmika Bhajanvali
  67.2.1: 'Cooly!'
  67.2.2: Narta Venkateswara Rao - 'Is There God or is There No God?'

* * *

67.1

TROTSKY JEEVITAMU [TROTSKY'S LIFE]

IN JUNE 1936, THE GOVERNMENT OF MADRAS INVOKED THE INDIAN Press Act of 1931 to ban *Trotsky Jeevitamu*, written by Dintakurti Bhaskarraju. The passages deemed objectionable were a call to arms to students.

Are we not witnessing all this in our young students who are turning out to be so many living corpses, so many pale lifeless slaves to white dogs, having lost their national wealth, eminence and prestige by virtue of their contact with the administration of the present British Government?... Why should our Indian students join Government colleges? Is it to carry on righteous administration or to maintain white dogs?....

Do you see what unbearable atrocities are being perpetrated at the present day in Government schools? When will the sacred and prosperous soil of India be free from the troubles of the Western system of education and when will Indian students shine with new life?.... Should one live in prisons which are bad, lifeless and dark? Is it valour to stay in prisons which are but abodes of deceit, roguery, cruelty and wealth?.... Should heroes who desire freedom, go to jail? They must either cut their enemies and drink the blood of the latters' hearts like valiant heroes, or they must give up their lives on the battle field....

If the Government do not agree to carry on the administration in accordance with the wishes of the people, we must subdue the Government even by shedding our blood profusely....

Is it proper to go to jail patiently in the name of Satyagraha? Having gone to jail, should one nicely bear all sorts of indignities at the hands of cruel persons? Thinking that such forbearance itself constitutes courage, is it proper to suffer like a slave? Having undergone all sorts of unbearable hardships, is it proper to simply leave the jail? What is the use of manliness, if one should join innumerable movements, without any regard to propriety? To discharge the mother's debt (Lit. in return for the mother's breast-milk), one should devoutly make offerings of blood. Such being the case, how mean and unmanly is it that man should be imprisoned in jails and taken to strange places like brutes, birds and other creatures of a lower order?... Is imprisonment intended for the body or for the soul? What can the Government do to the soul? It would imprison the dirty, worthless body alone. Where there is a will there would be a way also (for escape)....

Find swords for your countrymen, slaughter the enemy-groups, shatter the hearts of obstinate rulers and dance upon their breasts, standing by the side of the Mother (country) with the banner of victory in hand and uttering cries of victory -- Wake up, etc....

Rise very quickly to redress the hardships of the people, to kill the obstinate ruler who exercises authority over serfs, kick his crown with our left foot as though it were a worthless trifle and drag it away to thick forests....

Glorious Indian heroes! Indian youths! Give up your selfishness and look at the country's condition. Note the eminence of other countries. Is it the inevitable lot of India with her population of 330 millions to be bound by the fetters of mean slavery to a foreign Government? Should she live like a corpse without freedom (Lit. Without scope to move the limbs or the mouth)? Should the massacre of 1,200 Indian men and women at Jallianwallah Bagh in Amritsar as a result of firing by their (the Government's) soldiers, be forgotten? Should the executions of men like Bhagat Singh without any consideration in spite of innumerable memorials by nationalists, be tolerated with unbounded joy and calmness? Are we to be mere on-lookers greatly enjoying the sight of eminent Indian Chiefs yielding to the luxuries provided by Britishers and casting away Aryan Ideals to the winds? God! Is this Thy drama? Is it not Thou that hast placed holy India under the Government of foreigners? What else can'st Thou not do? Thou hast brought British education into the midst of Aryans and blinded the latter. Are these Thy mean actions? Oh Indian parents!... Just recollect the Punjab atrocities and the other innumerable humiliations suffered by our Mother India having fallen into the hands of pleasure-seeking white people. Should we keep quiet in spite of all the countless hardships undergone by Mother

India having fallen into the hands of British rulers who are devoid of pity or mercy? (Indians.) Are lovers of independence dead in your country? Have you forgotten Chatrapathi Sivaji? Do you not know Thakur Durgadas [18th century Rajput general who fought the Mughals] at least? Have you forgotten patriots? Having thus forgotten them, what fate do you, your sisters and brothers propose to meet with? What was Trotsky and what was Russia? At least think of that and wake up from your sleep. Hold the National Flag.... Know that our existence is momentary. Cut asunder the shackles of Mother India's slavery, and let the trumpet of complete independence resound in the Indian Empire. Wake up and run! Otherwise, your Mother India will become an object of ridicule to other countries. Vandemataram!

* * *

67.2

1936

POEMS

IN OCTOBER 1936, THE GOVERNMENT OF MADRAS INVOKED THE Indian Press Act of 1931 to ban *Karmika Bhajanvali*, a Telugu book with verses in praise of Communism. The book was edited by Swami Narayananand. The introduction urged readers that since the songs in the book 'are conducive to the development of a man's independence, it is our conviction that it would serve the cause of world-welfare if every one reads them and chants them every day'. This application of religious vocabulary to further Communist ideals and objectives is a good example of what the historian Charu Gupta has called the 'vernacularization' of Communism in the Indian context. In the officially commissioned translation of passages and songs deemed objectionable, there was no explicit reference to the British, but several to rich and poor, serfs and merchants, and one to 'purna swaraj' or complete independence.

* * *

67.2.1

'COOLY!'

Your body is devoid of flesh and is full of dirt, Your anaemic face itself shows you out – Cooly!

While your wife and children are starving under a tree without food, it does no good to you to implore the relentless employer – Cooly!...

Has your master alone swallowed your hard-earned money? Let him – but will it go on forever like this? Cooly!

The relentless employer does not treat you like a human being. Will not the time (Lit. days) come (for you) to become the ruler and enjoy?

* * *

67.2.2

'IS THERE GOD OR IS THERE NO GOD?'

If there be a Lord of the Universe for whom all are equal, why should some (people) be joyful with superb riches (Lit. crores) and why should many (people) pine for food?

If there be on All-Merciful Providence, why should cruelty rule the world and peace roll in the dust?

If there be God who is the embodiment of love, why should hostilities increase beyond number and why should streams of blood flow?

If there be God who is the protector of the helpless, why should there be misery everywhere, and why should there be separation between the mother and (her) children

* * *

68

1936 ›› BANDAR VAND [DIVISIONS IN THE MANNER OF THE MONKEY IN THE FABLE]

Original: Punjabi (Gurmukhi) | Leaflet

THIS LEAFLET WAS DECLARED FORFEIT BY THE GOVERNMENT of Punjab in August 1932 under the Criminal Procedure Code under section 124A of the Indian Penal Code. It was in the form of a dialogue between a votary of the Congress party and a 'communalist', here referring to a supporter of the Communal Award of 1932. This was a government-devised scheme of seat allocation in legislative fora that allocated seats to different religious communities, and among Hindus, separately to upper and lower castes. As per its terms, members of the 'depressed classes' (then called 'untouchables') would have separate electorates (i.e. the right to elect representatives from their own community during elections to legislative bodies). The award was opposed by Gandhi and many other Congress members as it was seen as a move that would fracture the Hindu community, and also harden divides between Hindus and Muslims. This view was colourfully enunciated in this leaflet.

* * *

A Congressite: O friend! The distribution of rights on a communal basis amounts to the division (of a certain thing) in the manner of a monkey.

A communalist: O friend! What should we do then! The Government is very kind to the Mussalmans and is depriving us of our rights.

Congressite: This is the move of the Government. By giving more to one and less to the other, it wants to bring about riots like those that occurred at Bombay. We will remain fighting among ourselves, while the English will keep enjoying our money.

Communalist: True, O brother, true. The cream is being taken away and is being enjoyed by Goras (the whites). They gave sour curd or a few (lit. four) posts to the black.

Congressite: We belong to India and India belongs to us. The Government has no right to become an arbitrator to divide our own thing among us. The Government is gaining its own selfish ends with the help of a few country-selling black-coloured persons.

Communalist: How then should we free ourselves from the clutches of the Government?

Congressite: All (of you) should unite and become one Indian nation. Consider those who demand rights on a communal basis enemies of the country. Obey the order of the Congress. Use swadeshi and boycott foreign goods. Stir up the Congress *morchas* [rallies] at Lahore and Amritsar. Do not fear imprisonments, see, six thousand women have gone to jails, you are men. Are you worse than women even? The (legislative) council passed (a resolution) that land-revenue should be reduced by half. So take up your stand and do not pay a single pie in excess of half the land-revenue. Then see whether or not the Government comes to the right path.

Communalist: We are Jats [an agricultural community of North India]. We are putting (lit: throwing), through land-revenue, the whole of our income into the pockets of the Government. We are donkeys of the white Government.

Congressite: Cursed be such a life! A dependent person can find peace not even in a dream. Death is better than a life of hunger, trouble and humiliation. Get up. The Congress has unfurled the flag of freedom. Step into the field to keep it flying. O you who are called Punjabi lions! Follow in the wake of women and do not let any stigma be cast on your fair name. Get up. Act like men. Jump into the religious battle (field) and make the Government fall on its back.

Communalist: Very well. We will not pay more than half the land-revenue now. We will now make common cause with the Congress and will, acting together, make the Government lie on its back.

Congressite: Come, let us sing:

O, the Goras are going on enjoying eggs, butter, milk and cream.

The poor labourers and peasants are starving.

Unite and become one Indian nation if you no longer want to carry loads (lit. bags).

If you sacrifice your all-body, mind and wealth, you will get (lit, swing in the craddle [sic] of) freedom.

* * *

69

1939 ›› AN OPEN LETTER TO THE PEOPLE OF INDIA

Original: English | Pamphlet

THIS TWO-PAGE ILLUSTRATED PAMPHLET WAS ISSUED BY THE Hindustan Ghadr Party in the late 1930s, most likely on the eve of the Second World War in 1939.

* * *

DEAR FRIENDS:

We do not have to remind you, you all know how much we have suffered under British Rule. We all wish to get rid of this foreign tyrant, who has been bleeding us white. The time is coming when our united efforts will be able to throw off the yoke of this aggressor.

Another World War is approaching. We must take advantage of this opportunity. England is sure to get involved in the coming World War. Political wisdom demands that we must utilize this rare opportunity for our good. We must put forward our demand for complete independence when our enemy, British Imperialism, is engaged in a life and death struggle.

To save her life, Britain will need India's friendship more than anything else. We must demand complete independence as the price of our friendship.

We must let the British Rulers know in clear terms right now, that if they care for the friendship of India, they must be prepared to give India full independence at once. Otherwise India will resist to the limit their efforts to get any kind of help from India. It is beside the point, how we will resist, but resist we will.

Complete independence means India's control over the treasury, foreign affairs and military forces. Nothing short of that will do.

We must remember that we can no longer trust any more promises from the British Imperialists. To our sorrow, we have found out many times that we

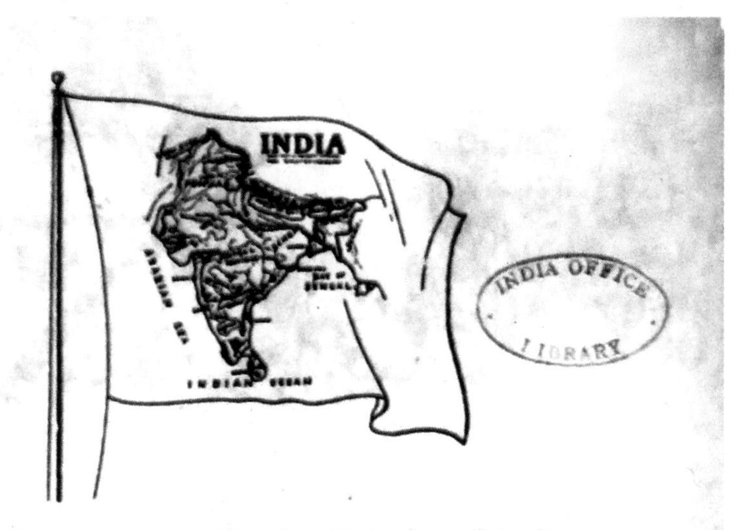
INDIA
An Open Letter To the People of India

Hindustan Ghadr, *An Open Letter, First Page.*

cannot rely upon their words. We must stand pat on our demands; we must not move one way or the other until our demands are met.

The world situation is such that the British will think twice before refusing India's demand. We must not miss this golden opportunity.

To get full advantage of the situation, we must put up a strong united front. All those Hindustanees who really work for independence must come together in a united front. Personal differences must be forgotten. Unity of purpose is essential for our cause. All of us who hold India's freedom dear to us, must work to establish a formidable united front. Our demands backed by our united front will have a telling effect.

Our demands must be popularised among our countrymen. Our people must be made to act in case our demands are not met.

Now is the time to educate our people; tomorrow may be too late. During the war, martial law will make things difficult. Unless the masses are made ready to act, our demands will not have much weight. The British Imperialists care little for empty resolutions unless they are backed by the united might of the masses.

War may start any day. We have not a moment to lose. We must do our best to educate and organize the Indian masses while we have time. Our slogans must be such as:

front. Our demands backed by our united front will have a telling effect.

Our demands must be popularised among our countrymen. Our people must be made to act in case our demands are not met.

Now is the time to educate our people; tomorrow may be too late. During the war, martial law will make things difficult. Unless the masses are made ready to act, our demands will not have much weight. The British Imperialists care little for empty resolutions unless they are backed by the united might of the masses.

War may start any day. We have not a moment to lose. We must do our best to educate and organize the Indian masses while we have time. Our slogans must be such as:

Complete Independent or non-Co-operation! Freedom, "or else!" No freedom, no soldiers from India! No freedom, no money from India! Freedom or resistence!

Yours for the cause,

Soldiers of Independence.

Hindustan Ghadr, *An Open Letter, Second Page.*

Complete Independent or non-Co-operation! Freedom, "or else!"

No freedom, no soldiers from India! No freedom, no money from India! Freedom or resistance!

Yours for the cause,
Soldiers of Independence.

* * *

70

1939 ›› THE CASE FOR INDIA

Original: English | Author: Will Durant
Book Excerpt: Conclusion – 'With Malice Towards None'

WILL DURANT (1885–1981) WAS A FAMOUS AMERICAN PHILOSOPHER and historian. He wrote this 210-page book in 1930, and it was published in New York. Two editions were banned: the original one as well as the one reprinted in India in 1939 to commemorate the 52nd annual session of the Indian National Congress at Tripuri in 1939. This was an inexpensive Indian edition, published after taking permission from Simon and Schuster, the publishers. The book was dedicated to two American authors, whose books on India too had been banned – John Maynard Holmes and Jabez T. Sunderland. In addition, it contained 'substantial excerpts' from the latter's banned book *India in Bondage*, which is why from 1930 onwards it was intercepted under the Sea Customs Act as well. Since Durant had commended Sunderland's book as 'so good that its circulation is prohibited by the British Government in India', he could not deny knowledge of that ban either.

In his note to the reader, Durant admitted that it was his trip to India that prompted him to write the book. He had not 'thought it possible that any government could allow its subjects to sink to such misery.' He further termed the 'apparently conscious and deliberate bleeding of India by England throughout a hundred and fifty years' as 'the greatest crime in all history'. Durant did not advocate complete independence in his book, but suggested that it transform into a Commonwealth of Free Nations, of which India would be a part. Chapters bore titles like 'The Rape of a Continent', 'Economic Destruction', 'Social Destruction' and 'The Triumph of Death'. Durant saw the United States' past (in terms of its anti-colonial movement against the British) in India's present. His renown made the appeal of his words dangerous.

* * *

THE
Case for
INDIA

WILL DURANT

1930
Simon and Schuster, New York

PRICE] [RE : 1/- Net.

Will Durant, The Case for India.

CONCLUSION (CHAPTER)

'WITH MALICE TOWARDS NONE'

I have tried to express fairly the two points of view about India, but I know that my prejudice has again and again broken through my pretense at impartiality. It is hard to be without feeling, not to be moved with a great pity, in the presence of 320,000,000 people struggling for freedom, in the presence of a Tagore, a Gandhi, a Sir Jagadis [sic] Chandra Bose, a Sarojini Naidu, fretting in chains; there is something indecent and offensive in keeping such men and women in bondage. To be neutral in this matter is to confess that we have lost every hope and every ideal, and that our American experiment, and indeed all human life, have become meaningless. Our gratitude for our own national liberty, for the opportunity which our Revolution gave us to develop ourselves in freedom, obliges us to wish well to the Washingtons and Jeffersons, the Franklins and Freneaus and Tom Paines [American nationalists who fought against British colonialism in the 19th century], of India. We may still believe that taxation without representation is tyranny.....

Therefore, though Home Rule must not come over night, neither must it be much longer delayed; for it may be as vital to England as to India. To India it will mean at last full opportunity for self-respect and growth; for self-protection in industry, tariff, taxation and trade; for self-reform in religion, morals, education and caste; and for the free development of a unique and irreplaceable civilization. To England it will mean a dominion saved; for an India longer forced under a hated yoke may abandon the methods of Gandhi for those of Lenin, and turn all Asia into a mad revolt against everything European or American. Already China is in flames; Islam in Turkey, Persia and Afghanistan is rebellious, and Russia is at India's gates. The British Empire, if it continues to be based upon force, will consume England in taxes and wars; if it can transform itself into a commonwealth of free nations it will be stronger than ever before. The Revolution may be suppressed successfully today, but it will be break out again tomorrow; its causes are wrongs far worse than those which led Ireland to bloody revolt, and lost America to England. These causes continuing, the revolution will go on; and England will find it troublesome to put 320,000,000 people into jail.

* * *

PART V: 1941-1947

71

1943 ›› A PHASE OF THE INDIAN STRUGGLE

Original: English | Author: S.P. Mookerjee
71.1: Letter to Sir John, 7 March 1942
71.2: Letter to Sir John, 26 July 1942
71.3: An Appeal to the Viceroy, 12 August 1942
71.4: Letter to Sir John, 16 November 1942

SYAMA PRASAD MOOKERJEE (1901–1953), EDUCATIONIST AND lawyer, served as president of the Hindu Mahasabha, opponent of the Indian National Congress, between 1943 and 1946 and went on to establish the Bharatiya Jan Sangh in 1951. In 1942, when he wrote the letters published in this book, he was the finance minister of Bengal, working closely with the British governor, Sir John Herbert (1895–1943; in office from 1939–1943) to whom most of the letters were addressed. The book contained Mookerjee's three letters to the governor of Bengal and one to the viceroy, written during the period March–November 1942, in addition to other documents. The book was banned by the Government of Bengal in January 1943 by invoking certain clauses of the Defence of India Rules that gave the ban all-India validity. Much before this, however, excerpts had already been published in newspapers all over India. Viceroy Linlithgow (1887–1952; in office 1936–1943) considered the letter of 16 November a 'most objectionable document'.

A brief note in the book titled 'Publisher's Apologia' described Mookerjee as 'one of the foremost nationalist leaders of India and at present the only personality who guides public opinion in Bengal'. It said that the letters were unique because 'for the first time a responsible Minister under the so-called provincial autonomy boldly challenges the iron grip that the bureaucracy still maintains over the administration in India, and exposes how Indian ministers though burdened with great responsibilities have little power to guide and control State policies in accordance with the real interests of the people.' This note itself explains why the book was banned – it was seen as a criticism of colonial war-time policy by an insider, and was deemed all the more dangerous for it.

In these letters, Mookerjee raised issues of discrimination against Bengalis specifically and Indians more generally, and urged the British to hand over

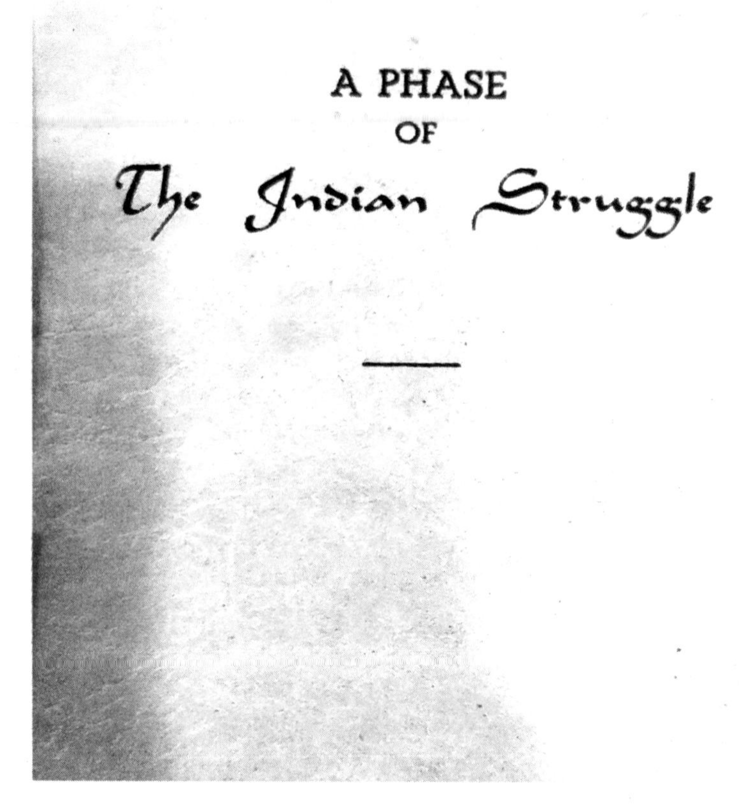
Syama Prasad Mookerjee
A PHASE
OF
The Indian Struggle

Cover, A Phase of The Indian Struggle.

power to Indians in the interests of national defence. However, as is clear from the letter of 26 July 1942, reprinted in part here, he also helpfully suggested ways and means to the British government so that they could put down the Congress-led anti-colonial mass struggle.

* * *

71.1

7 MARCH 1942

LETTER TO SIR JOHN

[Published in this book with the title 'Momentous Issue']

My Dear Sir John Herbert,

...I yield to none in my anxiety to see that we are not enveloped in a state of defeatism, but this does not mean that you or we can or should ignore the realities of the present grave situation. For nearly two hundred years we have had nothing to do with the task of organising the military defence of India. The British Government and its chosen representatives took upon themselves the responsibility for protecting India from foreign aggression. India's wealth has been lavishly spent for this purpose. We have been kept unarmed and untrained...

The fact that everywhere in the Far East the enemy is finally proving superior to ourselves is a terrible blow to British prestige. If we could have resisted somewhere and beaten down the enemy, something might have been said to keep alive British prestige. Over and above this, the scorched earth theory, which is being applied in practice elsewhere is capable of most serious consequences in India. This means that is military resistance fails, important zones will be destroyed by our efforts so that the enemy may not get any advantage whatsoever. This was done in some parts of Russia. But there the people did this themselves after a relentless fight under national command.

You should impress upon the Viceroy that even at this late hour there should be an immediate settlement between England and India so that Indians may spontaneously feel that it is really a people's war. A strong representative national government with power to direct the defence policy of India in India's paramount interest has to be set up immediately if we are to win the war....

* * *

71.2

26 JULY 1942

LETTER TO SIR JOHN

[Published in this book with the title 'A Warning Voice']

Dear Sir John,

I have been thinking over the questions which we discussed at some length at the last Cabinet meeting...

We shall have to examine immediately the special spheres of activity and classes of people who may be liable to be influenced by a mass movement and see how far their just grievances can be properly adjusted. I would proceed somewhat in the following manner:

Middleclass Hindus - They form the backbone of every political struggle. It is no use trying to crust their spirit or throw them into prison cells.... They must at once be imbued with the passionate idea that India's freedom is India's birth-right, and Japan which is coming to occupy India, must be resisted at any cost. They must be given proper occupation and scope for serving their country. I would immediately adopt a scheme of militarization under proper military control. I have repeatedly asked you to obtain permission to raise at least one lakh of Bengalee soldiers for the defence of Bengal.... Would you have liked your own country to be defended by people belonging to other countries and you be treated with a similar excuse by your rulers as we are accustomed to hear from you? The real obstacle is distrust. Are you prepared to trust Indians and Bengalees with arms? There should be no difficulty on this point either, if you say that you have no desire to remain here after the war. When you withdraw, this army will be handed over to the new National Government that is to come in future as a result of the Indo-British settlement.

There is one point regarding the pay of Indian sepoys and non-Indian soldiers and others in higher ranks. Why do you maintain discrimination of pay? I believe an Indian gets Rs.16/- p.m. and a non-Indian soldier receives Rs. 90/- p.m. So also is the case in higher ranks. These are factors which breed discontent which no argument can answer. The Bengal army that will be formed should consist of an equal number of Hindus and Moslems, subject to qualifications. I think if we commence recruitment within one week and give a call to the people properly, we shall not only get immediate response but also take away a considerable portion of the support that the Congress may hope to get out of its movement....

* * *

71.3

12 AUGUST 1942

AN APPEAL TO THE VICEROY

[Published in this book with the title 'An Appeal to the Viceroy']

Dear Lord Linlithgow,

May I take the liberty of making an earnest appeal to you and through you to the British Government to reconsider the Indian political situation?...

The demand of the Congress as embodied in its last resolution virtually constitutes the national demand of India as a whole. It is regrettable that a campaign of misrepresentation is now being carried out in some sections of the foreign press characterizing the Congress demand as a virtual invitation to Japan and a surrendered to chaos and confusion. No one desires that India should be plunged into a mass movement resulting in disorder and anarchy. At the same time a refusal on the part of the British Government to deal with the real demand of the people in a spirit of true statesmanship will be an even greater disaster; for by this unwise decision it is they and not the Congress who will precipitate a crisis in India.... Repression is not the remedy at this critical hour. Indeed the history of all countries struggling for freedom amply discloses that the greater the repression from the ruling power, the more intense is the spirit of resistance of the people who regard themselves as oppressed and downtrodden. You may keep down by a severely repressive policy the external manifestations of discontent, -- even that may become difficult to achieve without using extraordinary force, which again will have the most disastrous effects on the public mind of India. But even if you succeed, discontent is bound to be driven underground and anti-Government, especially anti-British feelings will stiffen throughout India. The enemy's object will be attained, for he cares not about Indian freedom but merely wants a chaotic condition in India, of which he will not fail to take the fullest advantage at the right hour. Indeed a blind pursuit of a repressive policy and a failure to satisfy India's legitimate aspirations may well create an atmosphere in India which will make us look upon the enemy as a virtual liberator from the hands of the British oppressors, a state of feeling with which many Indians hailed your ancestors under different surroundings in this very country about 200 years ago, when they gradually changed from their role of traders to that of masters of Indian affairs....

* * *

71.4

16 NOVEMBER 1942

LETTER TO SIR JOHN

[Published in 'Provincial Autonomy - A Colossal Mockery']

Dear Sir John,
I have decided to resign from my office as Minister...

...The demand of India is simple and straightforward. A slave cannot fight whole-heartedly for any noble cause. India wants that she should be a free country and she should fight along with other free nations for the liberation of humanity against the onslaught of Axis Powers. You have enjoyed freedom in your own country for too long a period to realise fully what it means to be a subject-race that feels oppressed and down-trodden...

If it is a crime to see one's country free and shake off its foreign domination, including British, every self-respecting Indian is a criminal. There are administrators in India who dream constantly of fifth columnists walking on the roads and lanes in Indian towns and villages. These estimable gentlemen themselves belong to this category, if treachery to India's genuine interests is the real criterion of a fifth columnist in India. The great bulk of the Indian people can have possibly no sympathy with Japan or with any other Axis Power. Why should we Indians be at all anxious to invite Japan to this country? We want you to return to your own home safely and as speedily as possible, and does it stand to reason that we would welcome a new master with fresh vigour and unsatisfied lust for widespread possession. We want to be rid of alien rule altogether. We want this country to belong to and to be governed by ourselves. India has for a long time allowed itself to be sacrificed at the altar of Imperial greed. The doctrine of benevolent trusteeship stands exploded and you can no more throw dust into our eyes. Indian representatives therefore demand that the policy of administration of their country in all spheres, political, economic and cultural, must be determined by Indians themselves, unfettered by irritating acts of unsympathetic bureaucrats and bungling Governors....

* * *

72
1943 ›› THE ORDEAL BEGINS [GANDHI'S CORRESPONDENCE WITH THE VICEROY]

Original: English
Gandhiji's Letter to Viceroy, 14 August 1942

THIS PAMPHLET, PUBLISHED IN BOMBAY BY HAMARA HINDUSTAN Publications, contained Gandhi's correspondence with Viceroy Linlithgow as well as excerpts from Gandhi's statements on his fasts and their connection with Satyagraha. The letters were written by Gandhi after his arrest in the immediate aftermath of the launch of the Quit India movement on 8 August 1942. The Intelligence Bureau expressed concern about these publications because they were best-sellers among students, especially in Delhi, who then passed them on to American servicemen stationed in the capital, thereby influencing their views of British rule in India. The pamphlet also reprinted published Muhammad Iqbal's (1877–1938) poem, 'Hindostan Hamara' (better known today, and highly popular as, 'Sare Jahan se Acchha' – Better Than the Entire World).

The cover carried the following statement:

> 'I have spent a good deal of my time in Jail. I have been in Jail seven or eight may be ten times. I shall probably spend a great many more years in Jail and may die in Jail' - GANDHIJI

In this pamphlet, the original letters were published with certain sentences highlighted bold, and with the addition of section titles and some rearrangement of the paragraphs. The formatting of the text as it appeared in the pamphlet has been retained. It was banned by the Government of UP under the Defence of India Rules. The first letter is reprinted in full in the following pages. In it, Gandhi repeatedly asserted the legitimacy of the Congress and its political demands, and excoriated British imperial policy in harsh terms.

* * *

"Hamara Hindostan" Special 3

The ORDEAL BEGINS

I have spent a good deal of my time in Jail.
I have been in Jail seven or eight may be ten times.
I shall probably spend a great many more years in Jail
and may die in Jail —GANDHIJI

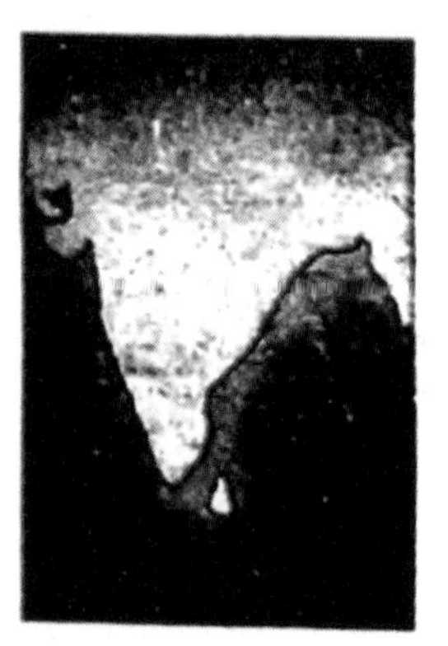

"A Hamara Hindostan Publication"

As. 2

Cover, The Ordeal Begins.

AUGUST 14, 1942

GANDHIJI'S LETTER TO VICEROY

Dear Lord Linlithgow,

The Government of India were wrong in precipitating the crisis. The Government resolution justifying this step is full of distortions and misrepresentations. That you have the approval of your Indian 'colleagues' can have no significance, except this that in India you can always command such services. That co-operation is an additional justification for the demand of withdrawal irrespective of what people and parties may say.

INTENDED APPEAL

The Government of India should have waited at least till the time that I inaugurated mass action. I had publicly stated that I fully contemplated sending you a letter before taking concrete action. It was to be an appeal to you for an impartial examination of the Congress case.

As you know the Congress has readily filled in every omission that has been discovered in the conception of its demand. So could I have dealt with every difficulty if you had given me the opportunity. **The precipitate action of the Government leads one to think that they were afraid that the extreme caution and gradualness with which the Congress was moving towards direct action might make world opinion veer round to the Congress as it had already begun doing, and expose the hollowness of grounds for the Government rejection of the Congress demand.**

They should surely have waited for an authentic report of my speeches on Friday and on Saturday night after the passing of the resolution by the A.I.C.C. [All India Congress Committee]. You would have found in them that **I would not hastily begin action.** You should have taken advantage of the interval foreshadowed in them and explored every possibility of satisfying the Congress demand.

A CHALLENGE?

The resolution says: **'The Government of India have waited patiently in the hope that wiser counsels might prevail. They have been disappointed in that hope.'** I suppose 'wiser counsels' here mean abandonment of its demand by the Congress.

Why should the abandonment of a demand legitimate at all times be hoped for by a government pledged to guarantee independence to India?

Is it a challenge that could only be met by immediate repression instead of patient reasoning with the demanding party?

I venture to suggest that it is a long draft upon the credulity of mankind to say that the acceptance of the demand 'would plunge India into confusion'. **Anyway the summary rejection of the demand has plunged the nation and the Government into confusion. The Congress was making every effort to identify India with the allied cause.**

DISTORTION OF REALITY

The Government resolution says: 'The Governor-General-in-Council has been aware, too, for some days past, of dangerous preparations by the Congress party for unlawful and in some cases violent activities, directed among other things to interruption of communications and public utility services, the organization of strikes, tampering with the loyalty of Government servants and interference with defence measures including recruitment.'

This is a gross distortion of the reality. Violence was never contemplated at any stage. A definition of what could be included in non-violent action has been interpreted in a sinister and subtle manner as if the Congress was preparing for violent action.

Everything was openly discussed among Congress circles, for nothing was to be done secretly. And why is it tampering with your loyalty if I ask you to give up a job that is harming the British people?

Instead of publishing behind the backs of principal Congressmen the misleading paragraph, the Government of India, immediately they came to know of the "preparations", should have brought to book the parties concerned with the preparations. That would have been the appropriate course. By their unsupported allegations in the resolution, they have laid themselves open to the charge of unfair dealing.

The Congress movement was intended to evoke in the people the measure of sacrifice sufficient to compel attention. It was intended to demonstrate what measure of popular support it had. Was it wise at this time of the day to seek to suppress a popular movement avowedly non-violent?

GROSS LIBEL

The Government resolution further says: 'The Congress is not India's mouthpiece. Yet in the interests of securing their own dominance and in pursuit of their totalitarian policy, its leaders have consistently impeded the efforts made to bring India to full nationhood.'

It is a gross libel thus to accuse the oldest national organization of India. This language lies ill in the mouth of a government which has, as

can be proved from public records, consistently thwarted every national effort for attaining freedom and sought to suppress the Congress by hook or by crook.

The Government of India have not condescended to consider the Congress offer that if simultaneously with the declaration of the independence of India, they could not trust the Congress to form a stable provisional government, they should ask the Muslim League to do so and that any national government formed by the League would be loyally accepted by the Congress. Such an offer is hardly consistent with the charge of totalitarianism against the Congress.

UNREAL OFFER

Let me examine the Government offer. 'It is that as soon as hostilities cease, India shall devise for herself, with full freedom of decision and on a basis embracing all and not only a single party, the form of government which she regards as most suited to her conditions.'

Has this offer any reality about it? All parties have not agreed now. Will it be any more possible after the war, and if the parties have to act before independence is in their hands?

Parties grow up like mushrooms, for without proving their representative character, the Government will welcome them as they have done in the past, if the parties oppose the Congress and its activities, though they may do lip homage to independence, frustration is inherent in the Government offer.

Hence the logical cry of withdrawal first. Only after the end of the British power and a fundamental change in the political status of India from bondage to freedom, will the formation of a truly representative government, whether provisional or permanent, be possible. The living burial of the author of the demand has not resolved the deadlock. It has aggravated it.

Then the resolution proceeds: 'The suggestion put forward by the Congress party that the millions of India uncertain as to the future are ready, despite the sad lessons of so many martyr countries, to throw themselves into the arms of the invaders, is one that the Government of India cannot accept as a true representation of the feeling of the people of this great country.' I do not know about the millions. But I can give my own evidence in support of the Congress statement. It is open to the Government not to believe the Congress evidence.

FRIENDLIEST ADVICE

No imperial power likes to be told that it is in peril. It is because the Congress is anxious for Great Britain to avoid the fate that has overtaken other imperial

powers that it asked her to shed imperialism voluntarily by declaring India independent. The Congress has not approached the movement with any but the friendliest motive. The Congress seeks to kill imperialism as much for the sake of the British people and humanity as for India. Notwithstanding assertions to the contrary, I maintain that the Congress has no interest of its own apart from that of the whole of India and the world.

The following passage from the peroration in the resolution is interesting. 'But on them (the Government) there lies the task of defending India, of maintaining India's capacity to wage war, of safeguarding India's interests, of holding the balance between the different sections of her people without fear or favour.' All I can say is that it is a mockery of truth after the experience of Malaya, Singapore and Burma [where the British faced setbacks and defeats in their battles against the Japanese.] It is sad to find the Government of India claiming to hold the 'balance' between the parties for which it is itself demonstrably responsible.

CONVERSION OF NEHRU

One thing more. The declared cause is common between the Government of India and us. To put it in the most concrete terms, it is the protection of the freedom of China and Russia [the former threatened by Japan and the latter by Germany, both of which were Axis powers against which the Allied powers, including Great Britain, were ranged in the Second World War]. The Government of India think that the freedom of India is not necessary for winning the cause. I think exactly the opposite. I have taken Jawaharlal Nehru as my measuring rod. His personal contracts make him feel much more the misery of the impending ruin of China and Russia than I can, and may I say than even you can. In that misery he tried to forget his old quarrel with imperialism. He dreads much more than I do the success of Nazism and Fascism. I argued with him for days together. He fought against my position with a passion which I have no words to describe. But the logic of facts overwhelmed him. He yielded when he saw clearly that without the freedom of India that of the other two was in great jeopardy.

Surely you are wrong in having imprisoned such a powerful friend and ally. If notwithstanding the common cause, the Government's answer to the Congress demand is hasty repression, they will not wonder if I draw the inference that it was not so much the Allied cause that weighed with the British Government, as the unexpressed determination to cling to the possession of India as an indispensable part of imperial policy.

This determination led to the rejection of the Congress demand and precipitated repression. The present mutual slaughter on a scale never before known to history is suffocating enough. But the slaughter of truth accompanying the butchery and enforced by the falsity of which the resolution is reeking adds strength to the Congress position.

It causes me deep pain to have send you this letter. But however much I dislike your action, I remain the same friend you have known me. I would still plead for a reconsideration of the Government of India's whole policy. Do not disregard this pleading of one who claims to be a sincere friend of the British people. Heaven guide you!

I am,
Yours sincerely,
M. K. Gandhi

Hindostan Hamara

Sare Jahan se accha Hindostan Hamara,
Hum bulbulain hain uski woh gulistan hamara.

Gurbut main ho agar ham, rahata hai dil watan main,
Samjo wahi hamainbhi, dil ho jahan [illegible]mara.

Parbat who sab se uncha hamsaye asman ka,
Wo Santari hamara, woh pausbaun hamara.

Godi main khelti hain uski hazaron nadiyan,
Gulshan hai jinke dam se, rishke jeenan hamara.

Aye abe rude Ganga, woh din hai yad tujko,
Utra tere kinare jab Karvan Hamara.

Mazhab nahi sikhata [illegible]as me bair rakhana,
Hindi Hai Ham Watan Hai Hindostan Hamara.

Unano Misr[illegible]ooma sub mit gai jahan se,
Ab tak magar hai haqui namo nishan hamara.

Kuch baat hai ke hasti mitti nahin [illegible],
Sadiyon raha hai dushm[illegible]daore zamaun hamara.

Iqbul koi maheram apnanahin jahan me,
Maalum kiya kisi ko dardenehan hamara.

—IQBAL—

Printed by R. P. Shukla at the Vidyalaya Press, 23, Hama[illegible] St., Fort, Bombay and Published by J. P. Gupta, for 'Ham[illegible] Hindostan' Publications, 23, Hamam Street, Fort, BOMB[illegible]

Back cover, The Ordeal Begins.

73

1943 ›› UTHA JAGO BHOKI BANDI [ARISE, AWAKE, YOU THE HUNGRY AND THE CAPTIVES]

Original: Oriya
73.1: Poem: 'The Marching Song of the Red Army'
73.2: Poem: Bankabihari Biswal – 'We are Taking the Oath, Comrade!'

THE INTELLIGENCE BUREAU BELIEVED THAT THE PAMPHLET HAD been authored by prominent Communist leaders of Orissa, but that the publisher was not very well-known. It was the Government of India which directed the attention of the Government of Orissa to this pamphlet, one official terming it 'pretty bloody'. The Government of Orissa declared it forfeit for being seditious in September 1943.

* * *

73.1

'THE MARCHING SONG OF THE RED ARMY'

The trumpet of war is sounding, march forward,
you soldier angrily
Spill blood, you hero, delightfully for the sake of emancipation.
You are born in the family of labourers,
hunger and starvation is your badge
You have enhanced the prestige of those who sit on the Olympus
The palatial buildings, arms and ammunition are built by your hands
You build up the strength of Capital at the price of your own
blood considering life useless.
You beg out of hunger, your heart shivers under fetters
The day of freedom is approaching,
in this awakening raise up the tune of your victory song
Hold aloft the red banner,
Beat the drums of heroic march
The free breeze is resounding with the victory slogans of the destitute.

* * *

73.2

'WE ARE TAKING THE OATH, COMRADE!'

To-day near the bed of your grave-yard,
With unflinching resolve and bated breath,
Cast down with sorrow, we take the oath, comrade!
We will fight being inspired by the implication of your memory
For the happiness and comfort of the people of the world

Singing the songs of freedom
With clenched fists filled with warm blood,
We take the oath, comrade!
We take it trembling with the final wrath.
Oh! the red oleander of the new age!
Neglecting your nearest and dearest in the world
You laid down your life in the field of death
For the sake of the down-trodden people
Holding aloft the glory of freedom.
You stuck the banner near the heart of the nation
We take the oath quivering
Near the bewailings of your mother and wife
With the fullness of heart.
Adieu, friend! you choose a glorious path
Filled with the dreams of freedom
Unhesitatingly you make your gift
Know it the time will show how valuable it was.
By singing the praise of your sacrifice
and upholding the greatness of the human form
Oh the hero, the victorious and the pride of the destitute!
Friend, the time is fast approaching,
The autocrats are losing ground everywhere
Their seats are trembling and bestial strength decreasing
Frenziedly the great emancipated mass of humanity,
Piercing the stone well of oppression,
Are surging forward glittering like the new corn in the fields.
Adieu, friend! -- It is your sacrifice
That has filled the throats of millions with fiery songs.

Take the revenge, steel the hearts,
Let not this first expedition be unsuccessful
We swear comrade!
Bowing for a moment to the banner reddened with your blood
Holding it aloft on your grave, we shall expose our breasts

We shall awaken and slowly emancipate
All the down-trodden humanity of the world!
Adieu, adieu, we swear, comrade
By mixing our blood with yours
We will wipe out the darkness of bondage for ever.

* * *

74

1944 ›› THE NEW INDIAN ROPE TRICK

Original: English | Author: Reginald Reynolds | Pamphlet

THIS SIXTEEN-PAGE PAMPHLET WAS PUBLISHED IN THE MIDDLE of the Second World War by the Indian Freedom Campaign Committee in London, and banned the next year, in 1944. Reginald Reynolds (1905–1958) was an investigative reporter and an associate of Gandhi who had been to India in 1929. In 1930, when Gandhi decided to inform the British viceroy of his exact plans with regard to the conduct of the Salt Satyagraha (to protest against taxes on salt), it was Reginald Reynolds who was entrusted with the letter and acted as Gandhi's courier. As a British Quaker and pacificist, and member of the 'India Conciliation Group', he played an important role in keeping channels of communication open between Indian nationalists and British officials. His earlier book, *White Sahibs in India*, had also been banned under the Sea Customs Act. In 1952, he published his book *The Quest for Gandhi*.

* * *

....Every real debt is by definition, a present recognition of a past service; and British creditors have not yet suggested that their debtors should be absolved of all future payments because their debt originated "a long time ago." If, therefore, Indians are to pay for all [unclear] services rendered in the past, and often in the remote past, without any mandate from the people of the country, the least they can ask is that there should be some examination (a) of the reality and extent of these services and (b) of the total payments made, which should be set against such services. In each case the account must necessarily go back, as our official accounts do, to the beginning of financial relationships between the two countries.

It would, for example, be quite legitimate to include in such a contra-account the pension of £4,000 a year conferred—with other considerable benefits—upon Warren Hastings. Or the £5,000 a year pension paid from the Indian revenues—plus £47,000 prize money after the war with Mysore—to the Marquis of Cornwallis. Or again there was the Marquis of Hastings, who was

Cover, The New Indian Rope Trick.

gratefully presented on his retirement with a lump sum of £60,000 from the taxes. (An additional £20,000 was later given to his son.) Clive had estimated his own annual pickings at £40,000; and Macaulay [Law Member of the Governor General's Council from 1834-38], who considered that Clive would have made the figure as low as possible, said it was equivalent to £100,000 a year in his own days. But Macaulay himself was one of the thousands who took up Indian administration for very substantial reasons: he drew £15,000 a year and wrote to his sister that he proposed to "live in splendour" on £5,000 per annum "and return to England at only thirty-nine years of age, in full vigour of life, with a fortune of thirty thousand pounds." Not a bad fortune to accumulate in *three years*—and Macaulay had been earning only £200 a year up to that time. Money is worth less today, hut when one reflects that even now Macaulay's salary would represent the total annual income of 3,000 Indians it is easy to see why Indians feel as they do. Nearly 200 years of British officials bleeding India at that rate would be quite a large item in the accounts, and does help to explain frequent deficits in the Indian Budget. The Viceroy's salary of £ 19,000 to-day (plus liberal "expenses") is one of many indefensible instances of over-payment received by British officials, and it is obvious that had such sums not been dissipated in preposterous salaries and "gifts" for British administrators it would never have been necessary to borrow' so extensively—if at all—for productive purposes; on, alternatively, that sums so spent could and should have been spent in refunding such "productive" debts long since.

For years India has been in revolt. Successive governments have recognised that the only way to avoid a complete rupture is to make considerable concessions to the Indian propertied classes, and *by making them junior partners in British imperialism to enlist their support against the Indian revolution.* This policy has always existed as an integral aspect of imperialism. We see the creation, under the East India Company, of a landlord class over a large part of the country. We see it in the protection which "law and order" afford these landlords and the Indian usurers. We find it again in the general opposition of the Government to any social reforms, such as those which are aimed at the caste system. It is an explicit principle in Macaulay's decision to create a new interest—almost a new caste—in the Europeanised Indians who have since served, mainly in minor capacities, as an important part of the bureaucracy. The same policy is blatantly discernible in the protection afforded to the Indian princes, despots whom British bayonets defend when their misrule goads their subjects into revolt. It can even be seen beneath· the surface of the "Hindu-Moslem Problem," in the determined efforts of the Government to use the Moslem propertied classes (and through their influence, if possible, the Moslem masses) as India's "Ulstermen" [supporters of the British; an analogy from Irish politics]. It is the policy upon which successive constitutions have been based, with their property franchise, and the "federation" scheme, with its vast block of legislators nominated by the rajahs [rulers]. And it is to be found, as we have seen, in financial schemes as well.

Britain, we are told, is spending large sums on India's "defence". Actually the Indian defence estimates have been rising steadily (i.e. at India's cost) and most of the extra expenditure met by the British Treasury is not for defence at all, but in preparation for the re-conquest of Burma and Malaya. But in any case British expenditure on the "defence" of India means no more to Indians than German expenditure on the "defence" of Norway and Poland means to the Norwegians and Poles. (The Poles afford an excellent parallel, because they are as apprehensive of Russian designs as the Indians are of Japanese ambitions: which does not imply that they welcome German "protection" any more than Indians desire our own, on terms of national subjugation.) To talk of "protecting" a conquered country under foreign rule is nonsense: there is nothing left to protect, and to Indian eyes it is a case of shutting the stable door when the horse is stolen. However, were it not that the British Government is so obviously anxious to conciliate Indian capitalist opinion, there is little doubt that far more of the extra expense in "India's war effort," including the preparations for the re-conquest of Burma and Malaya, would have been charged to India, as were so many of our remote foreign wars in past years. Even now another "gift" from India, like that made in the last war, may yet be requisitioned to re-imburse Britain for her philanthropic efforts to force the benefits of British Rule once more upon the apathetic Malayans and the recalcitrant Burmese...

In India the taxes raised for such purposes (interest and refunding) fall far more heavily on the poor than they do in Britain. This does not mean that the poor pay more in India than in this country—it means that there is no poverty in Britain in any way comparable to Indian poverty; and that, in spite of this fact, the incidence of taxation hits the poor relatively much harder than the rich. Obviously you cannot take much in taxes from a country where the average income is about 3.1/2d. [pence] per head per day [India's per capita income was about Rs. 200 annually in 1945-46]. And if that means—as it clearly does—that a few are rich, while millions live on about twopence a day, the least one might hope for would be that the poor would be untaxed, and that the weight would fall upon the landlords, usurers, industrialists, etc. But as we have noticed in other matters, these classes are favoured in taxation; and even the Simon Commission in its Report marvelled at the low gradient of the Indian Income Tax. It is the poor peasant, paying land tax at the rate of 50 per cent on the rental value, who feels the weight of taxation most, while indirect taxation affects even the poorest. The Gandhi Campaign against the salt tax was a protest against this policy.... We talk of Germany "looting" her occupied territories in Europe: what word can better describe this system of taxing a poverty-stricken country to maintain a foreign army, high-salaried foreign officials and a vast horde of rentiers, whether these last are Indians or Englishmen?

The closer association of India's predatory classes with the Government of a foreign (and equally predatory) power means a broader and more stable base for the imperial pyramid. But for the Indian people it means that now, more than ever in the past, the only hope of social reform, the only possibility of dealing with their own parasites, pre-supposes the complete removal of that paralysing growth which has sapped India for nearly two centuries—The British Empire.

* * *

75
SUBHAS CHANDRA BOSE

Original: English
75.1: Book Excerpt: *The Indian Struggle*, 1920–34, 1935
  75.1.1: Chapter XVI – 'The Role of Mahatma Gandhi in Indian History'
  75.1.2: Chapter XVII – 'The Bengal Situation'
75.2: Testament of Subhas Bose, 1946
  75.2.1: A New Age is Dawning
  75.2.2: Report to Gandhiji

HAVING JOINED AND THEN RESIGNED FROM THE ICS (1920–21), and having served as Congress president in the 1930s, Subhas Chandra Bose (1897–1945) charted his own path during the Second World War. He sought alliances with Britain's enemies in that war, Japan and Germany, in order to hasten Indian independence. He formed the Provisional Government of Free India (in Japanese-occupied Singapore in October 1943) and revived the Azad Hind Fauj (Indian National Army) with the help of Indian prisoners-of-war in Southeast Asia. He retains hold of the popular imagination in India even today, and remains a central figure in what-if (counter-factual) histories pivoting on a hypothetical India had it been led by Bose.

The first excerpt comes from a book by Bose that was banned in 1935 (Bose later expanded it in 1942). Given that much is made of his differences with Gandhi today, the excerpt is a wonderfully revealing account of Bose's appreciation for Gandhi and impatience with Gandhian methods. Another excerpt from the same book contains his explanations for the appeal of revolutionary methods in Bengal. The second excerpt is from a banned book that reprinted the transcripts of Bose's radio addresses. Two speeches are reprinted in entirety. In one, from 1942, Bose addresses the Indian people and criticizes the methods of Congress. In the other, from 1944, he addresses Gandhi with warmth and affection, and explains why he himself needed to leave India and seek help from abroad.

* * *

75.1

THE INDIAN STRUGGLE, 1920-34, 1935

IN EARLY JANUARY 1935, AFTER CAREFULLY EXAMINING THE OVER 350-page manuscript of Bose's book (which had been seized by the police at Karachi), the Government of India (Delhi) communicated to the Secretary of State for India (London) their view that it was necessary to ban the entry of the book in India. The reasons for doing so were many: the book's object was to show that the British connection was undesirable; it accused the British of driving a wedge between Hindus and Muslims; it argued that left-wing methods were more successful than right-wing ones; and it took the line that all acts of terrorism were acts of retaliation in response to government excesses. In other words, the Government of India thought that the work justified terrorism, and would therefore 'encourage terrorist methods or methods of direct action.' The secretary of state concurred, and import of the book into India was banned on 21 January 1935 under the Sea Customs Act.

The next month, after a question was asked in the British House of Commons about the ban on the book, the secretary of state for India stated that he had read the book himself, that it was banned because it encouraged terrorism and direct action, and that in the matter of the ban he had to trust the opinion of 'the men on the spot', as they would be victims of violence if it occurred. The same month, the Government of India too was asked in the Legislative Assembly about the reason for banning Bose's book. Was it not the case, asked Pandit Nilakantha Das, that the book contained only historical analysis, and was not the government aware that there was a belief that the book was banned only as 'a measure of harassment'? Das also asked the Government of India to explain what it deemed objectionable in the book. In response, Sir Henry Craik (Home Member of the Viceroy's Executive Council) replied that the book had been banned – as had previously been mentioned in the House of Commons by the Secretary of State for India – because it 'tended generally to encourage terrorism or direct action'. In March the same year, the Government of India was again asked questions about the book by other members of the Legislative Assembly; one Indian member, Seth Govind Das, even went on to suggest that 'all books that are considered worth having in this country are generally proscribed by the Government of this country.'

* * *

In 1942 the Government of India considered this poster to be a 'prejudicial report' (prejudicial to the 'efficient prosecution of war') under the Defence of India rules since it suggested that Subhas Bose had gone over to the enemy.

75.1.1

'THE ROLE OF MAHATMA GANDHI IN INDIAN HISTORY'

The role which a man plays in history depends partly on his physical and mental equipment, and partly on the environment and the needs of times in which he is born. There is something in Mahatma Gandhi, which appeals to the mass of the Indian people. Born in another country he might have been a complete misfit. What, for instance, would he have done in a country like Russia or Germany or Italy? His doctrine of non-violence would have led him to the cross or to the mental hospital. In India it is different. His simple life, his vegetarian diet, his goat's milk, his day of silence every week, his habit of squatting on the floor instead of sitting on a chair, his loin-cloth – in fact everything connected with him – has marked him out as one of the eccentric Mahatmas of old and has brought him nearer to his people. Wherever he may go, even the poorest of the poor feels that he is a product of the Indian soil – bone of his bone, flesh of his flesh. When the Mahatma speaks, he does so in a language that they comprehend not in the language of Herbert Spencer and Edmund Burke, as for instance Sir Surendra Nath Banerji would have done, but in that of the Bhagavad-Gita and the Ramayana. When he talks to them about Swaraj, he does not dilate on the virtues of provincial autonomy or federation, he reminds them of the glories of Rama-rajya (the kingdom of King Rama of old) and they understand. And when he talks of conquering through love and ahimsa (non-violence), they are reminded of Buddha and Mahavira and they accept him.

But the conformity of the Mahatma's physical and mental equipment to the traditions and temperament of the Indian people is but one factor accounting for the former's success. If he had been born in another epoch in Indian history, he might not have been able to distinguish himself so well. For instance, what would he have done at the time of the Revolution of 1857 when the people had arms, were able to fight and wanted a leader who could lead them in battle? The success of the Mahatma has been due to the failure of constitutionalism on the one side and armed revolution on the other....

The Indian National Congress of today is largely his creation. The Congress Constitution is his handiwork. From a talking body he has converted the Congress into a living and fighting organisation. It has its ramification in every town and village in India, and the entire nation has been trained to listen to one voice. Nobility of character and capacity to suffer have been made the essential tests of leadership, and the Congress is today the largest and the most representative political organisation in the country.

But how could he achieve so much within this short period? By his single-hearted devotion, his relentless will and his indefatigable labour. Moreover, the time was auspicious and his policy prudent. Though he appeared as a dynamic force, he was not too revolutionary for the majority of his countrymen. If he had been so, he would have frightened them, instead of inspiring them; repelled them, instead of drawing them. His policy was one of unification. He wanted to unite the Hindu and Moslem; the high caste and the low caste; the capitalist and the labourer; the landlord and the peasant. By this humanitarian outlook and his freedom from hatred, he was able to rouse sympathy even in his enemy's camp.

But Swaraj is still a distant dream. Instead of one, the people have waited for fourteen long years. And they will have to wait many more. With such purity of character and with such an unprecedented following, why has the Mahatma failed to liberate India?

He has failed because the strength of a leader depends not on the largeness — but on the character — of one's following. With a much smaller following, other leaders have been able to liberate their country — while the Mahatma with a much larger following has not. He has failed, because while he has understood the character of his own people — he has not understood the character of his opponents. The logic of the Mahatma is not the logic which appeals to John Bull. He has failed, because his policy of putting all his cards on the table will not do. We have to render unto Caesar what is Caesar's — and in a political fight, the art of diplomacy cannot be dispensed with. He has failed, because he has not made use of the international weapon. If we desire to win our freedom through nonviolence, diplomacy and international propaganda are essential. He has failed, because the false unity of interests that are inherently opposed is not a source of strength but a source of weakness in political warfare. The future of India rests exclusively with those radical and militant forces that will be able to undergo the sacrifice and suffering necessary for winning freedom....

* * *

75.1.2

'THE BENGAL SITUATION'

...At the outset it should be pointed out that the revolutionary movement is not an anarchist movement, nor is it merely a terrorist movement. The revolutionaries do not aim at creating anarchy or chaos. While it is a fact that they do occasionally resort to terrorism, their ultimate object is not terrorism but revolution and the purpose of the revolution is to install a National Government. Though the earliest revolutionaries studied something about revolutionary methods in other countries, it would not be correct to say that the inspiration came from abroad. The movement was born out of a conviction that to a Western people physical force alone makes an appeal. It is not generally realised by Britishers, that it is they who have been primarily responsible for teaching the Indian people the efficacy of physical force. Two or three decades ago (and even till today in some cases) the average Britisher in India, especially when he was a member of the army, or of the police, was so haughty in his general behaviour towards Indians, that no Indian with a grain of self-respect could help feeling the humiliation of being under a foreign Government. In the street, in the railways, in the tram-cars, in public places and in public functions, in fact everywhere, the Britisher expected the Indian to make way for him, and if he refused to do so, the Indian would be assaulted. In such cases of friction, the forces of the Government were always on the side of the Britishers. Cases frequently happened in which Indians of the highest position and rank – even Judges of the High Court – would be insulted in this way. Even during the Great War, when India was fighting on the side of England, such cases of friction between Indians and Britishers would constantly occur in the tram-cars in Calcutta.* No legal or constitutional remedy could be found for such insults, for neither the police nor the subordinate Law Courts would venture to do justice. Then the time came when Indians began to hit back, and when they did so the effect was immediate and remarkable. Ever since then, in proportion as they have been able to hit back, Indians have been able to move about in their own country without losing their self-respect. Even in the colleges in Calcutta, British members of the staff would often be guilty of insulting behaviour towards Indian students and the fact that today such cases are not frequent, is because Indian students also made use of physical force in upholding their self-respect.

This then is the psychology behind the revolutionary movement; but a further explanation is necessary to show why Bengal has, comparatively speaking, become its stronghold. The trouble began with Macaulay. When he was out in India as a member of the Government, Macaulay wrote a scathing denunciation of the Bengalees and called them a race of cowards. That calumny went deep into the hearts of the Bengalee people. Simultaneously the Government took the step excluding the Bengalees from the army on the ground that they were not sufficiently warlike or brave. The climax came when the Grand Moghul, Lord Curzon of Kedleston, attempted to crush the Bengalees by partitioning their province. The people at first retorted with the help of Swadeshi and boycott. But when brute force was used — as at Barisal in 1906 — to break up peaceful processions and meetings, the people felt that peaceful methods would not suffice. In sheer despair, young men took to the bomb and the revolver. The effect was immediate. The behaviour of the Britisher began to improve. The impression gained ground that for the first time the Bengalee was being respected by the Britisher. Many of the revolutionaries were hanged but they were able to demonstrate that the race to which they belonged was not a race of cowards. They were, therefore, regarded as martyrs in many a Bengalee home and they had the silent homage of the Bengalee race.

On this soil and in this manner has grown up the revolutionary movement in Bengal. What is the remedy for it? Two courses are open to the Government — firstly, to demonstrate to the people that for winning political freedom it is not necessary to resort to revolutionary methods and secondly, to give individual revolutionaries a chance of serving their country along peaceful and constructive lines...

*The writer has had personal experience of many such cases.

* * *

75.2

1946

TESTAMENT OF SUBHAS BOSE

IN JULY 1946 THE CHIEF COMMISSIONER OF DELHI, W. CHRISTIE, banned a book titled *Testament of Subhas Bose*, which contained speeches broadcast by him during his exile from India, from locations as afar as Berlin, Tokyo, Singapore and Rangoon. In these speeches Bose had accused the British of causing starvation in India, claimed that their rule was based on deceit and loot, and exhorted Indian soldiers not to help the British. The anonymous editor of the volume, which contained not only the speeches but extensive comments on Bose's activity culled from radio broadcasts in Japan and Germany, thanked Indian National Army veterans for helping him obtain material for the volume. In his preface, he defended Bose from the oft-levelled charges of collaborating with fascist powers, by emphasizing on the purity and single-mindedness purpose of his intention to free India from British rule.

A raid was conducted on the office of the publisher (Rajkamal at Kashmere Gate, Delhi) and all copies were seized from there. The publishers then wrote to the Home Member of the Interim Government, Vallabhbhai Patel, in September 1946, appealing to him that the public deserved to know the viewpoint of Bose in his own words as given in the book. Although Christie considered the book 'very objectionable' and was opposed to its unbanning, the Home Department nevertheless, instructed him to remove the book from the list of banned publications, and this was duly done. Two months to the day after the book was banned, it was unbanned. Two speeches in entirety are reprinted on the following pages.

* * *

75.2.1

11 MARCH 1942

A NEW AGE IS DAWNING

Speech broadcast over Azad Hind Radio from a North German Station

Sisters and brothers! For some time I have watched the changes in the world calmly and quietly. The fall of Singapore [to the Japanese Army on 15 February 1942] is a prelude to the fall of the British Empire. A new era is setting in. By enslaving us, the British have entirely ruined our morality and our finances. We bow our heads before God, who has granted us such an auspicious occasion for freeing India. In this age there is no greater enemy of freedom and progress than Britain. Now is the time to wake up from your slumber. The end of British domination will mean the end of a tyrannous regime, and the beginning of a new life in the history of India. The British have heaped indignities and humiliations upon us. Again we thank God for giving us this auspicious opportunity. Today many nations of the world are the enemies of Britain. The friends of Britain are our enemies.

The Indian National Congress claims to guide the nation. But its half-hearted measures have encouraged British leaders to continue to follow the old and hackneyed course, namely, of making promises without meaning to fulfil them. I also know that there are such people in India who are anxious to preserve the British Empire. The majority of Indians do not want either British rule or their economic system. We will nor cease fighting until Mother India is free.

In the world is dawning a new age. A true patriot says that his own fate must be decided by himself. We are ready to co-operate with any nation that will help us in regaining our independence. I hope that all my Indian brothers and sisters will help me in this war against the British. Even with her cunning, and underhand policy, Britain cannot fool India, neither can she stop Indians from cherishing their ideal of nationalism. India has decided to fight for her freedom. She will not only free herself, but will free Asia and even the whole world.

* * *

75.2.2

7 JULY 1944

REPORT TO GANDHIJI

Full text of a message to Mahatmaji which Netaji broadcast over RANGOON Radio

Mahatmaji, now that you are healthy and you are able to attend to public business to some extent, I am taking the liberty of addressing a few words to you with a view to acquainting you with the plan and the activities of patriotic Indians outside India, Before I do so, I would like to inform you of the feelings of deep anxiety which Indians throughout the world had for several days after your sudden release by the British on grounds of ill-health. After the sad demise of Shrimati Kasturba [Gandhi's wife, Kasturba Gandhi, 1869–1944] in British custody, it was but natural for your countrymen to be alarmed about the state of your health. However, we leave it to Providence to restore you to comparative health so that 388,000,000 of your countrymen may still have the benefit of your guidance. I shall next like to say something about the attitude of your countrymen outside India towards yourself and your faith. What I shall say in this connection is the bare truth and nothing but the truth.

There are Indians outside India, as also at home, who are convinced that Indian independence will be won only through the historic method of struggle. These men honestly feel that the British Government will never surrender to the persuasion of moral pressure or non-violent resistance. Nevertheless, for the Indians outside India differences in the method are purely domestic differences. Ever since you sponsored the independence resolution at the Lahore Congress in December 1929, all the members of the Indian National Congress have had one common goal before them. For the Indians outside India, you are the creator of the present awakening in our country. In all their propaganda before the world they give you the position and respect that is due to you. For the world public we, the Indian nationalists, are all one, having but one goal one desire, and one endeavour in life. In all the countries free from British influence that I have visited since I left India in 1941, you are held in the highest esteem, as no other Indian political leader has been during the last century. Each nation has its own internal policies and its own attitude towards political problems. But that cannot affect the nation's appreciation of a man who has served his people so well and who has bravely fought with a first-class modern power all his life. The high esteem in which you are held by patriotic Indians outside India and by foreign friends of Indian freedom has increased a hundred-fold since you bravely sponsored the 'Quit India' resolution in August 1942.

From the experiences of the British Government while I was inside India, from the secret information that I gathered about Britain's policy while outside India, and from what I have seen regarding Britain's aims and intentions throughout the world, **I am honestly convinced that the British Government will never recognise India's demand for independence.** Britain's one effort today is to exploit India to the fullest degree in an endeavour to win the war. During the course of this war, Britain has lost one part of her empire to her friends and another to her enemies. Even if the Allies could somehow win the war, it will be the U.S. and not Britain that will be top-dog in the future, and it will mean that Britain will become a protege of the U.S. In such a situation, Britain will try to make good her present losses by exploiting India more ruthlessly than ever before.

In order to do that, plans have been already hatched in London for crushing the nationalist movement in India once and for all. It is because I know of these plans from secret but reliable sources that I feel it my duty to bring it to your notice. It would be a fatal mistake on our part to make a distinction between the British Government and the British people. No doubt there is a small group of idealists in Britain, as in the U.S., who would like to see India free. These idealists, who are treated by their own people as cranks, however, form only a microscopic minority and are without influence. So far as India is concerned, for all practical purposes the British Government and the British people mean one and the same thing.

Regarding the war aims of the U.S., I may say that the ruling clique and its intellectual exponents talk openly of the American century, i.e., in the present century the U.S. will dominate the world. In this ruling clique there are extremists who go so far as to call Britain the 49th State of the U. S. There is no Indian, whether at home or abroad, who would not be happy if India's freedom could be won through the method that you have advocated and adopted all your life and without shedding human blood. But things being what they are, I am convinced that, if we do desire freedom, we must be prepared to wade through blood. If circumstances made it possible for us to organize an armed struggle inside India through our own efforts and resources that would have been the best course for us. But, Mahatmaji, you know the Indian condition perhaps better than anybody else. As far as I am concerned, after 20 years' experience of public service in India, I have come to the conclusion that it is impossible to organize armed resistance in the country without some help from our countrymen abroad as well as from some foreign power or powers.

Prior to the outbreak of the present war, it was exceedingly difficult to get help from any foreign power or even from the Indians abroad. But the outbreak of the present war has opened the possibility of obtaining both political and military aid from the enemies of Britain. Before I could expect any help from them, however, I had first to find out what their attitude towards India's demand for freedom was. The British propagandists have been telling the world for years that the Axis Powers are the enemies of freedom and, therefore, of India's freedom. Before I finally made up my mind to leave home and my homeland, I had to decide whether it was right for me to get help from abroad.

I had previously studied the history of revolutions all over the world in order to discover the methods which enabled other nations to obtain their freedom. **But I had not found a single instance where an enslaved people won freedom without foreign help of some sort.** In 1940 I read history once again and I have come to the conclusion that history did not furnish a single instance where freedom had been won without the help of some sort from abroad. As for the moral questions whether it is right to take such help, I have repeatedly declared, both in public and in private, that one can always take the help as a loan and repay that loan later on. **Moreover, if a powerful empire like the British Empire could go round the world with a begging bowl, what objection could there be to an enslaved and disarmed people like ourselves taking the help as a loan from abroad?**

I can assure you Mahatmaji, that before I finally decided to set out on this hazardous mission, I spent days and weeks and months in carefully considering the pros and cons of the case. After having served my people so long to the best of my ability, I could have no desire to be a traitor or to give anyone any justification for calling me a traitor. By going abroad on the perilous quest, I was risking not only my life and my whole future career, but what was more, the future of my party. If I had the slightest hope that without action from abroad we could win freedom, I would never have left India during the crisis. If I had any hope that within our life-time we would another chance—another golden opportunity for winning freedom as during the present war, I doubt if I would have ever set out from home.

* * *

FURTHER READING

Topics are listed in alphabetical order, and under each topic key readings are listed in alphabetical order of the author's last name. Indian editions have been listed where available.

Bal Gangadhar Tilak/*Kesari*

Kamra, Sukeshi, 'Law and Radical Rhetoric in British India: The 1897 Trial of Bal Gangadhar Tilak', *South Asia: Journal of South Asian Studies* 39 (3), 2016.

Trial of Tilak (New Delhi: Publications Division, Ministry of Information & Broadcasting, Government of India, 1986).

British Supporters of Indian Anti-Colonialism/H.M. Hyndman

Claeys, Gregory, *Imperial Sceptics: British Critics of Empire, 1850–1920* (New York: Cambridge University Press, 2010).

Gopal, Priyamvada, *Insurgent Empire: Anticolonial Resistance and British Dissent* (New York: Verso, 2019).

Catalogues of Proscribed Publications

Barrier, N. Gerald, *Banned: Controversial Literature and Political Control in British India, 1907–1947* (Columbia: University of Missouri Press, 1974).

Patriotic Poetry Banned by the Raj (New Delhi: National Archives of India, 1982).

Patriotic Writings Banned by the Raj (New Delhi: National Archives of India, 1982).

Shaw, Graham and Lloyd, Mary (eds.), *Publications Proscribed by the Government of India: A Catalogue of the Collections in the India Office Library and Records and the Department of Oriental Manuscripts and Printed Books, British Library Reference Division* (London: The British Library, 1985).

Censorship and Sedition in Contemporary India (after 1947)

Bhatia, Gautam, *Offend, Shock, or Disturb: Free Speech under the Indian Constitution* (New Delhi: Oxford University Press, 2016).

Chandran, Mini, *The Writer, the Reader and the State: Literary Censorship in India* (New Delhi: Sage, 2017).

Sethi, Devika, *War over Words: Censorship in India, 1930-1960* (New Delhi: Cambridge University Press, 2019).

Singh, Anushka, *Sedition in Liberal Democracies* (New Delhi: Oxford University Press, 2018).

Sinha, Chitranshul, *The Great Repression: The Story of Sedition in India* (New Delhi: Penguin Random House India, 2019).

Chand - Phansi Ank

Kumar, Avinash, 'Nationalism as Bestseller: The Case of *Chand*'s "Phansi Ank"', in Abhijit Gupta and Swapan Chakravorty (eds), *Moveable Type: Book History in India* (Delhi: Permanent Black, 2008), pp. 172–199.

Communist Publications and Networks

Gupta, Charu, 'Vernacular Communism: "Marginal" History of Satyabhakta', *Economic and Political Weekly* 56 (23), 05 June 2021.

Gupta, Charu, '"Hindu Communism": Satyabhakta, Apocalypses and Utopian Ram Rajya', *The Indian Economic & Social History Review* 58 (2), 2021.

Manjapra, Kris, *M.N. Roy: Marxism and Colonial Cosmopolitanism* (New Delhi: Routledge, 2010).

Sethi, Devika, 'Stirring Up Strife: The Censorship of Communist Publications in Late Colonial India', in M. Deflem and D.M.D. Silva (eds.), *Media and Law: Between Free Speech and Censorship (Sociology of Crime, Law and Deviance, Vol. 26)* (Bingley: Emerald Publishing Limited, 2021), pp. 169–183.

Espionage, Intelligence Networks and Indian Revolutionaries Abroad

Bose, Sugata and Kris Manjapra (eds.), *Cosmopolitan Thought Zones: South Asia and the Global Circulation of Ideas* (Basingstoke and New York: Palgrave Macmillan, 2010).

Fischer-Tiné, Harald, *Shyamji Krishnavarma. Sanskrit, Sociology, and Anti-Imperialism* (New Delhi: Routledge, 2014).

Maclean, Kama, Daniel J. Elam and Chris Moffat, *Writing Revolution in South Asia: History, Practice, Politics* (London and New York: Routledge, 2017).

Popplewell, Richard J., *Intelligence and Imperial Defence: British Intelligence and the Defence of the Indian Empire 1904–1924* (London and New York: Routledge, 1995).

Gandhi/Gandhian Movements

Guha, Ramachandra, *Gandhi: The Years That Changed the World, 1914–1948* (New Delhi: Penguin Allan Lane, 2018).

Parel, Anthony J. (ed.), *Gandhi: Hind Swaraj and Other Writings* (Cambridge: Cambridge University Press, 2009).

Government Reports and Handbooks on Sedition and Revolutionaries

Hale, H.W., *Terrorism in India, 1917–1936* (Simla: Government of India Press, 1937).

Ker, James C., *Political Trouble in India, 1907–1917* (Calcutta: Editions Indian, 1960; originally published 1917).

Sedition Committee, 1918: Report (Calcutta: Bengal Secretariat Press, 1918).

Overview: Censorship/Press/Propaganda in Colonial India

Barrier, N. Gerald, *Banned: Controversial Literature and Political Control in British India, 1907–1947* (Columbia: University of Missouri Press, 1974).

Darnton, Robert, 'Literary Surveillance in the British Raj: The Contradictions of Liberal Imperialism', *Book History* 4, 2001.

Israel, Milton, *Communications and Power: Propaganda and the Press in the Indian Nationalist Struggle, 1920–1947* (Cambridge: Cambridge University Press, 1994).

Shaw, Graham, 'On the Wrong End of the Raj: Some Aspects of Censorship in British India and Its Circumvention, 1920s-1940s', in Abhijit Gupta and Swapan Chakravorty (eds.), *Moveable Type: Book History in India* (Delhi: Permanent Black, 2008), pp. 94–171.

Overview: Modern Indian History

Banerjee-Dube, Ishita, *A History of Modern* India (New Delhi: Cambridge University Press, 2014).

Sarkar, Sumit, *Modern India: 1885–1947* (Delhi: Macmillan, 1983).

Revolutionaries in Colonial Bengal/Jugantar/Bande Mataram/Aurobindo Ghose

Ghosh, Durba, *Gentlemanly Terrorists: Political Violence and the Colonial State in India, 1919–1947* (Delhi: Cambridge University Press, 2018).

Heehs, Peter, *The Bomb in Bengal: The Rise of Revolutionary Terrorism in India, 1900–1910* (Delhi: Oxford University Press, 1993).

Sanyal, Shukla, *Revolutionary Pamphlets, Propaganda and Political Culture in Colonial Bengal* (Delhi: Cambridge University Press, 2014).

Revolutionaries in the Inter-War Period (1920s–30s)

Lal, Chaman (ed.), *The Bhagat Singh Reader* (New Delhi: Harper India, 2019).

Maclean, Kama, *A Revolutionary History of Interwar India: Violence, Image, Voice and Text* (New Delhi: Penguin, 2016).

Maclean, Kama, 'Returning Insurgency to the Archive: The Dissemination of the "Philosophy of the Bomb"', History Workshop Journal 89, Spring 2020.

Moffat, Chris, India's Revolutionary Inheritance: Politics and the Promise of Bhagat Singh (Cambridge: Cambridge University Press, 2019).

Nair, Neeti, 'Bhagat Singh as "Satyagrahi": The Limits to Non-Violence in Late Colonial India', Modern Asian Studies 43 (3), 2009.

Vinayak Savarkar

Bakhle, Janaki, 'Savarkar (1883–1966), Sedition, and Surveillance: The Rule of Law in a Colonial Situation', *Social History* 35 (1), February 2010.

Chaturvedi, Vinayak, 'A Revolutionary's Biography: The Case of V D Savarkar', *Postcolonial Studies*, 16 (2), 2013.

Kumar, Megha, 'History and Gender in Savarkar's Nationalist Writings', *Social Scientist* 34 (11/12), 2006.

Pincince, John R., 'V.D. Savarkar and the Indian War of Independence: Contrasting Perspectives on an Emergent Composite State' in Crispin Bates and Marina Carter (eds.) *Mutiny at the Margins: New Perspectives on the Indian Uprising of 1857, Vol. VI* (London: Sage, 2014).

Sharma, Jyotirmaya, 'History as Revenge and Retaliation: Rereading Savarkar's "The War of Independence of 1857"', *Economic and Political Weekly* 42 (19), 12-18 May 2007.

World War Two/Quit India Movement/Subhas Chandra Bose

Bose, Sugata, *His Majesty's Opponent: Subhas Chandra Bose and India's Struggle against Empire* (New Delhi: Penguin India, 2013).

Greenhough, Paul R., 'Political Mobilization and the Underground Literature of the Quit India movement, 1942–44', *Modern Asian Studies* 17 (3), 1983.

Kamtekar, Indivar, 'The Shiver of 1942', *Studies in History* 18 (1), February 2002.

FILE SOURCES

National Archives of India

These are some of the files in which specific cases are discussed at length. Files containing periodical lists of banned texts or passing mention of texts have not been included. The banned text, or excerpts and translations from it, is occasionally to be found in the file, but more often than not has to be located elsewhere.

Chapter 3
Home Political A (Proceedings), 35-36, March 1908
Chapter 4
Home Political A (Proceedings), 18-21, February 1908
Home Political A (Proceedings), 114-118, July 1908
Home Political A (Proceedings), 99-104, August 1908
Chapter 5
Home Political A (Proceedings), 66, July 1907
Home Political A (Proceedings), 75-93, January 1909
Home Political A (Proceedings), 124-125, July 1909
Chapter 6
Home Political A, 11-17, January 1908
Chapter 7
Home Political A (Proceedings), 60-65, March 1909
Chapter 8
Home Political A, 61-108, October 1908
Chapter 9
Home Political (Deposit), 19, December 1908
Home Political A (Proceedings), 148-150, March 1909
Chapter 10
Home Political A, 38-42, January 1908
Home Political B, 86/115
Home Political A (Proceedings), 23, July 1914
Foreign Internal B, 208, May 1906
Chapter 11
Home Political A (Proceedings), 17-18, November 1908
Home Political A (Proceedings), 40-43, August 1909

Chapter 13

Home Political A (Proceedings), 88-97, April 1909

Chapter 14

Home Political (Deposit), 28, October 1909

Chapter 15

Home Political A (Proceedings), 13-13A, February 1909

Home Political A (Proceedings), 23-27, August 1909

Home Political A (Proceedings), 1, May 1910

Chapter 17

GOI Home Political A (Proceedings), 36-39, April 1910

Chapter 18

Home Political A (Proceedings), 34-40, July 1910

Home Political A (Proceedings), 59-70, August 1910

Chapter 20

Home Political B, 86/115

Home Political (Proceedings), 106-112, December 1909

Chapter 21

Home Political A (Proceedings), 88-91, December 1909

Home Political A, (Proceedings), 23, July 1914

Home Political B, (Proceedings), 61, August 1913

Chapter 23

Home Political A (Proceedings), 74-76, July 1914

Home Political (KWI), 9/V, 1932

Home Political A (Proceedings), 23, July 1914

Chapter 25

Home Political A, 110-111, June 1914

Home Political B, 33-40, August 1914

Home Political A, 110-111, June 1914

Chapter 38

Home Political, 33/III, 1925

Home Political, 214, 1925

Chapter 58

Home Political, 208, 1932

Chapter 60

Home Political, 208, 1932

Chapter 61

Home Political, 208, 1932

Chapter 62

Home Political, 116, 1932

Chapter 63
Home Political, 1937/5, 1934
Chapter 64
Home Political, 37/1, 1935
Chapter 65
Home Political, 37/2, 1935
Chapter 66
Home Political, 37/2, 1935
Chapter 70
Home Political, 22/151, 1931
Home Political, 9/III, 1931
Home Political (Internal), 41/7, 1943
Chapter 71
Home Political (Internal), 33/45, 1942
Home Political (Internal), 37/15, 1943
Chapter 72
Home Political (Internal), 3/47, 1943
Home Political (Internal), 37/5, 1943
Chapter 73
Home Political (Internal), 37/13, 1943
Chapter 74
Home Political (Internal), 41/1, 1944
Chapter 75
Home Political, 22/29, 1935

ACKNOWLEDGEMENTS

I AM GRATEFUL TO PRAMOD KAPOOR FOR SUGGESTING THE IDEA of this book, and for his passion for Indian history, reflected in Roli Books' carefully curated offerings year after year.

Brainstorming with Priya Kapoor and Chirag Thakkar on the possible contours of this project gave me clarity and a good sense of direction. Chirag's patient and gracious response to requests for deadline extensions, help with locating and acquiring source material, and cheerful guidance made the process of editor-author collaboration a pleasure. Neelam Narula and Ushnav Shroff steered this project ably, and it was a pleasure to interact with them during the course of the preparation of the manuscript. I am grateful to Lavinia Rao for her help. The entire team at Roli Books extended all possible support that an author requires, and did it with great good cheer. I will remember this entire experience and collaboration fondly.

All historians are indebted to archivists and librarians who, for decades if not centuries, preserve the raw material of history and make it readily available to those looking to retrieve fragmentary facets of the past. I would like to express my thanks to staff at the Nehru Memorial Museum and Library (New Delhi), the National Archives of India (New Delhi), the British Library (London), the Staatsbibliothek (Berlin), the State and University Library of Göttingen (Germany) and the Library of Congress (Washington, D.C.), where – over the last decade-and-a-half – I have been able to find banned texts, and texts about banned texts.

My students at the Indian Institute of Technology Mandi, with their curiosity about the past, and their questions both fundamental and nuanced, make me hopeful about the future of history as a discipline, and how it can help us understand where we have come from, and where we are headed.

I thank you all.